MW00891987

Blue Max Stories Inc.
Calgary, Alberta
Canada

www.bluemaxchronicles.com

Second Edition - 2019

I'LL TAKE MY CHANCES

For Elizabeth...and Sidney

Introduction

This tale is partly born out of love and respect for my paternal grandfather, Sidney Turner. I based the first book on his life and took the liberty of using his actual name. He served with the Lord Strathcona Horse (Royal Canadians) during World War One, although the deeds of fictional Sidney differ from those of the real Sidney.

His service with this famous unit remained one of his life's proudest accomplishments. Not all the events depicted occurred in his life; I took great literary licence with many. Gramps, I hope you do not mind too much.

When I was a boy, my excitement knew no bounds when he visited our home. Sidney was naturally one of my heroes, and he doted on me, his first grandchild. When he passed away, it felt I had lost not only my grandfather, but a spiritual comrade in arms.

Sidney's parents and siblings lived in the town of Chinnor, England. Based on historical records, and my visit in 2011, I determined Thomas was my great grandfather and a butcher. To the best of my knowledge, his wife Emily and their children also lived there.

Most of the major characters in this tale are based on real life individuals. People will no doubt recognize themselves and, in several instances, I employed their actual names. I beg their indulgence for such depictions.

My paternal great, great grandmother's aboriginal ancestors lived in southern Manitoba. I used their heritage as the basis for visions and spiritual messages depicted throughout the tale.

I am a serious student of World War One history and have walked many of the old battlefields described in the story. One major difficulty I experienced, was holding back my nerdy history side from taking over the process.

This story has been coming together for decades. The catalyst for putting it to paper, was the return of one person to my life.

Without that event, for which I am forever grateful, it is unlikely I would have written this tale. I hope you enjoy.

"This tale grew in the telling."
J.R.R. Tolkien

Prologue
Walking Thunder

An overhanging sandstone bluff shielded a youth from the searing noon sun. It was so hot it hurt to breathe the very air and one might fear their lungs were cooking. With no cooling breezes, all living things sought refuge in shady areas.

Fifteen-year-old Shadow, Ohanzee in Sioux, sat motionless in a gorse of berry brush while waiting for mid-day temperatures to fall. In the morning, he tracked three deer into a coulee but lost them in tall grass. The deer lay down to keep cool and remained vigilant for predators. Shadow knew his prey would not scatter if he sat silently and, so he waited.

A small pool of water at the shaded bottom of the coulee would eventually draw the deer; all creatures needed the waters. Survival dictated predator and prey drank from the same pool. The catch for prey, was drinking when predators were absent.

It was not simply a matter of predators waiting for prey to arrive. Prey on the Great Plains had finely honed survival skills developed over thousands of years. Nature provided keen eyesight, excellent hearing and superior speed to outrun hungry enemies.

The hunters were however, equipped with their own advantages. Wily coyotes and wolves possessed superior intelligence and often hunted in pairs or groups to offset their prey's superior speed. Deer and antelope ran faster than their enemies but only over short distances. Although unable to match those speeds, carnivores could run tirelessly for miles and run deer to exhaustion.

By strength of reason and experience, Shadow knew to sit quietly and be patient. The deer would succumb to thirst and break cover to drink from the pool. While they focused on the water, Shadow would slip an arrow to the bowstring. He knew to choose the smallest animal to ease his burden of carrying it back to camp.

The bounty would please his family and his father might even finally allow him to join a buffalo hunt. His chest swelled with pride knowing his efforts helped to feed his family. Perhaps his mother would reward him by making him a fine deerskin shirt.

As the sun inched across the afternoon sky in minuscule increments, the temperature dropped. Shadow's legs cramped from sitting still but he knew not to stretch his aching muscles. Shadow's patience had almost evaporated when the deer stirred. After sniffing the air and scanning their environs, they silently moved to the pool.

When the large doe dipped her head to drink, the smallest deer followed suit while the middle animal stood watch. Shadow took aim and loosed an arrow at the smallest deer. It pierced the fawn's heart and it immediately fell. The other deer bolted instantly but Shadow did not mind. Had he had been on a horse, he might have tried for another.

He quickly slit the deer's throat to bleed it out and keep the meat fresh on the journey back to camp. While the carcass bled, he expertly gutted the animal. Leaving the entrails would keep scavengers such as crows and coyotes, busy while he walked home.

Tying leather cord to the deer's rear hooves, Shadow dragged it out of the coulee. Crows and coyotes swept down to the small patch of bloodstained ground to bicker over the spoils.

Shadow was relieved camp was just a few hours away and he would not have to camp overnight. That meant staying awake to keep coyotes from stealing the dead deer. Too much attention might also bring other, larger predators that would not find the skinny hunter an intimidating presence.

Carefully threading his way out of the winding coulee, he followed the river back to camp. The band had camped here for many years as game was abundant and water nearby. Untold numbers of his ancestors wore a path along the grassy bank and Shadow followed their footsteps. But he did not relax his guard –

the path might invite an enemy to waylay unsuspecting wayfarers.

The walk proved uneventful and after two hours, Shadow reached the edge of camp. A small pack of dogs bounded up excitedly at the scent of fresh meat. Swinging his bow, he smacked several on the head when they came too close.

"Here, get away from me!" he yelled while turning a full circle and swinging his bow. "Get back. This deer is not for you."

Shadow proudly dropped the deer at his mother's feet. She rewarded him with a wide smile and praised his hunting prowess. His mother's name was Tatewin, or Wind Woman, and Shadow adored her. She was highly regarded by members of the tribe, even by men in the warrior society.

Although his father was a respected hunter and warrior, Shadow's mother was in charge. He wondered when the war party his father joined to go west against the Crows would return. A dozen men had left fourteen mornings earlier. Shadow was eager to hear of their exploits and learn who had counted coup.

The plains people rarely engaged in battles to exterminate their foes. Rather, the primary goal was demonstrating bravery to prove you were willing to fight. There was little honour in killing your foe with an arrow and much honour in closing in to strike him with a club.

Lives were occasionally lost during such melees although a death was usually considered a tragedy. For that reason, skirmishes between different tribes did not degenerate into the wholesale slaughter common to other societies.

The people did not use a calendar that was familiar to white society. They marked the passage of time by referring to a winter of big snow or a summer prairie fire. By the white man's reckoning, the year was 1856 ... and times were changing.

The plains Indians were about to experience a period of marked change that would end their traditional way of life. The final reckoning had not yet arrived, but life was notably different from earlier days.

By the white man's calendar, Shadow was born early in 1841, the winter of the hungry wolves. He was different by having piercing blue eyes that were virtually unknown among the plains people. His blue eyes made him special, born with medicine the Great Spirit might utilize through him.

Shadow played games with his friends and like all boys, learned the age-old skills of tracking and hunting. Despite his eagerness, he was too young to join the buffalo hunts or go on a war party. Despite that, he was proud when he and his best friend, Appears Brave, went along to hold the reins of horses belonging to hunters and warriors.

The next morning, he rounded up Appears Brave to return to the coulee to hunt. They began walking through the camp when a commotion on the far side drew their attention. When the piercing cries of wailing women reached them, they ran.

The war party had returned but with the bodies of two men draped across the backs of two horses. They had left camp to steal horses and possibly fight the Crows; the deaths proved they found war.

Several days before, the war party entered a Crow camp at dawn and stole some horses. To their dismay, a Crow scout quickly discovered the theft and sounded the alarm. A large group of Crow warriors pursued the Sioux to reclaim the horses and punish their mortal enemy.

Unfamiliar with Crow country, the outnumbered Sioux fled eastward across the rolling hills. In their effort to escape, the lead warrior plunged down a coulee, but it delivered them directly into another camp of Crows. The sounds of pounding hooves and shouting men alerted the encamped Crows.

Like soup boiling over a saucepan, the Sioux warriors and stolen horses burst into the open and tried skirting the Crow camp. Crow warriors fired a hail of arrows and a melee developed in the swirling dust and confusion.

The lopsided fight did not last long, and arrows struck two Sioux men. Discretion proved the better part of valour and the Sioux fled down the valley without the Crow horses.

The marauding Sioux rode for several miles and did not stop until the signs of pursuit ended. They laid the two wounded men on the ground, but they were beyond hope, and the survivors formed a prayer circle. A day that began with glory had become a day of mourning. There would be no victory songs on the ride home. The last man to die was Shadow's father.

Dumbstruck, Shadow watched as several men placed his father's body on a buffalo robe. In disbelief, he stared while his emotions madly twirled. His mother's shrieks shook him, and he knelt to hold her. Raising her face to the sky, she screamed aloud.

Such are the quirks of life upon which people's destiny changes. Stealing horses to prove their manhood lead directly to the deaths of two men. Their deaths might have served to warn that taking what does not belong to you only creates problems.

According to tribal custom, Shadow, his mother, younger sister and brother went to live with his dead father's younger brother, Horse Rider. The brother accepted the responsibility although he was not pleased with the additional burden. Four more mouths to feed were not part of the future this impetuous younger man expected. His young wife had already borne four children with another on the way. To his mind, the only positive was gaining four baby sitters.

Horse Rider shunned Shadow and that strained the familial bonds to near breaking. While Horse Rider was away from camp, the women bickered over caring for children and dividing food. When he returned, he expected the women to fawn over him and satisfy his sexual cravings.

Wind Woman refused to comply, which aggravated Horse Rider. Unease poisoned the air and Shadow's resentment of the situation scuttled all chance of bonding in this artificial family unit.

Shadow soon began staying away for days, hunting and camping alone in river valleys and on the plains. By necessity, his hunting skills sharpened, and he enjoyed the self-discovery that developed.

Watching the unhealthy interactions between the women and Horse Rider led to Shadow's distaste for female relationships. Young braves reinforced his beliefs when he saw their often silly and self-demeaning antics in attempting to impress women.

Band maidens thought Shadow attractive, but he spurned their advances and became more of a solitary figure. Maidens and their mothers gossiped that perhaps this future warrior might be a *winkte*. By using such innuendo, they soothed their wounded pride. Shadow ignored the rumours, he thought the maidens were gossipy, giggling, foolish girls.

Wind Woman worried Crows might capture or kill Shadow, but she need not have. He ensured his safety by not camping where an enemy might easily find him. His cooking fires gave off little smoke and he never lighted a fire at night. He lived up to his name; he had become a shadow.

During these days of solitude, dreams of an unsettling nature left him confused. Confiding to Appears Brave provided no insight beyond suggestions that Shadow should consult the band's medicine man. Approaching a medicine man about the disturbing dreams was something Shadow approached with trepidation.

He did not know if he could even describe the dreams. Most were a hazy swirl of faces and often the faces were white. Shadow had never seen a white man although he'd heard descriptions from other warriors. He occasionally dreamed of riding across the plains aboard a magnificent painted horse. In one dream, he possessed a powerful voice that carried to the horizon and commanded buffalo to present themselves before him.

In another dream, he saw a white man on a horse. The white man had long whitish hair of a colour Shadow had never seen before. He was dressed in clothing strange to Shadow and the setting seemed to be in the future.

On occasion, he dreamt of a young white man with a happy smile, a man of peace and solid character. That perplexed him because the white man seemed familiar, almost like a friend. This was totally at odds with Shadow's waking thoughts and his growing dislike of the whites for encroaching on Sioux land.

Hoping for guidance, Shadow returned to camp to speak with Crawling Bear, the band's spiritualist and medicine man. After respectfully shaking the tipi entry flap, he entered when he heard the elder's welcome. Protocol dictated the young man attend with his father or guardian, but Crawling Bear knew the youth's situation and overlooked this minor breach.

Crawling Bear listened as Shadow shared his unusual dreams. That Shadow saw a race he had not witnessed while describing it in the future, was puzzling. Such a revelation was new to the older man and he had no frame of reference for counsel. He wanted to ponder this and asked Shadow to return in two days.

As instructed, Shadow returned to Crawling Bear hoping to receive the elder's guidance. The medicine man was still flummoxed, and his answer was simple. Crawling Bear told Shadow it was time for him to seek answers in a vision.

It was late spring and the time of year when the band camped near the base of Bear Butte. This mountain stood several miles north of the Black Hills or in Sioux, Paha Sapa. The Black Hills were sacred to people of the Plains and Bear Butte was a place of prayer and ritual ceremony. It was in this place where Crawling Bear counselled Shadow to seek his vision. There he might gain insight into the meaning of these strange dreams.

In early June, the band arrived and camped on flat land near Bear Butte. Shadow found a quiet spot away from the camp and sat down to offer prayers. After returning, he followed custom and purified himself in a sweat ceremony. Elders reminded him the vision seeker did not eat or drink.

Shadow left camp and by mid-morning, he reached the half-way mark and sat down to catch his breath. From this high vantage point, the camp looked minuscule. The breeze refreshed him and all he heard was the rustling of grass. It was a good day to be alive and hope for being on the verge of manhood coursed through his veins.

By late afternoon, he reached the top and sat down to survey the world. The view astonished him. A brown smudge on the eastern horizon he knew to be a vast buffalo herd. Hunters were tracking the animals. To the west, he saw wisps of grey smoke from a prairie fire. Looking north, he saw endless prairie and to the south, the hills of Paha Sapa.

The cool breeze reminded him to find a sheltered spot to spend the evening. He made his bed in a shallow ravine filled with long grass and stunted brush.

When night fell, he studied the stars and gave thanks. Many plains people believed stars to be spirits of ancestors that shone down to help guide them. To date, there had not yet been a sign from his father. Shadow took that to mean his father felt the son did not need guidance.

The second day passed uneventfully although hunger pangs and thirst became distractions. Elders had briefed him that foregoing food and drink made it more likely he would have a vision. Shadow passed the afternoon idly drawing pictures in the dirt with a pointed stick.

On the third day, his strength ebbed, and thirst parched him. He stared at the fluffy clouds and fantasized about rain. At sunset, he returned to the grassy hollow and huddled under his buckskin shirt while his spirit weakened. Never had he known hunger or thirst and the depravation offended him.

By the fourth morning, doubt assailed him. At midday, he lay down, and shielding his eyes, fell asleep in the warm sunshine. While he slept, clouds far to the west started building into formations thousands of feet high – the harbinger of thunder and lightning headed directly for Bear Butte.

As the storm relentlessly advanced, Wind Woman watched anxiously from far below. She did not know where her son might be on the mountain but guessed he was high above. Several women joined her, they knew Shadow was up there. A small crowd gathered and shared opinions of where he might be.

Lightning split a darkening sky and thunder rolled across the village. Concern for Shadow's safety grew as the menace in the sky drew near to Bear Butte. Several men spoke of searching but Crawling Bear stopped them. Their presence would distract from the vision setting.

After four days without food and water, Shadow was delirious. He awoke and saw the clouds marching directly toward the mountaintop. Brilliant flashes of lightning arced to earth leaving smouldering grass as proof of their astonishing power. High voltage filled the air, but Shadow revelled in it and his imagination raced at full speed.

He turned to face this coming fury and saw a pink glow shimmering inside the clouds. As the clouds madly writhed, he stood mesmerized and surging adrenaline levels fueled the power of his delirium.

Bizarre images raced in and out of pink, grey and blue clouds. In this aerial tumult, groups of horse-mounted warriors screaming war cries raced across a river and charged to the brow of a hill. The scene moved swiftly and revealed white men standing behind horses while frantically waving. Then to Shadow's astonishment, a smiling maiden appeared with a baby.

Who were these people? Where was all this happening and when? The visions were strange and pointed to death.

Who was the young maiden carrying a child?

Visions continued dancing across the gossamer clouds. The young white man from the dreams rode by on horseback and waved. He rode away and disappeared into a cloud that ominously grew dark. Against that backdrop, red flashes belched from monstrous objects that were beyond Shadow's wildest imagining.

Lightning hit the mountain and singed his hair. Thunder boomed like a huge bass drum and the shock waves staggered him. He panicked, fell off a ledge and tumbled head over heels before coming to rest on his back.

A hammer blow of jagged lightning scorched the earth with a stupendous roar. The supercharged air and flash blinded him for several seconds and he cowered on the ground.

Opening his eyes, he saw the young white man had returned. He told Shadow to turn from the warrior path and help make peace between white and red men. As a matter of course, Shadow presumed being Sioux meant being a warrior. Although he did not understand the reason for such messages, he might learn more one day.

At this moment however, he could no longer ignore this dangerous and violent storm. A lightning bolt shattered a nearby rock outcrop with energy hotter than the sun's surface. The exploding rock peppered Shadow's ribs with fragments of super-heated stone.

That fueled his anger and he bellowed insults, daring the bad spirits to try striking him again. His fierce cries carried above the uproar. Then Shadow heard human voices calling him. Astonished, he saw two men had defied Crawling Bear's command not to search for Shadow. Through the tumult, the men waved for him to join them.

A brilliant flash of bluish-white lightning struck the ground close to Shadow. Laughing maniacally, he pointed an arm to the heavens and the other to earth, taunting the weather demons.

Moments later, the demons obliged and delivered a bolt of raw energy that barely missed. Scorched earth burned his moccasin soles and he hopped on wet grass to cool his feet. The lightning terrified the two rescuers and leaving Shadow to his fate, they ran down the mountain.

Shadow watched them flee as he stood and dared the storm to strike him. The lightning struck all around him. Sheet lightning seared the sky while invisible hands hammered a soul-shaking beat across the heavens.

Far below, people anxiously scanned the mountain for signs of the three men. Thunder unexpectedly boomed directly overhead, and people collapsed in terror. Then an unexpected hush occurred, and the people opened their eyes. A seam opened in the clouds cloaking the lower mountain slopes. Far above, a funnel of sunshine backlit the seam and through the spinning vapors, a silhouette emerged.

It was Shadow, arms raised to the heavens and howling his wrath and disdain. Shaking his fists, he stomped down the mountain through the tear in the cloud cover while the thunder boomed.

The people were shouting and clapping in astonishment. A man yelled, "Look, he is not afraid of walking in the thunder" and in an instant, voices were calling Shadow's new warrior name.

"Walking Thunder! Walking Thunder!"

Chapter One

The following years were times of plenty for the band. However, the good times bore a blot - Washita, white men, who trespassed across the western boundaries of their traditional lands. Several years before, a treaty had ceded the lands in perpetuity to the Sioux.

Walking Thunder knew little and cared less about the treaty, but the trespassers angered him. Meanwhile, rumours reached the people about a far-off war between the whites and that was satisfying news.

"Let the war be big so the whites all kill themselves," harrumphed Walking Thunder.

His fellows around the evening campfire chuckled in agreement; none missed the whites. All the men respected him, but he had one belief they could not understand. He refused to count coup among the Crow or Pawnee. His steadfast belief was the true Sioux enemy, were the white men encroaching on Indian lands.

Walking Thunder questioned the time-honoured mantra of counting coup. Simply put, the definition of counting coup was 'A feat of bravery, performed in battle, especially touching an enemy's body without causing injury.'

He had no wish to fight his fellow red man. He believed Indians needed to stand together as one people. Stealing horses from one another stirred ancient animosities. He claimed it only served to divide and weaken the common front necessary to repel this aggressive and greedy invader.

His counsel was to urge the Sioux to reach out to other Indian bands to present a unified force. If thousands of warriors banded together, he believed the whites would leave and let the plains peoples live in peace. The task however, would not be easy to accomplish. Sioux men believed anyone not of their blood was an enemy and they struggled to follow his reasoning.

Nevertheless, by following his own counsel, even if no others did, earned him respect. He began to emerge as a voice of reason and wisdom despite his youth. Young men in the tribe looked to him for guidance and considered him a leader.

Setting out on their annual summer buffalo hunt, the band followed the herds. Over thousands of years, they had learned to use virtually every part of the animals. The hides became tipis or blankets, bladders held water, fat waterproofed clothes and meat provided protein.

The band steadily moved north into lands where other Sioux also hunted. Relations between the tribes were normally hospitable although there had been skirmishes with the far northern band of Assiniboia. The relationship between the northerners and southerners was about to be put to the test.

Walking Thunder's hunting party tracked a vast herd of buffalo to a grazing ground in a river valley. From atop the bluffs, they spied another band that had already made camp.

While discussing that, scouts from the other band surprised them. It was a humbling experience; rarely were the southern Sioux tracked without their knowledge. While the Sioux were watching the other band, Assiniboine trackers crept close enough to hear their voices.

Using their common speech saved the hunting party from attack. As each group was away from their normal hunting grounds, neither could claim jurisdiction. Rising from their hiding places, the Assiniboia raised their shields in a gesture of peace and slowly approached the Sioux. With greetings exchanged, the Sioux hunting party received permission to hunt alongside the Assiniboia.

At midday, the rest of Walking Thunder's band arrived and set up camp on the bluffs across the valley. Hunting parties discussed a plan to separate a group of animals from the enormous herd. Hunting bison on horseback held great danger; the large animals could often outrun a horse. Like most young Sioux men, Walking Thunder revelled in the thrill of a buffalo hunt and in knowing he helped provide for his people.

The bands hunted together for several days to get enough meat to carry the people through the winter. Women and older children then spent hours drying the meat and making stores of pemmican.

While that work continued, Walking Thunder decided to visit the Assiniboia camp and he left his knife and bow behind. Threading a path through the camp, he nodded greetings at the men but ignored the women. When turning to walk back to his camp, he sensed eyes on him and turned to look.

A maiden sitting on the grass was scraping a buffalo hide clean of flesh and blood to begin the tanning process. She saw him enter the camp and his manner and bearing intrigued her. Most young men made a show of bravado that she found juvenile.

This man walked with quiet self-assurance and radiated a leader presence. When he discovered who had been watching him, he affected an air of nonchalance while examining the hide.

She surprised him by putting aside the scraper and calmly regarding him, as though appraising a buffalo roast to cook. She displayed neither impetuousness nor immaturity, but self-assurance. Walking Thunder had seen much giggling and brazen shows of raw sexuality from young women. It left him jaded.

The thrill was in the challenge and most women bored him. This maiden sparked his curiosity, but he had felt attraction before and his interest was always short-lived. However, he employed a polite but direct manner in making the opening move.

"Maiden, what is your name?" The man's approach confirmed and intrigued her instincts about him. Nevertheless, an opportunity for a verbal sparring match was not one to miss.

The maiden's name was Deer Runner. Fleet of foot, she could run faster than many men. Young braves who failed to woo her claimed the name reflected how fast she ran away from them.

"Why do you need to know my name? Will you be staying in our camp and need to know our names?" Taken aback, he found her reply amusing and never one to back away from a challenge, he continued.

"What may happen later is not yet known. Tell me your name."

"You act like a chief, but I know you are not. Tell me your name first and maybe then I will tell you mine."

Walking Thunder let slip the hint of a smile and decided to introduce himself but the need to give in first proved unnecessary. An older woman inside the tipi listening to this conversation decided to come outside. She knew the young man's identity and did not want her daughter to run him off with her saucy replies.

"Deer Runner, hurry up, there are more hides to clean." After giving a friendly nod to Walking Thunder, she strode away. Her daughter was often too smart for her own good.

"That is a good name. Has it always been yours?"

"Not always but for most of my life. When I was old enough, I ran faster than boys did, and people said I ran like a deer. That is how I got my name. So now you know mine. What is yours?"

While she spoke, he looked down at her. Finding that intolerable, she stood up. Although he was a head taller, it sent the message that no man was better than she. He was impressed. This woman would be a challenge to court. She might also be a fiery bedmate.

"The name my people gave me five summers ago, is Walking Thunder. Do you want to know why they gave me this name?"

In her own turn, she was impressed. Word of this young man had reached their camp. Still, she could not resist impish behavior and decided to ridicule him. If he could not take a small joke, she had no interest in him.

"I would think it is because when you walk, your feet are so heavy it sounds like thunder." His eyes flashed in response to the challenge. She had not angered him, but her words stoked his competitive spirit to nearly full boil.

"If you think that, you do not hear well. My feet made no sound when I walked into your camp. Maybe your name should be No Ears."

She tried putting on an angry face but failed and giggled at his quick-witted comeback. "That is true, you made no sound. Now tell me how you came to have your name."

He sat down across from the hide and spoke while she resumed working. His lack of bravado pleased her; she had heard enough boasting from her brothers to last a lifetime. This man calmly spoke of the near-death experience in gaining his warrior name. He relayed the tale as coolly as if he were describing a quiet walk by the river. Later, she would make inquiries to confirm the tale although she did not doubt he spoke the truth.

Finishing his explanation, Walking Thunder rose and with a nod, returned to his camp. Deer Runner and Walking Thunder already had privately decided each was the person they would marry. Deer Runner's only concern was gaining her father's approval. He would not want his daughter marrying a man from so far away.

However, to her surprise, that did not become an obstacle. Her father knew of the future son-in-law's prowess as a spiritualist and leader - a born leader who won the respect of men.

Winning her father's approval would require the gifts of horses and fine clothing. To offer such a dowry, Walking Thunder needed his band's support.

The bands camped together for several more weeks. Chiefs and medicine men used the time to strengthen tribal bonds. A day might come when the bands needed one another for self-defence.

Walking Thunder's courtship of Deer Runner continued. Their marriage had been a foregone conclusion from the first meeting. Following their marriage, brides customarily left home to join her husband's tribe. The couple occasionally would return to hunt and to introduce their children.

The hunt ended, and the southern Sioux moved to their winter camp in the Powder River Basin east of the Bighorn Mountains. For now, life was good, and they settled into their winter routine. However, they continued to receive disturbing reports of Washita, white soldiers. The people had believed the whites would stay away from their traditional hunting lands. Some whites followed the treaty, but others scoffed at the notion 'savages' should dictate terms.

Skirmishes broke out between red and white people. The death toll and tempers rose steadily. Then came a gold discovery to the north in Montana territory. Prospectors and miners stampeded onto native lands in direct violation of the treaty.

Deadly confrontations between Indians and whites grew in number and intensity. Whites demanded the army provide safe protection along a route known as the Bozeman Trail.

Then came word of a white atrocity to the south; history would know it as the Sand Creek Massacre. White militiamen attacked a peaceful Indian camp and indiscriminately killed men, women and children. Survivors of this outrage fled north hoping to escape the whites and find protection with the Sioux. By the spring, open warfare had broken out and deaths on both sides added to the bad blood.

Red Cloud was chief of the Oglala Sioux and these broken treaties angered him. The Arapaho and Cheyenne also were angry, and their warriors allied with the Sioux to attack whites. Walking Thunder reluctantly became a participant in what history would call Red Cloud's War. He remembered his vision of working for peace between the two races but in his view, the whites were taking Sioux lands by force.

To protect white travellers, the federal government began building a trail through the heart of the Powder River country. Nearly a decade earlier, the government signed a treaty promising the area to remain Sioux territory. With the army constructing forts, Red Cloud began attacking forts along the Bozeman Trail in 1865 to protect Sioux lands.

Walking Thunder and hundreds of his fellows, were rarely home that summer. Had the Sioux gone against the Crows, he would have opposed it. This was different; the whites would never keep their promises of staying out of Indian lands.

Red Cloud sagely pronounced the only promise white men would ever keep was the one to take Indian lands. He refused to live on a reserve and could not understand why the whites would not let Indians continue their traditional lives.

Walking Thunder watched warriors such as Red Cloud, Young Man Afraid Of His Horses and Crazy Horse. The warriors chose when and where to strike, and their tactics often made the soldiers look like fools.

Hit and run strategies drove army commanders to distraction. They had trained to wage war with large armies standing toe-to-toe in brutal slugging matches. This war on the plains was new and strange for the soldiers but it suited the Indians very well.

Their primary weapons were the war club and bow and arrow, both close-range tools. The Indians learned some painful lessons that charging headlong against soldiers armed with rifles would not win a war. Wiping out small groups of soldiers and miners in surprise attacks paid far greater dividends.

One aspect of the fighting Walking Thunder found repugnant, involved the practice of mutilating bodies of the dead. He understood stripping clothes from dead soldiers nor did he object to taking scalps. But he objected to hacking off legs, arms and penises.

Walking Thunder believed that although the soldiers were his enemy, a man who served knowing it might take his life was worthy of respect.

Not all the summer days were out on the warpath. He and other warriors took time away and returned home to their families. Married life suited him well, at least when he was home to enjoy being a husband.

Deer Runner was passionate and loving in equal measure to her independence and self-assuredness. She delighted in pleasing her husband, preparing meals he liked, making soft deer hide garments and adorning his war shield with colourful symbols. At night, under their warm buffalo robes, she learned how to delight him.

Being healthy young adults, Deer Runner was soon pregnant. Walking Thunder found a quiet place to thank the Great Spirit for blessing them with a child. Knowing he would soon be a father, excitement quivered in his chest.

He prayed for guidance to be worthy of this great responsibility. Assuming the child would be a boy, he wanted to share the ways of the hunter, to respect all things in life and only if forced, to be a warrior.

Pondering this last aspect at length, he felt concerned about the changes occurring in their way of life. The traditional enemies of the Sioux held to a code each tribe understood.

Nomadic people moved with the seasons, following game they hunted for survival. The notion of living in one place and growing crops was foreign to a life based on hunting. Planting seeds and waiting to harvest it months later, was anathema.

The whites made war very differently than the people. Whites formed into groups and fought battles that claimed thousands of lives in a single day.

In contrast, warriors met in pitched battles that rarely claimed lives. Annihilating a foe was not the point of such struggles. Facing off against one another, closing to strike an opponent, counting coup without showing fear, that mattered.

They fought to keep intruders from their ancestral land and to sustain their way of life. Their battles were not to seize lands for an empire, subjugate people or gain mineral riches. Those were the reasons why whites waged war. Would his child be able to live free as his ancestors had done for thousands of moons?

Walking Thunder feared his people might not be strong enough to turn back this invasion of newcomers. They were learning that killing one white man meant ten more arrived to take the dead man's place.

White men built strange homes of wood and owned strange animals. They did not follow the buffalo and live with what the earth provided. Instead, the whites chopped down trees, blew up rocks with black dirt and dug holes in hills and mountains. They had no concept of living with the gifts of the Great Spirit. How could they not understand and respect such a simple code?

Shaking his head sadly, he reproached himself for dwelling on such a subject on this fine autumn morning. Returning to camp, he found a council about to begin. There he learned their warriors were joining warriors from other bands to attack a newly built soldiers' fort.

Throwing a leg over his horse's back, he reached down to hug Deer Runner. She hated displaying 'young girl' emotion but her tears spoke to the emotion she wished to hide.

"Look after yourself and the child," he stuttered while choking back his own sadness. The warrior party moved off and waving farewell, he rode away.

Bowing to public pressure, the U. S. government had authorized building army forts along the Bozeman Trail. This blatant violation of the 1851 Fort Laramie Treaty outraged the Sioux. According to the treaty terms, these lands were off limits to white men.

Unfortunately for the Indians, a gold discovery in western Montana touched off a gold rush. Prospectors and miners stampeded across Indian lands without regard to the treaty. Warriors ambushed the trespassers and that brought calls for the army to protect the miners.

In June of 1866, the government arranged for a council between themselves and Indian leaders. There the white authorities revealed the plan to build forts along the Bozeman Trail. That infuriated native leaders and Red Cloud rose to denounce the whites and led the Sioux away. He vowed to fight all whites who intruded onto their lands.

The great warrior kept his promise and through the summer and fall, wagon trains, soldiers and forts came under attack. The Indians employed hit and run ambushes and then simply melted away into the grassy plains. Frustration with their inability to engage Indians in battle finally boiled over with disastrous results for the army.

Just as winter snows set in, the large warrior group Walking Thunder had joined, camped near an army fort east of the Bighorn Mountains. Warriors continually watched the fort and attacked whenever whites ventured outside to gather firewood. The chore was fraught with danger, but the inhabitants had little choice. It was either freeze or risk death from the Indians.

Protected by army patrols, woodcutters trekked several miles from the fort. The Indians always attacked, and soldiers died in ambushes. Unsurprisingly, many soldiers burned with feverish desire to catch their foes in the open and annihilate them.

This was the situation when Walking Thunder and the war party arrived. There he heard of daring acts and saw white scalps on display. He attended remembrances for dead warriors, angered that so many good men died to keep out the whites.

Knowing he would be a father, his goal was protecting his family, people and homeland. He remembered his vision to work for peace between the red and white man. Did whites have no honour? He resigned himself to the belief the time to drive out the invaders had arrived.

The warriors had watched the impetuous and often foolish actions of some soldiers and those observations helped Red Cloud and Crazy Horse formulate an ambush plan.

When a woodcutter party ventured out, a small group of warriors would attack hoping to lure more soldiers from the fort. If the soldiers took the bait, the warriors hoped to draw them behind several hills where a large group of hidden warriors, would ambush them.

Red Cloud chose ten young men to act as decoys and Crazy Horse and Walking Thunder were among them. On a cold winter day, three miles from the fort, warriors attacked a party of woodcutters. As hoped, a company of soldiers marched out to protect the woodcutters. Soon after, a group of horse soldiers joined the foot soldiers and chased off the attackers.

The woodcutters finished and returned to the fort. Crazy Horse now led the decoys back down toward the fort. They came close enough to draw artillery fire and then drew back to the hills.

From the hilltop, they yelled insults hoping to anger the soldiers. The warriors pantomimed fear while pointing at the fort. Seeing that the soldiers would not leave the fort, angered Walking Thunder but a rumour also fueled his anger. Some braves believed he lacked the courage to count coup. On this day, he would prove the rumours false.

As hoped, foot soldiers left the fort and began marching up the hill. Horse soldiers also formed up to support the infantrymen while the warriors continued taunting the soldiers.

Watching the soldiers advance, brought Walking Thunder's blood to a boil and he lusted for battle. Leaping from his horse, he walked a dozen paces and grabbed his crotch as though inviting the soldiers to look at his manhood.

Not to be outdone, Crazy Horse pretended his horse was too lame to ride. The foot soldiers took the bait. Crazy Horse led the decoys beyond the hilltop and disappeared.

The horse soldiers charged past the infantry to pursue the apparently fleeing Indians. Their charge carried them out of sight of the fort and foot soldiers. To their shock and horror, the reckless cavalrymen found two thousand warriors waiting for them.

Wheeling his horse around, Walking Thunder charged into the panicked cavalrymen. He saw a soldier withdrawing his sabre and clubbed the man out of the saddle.

Horses snorted in fear and stampeded into one another while slipping on the snowy grass. Most of the horse soldiers died in the first wave but a few broke through trying to fight their way back to the fort.

Hearing sounds of battle, the foot soldiers continued their advance up and over the hill. Coming face to face with the deadly peril facing them, they crouched in a circle to defend themselves. Mounted warriors running down the surviving horse soldiers, plowed into the foot soldiers. Hundreds of battle-crazed warriors jumped down to fight hand-to-hand.

Walking Thunder ducked under a swinging rifle butt and plunged a knife into the man's chest. Coughing up blood from his severed windpipe, the soldier grabbed at Walking Thunder's throat, but his life energy bled away too quickly.

Bodies crashed to the ground. Curses and screams of fear and pain from man and beast rent the air. Such intense hatred and violence quickly brought the battle to a bloody end. In less than half an hour, all the soldiers were dead. Triumphant victory cries mixed with sorrowful wails; the soldiers had killed nearly the same number of Indians.

Walking Thunder suffered a minor sabre wound to his arm during the melee. Cutting a long strip of cloth from a uniform, he bound the wound. With the fight over, the enormity of what he had survived began to sink in.

Nervously shivering, he realized the reaction was more than a response to the cold air. Returning to the dead soldier, he stripped off the heavy blue coat to wear. A warrior shook Walking Thunder's shoulders to express admiration for his courage.

Warriors still full of blood lust began mutilating the dead soldiers. Walking Thunder did not object to scalping but he considered these acts a desecration. The dead had limbs, noses and even genitals hacked off, their eyes gouged out and skulls crushed with stones.

Many warriors believed this ensured the dead soldiers would be helpless in the spirit world. Walking Thunder wondered if, in a reversal of fortunes, would spirits of dead warriors be as helpless? Unable to answer the question, he rode from the field of slaughter to begin the long journey home.

Chapter Two

Returning home, he found more death. Before the battle, Deer Runner dreamed a soldier had killed her husband. Awaking in the early morning hours, she mourned and refused all food and water.

Wind Woman sat beside her daughter-in-law and softly sang, hoping to soothe her spirit. Deer Runner laid under her robes and without food or water grew weak. Wind Woman urged her to eat and drink to keep the child safe, but her efforts were for naught.

Four days after beginning to fast, Deer Runner fell ill with chills and fever and moaned disconsolately. She firmly believed the dream of her dead husband was real.

The self-deprivation meant trouble and after the fever began, Deer Runner awoke with severe cramps and her cries of pain woke Wind Woman. Groaning in pain, Deer Runner complained of shooting pains in her abdomen.

Her discomfort increased and following an excruciating cramp, Deer Runner fell unconsciousness. Wind Woman summoned the medicine man to drive out the evil spirits contaminating Deer Runner's mind. Kneeling over her inert body, he worked with his medicine bundle to banish the bad energy. Although she was not awake, knots of tension on her forehead relaxed. Unfortunately, his efforts did not save the baby.

Losing the child, mourning Walking Thunder and longing for her family, drove Deer Runner to deep despair. No words of encouragement brightened her outlook and Wind Woman began preparing for a death ceremony.

Walking Thunder returned, and Wind Woman warned him of Deer Runner's condition. Astonished by these happenings, he paused to collect his thoughts. His own visions were powerful enough to direct his life and he could not fault his wife for her reaction.

Recalling the despair he experienced when his father died, he forgave Deer Runner. Following his father's death, sorrow turned to anger, and he left home. His wife's spiritual malaise caused by thoughts of Walking Thunder's death, had almost ended her life.

When they married, Deer Runner left her family to live in the land of her husband. Walking Thunder had unwittingly brought her to a place where war had become a part of life and he left for months to fight, defending his people and home.

Where the latest warrior victory might lead, he could not guess. Perhaps the whites would leave as many believed, but he doubted that. Walking Thunder's intuition foretold that defeating the white man would require many more victories. He feared the whites would eventually overwhelm the Sioux.

Life in this part of Sioux country had become far too unsettling. Newly married and wanting to start a family, he weighed his options. The months of being away from his wife and risking his life had wearied him.

Perhaps it was time to return north to Deer Runner's people. Life there seemed to offer more chance of living lives their ancestors once took for granted.

Pulling back the tipi entry flap, he sat beside his sleeping wife and held her hand. After several minutes, her eyes opened and widened in surprise. She tried rising but he gently held her down. Calling for food, he fed her tenderly.

Over the following days, Deer Runner recovered her strength and spirit. Walking Thunder's proposal to take her home to live among her people, proved the most effective tonic. They would leave once winter eased and head north, hoping to find peace.

Spring came early and taking two packhorses, Walking Thunder and Deer Runner set out. After weeks of riding, they reached the land of the Assiniboia. Welcomed with open arms, they settled down and times were good.

Game was plentiful and although the buffalo herds were not as populous as before, there was no risk of famine. Since the whites were far away and in smaller numbers, the people's ways had not changed to the degree they had in the south.

Walking Thunder found the peace to his liking and band members appreciated his tracking and hunting skills. Confident he had found his place, they busied themselves making a baby. The next spring, Deer Runner gave birth to a baby girl whom they named Ehawee, or Laughing Maiden. She would be their only child.

Walking Thunder taught her to walk quietly and stay down wind while hunting. On starry nights, she sat on his knee while he spoke of their ancestors' guiding spirits.

The little girl loved her mother but idolized her father, often lamenting she had been born a girl. Little boys who bullied her quickly learned she was a fearless warrior who could beat them up. Mother and father laughed to hear stories of the camp's girl warrior who always wore a happy smile.

Walking Thunder had never aspired to lead others and wished only to develop skills in reading the spirit world. After putting Laughing Maiden to bed, he often sat watching the stars. The future remained unknown, but he believed the answers were in the stars. Messages often came, and his confidence grew as he came to understand their meaning.

One night, he quietly meditated and saw a grassy hill with white men on it. Dust rose in the air and the whites pointed wildly while warriors rode in and out of the dust cloud. They were fighting, and he presumed this was a replay of the fight of several years earlier. Whatever the vision portended, he resolved not to take his family near such danger.

Walking Thunder went out on a buffalo hunt and a large bull broke free of the herd. Several arrows and a spear had already wounded the bull and the beast was in agony. With bloody, raging eyes, it charged directly at Walking Thunder. His horse could not dodge the enraged beast and it knocked down horse and rider. Fatally wounded, the horse's squeals carried over the tumult of the hunt.

Knowing he faced mortal danger, Walking Thunder scrambled to his feet. Snatching his spear, he whirled to see the bull pawing the ground with a sharp hoof. Snorting angrily and lowering its shaggy head, the bull charged. Walking Thunder knew it was a life and death moment - perhaps for both man and beast.

Only feet from the spear, the bull skidded to a dusty halt and grunted through bloody nostrils. The eyes of man and beast locked, and Walking Thunder knew the bison was aware this was the end. The bull slowly sank on all haunches and shuddered. On the breeze, it sent a message. '*Remember your buffalo brother, your time soon will be no more.*' The light in its eyes dimmed and drifted away.

Two days later, Walking Thunder saw buffalo grazing in the distance. While he watched, the herd galloped over a low ridge and out of sight. Their thundering hooves reinforced the message of the dead bull; freedom to roam the plains was nearly at an end. Reining to a stop, Walking Thunder bowed his head and offered thanks to be among the last to live so freely.

Laughing Maiden was nearing her eighth birthday when her parents came to a decision. Children become curious as they grow, and the little girl was asking questions. She knew her grandmother and grandfather but wondered where her father came from and where his parents lived. Walking Thunder explained his father had joined the spirits years earlier and his mother still lived with her people.

The explanation naturally lead to a request to see her other grandmother. They discussed the idea and Deer Runner urged him to take them to Lakota country. Nine years earlier, they had come north and not once had Walking Thunder spoken of returning home. Deer Runner wanted to be fair, so they prepared for the trip.

The spring days grew warmer and with the prairie turning green again, they set out. During their years away, much had changed in the ancestral lands of Walking Thunder's people.

Red Cloud's War ended when the whites signed the Treaty of Fort Laramie in 1868. It granted land to the Lakota and ceded them the sacred Black Hills in perpetuity. The treaty stipulated the hills were to remain free of the white man, but future events would prove that was nothing more than false hope.

In 1874, Lieutenant Colonel George Armstrong Custer led an army expedition, including geologists and surveyors, into the Black Hills. When they found traces of gold, it touched off a gold rush. Skirmishes erupted between the whites and Indians and The Black Hills War began. All this was unknown in the north and Walking Thunder, Deer Runner and Laughing Maiden rode south to a land rocked by war.

They found a land strangely silent and empty. There were no signs of man and rarely did they see evidence of buffalo. Walking Thunder was perplexed; this land was home to vast buffalo herds. At Mato Paha, or Bear Butte, they finally found his people and he learned of recent events.

Although most refused, some Lakota had moved onto reserves following the treaty of 1868. It took little time for the white government to fail in meeting their treaty obligations. Young people rapidly grew disillusioned with their elders and moved off the reserves to follow Sitting Bull and Crazy Horse.

The gold rush and resulting public pressure for the army to protect miners from marauding bands of warriors, prompted the government to make an offer to buy the Black Hills from the Sioux. New offers were made of splendid reserves outside the disputed territories with the usual promises of good treatment.

Crazy Horse scoffed and suggested that if these reservations were so good, the whites should live on them and leave his people alone. With the refusal of this offer, the government ordered all Indians onto reservations by January 1, 1876. Those who rejected to obey the edict would be considered hostile and committing an act of war. The army received orders to round up and move the Indians, by force if necessary, to these reserves.

Sitting Bull and Crazy Horse refused the order and defiantly continued to live as their ancestors had. It was into this turmoil that Walking Thunder innocently led his family.

They eventually found a large camp of Sioux and Cheyenne who had joined for safety in numbers and mutual support. Walking Thunder found his mother, Wind Woman, who was overjoyed to see him. Laughing Maiden shyly greeted her grandmother and extended family.

The large camp astonished Walking Thunder; he never imagined there were so many warriors. Finding some he knew, they spoke of the dangers everyone might face should the army find them.

Two days later, the camp began moving west to a place the Sioux called the greasy grass. Clouds of dust rose into the air from horse-drawn travois and thousands of feet. Walking Thunder knew the dust was visible for miles and unfriendly scouts could easily follow their tracks.

Reaching a small river, the camp spread along the banks for several miles. The air held tension but for all that, Walking Thunder was happy to be among his people. After discussing the situation with Deer Runner, they decided to cut short their visit and return north. However, first he went hunting to re-provision.

After his return, they rested several days along the banks of the slow-moving river before leaving. The weather was hot and sunny, and people moved slowly in the heat. A disquieting rumour swept through camp that soldiers were moving toward them. Because the camp was large and full of warriors, people were unconvinced an attack would occur.

Late in the morning, Walking Thunder told Deer Runner he was going to the river for a bath. While splashing about in the cool waters, he looked over to the hills on the east side of the river. The hills looked familiar and with a shock, he recalled the vision at Bear Butte and the dream he had the year before.

These hills were the setting for his vision and dream. The reason for the visions he had never understood, was about to become reality. Shouting men, screaming women and shrieking children startled him and a man cried out, "Washitas!"

Warning calls rang out and sounds of gunfire came from the southern end of camp. Warriors scrambled for their horses and raced to the surprise attack. Streaming towards them, women and children desperately ran for their lives.

Savagely sawing his horse to a stop, Walking Thunder shouted for his wife and daughter to run north and hide in the trees along the river. His blood boiled seeing soldiers haphazardly shooting and hitting children, women and old people. All thoughts of living peacefully vanished as bullets cracked past his ears. Bodies littered the ground and a desire to kill seized him. Whipping his horse, he raced after warriors who were closing on the soldiers.

Horse soldiers had come down from hills and charged the south end of the camp. Surprised to find so many warriors, they dismounted to form a skirmish line. Waves of rushing Indians unnerved the soldiers who then panicked and ran for their lives.

Shrieking warriors chased them, stabbing and clubbing their enemy. A soldier shot at a charging warrior but the bullet only grazed Walking Thunder's shoulder. With his war club, he shattered the trooper's head. Blood and brains sprayed into the air and coated Walking Thunder's face in a gory war paint.

Urging his horse down the bank to cross the river and pursue the fleeing soldiers, he heard warning cries behind him. Reining in and listening, he discovered other soldiers were gathering to attack the north end of the camp.

It was exactly where he told Deer Runner and Laughing Maiden to hide. Fear and anger exploded in a fiery ball in his chest and racing back through the camp, he saw a column of horse soldiers fording the river.

A howling wave of mounted warriors, firing showers of arrows and bullets, charged headlong into the soldiers. As their attack failed, the soldiers turned and galloped away to escape. Hundreds of warriors crossed the river and chased them up the hills where soldiers tried forming a defensive circle.

Firing at any Indian who moved, the panicked soldiers hoped to defend themselves. Clever warriors evaded the volleys of gunfire by crawling through the long grass. Popping up to find targets, the warriors shot arrows at soldiers. Walking Thunder raised up to find a new target and a bullet snapped past his ear. He ducked but not before felling the soldier with an arrow.

Dust swirled, and horses shrilled in fear. Men were shouting and cursing while screams of pain filled the air. A warrior in front of Walking Thunder fell with half his skull missing.

Several other warriors died from arrows fired by their adrenalin charged comrades. Inexorably though, like a tide advancing on the shore, warriors crept ever closer to the soldiers.

A large group of screaming warriors on horses, charged over the hill and in minutes sealed the fate of the remaining soldiers.

Peeking above the grass, Walking Thunder saw victory was at hand and charged headlong into the fracas. A soldier swung a jammed rifle by the barrel, but Walking Thunder dodged the blow. His war club crushed the man's skull and splashed gore that recoated his face and shoulders in the hideous war mask.

Walking Thunder spun around to find another target and came face to face with a white man dressed in buckskin. Screaming his hatred, Walking Thunder raised the club to kill but he was too slow. Although the man's eyes bulged in terror, his hand was steady. Walking Thunder's last earthly sight was a long-barreled revolver flashing in his face.

Epilogue

The fight at Greasy Grass became known as The Battle of The Little Big Horn or Custer's Last Stand. The next day, the Indian camp moved and carried away most of the dead warriors. Somewhere on the open plains, warriors left Walking Thunder to allow his spirit to join their ancestors among the stars.

Deer Runner left the Lakota lands and returned to her people to live the remainder of her life in peace. She eventually married a white trader at the local trading post. Deer Runner and Laughing Maiden slowly adopted white customs and dress. Deer Runner's white husband changed Laughing Maiden's name to Florence Helen, although he never convinced Deer Runner to adopt a white name.

The young girl learned to read and write. White people condescendingly considered her one of the smarter Indians. Mother and daughter lived as white people, although Deer Runner never lost her pride of being one of the last nomadic people. She taught her daughter how to communicate with her ancestors.

And Deer Runner made certain her daughter knew the life story of the honourable man who was her father.

Foreword

Cursing another sneezing outburst, a shirtless young man slung another stook onto a hay wagon drawn by two plodding dray horses. An endless blue skyline stretched out to meet the equally endless prairie horizon. The only relief in the flat plain were other men engaged in the identical monotonous dance of collecting hay stooks standing sentinel in the silent fields.

The men grumbled as a matter of course at commencing their daily toil but the words quickly faded as they bent to the rhythm of their task. They knew their labour was essential to feed the dairy herds and cattle all families depended upon for survival through a harsh prairie winter.

Howling blizzards and deep snowdrifts would replace the blazing summer sun riding high in the sky. The work schedule would then be less hectic as their duties were primarily tending the livestock. Spring, summer and autumn months demanded long hours working the fields while also caring for the animals.

The young man's pace matched that of the horses as he strode alongside. Reaching onto the wagon, he ladled out water to cool his sweaty brow and scooped another to drink. Refreshed, he stretched his limbs and, hoisting another stook, swung it in an arc. It landed with a satisfying thump in the middle of the wagon.

Years of strenuous physical labour were obvious in the hard muscles of his upper body. Hearing the wagon driver chuckle at his youthful exuberance, he grinned in reply.

Sidney Turner was in the prime of his life that glorious month of July 1914. Three years earlier, at the age seventeen, he left the English village of his birth and came to Canada. That action was proving to be the most momentous of his life.

Periodically, he missed the familiarity of family, friends and the daily routine of his childhood home. Despite that, the vastness and promise of his adopted country quelled any question about the wisdom of his move. A disciplined and honest work ethic had served him well in creating a place for himself in this new land. When he thought of the future, his heart raced imagining the prosperity that was surely only months away.

A distant noon bell rang and as the wagon came to a stop, they unhitched the giant horses and led them to a shaded creek. The animals gratefully stretched their necks to the cool water before grazing grass on the bank.

Both men slipped off their work boots to dangle their hot feet in the water and unwrapped ham sandwiches that they ravenously wolfed down. When the last crumbs had vanished, they leaned back on a tree and Sidney closed his eyes. The driver followed suit but had no wish to sleep and as usual, he wanted to talk.

Although he was only two years older, John treated Sidney as a younger brother. Sidney met John's father, Percy MacDonald, literally within hours of arriving off the train. The elder man sized up the new arrival and extended an offer to work on his farm that included room and board. The MacDonalds had recently purchased more land and it was proving too much to handle for just himself and his son John.

Quickly proving his worth, Sidney settled into the routine and became one of the family. Mr. MacDonald asked Sidney to call him Dad rather than the stilted mister or by his given name of Percy that he hated. Sidney took to thinking of them as his Canadian family and it was a good arrangement for all concerned.

Mr. MacDonald had emigrated from England following the completion of Canada's trans-continental railway in 1885. He came west on the railroad, established himself in southwest Manitoba and began farming.

Shortly after starting on the land, he met the daughter of a neighbour and within a year they were married. Their son was born a year later, and he was proud to be the firstborn in this vibrant new land. To honour their adopted country, his father named him John after the first prime minister of Canada.

Unlike his father and Sidney, John's speech was free of the old country accent; his dialect was the twang of the new west. John would never admit his admiration of Sidney for venturing out alone this vast distance without the benefit of family, friends and with only the clothes he wore.

Stories of hardships in the old country cured John of all curiosity to see a place where life sounded so unfair and harsh. John could not understand why men would submit to lives of virtual economic and social slavery. Based on the tales he had heard all his life, it boggled his mind such a system even existed.

He was too innocent to understand the bias of family and friends was only one side of a complex story. John often asked to hear the stories and he never tired of hearing them repeated.

"Hey Sid, how long you been over here now?" Although his eyes remained closed, a patient smile crossed Sidney's face. John loved to talk, and he could not bear to sit silently more than a few minutes.

At their first introduction, he pressed Sidney for details of his personal life and travel stories. Sidney was reluctant to reveal much to a stranger, but John's honest nature and curiosity had won him over. Since their first encounter, the young men had become fast friends.

John marvelled to hear the story of how a near vagabond beat the odds stacked against him. This young Englishman arrived on the fertile western plains with only his wits and work ethic to claim fortune and fame.

Sidney had proven he was a different breed from many of his fellow compatriots. Many Britons arrived in the new world armed with a belief their birth as Englishmen granted them immunity from working. The discovery that able-bodied adults were expected to support themselves, rudely dashed this conviction.

Many Englishmen were nothing more than complainers and malcontents who would not give an honest day of work. As a result, it was often difficult for a newcomer from the islands to secure employment.

Sidney had shown he wished to succeed and make a productive life for himself in his adopted country. John heard a rumour Sidney had arrived with a hint of scandal trailing him. Despite repeated attempts, John was unable to prise details from his young companion.

Sidney still possessed the accent of his homeland but some of the spoken idioms of Canada were creeping into his daily speech. Although some of the old country slang was unfamiliar, John loved hearing the spoken lilt of the old country.

"John, are you so feeble minded you've forgotten we talked about that two weeks ago? I'm bloody glad the horses know where to go every day or we would never get to work. We'd be completely buggered, mate, if it was up to you to remember where we are supposed to be working." John laughed and picking up a pebble, playfully threw it at Sidney.

"You sound like a typical know-it all limey! Oh wait. You are just a limey, so I have to forgive you for being born with a bone between your ears." Sidney sat with eyes closed and raised a middle finger in reply. John chuckled and carried on with his verbal assault.

"By you asking the same questions, I'm trying to help you get out of that English fog you're all stuck in. At school, they taught us continuous practice helps you remember your letters and numbers. Oh, that's right. You never got past first grade!"

"Well I learned more in just one year than you learned in the six years it took you to pass grade two!" More pebbles were good naturedly tossed back and forth for several moments.

"All right then colonial dimwit, listen up to a story from one of your betters and maybe, just maybe, you can finally learn something."

Sidney gazed across the fertile fields as memory returned him to far away England. Closing his eyes, he heard familiar voices in the village and saw the activities of people there. A shudder rippled down his spine recalling the violent confrontation at home that led to expulsion from his birthplace. He drifted back to the bygone days of his truncated childhood.

The Voyage

Chapter One

Tightly twisting leather straps around a soccer ball-sized rock, twelve-year-old Sidney Turner snapped the reins. A black Percheron horse strained into the harness and a stone, held in the ground for an eternity, began quivering.

Sidney yelled encouragement to the animal while pulling back with all his strength on a steel pry bar. The rock teased with tiny movements of the sod holding it fast but refused to budge. He eased up on the reins and as the horse relaxed in the harness, the boy dropped them and wearily picked up a spade.

He jumped on the spade and his weight drove it down several inches. By slowly working his way around the stone, Sidney hoped to loosen it. Perhaps he and the horse might then pull it free.

Again, he snapped the reins and the mighty Percheron lent his enormous strength while Sidney hauled back on the pry bar. With a tearing noise of sod, the rock finally rolled up and out of the ground. Free of that resistance, the horse dragged it to the edge of the field where a pile of stones lay.

Reining to a stop, Sidney untied the harness from the rock and gazing up, guessed it was lunch time. He led the horse under several shade trees where it could drink from a brook bordering the field.

Despite his youth, Sidney was skilled in handling horses, the most valuable possession on a farm. The young boy loved working with this huge Percheron.

During the long work day, he continually spoke to it with boyish enthusiasm. When he stopped to let it drink, he massaged its forelegs and using a wet cloth, sponged the head, neck and flanks of the mighty beast. The horse repaid this kindness with a gentle whinny and nuzzled the boy's shirt.

They were a good team, very much in tune considering Sidney's tender years. Boys his age were rarely trusted with such a precious working animal. The farmer saw how fastidiously Sidney behaved with the horse and as a reward, taught him the art of being a farrier.

Sidney learned to trim horse's hooves and shape them to accommodate metal horseshoes. He learned and applied the knowledge with patience and always with the utmost of concern for the welfare of the animals.

Sidney's father owned the village butcher shop and he bought sheep from this farmer. That arrangement led to the elder Turner's sons working summers on menial chores the farmer did not have time to attend.

Both of Sidney's older brothers had worked on this farm for two years each. Their energies were now devoted to learning the butcher trade from their father and it was Sidney's turn to work on the farm. Unlike his brothers, he enjoyed his work.

As the third son, he had no chance of becoming part of the family business. The village and the shop were too small to support more than two sons and their future families. Sidney could expect more years of toiling at farm duties before necessity forced him to leave home.

He would never own a farm in this region of England. Wealthy landowners owned the larger farms in the parish. Men whose families had toiled for generations to save money to buy land, owned the small farms. Sidney already knew there were few options available in this small village. Whatever the future held, it lay elsewhere.

For the time being, his labours earned pennies for his family. His father took those earnings but did not know his wife secretly gave Sidney several pence each week to save. Sidney knew that small detail would earn him a thrashing from his stern father were he to learn of it.

The boy unwrapped the gingham cloth holding two thick slices of homemade bread slathered in bacon grease from the morning meal. Sidney was hungry and grateful his mother did her best to make him appetizing meals. He yearned for a thick slice of cheese – that would transform his lunch into a gourmet feast!

Once he devoured the bread, Sidney strolled to a nearby apple tree and shinnying up the trunk, seized several juicy apples. He slouched back under the tree to munch his ill-gotten gains while pondering the world about him. The horse listened without comment to the dreams of a boy who planned one day to earn a fortune.

Then he would buy this horse and the two of them could dine on whatever they wished. They might even sit idly under this shady tree all day. Neither would want for anything and meals would be served to them rather than earning only crumbs of bread and dried straw. His noon hour reverie ended far too soon. It was time to harness the horse and resume their chores.

The afternoon sun was agreeably warm and so the work did not quickly play them out. They made good progress and the pile of rocks beside the field steadily grew larger. Sidney was tying the harness to another large stone when he heard a voice.

To his pleasant surprise, his younger brother Albert was calling to him. It was nearly five p.m. and their mother sent Albert to fetch his brother home for dinner. Glad the work day was done, Sidney unhitched the horse. Holding a rein, he guided the great beast home to the farmer's yard.

Calling out a greeting to the house, he led the horse into a stall and filled the water trough before closing the gate. He knew that later in the evening, the farmer would give the animal fresh hay and a nosebag of oats. Cheerfully whistling, Sidney draped his arm affectionately over his younger brother's shoulder as they walked through their small village.

Pushing open the rear door of the shop, the boys climbed a dozen steps to the flat above that served as the family home. Rich aromas from the evening meal stoked hunger pangs they could not ignore. The boys followed these delicious scents into the kitchen where their mother met them.

Emily Turner was a stout woman of medium height who ruled as the benevolent matriarch of her brood of six children. She affected an air of iron discipline that even the youngest child knew was a façade. Try as she might to appear stern, Emily could not long hide her generosity and loving nature. Gathering the boys to her apron, she hugged and kissed each in turn.

"Enough now boys, run and wash your face and hands before dinner."

Cheered by their mother's affection, the boys scampered away to do her bidding. Along the way, they dropped to the parlour floor to talk with the two youngest children, Constance and Victoria. Emily doted on her girls. She loved their sweet innocence while they trailed along to help with the daily housework.

While Emily would not trade her four boys for the world, their need to be so rough and tumble puzzled her. Sidney wondered why girls wished to play house when they could be outside exploring, climbing trees or swimming in a pond. He had long ago decided that girls were just too different to take seriously and thought himself extremely fortunate to be a boy.

With their sisters in tow, the boys dutifully washed their hands. Naturally, they splashed just enough water to pass the wet hands test their mother would administer. All four children trooped into the kitchen and squeezed onto the bench between the table and wall.

Heavy footsteps on the stairs signalled the approach of the two elder brothers and Thomas. The eldest son went by his father's name and to avoid confusion, everyone referred to him as Junior.

The second son, Reginald or Reg in daily use, bore his name in honour of a favourite uncle. Junior was sixteen, Reginald had just turned fifteen and they would take over the family business.

Junior worked full time in the shop as schooling for him ended at age sixteen. Reg had one more year of studies before he entered the shop on a full-time basis. Their extended schooling was to groom them for taking over the family business and the sole reason each boy finished school.

The middle child of six siblings, Sidney did not differ from other family members save for one detail. Unlike the hazel eyes of the other Turners, he had blue eyes. It was cause for wonderment since only one in the family of eight had blue eyes.

As he matured, Sidney grew into a young giant and refused to allow anyone to strike him. He did not try to intimidate others but defended himself as necessary. When asked to stand for an incorrect lesson answer, he usually towered over the teacher. Time passed until only his father dared punish him.

To Sidney's credit, he did not bully or take advantage of his smaller classmates and siblings. He knew his size spared him from the abuses a tormenter might wish to visit on him. That truth formed his basis for understanding not to harm others simply because it was within his capacity.

Thomas eased some rules that demanded absolute obedience as the boys matured. Failure to do so had always resulted in a sound thrashing with a leather belt. The three older boys had experienced the stinging lash of a belt. Albert was still too young for such punishment.

During the last beating, Sidney raged he would beat his father senseless should the older man ever strike him again. For the last year, his father had not struck Sidney with belt or fist. The older man appeared to be easing up on the strict decrees.

There remained one rule their father still demanded they follow. The boys were not to play in the butcher room with the tools of the trade. Thomas had once caught Sidney and Reg playing a game of chicken with a meat cleaver.

One boy laid a splayed hand on a chopping block. The other boy swung a cleaver down trying to land the blade in the space between two fingers. Each boy received a sound thrashing for breaking that hard and fast edict.

Emily rarely spoke contrary to her husband. Regarding Sidney however, she voiced her absolute opposition to him leaving school to work full time before he turned sixteen.

Before reaching that age, many boys went out into the adult work world. Emily considered it a sin to force their son to leave school and home early for economic reasons. Thomas explained once more, the shop could not provide for three sons. Moreover, the village did not offer full time employment a workingman required to support his family.

"Very well then," Emily declared, "We owe it our son to give him the best chance possible. Both Sidney and Albert will live at home until they finish their schooling."

Thomas knew most of the village children left home barely able to write their own names. That condemned them to a life of toil with little hope for advancement. He grudgingly acknowledged it would be to Sidney's advantage to know more than how to scratch his name on a piece of paper.

Thomas viewed life through a purely economic lens. Sidney was growing older and providing for him had become more expensive. Emily always became angry when Thomas spoke of their child as a monetary expense.

"How dare you speak of our son that way? We brought him into this world to love as one of God's treasures. At least I always believed that."

Thomas shifted in his chair to reply but Emily's scowl at the intended interruption caused him to reconsider.

"Do not speak of Sidney or any of our children as though they are nothing but an expense. Sidney works after school, on weekends and gives you all his earnings. He is still a boy and he will not leave school early just to bring home a few more pence each day."

Her husband stared at the floor knowing there was no point offering further counsel on the subject. Emily however, wanted to be certain there was no room for doubt.

"Thomas, you know how dreadful it is working on a factory floor or in a coal mine. Sidney will be a workingman long enough in this life without starting him out early. Husband, do not force our son out to work now. I will never forgive you for that."

Sighing and thinking better of replying, he walked downstairs to his shop. Lighting a lantern to chase away the gloom, he picked up a carving knife to work on a mutton shank. The silence calmed him as he sat on a stool pondering the words Emily had spoken; she rarely challenged him.

Throughout their marriage, he had worked hard to provide for his family. The costs were increasing, and he was unsure if the shop could sustain them all. Sidney's earnings were small but covered expenditures for both he and his younger brother. That freed earnings to spend on expanding the family business. Why could Emily not accept that? Did she not worry about their survival as he did?

Thomas loved Emily for her loving, compassionate nature and he could not now find fault with her for it. He remembered well the night Thomas junior was born and how that awoke fears, he might not be able to provide for his son.

Primarily due to his marriage to Emily, they managed, and their family had grown to six children. Sighing, he reminded himself that if he kept his faith, those concerns would vanish. Extinguishing the lantern, he rose and returned upstairs.

Chapter Two

Several years passed since the evening Emily took a stand in defiance of her husband. It was the only time in their marriage she had flouted his will. There was an unspoken truce between husband and wife pertaining to Sidney's place in the family.

The result of the truce was Thomas grew resentful of Sidney and saw the boy as an impediment. Try as he might, his frustration with this situation festered.

Albert now worked with Sidney on local farms and the boys still paid all earnings to their father. Thomas kept half for the business, gave half to Emily and she surreptitiously gave each boy a quarter of her share. Emily had three years earlier emphasized to Sidney he must save this money for future needs.

A husband traditionally controlled family finances. Truth be told, Thomas knew Emily was the better money manager. Their partnership proved a success and slowly they prospered. With satisfaction, Thomas saw the days of scrimping and sacrifice were finally paying off. He had borrowed money years before and soon he would have it paid back.

Thomas planned to expand by opening another shop in a neighbouring town. One of the older boys would move over and operate the new shop. Thomas hoped that would allow each son to be self-supporting in his store. The unspoken problem with his plan was only the two oldest boys would benefit; Sidney and Albert remained unaware of the plan.

Thomas Jr. had worked as a cutter in the butcher shop for the last three years and could cut a side of meat to maximum effect and profit. After completing his grammar schooling the previous year, Reg took over the sales counter. His cheerful disposition ensured a visit to the shop was a pleasant experience.

Thomas was grateful the two eldest sons still accepted his directions with little question. One day they would wish to put their own stamp on matters. For the time being, however, he and the two oldest boys worked well together.

His third son was of much different character and Thomas grew ever more frustrated with him as time passed. Sidney stood six feet and taller than his father and brothers by five inches.

Years of farm work were transforming him from a boy into a broad- shouldered man with powerful upper body strength. He was a good-natured lad but the years of arguments and thrashings by his father changed the dynamics of their relationship. Sidney refused to be intimidated, disrespected, or to lose his possessions, and he made those principles known.

To treat him as his father often did was courting disaster. An angry retort was the least transgressors could expect. Not once did Sidney raise a hand to his father and Thomas grew complacent believing he never would. He ignored warning signs presaging the coming storm.

Sidney and Albert continued surrendering their wages. Emily still returned a small amount to them and insisted they save it. Unbeknownst to anyone else, she also set aside a portion of the house money for the two younger boys.

She was saving money for each boy in anticipation of a day she knew would arrive. Emily feared the explosion when Sidney discovered his earnings would be used to expand the family business.

With a mother's premonition, Emily sensed the day of reckoning was near. One morning, she went out to her vegetable garden. In a sunny corner of the bricked yard stood her prize English rose bush.

She alone tended the plant and told the children it was her special 'pet' plant. Her reason for cultivating this rose was a small clay pot buried behind it at the base of the brick wall. Inside the pot were two small leather pouches holding coins she had saved over the years.

Glancing over her shoulder, Emily pulled the pot from its secret place. The heavier pouch belonged to Sidney. The pouch disappeared into her apron; she reburied the pot and smoothed over the black soil.

Returning to the house, she climbed the stairs and checked to be certain she was alone. With a relieved smile, she entered the boys' bedroom and knelt behind Sidney's headboard. There she found the small leather pouch where Sidney hid his treasure, unaware his mother knew it existed. Emily poured the coins into Sidney's pouch and slipped it into the hiding place.

The prudence of Emily's actions was about to be justified. Thomas continued to ignore her pleas to stop taking the younger boys' money. Thomas could not forget the crushing poverty of his childhood due to his alcoholic father. The man died a drunkard and left his wife and four children destitute.

Thomas swore not to squander his own life in such a careless, selfish manner. The vow formed the basis for all his decisions and actions. While good intentioned, it blinded him to all else. He failed to recognize the contradictions of favoring two sons might ignite a conflagration and destroy the family dynamic.

On Saturdays, the farm work day ended at noon. Albert walked over to the distant field where Sidney was deep in thought. He and the black Percheron were still a team and today they were breaking sod. The farmer hoped to convert this pasture over to planting and grow a crop of sweet corn.

Albert stole to within fifteen feet of his older brother and tossed a small clump of sod at his back. Snapped from his concentrations, Sidney whirled to face his attacker. Laughing, he charged, and they tumbled to the sod sniggering and squirming.

Sidney always let Albert win but forced him to the point of exhaustion for every victory. He was proud Albert had learned not to fear anyone or surrender, no matter who his opponent might be. After a minute of rough housing, Sidney allowed Albert to pin him and declare victory.

"Well Sid, I hope you've learned it's hopeless to take on your younger brother. Maybe you should pick on our little sisters, you might have a chance!" Sidney bowed and asked Albert's forgiveness for his transgression.

"Sid, I'll think about it tonight and let you know whether you'll live until tomorrow morning."

Bowing again, Sidney unhitched the horse and walked it to the barn. He called out to the house and guided the horse to its stall.

Ensuring the water trough was full, he patted the horse on the neck and the boys chattered on the walk home. Their conversation ended when they reached the doorway leading into the shop. They heard the voices of Thomas and Reg, who were having a vigorous discussion.

"Dad, when will we open the new shop in Thame? I'm ready to give it a go. Junior has the shop here well under control and Connie is old enough to tend the counter. No time like the present, as they always say."

His father grunted a reply, "Who is they?"

Working in the meat locker, Thomas did not see Sidney and Albert. The boys looked at one another in surprise. This was the first talk they had heard about a new shop. Sidney's spirits jumped at the news and he hoped his father would ask him to work at the new venture, but his hopes vanished almost instantly.

"Whoever 'they' are, they're not the ones spending our money. Things are well along so give it another two months. With my savings, we are nearly there and then you can try running a shop."

Their father's plans obviously did not include the younger boys and Sidney viewed it as a betrayal for turning over his earnings. Emily's fears of a violent confrontation between Sidney and Thomas were about to be realized.

Albert turned to Sidney. Seeing the thunder on Sidney's face, Albert realized his brother was hearing the plan for the first time. He tried blocking the shop entrance, but Sidney brushed him aside like a wisp of smoke.

Reg was asking his father when he planned to tell the younger boys when Sidney darkened the doorway. His face a mask of fury, he closed on Thomas. In a voice of icy rage and menace, he stopped mere inches from his father.

"What the bloody hell is all this about then? You've been taking my money so Reg can have his own shop and I'm left with bugger all?" That his son would speak to him with such anger and language stunned Thomas.

"Who in blazes do you think you are, talking to me that way? I am your father! Apologize and then you can leave. I will..." The sentence ended when Sidney contemptuously pushed his father backward into a counter.

"Piss off you bastard! What kind of man takes from one son to give to another and keeps it a secret? All of my money, and probably Albert's too, is going for your grand ideas!"

Face to face with his furious son, Thomas feared one of his boys for the first time. Naively, he had never considered a physical confrontation with one. Sidney's eyes blazed as he roughly jammed a finger into Thomas's chest.

"You thieving bastard! Give me back my money right now! You've taken it for years, saying it helped our family. Here you've kept it all along. I bet you've never spent any of it on the family!"

Hearing the uproar below, Emily guessed the reason and ran downstairs. As she stepped across the threshold, Thomas raised a fist to strike Sidney.

The boy caught the fist in one hand and twisting his father's arm around, he struck his father and shattered his nose. The blow staggered Thomas and he grabbed the cutting table to keep his feet. Emily screamed which caused Sidney to turn.

Now completely enraged, Thomas raised a meat cleaver in hopes of intimidating Sidney but failed to consider Sidney's quick reflexes and enormous strength.

Sidney seized his father's arm and squeezed until the blade fell. He punched Thomas again who sank to the floor.

The heavy blade bounced from the cutting table, but Sidney caught it before it fell on his foot. His own fury had boiled over and he went to imbed the cleaver in the thick wooden table. Albert misinterpreted Sidney's intent and reached across to grab his arm.

Albert was not strong enough to prevent Sidney from swinging the blade down. All he accomplished was pulling Sidney's arm off course and with a horrifying thud, the blade cleaved the wooden table. Albert gave a shriek of pain when the cleaver chopped off two of his fingertips.

Emily screamed and furiously pushed Sidney aside. She wrapped a towel around Albert's bleeding hand and knelt to cradle Thomas' bloody head.

"Enough of this! Sidney, get out of here and stay out. Reg, help your father. I'll look after Albert and get him to the doctor."

Sidney stood glowering over his father and saw the fury and heartbreak on his mother's face. It shamed him. Turning on his heel, he left the shop and vaulted the stairs two at a time.

Reaching under the headboard, he grabbed the leather pouch. It was heavier than he remembered but there was no time for wondering about that now. Stuffing the pouch in a pocket, he pulled open several drawers and grabbed a pair of trousers and a shirt.

Turning around, he saw Constance and Victoria, and their tears proved they knew what this moment meant. Crossing the floor, he wrapped them in a bear hug.

Kissing each on the cheek, he huskily whispered, "Tell Ma I'm sorry and not to worry. I'll write so you know I'm all right." With tears threatening his composure, he brushed past and his boots thundered down the stairs and out the door.

Sidney knew there was no chance of reconciling with his father. He had committed the mortal sins of cursing and striking the man who led the family.

News of their brawl would spread throughout the village and make him an outcast no matter the provocation. For a young man to fight with his father was inexcusable in the eyes of townsfolk and Sidney knew he would be a pariah.

Fighting with his father was enough of a disgrace; that he also seriously injured his younger brother was the final nail in the coffin. He thanked the stars Emily forced him to save his money. Heaven knew it was not much but with a bit of prudence and by finding a job, he just might make it.

Several miles from town, he remembered the extra heft of the pouch and pulled it free to examine. The mystery ended when he found a note: "My boy, here is a little help. Take care and remember, a mother's love is forever."

At some point in a boy's life, he realizes one of the most powerful forces in the world is his mother's love. Leaving the road, Sidney crouched under a large tree and sobbed.

After a few minutes, his composure returned, and he realized today was the first as his own man. It was all up to him from here on; there would be no relying on his parents. He grimly admonished himself, *'No more bloody crying either, you pussy.'*

With a burst of pent up energy, he vaulted the stone fence. He had no plans for shelter or meals as he trod along a dirt road leading away from the only home he had known.

About all he knew was the great seaport of Southampton lay to the south. As he could think of no other course of action, he followed his instincts. All his life, five miles was the furthest he had been from home. Without a map, he would need to ask directions but right now, it was too soon. He did not want local folk to know or guess his destination.

Unsure if his boots would survive the long trek, he decided to walk barefoot the ninety odd miles. He always worked barefoot on the farms and tough calluses had grown on his feet. The warm sun tanned his skin and helped him appear several years older than his seventeen years.

Chapter Three

At noon on the journey's fourth day, he stood on the crest of a hill and gazed at one of the busiest harbours in the country. The city of Southampton was the largest he had ever seen and although he had heard stories, he was still unprepared for the vista that lay before him.

Adding to the wonderment, his timing coincided with the arrival of several squadrons of the Royal Navy's new battleships that were anchored in the Solent. The silent menace of these sleek grey warships, stirred deep feelings of patriotism; he wondered if joining the navy might satisfy his curiosity of what lay beyond the horizon. Could he find prosperity in His Majesty's navy?

England had been secure behind the wooden walls of her navy since the days of the Spanish Armada of 1588. The ships were now steel and although a threat across the North Sea had arisen, most Britons did not doubt their superiority. Recruitment efforts urged young men to serve and meet the navy's increasing manpower needs. Perhaps becoming a blue-jacketed sailor could satisfy the wanderlust assailing him.

Sidney knew leaving home had been spur of the moment. With no plans, apprehension about the unknown plucked at his youthful confidence; he knew not a soul in this great city. For several moments, fear of the unknown caused him to consider returning home and beg forgiveness. Then his spirit flared and slammed the door on the idea. No matter, the future lay somewhere ahead and taking the road down this hill was the first step.

An hour of walking brought him to the centre of the great city. The hustle and bustle swept him along and he followed a scent of the sea to the harbour. The docks of any major port are rough and tumble areas with many perils to waylay a young man.

Despite the tender years, his survival instincts were sharp after fistfights with school bullies, tussles with older brothers and his father. It served him well in his first hours by the docks where toughs, thieves and prostitutes preyed upon the naïve and innocent. His size and broad shoulders deterred those who might consider him an easy target.

He still had no clear idea what to do when the road reached its terminus at the docks and he looked about in wonderment. Ones' future course is, at times, determined by chance.

Advertising posters were plastered everywhere. A large coloured poster for the Canadian Pacific Railway caught his eye. It encouraged readers to join thousands of other Britons who had sailed to Canada for a better life.

Sidney was a true product of his country and people of their island nation believed in the supremacy of the British race. They considered the planet was civilized and primarily at peace due to missionaries, scholars, explorers, physicians, industrialists and the Royal Navy. Their belief lay in the certainty God led and guided the people of their islands.

England had known peace for nearly a century because men such as Nelson and Wellington had defeated their enemies. Nelson thwarted Napoleon's invasion plans by crushing the French and Spanish fleets at Trafalgar in 1805. Wellington helped end the threat of Napoleon, ten years later at Waterloo.

The British Empire became global, an empire upon which the sun never set. Sidney accepted this truth with the same certainty he had that tides rose and fell each day. To consider a time might come when this order could end was simply beyond imagination.

He felt energized by considering leaving the land of his birth. The idea had sprung from thin air in only the last two minutes and was a future he had never imagined. His entire existence was rooted in the village where generations of Turners made their lives. He had never known anyone to leave England; it was entirely a foreign concept.

A fresh breeze sprang from the water and filled his lungs. A shiver of excitement ran up his spine and burst in a wide smile on his face. All he knew of Canada was it had been part of the empire for centuries. In his youthful ignorance, he presumed it would be like England.

Canadians spoke English and as a former British colony, for Sidney, it naturally followed they were civilized subjects of England. Although he did not yet realize it, this instant of decision defined the remainder of his life, the poster details etched forever in his mind.

An unseen magnet pulled him to the docks where ocean freighters lay. The ships were hives of activity as dockside cranes raised large nets filled with goods from the cargo holds. Stevedores swarmed over the nets and manhandled the goods onto horse-drawn wagons. When fully loaded, the wagons moved off at a command from the horse drover.

Once the cargo holds were empty, other wagons pulled alongside and the process reversed. Crates of manufactured products destined for far off lands were hoisted high overhead and disappeared into the belly of a freighter.

From decks deep below came muffled shouts as stevedores emptied the nets. Using dolly carts, they vanished into the dark steel cargo holds and stacked each to full capacity. Sidney saw the frantic activity and despite appearances, it was anything but chaotic.

Foremen bellowed orders via megaphone to the stevedore gangs, used arm signals to guide the crane operators while making certain all stayed on schedule. The oily smell of cranes, horse droppings, sweat and hemp netting combined with ocean scents to fire his imagination.

Perhaps here was a chance to realize ambitions the travel poster had stirred. Sidney would learn quickly the perils of youthful naiveté in this place of hurly burly hustle.

Sidney had learned about physical labour in the farm fields. Though his father was a stern taskmaster, he instilled in his sons that hard work was the key to prosperity. Sidney took the lesson to heart and the time for action had arrived. Considering his finances, he mulled over the options.

In an era when many working men earned the annual salary of 50 British pounds, Sidney had no hope of paying for a steamship ticket. The sum of funds in his trouser pocket totalled only two pounds. Even with his mother's help, saving that small amount had taken five years. A third-class steerage ticket on a humble Trans-Atlantic steamer cost two months' wages. He might as well dream of growing wings and flying across the ocean.

In common with many people, he had no identity papers or even a birth certificate. His birth was on record at the village church but other than the national census taken every ten years, he did not exist. No matter, his rudimentary reading and writing skills were enough for his entry on the world stage. He could cross the ocean on one of the freighters by volunteering to work for his passage.

Necessity spurs people to push beyond their normal boundaries and so it was with Sidney. At seventeen he was already the height of many older men and stronger than most. Spurred by need, he strode to the gangway of the nearest freighter. With no one in attendance, he began walking aboard. Very quickly though, a scowling man stepped from a doorway near the bridge.

"You there. Stop right now! Where the hell do you think you're going, sonny?" Although caught by surprise, Sidney was no stranger to a rough greeting.

"I want to cross to Canada by working for my passage." A rude peal of laughter and rough talk was the reply.

"Piss off laddie, you and ten thousand other rabble who can't buy a ticket! Be gone before I kick your arse into the water!"

Sidney's anger flared at such rudeness. He took a step forward to confront the man so brusquely trashing his aspirations. When the man drew a club from his waistband, Sidney saw there was no chance of a fair fight.

"Mate, if I see you ashore without your stick, you'll be the one getting his arse gets kicked into the water. Depend on that, you bastard."

The man thought of attacking but seeing the young man's size and fire in his eyes, he held back. With a glare and a one-finger gesture, Sidney retreated. On the dock, he looked back and saw the man had vanished.

"Surely not everyone here is such a bastard! I just need a ship to sail away from this place."

With that in mind, he resumed his quest. While not greeted so curtly elsewhere, no one was willing or able to help him. Unsure how to solve his dilemma, he sat on a bollard to think.

He remembered his father's words. It was not what you knew, it was who you knew. Rapidly learning the truth of these words, he needed to think of how best to use the advice. The first step was getting off the bollard, as it had not yet offered a single recommendation.

Passenger ships of large steamship lines belonged to the Cunard or White Star firms. It would have been posh to cross aboard a liner like the *Lusitania* or *Olympic*. Such are the dreams of a young man, but reality brought Sidney back to earth.

The steamship lines forbade taking on passengers to work for their passage. No officer would risk dismissal and being black listed should he break those rules.

Sidney did not have the money to bribe his way aboard by approaching an ordinary seaman. He could try stowing away but did not relish hiding for a week under a lifeboat, cold, wet and hungry.

The prospect of being arrested, clapped in chains and thrown in the brig, was unappealing. He would return to England branded a criminal and serve a prison term. After several moments, a solution presented itself. If he hired on as a crew member, that would solve the problems of meals, lodging and avoid a stay in jail.

With that in mind, Sidney set off to find a ship needing men. By way of naïve confidence and ignorance, he went to the largest passenger liner. Remembering his last experience, he knew not to simply walk up the gangway. Dock side, he saw a man in the black tunic uniform of the Cunard line.

"Pardon me sir. Are you taking on men for work? Even if they will work for free?"

The man had a lifetime of sea service and surmised the young man was leaving or running away from home and his countenance softened. With a wife and family, the man knew the anguish it would cause his wife if one of their boys ran off to sea.

"Laddie, what are you doing down here on these rough docks? Son, you should be at home with your family." Sidney flushed and considered the kindly advice but remembered why he left home.

"Sir, there is nothing for me there and I am off to seek my fortune in Canada."

Although the officer smiled, Sidney recognized no derision was involved. With only the clothes on his back, it must be obvious how unprepared he was. If there were other avenues of opportunity, none was apparent at this moment.

"Sir, there is no home for me there. I hope to find one ahead of me. Can you tell me where to find a job aboard a ship?"

Bound by regulation, the officer knew there was no possibility of this lad boarding the liner. Working aboard a transatlantic liner was highly prized for the working conditions and usually higher wages.

There were long lists of men hoping to work aboard the liners and this was not the only obstacle - there were trade and labour unions to consider. That required a membership card, signing at the bottom of a long list of names and waiting for an opening. The officer grimly chuckled and hoped Sidney would heed his words of advice.

"Lad, there is no chance of you working aboard this ship. There are hundreds of men hoping to work aboard. Union men are on board and trouble would find you if a unionist discovered you working and not signed up. I don't want that kind of trouble and neither do you. Why do you want to go to Canada so much?"

"Sir, I come from a small village and there's no work there. All I had was leaving to work in a factory or coal mine. None of that interests me so I packed up what was mine and left."

The older man knew there were holes in Sidney's tale but there seemed little point asking further questions. He listened while the youngster finished speaking.

"I didn't really know where to go, just that Southampton was away south, so I started walking. Once I got here, it seemed as good a time as any to decide where to go."

"Are you sure you wouldn't be better off back at home, boy? How much do you really want to go to Canada? More to the point, do you know anything about Canada? About all I know about the place is it takes a week to cross by train. There are thousands of miles of wilderness and little else."

Sidney smiled as he tried to determine how to answer the questions posed to him.

"Sir, to be honest a week ago, I had never thought about Canada. I never went beyond my village and always thought England as home. Being here talking to you, was not in the cards." He paused to catch a breath and organize his thoughts.

"I saw a railroad poster for Canada and seeing the offer of free land made up my mind. Here, I can never have anything like that and it seems a brilliant idea. Can you help me, sir?"

"Lad, I have a wife and kiddies at home. If one of our boys ran off, it would break my wife's heart. It goes against my better judgement to help you leave your family." Seeing the impetuous youth's determination, he wrapped up his speech.

"You've made up your mind, so I will try to steer you right. If I were young again, I might ask if you want company. The thought of owning your own land is mighty appealing." The officer paused to relight his pipe before finishing.

"Lad, you won't find a ship on these docks, but you might find a ship to Canada, across the harbour. A ships mate will quickly size you up, and down below you'll go." The officer offered several words of caution and advice to Sidney.

"First, ask if men are being hired before offering to work for free. A fellow who sailed with me long ago, is first mate on a steamer across the way. Find him and say a Cunard fourth officer sent you. His name is Thompson and he is a good sailor. He's a bit quick-tempered and his love of whiskey gets him in trouble." Sidney wondered what sort of situation he might face but politely continued listening.

"If you are hired, keep your mouth shut, keep a hand on your wallet and sleep with one eye open. The ship is the *Angus Celt*. She is old and slow but will get you to Canada. Good luck boy, and I hope you find your bit of paradise in Canada." The officer held out his hand which Sidney shook gratefully.

"Sir, I do not know how to thank you beyond saying so. I will remember your kindness."

"Lad, going to Canada to make something of yourself that you could not do here will be thanks enough." With that, the officer turned and strode up the gangway.

Fate often redirects a life path in completely unexpected directions. The old merchant ship Sidney sought would provide far more than transportation and remuneration. This chance suggestion of securing work would reward Sidney with a lifelong friend and gain beyond his wildest reckoning.

With hope surging in his breast, Sidney searched for the ship to carry him to the Promised Land. Numerous ships tied to the docks, made him wonder about ever finding it.

After a long trek, he found it, and his heart sank at the sight. An apparition straight from a nightmare replaced the ocean liner of his dreams. His anger boiled up for it appeared the officer had cruelly played him for sport.

This diminutive vessel appeared unfit to be towed across the harbour, much less to attempt an ocean crossing. Sidney guessed the entire boat might fit on the foredeck of the ship he just left. A solitary smoke stack poked up amidships between the fore and aft masts. The bridge and wheelhouse were visible just above the railing.

The black sides were streaked red and patches of rust pockmarked the white superstructure. Perhaps this was not the right ship and he had taken a wrong turn. However, as his eyes drifted aft, he read the faded white remnants of a painted name; the *Angus Celt*.

A pall of neglect hanging over the ship accompanied scents of coal dust, rust, old rope and oily timber. Foul green bilge water dribbled from drains several feet above the water line to spatter into the harbour water.

At first, he saw no signs of life, but then a figure emerged from a doorway on the bridge. Surprised to see anyone showing interest in the ship, an older man stepped to the railing and peered down at the visitor.

He said nothing but took a pipe from between his stained teeth and spat a stream of brown tobacco juice into the water. He coughed, spat again and returning the pipe between his uneven teeth, resumed examining the young man on the dock.

Mindful of his earlier exchanges, Sidney felt unsure whether to speak or walk away. He decided to move along and as his intent became obvious, the older man hailed him.

"What are you doing there, boy? Are you lost, or do you want to buy this ship? She can sail anywhere and do it for years to come. You look like a smart fellow who knows a good ship when he sees one. Want to buy her and make a fortune, boy?"

The man laughed at his own wit and began coughing when the guffaws overwhelmed his rheumy lungs. He spat again and lounging on the railing, returned to staring at the young man.

Unprepared and astonished by such an approach, Sidney could not believe the man thought him foolish enough to believe this scow could possibly sail anywhere. Even with no experience with the ocean, Sidney doubted this ship could reach the shores of a country thousands of miles away. Raised to respect his elders, even one such as this, he answered the man in a civil tone.

"No sir, I am not here to buy a boat. I hoped to find a job aboard a ship sailing to Canada. I was sent from across the harbour but seeing this boat, makes me think someone played a game on me." His impertinence made the older man's temper flare.

"What do you know about ships, you smart ass pup? I bet you've never even been on a ship. Keep your stupidity to yourself!" The old mate angrily seethed in response to Sidney's cheek.

"I'm the mate of this ship and I hire the men. You don't know shit about the sea to think you can speak badly of my boat! How dare you stand there, lobbing words at me?"

For the second time that day, Sidney found himself on the verge of fisticuffs with an older man. His first encounter had been unsuccessful and though his second experience went much smoother, he did not find work. Common sense dictated he walk away to find another ship.

Growing desperate, he decided to change tack. Choking back his own angry retort, he demonstrated unusual maturity and furthered his cause.

"I did not mean to give offense, sir. As you guessed, I've never been at sea. The fourth officer of the Cunard liner yonder told me to ask for first mate Thompson of the *Angus Celt* about a job. As you say, I don't know ships and thought I was at the wrong one."

While not entirely the truth, Sidney prayed the man would not see through his white lie. For a long moment, the man glowered, and Sidney wondered whether he was about to be shot.

As the moments ticked away, a drop of sweat ran down Sidney's spine. No one was at hand if matters turned against him. To his surprise and immense relief, when the man spoke again it was in a conciliatory tone.

"You say the fourth officer told you to find me? I've known Harold many years and he would never send me a boy that could not sail with a ship's crew. Well, come here boy, and show me your hands. I don't want you if your hands don't know what hard work is all about. Hard work is all you'll get if I decide we need you." When Sidney joyfully whooped, old Thompson could not hide a smile.

"Step lively now, we load this afternoon. I'm short two hands who got drunk and wound up in jail. You've got to be at least twenty and if the captain asks, remember you're twenty.

"So, if you really do want to go to Canada - and God knows why anyone would – get your ass up the gangway." Fierce joy bubbled up, and like a soul offered salvation, Sidney leapt aboard.

Chapter Four

"Please, please, please, please. If there really is a God, help me puke up my stomach and be done with all of this shit."

Sidney's attempt to straighten up from the rusty rail failed when more retching again forced him to lean over the side of the ship. Once more, he thought of ending his misery by diving into the heaving green sea.

"I can't stand this anymore, Bert. Get a gun and bloody well shoot me. I won't mind at all so just dump my arse overboard." The mate chuckled grimly while shaking his head.

"Not a chance, boy. Think I want to be up on charges for destroying company property? You haven't worked a minute in the last two days. You aren't eating though so maybe old Thompson will think it's an even wash. Being seasick don't last much more than two or three days, so right quick, you'll be able to eat stew again."

Bert laughed when Sidney gagged again at the mention of food and he eased the youngster to the deck. "I guess your guts don't think that's funny."

"If I had any puke left, I'd gladly die if it hit you." Wearily passing a shaky hand over his forehead, Sidney hoped to quiet the pounding drums for just a blessed minute. Looking askance, he glanced up at Bert and smiled wanly.

"Here you prick, help me up so I can sit down and catch my breath." Bert eased Sidney to a locker where he could sit down and repeated his advice.

"Look straight ahead, not at the horizon. I brought some ginger ale. You best get over this or you won't make much money. Can you get back to it by tomorrow?"

Several days earlier, Sidney had joined the black gang deep below in the boiler room. Given his size and youth, he was perfect for such physically demanding work. Before they left

Southampton, he found a trimmer's job required no technical skill.

The only prerequisite was an ability to shovel huge amounts of coal. Hundreds of tons of coal slid down chutes from topside where it piled up in lopsided pyramids. This coal needed to be stored in dark, grimy bunkers along the ship's steel hull.

A trimmer's unenviable task was spreading the heavy coal evenly throughout the bunkers; coal stacked haphazardly could cause the ship to list to one side. In rough seas, this might cause the ship to founder.

It was imperative to rearrange, or trim, the coal before the ship sailed and it demanded a fast work pace. Larger ships had bigger crews and the work was not as onerous as on smaller vessels.

Such was Sidney's introduction to life aboard a freighter and the punishing duties astounded him. Unless a person performed this job, words failed to describe such toil. His muscles screamed for relief from continually jamming a shovel into piles of coal and heaving it into a steel wheelbarrow.

Sidney had heard vague references to the term black gangs that richly described men blackened by coal dust. A boiler boss yelled for the black gangs to trim the coal, so they could get under way. With trimming nearly complete, the men rushed to supply the boiler rooms with coal.

There they fed the insatiable furnaces to create a hellish heat that fired the steam boilers. Steam created power to drive the massive pistons that spun a long steel shaft and a bronze propeller.

If the black gangs shovelled enough coal, in three weeks the vessel should arrive at the destination port. The crew then off-loaded the cargo, reloaded with lumber, grains, ores and other goods vital for the survival of their island nation. All it required was the back-breaking labour of the black gangs.

Before the first day ended, Sidney vowed this was his last voyage working aboard an old merchant ship. Sidney's youthful energy barely sufficed to complete his shift. He hoped to make his way topside and collapse in the cool night air. Never had he known such demanding physical work, noise or heat.

No matter how he pushed himself that day, he lagged. His days on the farms seemed idyllic compared to this nightmare of dust and heat where the only light flared through boiler door peepholes.

All day he stumbled, causing the heavily laden wheelbarrow to tip over and spill coal everywhere. The boiler boss and fellow trimmers cursed him while Sidney frantically refilled the wheelbarrow and tried staying clear of the rushing men. The day wore on in a delirium of struggling for breath while sweat streaked with stinging coal dust ran in his eyes.

The shift finally over, he crawled to the main deck for fresh air and saw, in surprise, night had fallen. On the northern horizon, he could see a black smudge of land. Lights twinkled, and Sidney realized this was his last view of England.

A quarter moon rose above the eastern horizon in reply to sunset's fading glow. Refreshing western breezes blew the acrid black funnel soot well astern. Sidney saw the North Star high in the black vastness and his eye traced a path in the Milky Way.

Overhead, a shooting star flared and trailed away to the west. Despite the arduous labour, his spirits rose, and he reminded himself it was only three more weeks. *'That is, if I live through this shit ...'*

A burly seaman came up from below, lit a cigarette and leaned on the railing. Sidney recognized Bert, the black gang foreman. Only in his mid-thirties, Bert had already been at sea more than twenty years. Most of the crew considered Bert a first-class bastard for more reasons than just his birth.

Sidney heard the big man had served in the navy and was the fleet boxing champion. Whatever his reasons for being aboard this poor steamer, no one knew, and none dared ask.

Bert's life story was one of defying the odds stacked against him. Through sheer force of will, he created several lucky breaks he used to full advantage. His life was a tale fit for telling about the law of the jungle.

His full name was Bertrand, a name too dandified for the hard scrabble life of a tough sea port. Born to a teenage prostitute, she left him on an orphanage doorstep. The mother scribbled his name on a scrap of paper and tucked it in a small wooden box.

After wrapping the child in a filthy blanket, she vanished from the doorstep of the Westhaven orphanage. For all his life, Bert carried the facility's name.

He lived his early days in a series of foster homes where he was always last in line for meals and clothing. Little wonder then Bert grew up tough and the miracle was he survived. The lesson he drew from those experiences was to always be ready to fight. He fled the last home after slashing the foster parent who tried to rape him.

Bert took to roaming Southampton's dirty streets and joined a gang of homeless youngsters that prowled the docks. A brotherhood of wolves, quick to run after a theft and quick to fight when cornered.

His life changed late one night near the navy yards. The gang tried robbing three drunken sailors when six large sailors of a shore patrol turned the tables. After subduing the gang with the liberal use of night sticks, they hauled Bert before a navy captain for sentencing. The captain offered him two choices: a lengthy prison sentence for attempted robbery or a four-year stint in the navy. The thought of losing his freedom terrified Bert and he accepted the lesser of two evils.

The navy changed his life. He learned to read, write and basic arithmetic. His reward was a promotion to gunner's mate aboard a battleship. That was not the end of his lessons either. Following scuffles with several crewmembers, an older petty officer taught Bert to box. Honing his skills, he eventually became a heavyweight navy boxing champion.

Sidney knew none of that tale when Bert came up on deck the first evening. He knew to be careful around the big man, that he was as liable to take a swing as speak. Flicking a cigarette away, Bert turned to see Sidney sitting on a chain locker.

When the young man nodded in greeting, Bert unclenched his fists and returned the gesture. Bert met each new situation ready for a battle to the death until he knew there was no hazard.

Sidney had never known a man so full of menace and potential violence and wondered if he invited disaster simply by speaking. But *'in for a penny, in for a pound'* and casting caution to the wind, he asked the older man a question.

"Can I ask how long you have been at sea, sir?"

Bert guessed the young man knew of his reputation and ferocious temper he most certainly had earned with the crew. But this youngster had taken a chance and addressed him respectfully.

Bert witnessed Sidney's heart and determination in the boiler room. The lad kept his mouth shut despite hearing harsh curses for his clumsiness and inexperience. Other men might have argued, worked at a slower pace or become violent.

Bert saw the big lad's strength and while he had struggled with the heavy loads, knew he would grow stronger in the coming days. Sidney spoke intelligently and hopefully would avoid shipboard hazards that often befell young men. That he was polite and respectful clearly indicated the youngster would think before speaking.

"How old are you boy?"

"I am seventeen, sir." Sidney answered before belatedly remembering his instructions to answer twenty if questioned. "At least I was seventeen three years ago, sir." Bert laughed at the display of quick thinking.

"Boy, you worked hard enough today to be twenty. Not to worry, if you can stand the pace, no one will wonder about your age. But don't tell anyone else or by law, the captain will turn you in at Montreal. And don't address me as sir, I'm not an officer. I'm just the first mate below decks. Can you read and write, boy?"

"Yes sir." Sidney proudly replied before recalling the directive not to address Bert as sir. "If I'm not to call you sir, how then shall I speak to you?"

"Bert works fine off shift. Mr. Westhaven down below. You've never been to sea boy. What in hell are doing out here on this old bucket? Won't your family wonder where you are?"

Sidney knew to be cautious with people he did not know. He had struck up a conversation with a man others had warned him to avoid. Now he wondered if his hesitation might offend.

Without his father's written permission, Sidney could not legally work aboard ship; the captain could clap him in irons. That would be highly unlikely if Bert spoke in his defence. All the same, Sidney wished to share just enough to ease his way out of the current moment.

"My father and I had a bit of a disagreement. It seemed best to clear out and let matters calm down." The innocuous answer sounded plausible to Sidney and he waited for Bert's reply.

Bert knew Sidney had not really told him anything. Until he heard more, his curiosity would remain unsatisfied. He wanted further details before deciding on how much protection this lad might need.

"Sonny, I ain't asking just to make simple talk. You busted your ass down below and not every man survives his first day. But you did, kept your yap shut and earned a day's pay." Pride for a job well done, especially from this big man, felt gratifying.

Bert continued, "Most of these dullards don't know I'm part owner of this old tub and there's no need for them to know. I've been working my ass off my whole life but five years ago, I wised up. When this old boat came up for sale, we bought it. Didn't have much money but we had a plan. The captain knows a Southampton businessman who loaned us the scratch.

"We're working to pay off the loan, meals and clothes. The boat pays for the coal and crew, as few repairs as we can manage. His lordship takes the rest. Next year it's paid off and then we can start paying ourselves.

"The captain captains, Thompson runs the ship and I keep the peace. I make damn sure no unionists get on board and if one does, well he gets wised up right quick and he doesn't get aboard again."

Bert quietly chuckled at a memory in a tone so filled with deadly humour, Sidney shivered. Reading his thoughts, Bert reassured the boy.

"Lad, I don't see you as a unionist. One of those bastards would never have worked like you did today or kept his scurvy mouth shut. I'm not afraid to use my fists to keep the peace.

"Don't believe everything you heard about me, probably most, but not all. Give me an honest effort, keep your yap shut and don't ever think of crossing me. Now it's your turn to talk before I tell you more."

A man who gave every indication of being nothing more than an oafish brute had astonished Sidney with these confidences. Sidney realized not all people were what they wished others to see. Throwing caution to the wind, Sidney decided to share his story. If Bert did not care for it, he might well toss him overboard.

"My family lives in the town of Chinnor on the old road between Oxford and London and my father owns the butcher shop. I'm the third son of four and the shop is too small for me to work in.

"My only choice was leaving home to work in a factory or coal mine, so I decided on going to Canada. Not sure if sailing to Canada is best for me to do, but it can't be any worse than staying in England. No offence intended either." Bert smiled hearing the story and admired Sidney's pluck.

"A fine tale, but nothing bad enough to get you out here."

Sidney thought about recent events and his mother's tears, fury and fear. While heartbroken to leave his mom, brothers and sisters, he was determined to make a success out of the hand dealt by his father.

"My old man and me had a row. I lost my temper and pushed him. He took a swing, so I punched him. He grabbed a meat cleaver and I thought he would hit me with it. I grabbed his hand, made him drop it, and hit him again. I tried throwing the cleaver away, but my little brother Albert thought I meant to use it. He pulled my arm down and I chopped off two of his fingertips. My mom got in the middle and screamed at me to get away from them. What a shitty feeling, but I did what she said.

"There's a couple of pounds in my boot but it's all I have. No idea how much I'll need in Canada. I hope that and what I make here, will be enough."

Hearing the grandiose plans of a boy barely old enough to leave school astonished Bert. While his life had not been smooth, never had he considered leaving England. His life and future fortunes changed when he joined the navy to avoid a lengthy prison sentence.

Training cruises took the ship to many ports of call. To see warm climes and tropical islands revealed a wider world than that of often gloomy England. Imagination soared to think of charting his own destiny and where to drop anchor rather than the navy making those decisions for the remainder of his days.

Bert began deliberating where he would be, what his life might be versus staying in the navy for thirty years. Thoughts of living his twilight years on a small pension near the navy port did little to excite. He decided to leave at the end of his twelve-year enlistment period.

His decision to leave came following an all-night poker game in a seedy Portsmouth pub. Upon winning a high stakes game, his expression did not reveal he won the equivalent of four years pay. Returning to his ship, he decided to leave the navy even though it had been home most of his life.

Bert met Thompson and the future captain two days later. By pooling their capital, they had just enough for a down payment to finance the boat. However, Bert would discover one final item to address before they sailed.

The money he won playing poker did not belong to the opposing player. That poor unfortunate borrowed the money to play cards. Adding to his problem, he borrowed from two separate bookies. When he lost, the gambler lost all ability to repay the loans.

Two days later, police found the unsuccessful gambler floating in Southampton's harbour. Beaten to a pulp, the coup de grace came from a bullet in the head – a grisly warning about failing to pay gambling debts.

Rumours quickly spread about who ordered the hit and Bert guessed trouble might be brewing. It came as no surprise one morning to receive a message requesting Bert attend a meeting.

That evening, Bert waited on the docks and a horse-drawn taxi arrived. "Get in and shut up," came an order from behind a curtain. He climbed aboard and saw two masked men with guns. One blindfolded him, and Bert growled when the other grabbed his arm.

"Shut the fuck up mate. Make another noise, or even move, you'll be the next one floating in the harbour." The taxi took a circuitous route designed to confuse. When it finally stopped, they pulled Bert inside a building and pushed him onto a chair.

After removing the blindfold, Bert blinked rapidly in the harsh light. His heart sank seeing who sat on the far side of a large desk. It was the most ruthless crime boss in southern England.

The man nodded and with a thin, cruel smile, extended greetings. Icy vapour seemed to flow from him. Bert knew the man would kill him with as little thought as he might give a worm. He had no option other than agreeing with whatever proposal the man put forward.

With a mocking smile, the boss explained his reason for the summons. The dead gambler had borrowed from the crime boss and did not repay the loan. His demise was unfortunate but who could have seen that coming?

'Yeah, who could have seen that coming?' Bert silently mused.

In addition to the financial loss, the dead man also delivered opium to North America for the boss. Lowering his voice in mock sorrow, the boss bemoaned he had no chance of recovering his loss. He also wondered how he might resume the opium shipments.

"I need someone trustworthy. Someone who keeps quiet and gets things done properly." Like a viper judging a striking distance, he leaned forward.

"Shall we look at this reasonably, Mr. Westhaven? As businessmen, we both want to make money. No doubt, I made clear whose money you won. I am prepared to accept that loss and let bygones be bygones. Keep the money, you won it." Bert's heart sank knowing where the talk was heading.

"I need someone to make deliveries to North America. That someone will be highly paid. I expect this person to make six deliveries a year. Do you know anyone who could do that for me?" Bert nodded, knowing he had only one correct reply. Were he to refuse, he would die where he sat but he had a question the boss foresaw.

"Not to worry Mr. Westhaven. Certain customs officers in North America are part of the operation." The boss then casually mentioned the amount each successful delivery paid. It staggered Bert to learn it matched his annual pay as a petty officer.

"May I trust we have agreement, Mr. Westhaven? Oh, one last detail. I always ensure things go smoothly and those who fail..." he paused for effect.

"They only fail once, no matter how long it takes to find them."

That meeting occurred four years earlier and the arrangement worked smoothly; the proof was Bert remained alive. Safeguarding the shipments was the reason for his terrifying reputation.

The sailors feared him and only a few had ever dared to challenge him. His brutality was so legendary, men rarely even dared speak to him. That suited Bert and he rebuffed all attempts to befriend him. To his surprise, he had decided to listen to a young man's dreams.

"Well boy, keep word of having a couple pounds to yourself. There are some aboard who would happily take it." Sidney's eyes narrowed at the warning.

"Any bastard who tries that is going to be bloody sorry." Bert knew the naïve youngster meant it.

"This is a rough crew. Not really their fault; this is a tough life. The best way for things to run smooth is having my reputation. Letting little things go leads to trouble and it's why I don't put up with anybody's bullshit." When Sidney nodded he understood, Bert continued.

"You don't want grief coming your way and it would if you hadn't come to me. If you keep your mouth shut and do what you're told, I'll keep an eye out for you. That way you'll get off this ship just the same as when you walked on." Bert had a final point he wanted Sidney to grasp.

"I'm not friends with anybody but so long as you don't bring on trouble, I've got your back. Now go get cleaned up, get some grub and sling a mic, you've got another long day tomorrow."

Sidney stared at Bert, confused yet again by a term he did not understand. "A mic? What is that?"

Bert shook his head in disbelief. *'Fuck, I'll have to babysit this kid all the way across.'*

"A mic is short for hammock. Now go sling yours and get some sleep."

Grateful the big man had confided in him and been patient, Sidney vowed not to disappoint. Sliding from the sea locker, Sidney extended his hand. After a cautious glance about for other crew members, Bert shook hands.

Chapter Five

With relatively calm western winds, the voyage proceeded smoothly. Having never been out of sight of land, Sidney marvelled to see horizon in every direction.

The sea air invigorated him and when off duty, he tried guessing from where the waves originated and how far each travelled. Was it possible for a wave to leave North America and wash up in England?

After a week, he realized there were no shrieking gulls. His whole life, he took their cawing for granted but now the birds were far behind. On the featureless ocean, he saw only sunshine and white clouds. At night, millions of stars and a moon far more brilliant than he saw on land fascinated him.

Typical of his young heart, he entertained thoughts of sailing the world's oceans. By working hard, he would prove worthy of duties above deck and be seen capable of more than mindlessly shovelling coal. Swinging in his hammock, he fell asleep with thoughts of becoming a sailing master.

Just like the fickle nature of a youth's impetuous whim, the weather changed. Dawn's first grey streaks seeping through the portholes were a harbinger of the agony about to shatter Sidney's whimsy of a life at sea. The *Angus Celt* had now crossed a third of the way. After sailing the route for decades, Thompson's sea sense warned of an Atlantic storm assault before daybreak.

His hunch proved correct when the winds gained strength and sea swells grew. The old freighter started to pitch and as winds shifted from the northwest, it began to yaw.

Sidney awoke to bodies swaying and muttering curses as the old hands grimly dressed. Swinging out of his hammock, his knees buckled, and he fell face down on the damp steel deck.

The first wave of nausea hit, and he crawled to the puke bucket. He gripped it with both hands but to his horror and disgust, it had already overflowed, and his hands were slimy with vomit.

Trying to swallow the volcano brewing in his gut, he stood to run for the heads. A torrent of vomit launched itself and fouled his shirt, trousers and boots. Slipping in the waste, he crashed to the deck and knocked over the puke bucket.

The stench and vile liquid flowing over his legs and chest horrified him. Primal fear seized him as his tortured body and mind reacted to being filthy with his own waste and that of other men. The rolling deck sent streams of vomit toward him and defeated all attempts to stand.

Sidney tried pulling himself from the revolting liquid, but the slick deck overpowered his efforts. His stomach heaved again, and bitter bile mixed with that of other men. Sidney felt the mess congealing in his hair and the clothes stuck to his skin. While some men vomited, two others cruelly laughed. Then a roaring voice penetrated the agony and panic assaulting Sidney.

"What the fuck is going on here?" Bert stood in the doorway surveying the scene and he barely recognized the sailor lying on the deck. Sidney's pathetic movements resembled a fish flopping in the sand.

Bert had not been seasick in years, but this mess nearly brought up his breakfast. Turning into the passageway for several clean breaths, he returned and furiously bellowed again.

"What the hell is going on? One of you lazy pricks grab a hose and spray all this shit down the scuppers." One of the healthier hands objected to the demand and voiced his opposition while pointing at Sidney.

"He's the one who knocked over the bucket and made most of this bloody mess. Why do we...?" The sailor stopped in mid-sentence, his features blanched upon seeing Bert's fury.

"Do it right fucking now, or I'll swab this deck with one of you bastards! I don't give a shit whose shit this is. Hose him down too and get him out on the aft deck."

The healthy men ran to follow Bert's orders. None had seen him so angry and they knew not to trifle with the big man. To be the target of his huge fists would leave at least one of them nursing broken bones.

Blasts of cold water folded Sidney into a fetal position and he tucked his face into a shoulder. While he gasped for breath, the water helped rinse away some the bitterness in his mouth. With gratitude, his surviving corner of consciousness knew the water had washed away another bout of vomiting.

A hand dragged him by the collar to a clean space on the deck. Though his stomach had emptied, the retching continued, and it felt like a trapped animal trying to claw a hole to freedom.

By taking deep breaths, Sidney hoped to quell his misery and discovered closing his eyes worsened the vertigo of the pitching deck. Gasping in resignation, he opened his eyes and accepted the world remained these steel walls. Rolling to his knees, he reached for a bulkhead and staggered upright.

Bert grabbed Sidney by the arm and the young man trailed along as a young pupil might a school headmaster. They climbed several steep stairs until reaching the after deck.

Although deathly ill, even that failed to quash Sidney's terror at seeing huge waves pounding aft past the ship. Howling winds whipped foam from wave tops and hurled stinging spray against the ship and into men's eyes. Despite his panic, he greedily gulped air free of the stench of vomit. Over the shrieking winds, Bert leaned close to yell in Sidney's ear.

"Listen up. You'll be sick three, maybe four days. You won't be any use down below and if you don't work, you don't get paid. Much as I need swinging dicks shovelling coal, a man this sick gets in the way.

"I'll tell Thompson you're too buggered up so just stay out of sight. After a couple days, you'll be better, and I'll put your sorry ass to work. Anyone bitches about it, tell them to see me.

"Me and most of the other tars haven't been seasick in years. Most get used to it and then it ain't too bad. Some never really get over it, but they learn to live with it." Sidney groaned at the idea of living a life filled with such torment.

"This is your first trip and there's nothing for it but toughing it out. You feel like shit and the last thing you want to do is eat. But believe me, it keeps your strength up and gets you past it quicker." An uptick in the shrieking wind silenced Bert for a moment and further terrified Sidney.

"You're gonna puke some more so drink lots of water. Don't jump overboard either, I'll kick your sorry ass if you do!" Seeing Sidney's miserable nod, Bert finished his lecture.

"I've got to make sure the black gang is working but I'll check on you. Spread a couple lifejackets in a corner and try to sleep. Don't get in your hammock because that will only make you sicker."

The thought of swinging sideways brought on more nausea and Sidney gagged over the side railing. Following Bert's advice, he found several lifejackets and crawled into a tool locker. Thoroughly exhausted, Sidney fell into a fitful sleep. While he slept, the weather worsened, and cold rain lashed the unfortunate men standing watch at exposed duty stations.

Sidney awoke as the seas grew rougher. Nausea struck, and he vomited on the steel deck until his stomach corkscrewed and his throat felt sandpapered.

Emerging from the locker, he saw huge waves charging past only a few feet away. The waves roared away into the gloom and vanished from view as the ship careened down deep troughs.

Sidney's first experience with a wild ocean storm paralyzed him with fear. As though giant and invisible fingers were plucking bass strings, gale force winds thrummed the steel cables supporting the masts and funnel. Steel beams flexed and screeched in rivet joints. Canvas covers on lifeboats flapped madly, threatening to tear free and disappear.

Shutting his eyes only made his stomach rebel again. Torn between nausea and fear, he knew to open his eyes and face the roaring elements. Better to die eyes open than like a sobbing child.

He needed to stay outside to fight the nausea and that meant finding warm clothes and rain slickers. It spoke volumes of his courage that he decided to search below decks. Fortune smiled though as footsteps pounding up a stairway belonged to Bert.

"What the hell are you still doing here in just trousers and a shirt? Want to catch pneumonia and die? You won't get to Canada that way. I'll get some clothes and a Mac to keep the rain off."

Through his nausea, Sidney smiled and wheezed, "Thanks mate, you're a good man." He turned back to the open air and missed the look of concern on Bert's face.

Sidney had stirred paternal feelings Bert had no inkling existed. He had never known family or even a trusting friendship. His early days on the hard streets of Portsmouth had ground away any possibility of fraternity. He felt unsure how to deal with sentiment far beyond the familiar.

The boy's naïve confidence struck a chord in Bert. Owning a share of this ship was the extent of all things Bert thought possible. This youngster had left behind family, friends, home and all things familiar. He spoke from the innocence of youth. Bert knew Canada existed; he had sailed into Montreal, Quebec City and Halifax dozens of times.

However, he had not gone far beyond the docks. In port, the ship delivered cargo and rapidly reloaded for England. In Montreal, Bert conducted business his partners knew nothing about; that story could wait for another day.

Compared to Bert's structured environment, Sidney's plans were astonishing. The boy presumed he could buy a train ticket and travel thousands of miles west. There he planned to claim the one hundred sixty acres of land the Canadian government offered to immigrant settlers.

Bert had never met a youngster with such aspirations for a new life, in a different occupation, in a foreign land. Sidney did not know anyone in Canada and barely had money to buy a one-way train ticket. Bert shook his head in admiration of this impetuous young man.

Chapter Six

The weather was just as bad the next day. Howling winds and high seas pitched the old freighter like a cork bobbing in a bucket. The ship made little headway and at times felt motionless. They made only a few miles each day, slow progress on the three-thousand-mile voyage. Bert's dark mood matched the foul weather and as the crew bent to their duties, all avoided eye contact with the big man.

On the third day, a faint sunset tinged the clouds. Winds still blew strongly but the heavy cloudbank began to tatter and fleeting glimpses of blue sky, and later, stars began dappling the grey seascape.

Sidney had prayed for death as he suffered the ravages of seasickness. Afraid of the nausea, he did not go below decks and ate little. He kept down ginger ale but suffered bouts of diarrhoea on the liquid-only diet. As the third day ended, he sensed the changing weather pattern. Deciding to risk a trip to the galley, he found Bert there.

"It's about time you ate. Can you work in the morning if this storm breaks up? I could use your mighty muscles." Swallowing a bite of mutton stew, Sidney nodded knowing he had to work and earn some money.

"Yeah, if I can get a decent sleep, I'll give it shit in the morning. Maybe I'll work a double to make up for lost time."

"Take a day or two to get your strength back. You'll be sick again if you go back too soon. Let me judge when you're ready for a double shift."

Sidney deferred to Bert's experience and cleaning his plate, he went to his hammock to sleep. Kicking off his boots, he pulled the rough woollen blanket close and fell asleep in seconds.

The night crew roused the day crew and after a quick breakfast, they shuffled down to the boiler rooms. Sidney quickly began sweating as he filled the wheelbarrow. His youth helped him shrug off the sickness that assailed him for three days.

When the storm eased, it made sailing easier as the waves reduced to long swells. That meant lower coal consumption and a less hectic work pace. Sidney fell into a rhythm and felt confident of working the rest of the voyage.

Although able to complete the shift, he knew not to try working a double shift. After showering off the grimy coal dust, he ate dinner and went up on deck to sit near the bow.

The clear evening sky and a brisk breeze invigorated him. Stars stretched across the heavens like a finely woven needlepoint diamond shawl.

Sidney marvelled at the sight and understood why men fell under the spell of the sea. The hours of back breaking toil now seemed a reasonable price for this serene moment.

He leaned back and saw a crescent moon rising far astern. A thrill shivered up his spine and his hair waved in the breeze. Joyously laughing aloud, he jumped up to dance a jig while humming a tune.

Imagining a pretty girl in his arms, he swept his feet back and forth and twirled his partner. *'By Christ mate, aren't you acting like a right barmy bastard?'* he giggled. *'You daft bugger, sit down before someone sees and throws you in the loony bin!'* Sitting on a bollard, he focused on the breeze and twinkling stars glued on the canvas of a night sky.

At home, Sidney read about the Indians who lived on the great plains of North America. They believed stars were the guiding spirits of their ancestors and often part of a vision.

For thousands of years, these people lived a nomadic existence by following the buffalo. The stories explained how natives felt a connection to all things in their world.

The land provided their necessities of life without any need for manufactured goods. This uncomplicated way of life had evolved over millenniums and Sidney tried picturing their lives. While naively assuming civilization improved their lives, he still wished to have seen it.

The constraints imposed by society usually leave little room for anything but the easily explained. But on this night, a young man's imagination and desire to see the past was rewarded.

On the horizon, a translucent light began shimmering and his mind's eye carried him to the luminescent curtain. Halting before it, he marvelled at this apparition while the scent of unplowed soil wafted in the air.

He leaned closer to peer inside but sensed that touching it would destroy the moment. An invitation encouraged him to sit quietly and not question this strange energy. A gentle but powerful vitality urged him to surrender doubt and accept the ancient knowledge it wished to share.

A kaleidoscope of unfamiliar images flashed into view. After the passage of many frames, the curtain wrapped Sidney in radiant light. As the brilliance eased, he saw an immense panorama that somehow looked familiar.

Rich colours began defining a grassy plain and the indistinct smudges that were thousands of buffalo. In surprise, as though viewing the sight from afar, he saw himself as a hunter and part of the scene.

A large bull left the herd to come near and from a long ago past, a warrior touched Sidney. The warrior urged Sidney to understand the buffalo were sacred to plains peoples. He should view the hunt not as death for the buffalo, but as a joining of two spirits.

After calming himself, Sidney shot an arrow, but it did not reach the buffalo. He had questioned the moment. Having never taken the life of a living creature, he thought the entire situation unlikely. His scepticism severed the spiritual thread and removed him from the wisdom of the intended message. In time, he would understand physical death did not mean the death of spirit.

"What was that?" The mesmerizing vision unsettled him. He had never known anyone to speak of such things. The vision's beauty and energy seeped away though he pleaded for it to stay. If it returned and he banished negative thought, then he might accept the vision.

In the morning, as Sidney resumed work that required little mental attention, he focused on the previous evening's apparition.

Maybe he had gone directly to bed and dreamed of hunting the buffalo. *'You were born in England. So how would you know anything about hunting a buffalo?'* Perhaps the days of seasickness brought on a hallucination. *'Hey, don't think that. It ended when you thought like that.'*

Why had the past invited him to join a buffalo hunt? Knowing he was changed, but unaware how, made him uneasy. When the shift ended, he went up on deck so deeply preoccupied, he failed to hear Bert calling him.

"Hey! I'm talking to you. How are you feeling?" Spinning round, Sidney saw the big mate and organized his thoughts.

"Sorry Bert, my mind was elsewhere."

Bert looked closely in case the youngster had been drinking but he did not smell of alcohol. Sidney looked pale and in a wilderness of emotional turmoil.

"Can you work a double tomorrow? We're trying to make up lost time, but you look like you saw a ghost. You all right?"

"I'm okay, just thinking about home and where I'm going," Sidney replied in an unconvincing tone.

Bert knew Sidney had dodged the question but decided not to pursue the matter. Whatever it might be, Sidney could decide whether to talk.

"Tell me in the morning about working a double. Go get some sleep, tomorrow could be a long day for you."

Swinging in his hammock, Sidney hoped for guidance with the puzzling vision before snorting derisively. *'You're no more a great hunter than a brilliant scientist.'*

His thoughts were typical for a seventeen-year-old boy – girls, sex, fame and fortune. He wondered if by speaking of the vision as a dream, it might sound saner than speaking of it as an actual event. How could he explain that which he did not understand?

Perhaps he should dismiss it as fatigue brought on by seasickness and exhaustion. *'That's a better idea, so no one thinks you've gone crazy.'* Forgetting what he had seen would not prove as simple as erasing a chalkboard. The vision had been preordained years earlier.

The next afternoon, Bert hollered at him through the mechanical clatter of the boiler room. "Hey! Can you swing four more hours?"

Wiping a grimy forearm across his forehead smeared the coal dust and burned his bloodshot eyes. His first thought was *'Please God no'* but he remembered there were earnings to catch up.

"Sure. Will any supper be left when I'm done?"

"Cookie has already saved it for you, boy."

The next day, Sidney toured above decks on his noon break. He found his favourite perch on the bow bollard. The bright sunshine made it an exceptional day to scan the horizon.

Slowly spinning, he saw several men on the bridge pointing to port. In the distance was a smudge of black smoke and the tips of tall masts. Below the masts were four black topped buff funnels and Sidney understood the reason for his crewmates' excitement.

Approaching at high speed was the new liner R.M.S. *Olympic*. All England knew about this new class of trans-Atlantic liner, the *Olympic* being the first of three to enter service. Crossing the ocean on such a ship would have been grand.

As the *Olympic* sailed past, the *Angus Celt* saluted with a steam blast whistle and crew waved their sea caps to honour such a stupendous vessel. Moments later came a deep bass response from the great liner.

Sidney marvelled at the huge vessel as it sped away. Perhaps when he made his fortune in Canada, he would visit England aboard one of these wonderful ships.

Chapter Seven

"Lad, wake up. Come on, you should see this." Typical of youth, he did not readily awaken and tried burrowing under a blanket that Bert pulled away.

"Come on boy, you'll only see this once and you ain't sleeping through it. Get your sorry ass up and let's go on deck."

Sidney yawned, rubbed his eyes with balled fists and moaned while rolling out. Owlishly eying Bert in the dim light, he stumbled into his boots and followed him up the ladders.

"Why in blazes did you get me up? I had two more hours to sleep. Hope this is quick, so I can get back under the blankets."

Smiling over his shoulder, Bert led them on deck in the thinning dark. At the bow, he pointed to the western horizon. Sidney peered ahead and for several moments, failed to register anything other than night sky.

"I don't get it Bert. What am I looking for?" Bert said nothing and simply pointed ahead. Then Sidney saw the navigation lights of an approaching ship. Other ships passed them on the horizon, but not this one, and Sidney wondered why.

About to comment, he detected a scent other than that of the sea. Turning to ask if Bert noticed, Sidney caught a fleeting pinpoint of light on the horizon.

Rooted to the spot, he strained to look, and a flash of light rewarded him. He suddenly understood the approaching ship, the scented air and flashing light were equal parts of one answer.

"Bert! Is that Canada? Holy shit, we've made it?"

With a triumphant whoop, Sidney jumped onto the railing and waved in the morning air. His exuberance nearly carried him over the rail. Bert's fortuitous grab of his collar saved Sidney from a watery, and fatal, entrance to Canada.

"Is that really Canada, Bert? Please tell me it is!" The big man smiled again watching Sidney's boisterous outburst.

"I've got not the faintest idea where we are lad." Seeing the despair on Sidney's face, he burst out laughing.

"If that isn't Canada, our navigation is the shits. Yes lad, it's Canada."

"Hip, hip, hooray!" Bert laughed again and gave Sidney a quick lesson in geography.

"The land to the southwest is Cape Breton Island and far off to the north, is Newfoundland. It's an English colony and possession of the Crown."

"Well that's how things are supposed to be, Bert."

"Maybe so, but the next part of Canada you'll see is Quebec, and most of them are French-speaking Catholics. I don't like them, they're a strange bunch. Seeing as how I don't speak much frog, I'm not always sure what they're saying.

"We should have made them speak English when we captured Quebec. But that's a story for another day. So long as they unload, and reload us, I don't much care if they speak English or not." Sidney pondered that, realizing he knew little about the country he wished to call home as Bert continued about Quebec.

"The freight bosses speak English and that's all I need. The two things I like about Quebec is the cooking and women. Both are Frenchie, just the way I like it." Bert glanced at Sidney, knowing Sidney had no experience with any French cooking.

"It takes a day or two to unload, so I've got time ashore. If your lordship has some time before he leaves for his Canadian estate, allow me to show you round old town Montreal."

Bert had been in many ports and Sidney knew nothing of the available treats. He chuckled knowing the ladies would quarrel over who looked after the big youngster. When Bert had a chat with his friend, and intimate, the house madam, it even might be on the house. Once they docked, Bert relished the opportunity of properly indoctrinating Sidney.

"Stay close to me in Montreal and everything will be fine."

The naïve youth presumed that meant being paid and Bert escorting him to the train station. What Bert had planned would horrify Sidney's mother and the village vicar.

"We'll be docking soon? I can't wait to walk on solid ground again." Bert surprised Sidney by answering with a laugh.

"Lad, welcome to Canada. We have about eight hundred miles yet before we hit Montreal."

"Eight hundred miles? Hell Bert, I thought we'd dock this afternoon. That's at least a couple more days away." Bert nodded in agreement and told Sidney further facts.

"This is the St. Lawrence River, one of the world's largest. It will take us nearly a week, longer if it's foggy, to get there."

"A week just to sail up a river? What the hell?"

"Get used to it lad. This is just where the country starts. It goes west for thousands of miles past Montreal." That information staggered Sidney.

"Thousands of miles? That's bigger than Europe, isn't it?"

"I've never been past Montreal and it's only about a quarter of the way across," Bert mused. "Maybe I'll take the train west one day to see what else is out there. Anyway, you won't see civilization until we get to Quebec City, and that's still far away." Swallowing his impatience, Sidney tried not to allow the news to dampen his happiness.

"So, boy, here's a chance to make some extra money before we reach port. Speaking of which, go have breakfast before you and your shovel become best friends again." Sidney looked out again but now with more satisfaction. After weeks of water, he saw land and his excitement returned.

"Well Bert, if you want to join a friend here in Canada, you have one in me." With that, Sidney bounced down the stairs, rejuvenated seeing his new country.

Sidney did not know Bert's desire to have his own place, had reawakened. When Bert won the unexpected windfall playing poker, it challenged him to create his own path and became impossible to ignore. The navy represented guaranteed earnings, meals, lodging and a pension in ten more years. Winning so much money, removed the anchor securely holding him to the navy.

Buying an equal share of the *Angus Celt* originally appeared to be his whole future. He and his partners were making good progress toward becoming debt free and they were considering buying another ship. The logical choice for captain, Bert smiled imagining himself as Captain Bert. He had made the best of the hand dealt him by coming so far from the orphanage where his teenaged mother left him.

Bert returned those thoughts to the shelf, knowing they were hundreds of miles away from Montreal. Below decks, Sidney excitedly told the black gang they were only days from port, which energized everyone.

At sunset following his shift, Sidney returned to the bow bollard. Having showered and eaten, he watched a magnificent summer sunset. They were now in the channel between Anticosti Island and Gaspe and he marvelled at the breadth of the water and sweeping sky. After weeks breathing coal dust, the pure evening air stung his nose. Surely somewhere in this immense country, he would find his place.

Thoughts of the vision from several evenings earlier came to mind but offered no further clarity. Just as well, he had no wish to trade the grand scene before him, for such a distraction.

The sun dipped below the Gaspe Peninsula and the stars grew brighter. Fresh water of the great river that drained half a continent, mixed with Atlantic brine and the air smelled differently. *'You're a long way from home Sid old boy.'* With a contented chuckle, he surrendered to weariness and went below to sleep the sleep of the innocent.

Nearly a week later, the *Angus Celt* lay roped to a dock in Montreal. Up on deck, Sidney offered a silent prayer of thanks for surviving his first, and maybe last, ocean crossing. He thanked old Thompson for hiring him and Sidney knew he had earned his place aboard ship.

Sidney owed Bert a sincere thank you for looking out for him while he struggled in the coalbunkers during the first days. The big man allowed Sidney time to recover from seasickness. When they went ashore, he wanted to buy Bert lunch. He could not afford a fancy meal, but he wished to show his gratitude.

While waiting, he marvelled at the sight of Canada's largest city. The buildings stood straight and true, streetcars clanged along busy avenues, and steam rose from the train station. The city appeared much bigger than Southampton along with a newer texture, and as he watched, a ship slipped free from a dock.

Crossing the deck, he saw the river flowing with water from thousands of miles away. An ancient, primal instinct summoned, compelling him to obey. Knowing the water came from mysterious forests, firmed his resolve to journey further west.

"Sid! For Christ sakes, I've called you three times. Where is your head at boy?" Turning around, he saw Bert standing on the gangway with a sea bag.

"Grab your bag and let's go. I want to get you a good dinner before you leave. Come along and I'll introduce you to old Montreal's charms."

Bert's eyes twinkled merrily, and Sidney mistook that as his pleasure to be ashore. Jumping up, Sidney grabbed his bag and joyfully stomped down the gangplank. Dropping the bag and falling to his knees, he kissed the ground and chortled.

"I know it looks foolish, but I could give a flying fuck what anyone thinks! That's how glad I am to be a free man. Maybe I should say boy, but whatever. I've a shot at the good life. What do you say to that, my friend?"

Without waiting for Bert's reply, Sidney jumped up and pirouetted with one fist high over his head. Standing tall, he held the canvas sea bag to his chest and danced a joyful jig.

"Lead on fearless leader, I'll follow you to the gates of whatever, wherever they are!" A smile creased Bert's hard hewn features as he watched Sidney's antics.

"Come along then, let's get this show on the road! Oh, and even though you seem to have forgotten this minor detail, I'll pay you at dinner, future king of Canada." Passing through a dockyard gate, Bert winked at a custom official and called out.

"Later."

Chapter Eight

Slinging the bag over a broad shoulder, Bert strode off and Sidney fell into step beside him. The workday had ended and at dinner hour, few people were on the sidewalks. While Sidney had no idea where they were going, Bert obviously did.

People were well dressed and Bert and Sidney, in their rough clothing, looked out of place. Men wearing expensive suits cast disapproving looks but none met Bert's eye. He saw their glances but did not care. The value of his sea bag was greater than the snobby businessmen dreamed.

For several years now, Bert had been bringing sea bags from Southampton to quietly deliver in Montreal. The proceeds earned from this enterprise, he deposited in a Canadian bank account under an assumed name.

Bert knew one day his surreptitious dealings would end. Some unfortunate might talk after being arrested, a customs officer might grow greedy, a politician's daughter could overdose, or an honest cop might stumble into the scheme.

With no intention of spending time in jail, Bert was prepared to silence anyone that could put him there. Knowing he would take a life to avoid that fate, did not sit well with his conscience.

As he grew older, time eroded his willingness to be ruthless. Hesitation could be fatal in the cutthroat business where he so handsomely profited. Men of this trade struck at any sign of weakness.

Bert began planning, knowing one day he would leave the business and the gypsy life of a seafaring merchantman. Years of sailing had begun to weary him and the day to drop anchor approached. By necessity, it had to be where old money did not enquire about the origins of new money.

The chance meeting with Sidney caused Bert to consider putting his plan into action. It had piqued Bert's curiosity about what lay beyond Montreal. Genuinely surprised, he regarded the youngster as a potential friend for life.

At Dorchester Square, Bert crossed through the park and into Windsor Station's vast confines. Sidney gazed in wonder as he walked through the towering structure. It spoke of power, organization and vast wealth.

Signs directed passengers to boarding gates for distant places. Sidney laughed while reading some of the outlandish sounding place names. He thought the word Quebec strange, until seeing some other names.

Could there actually be a place named Saskatchewan? It did not sound like part the British Empire. On closer inspection, he took heart reading the city name of Regina, a tribute to the English Crown, and nodded in satisfaction. These colonials still revered the institutions and traditions of the mother country. After standing for a minute in astonishment, he saw Bert regarding him with patient amusement.

"Welcome to Canada boy, but you didn't come all this way just to stand around in a train station. If it is all right with you, sir, can we continue on our way?" Bert mocked.

"First, I have some business to attend and then we'll go to dinner. After that ... well, you will see what comes after that. I think it will be worth remembering. Let me take care of this one matter before your proper welcome to Canada."

Bert turned and waved for Sidney to follow. At the entrance to a restaurant, he told Sidney to sit at the long counter.

"Order a cup of coffee and wait, I won't be long."

Sidney took a stool and laid his jacket across another for Bert. Ordering a coffee, he saw the large restaurant offered many dining choices. A hubbub of voices rose as patrons ordered meals, discussed destinations or a hundred and one other topics.

Unlike England, the people appeared healthy and well fed. They wore better clothes and looked more prosperous. When his coffee arrived, and before Sidney offered payment, the waiter moved off to serve other customers. *'Must be your honest face Sid old boy.'*

Minutes later, Bert sat down and looked over his shoulder as though searching for someone. The behaviour seemed odd, but

Sidney thought it best not to ask questions. Bert was looking for someone, he just did not know who. Sitting in the restaurant was part of the delivery process, the final step.

Bert had taken the sea bag to a large bank of coin-operated lockers. After pushing the bag inside one, Bert closed the door and put the key in his pocket. He knew that somewhere in the crowd, a man had been watching his every move.

The pickup man was not the same twice in a row. The routine never varied though and while Bert did not relax until completing the switch, it always went smoothly.

Several moments after Bert's return, a well-dressed man along the counter stood up. Leaving some coins on the counter, he walked toward them and with a friendly air, offered Bert a folded newspaper. Bert nodded, took the paper with thanks and they shook hands. The man tipped his hat, left the restaurant and disappeared.

The exchange went so smoothly, Sidney did not realize anything had occurred. Tucked inside the newspaper, was an envelope containing cash. With the handshake, Bert slipped the locker key to the man. From the corner of his eye, Sidney noticed Bert stand up and heave a sigh of relief.

"Come along my young friend. Let's dine at one of Montreal's finest establishments and then we will enjoy some nightlife. Over dinner, I'll pay you for all the hard work on the boat. You did well lad, many a man could not have matched your pace."

With that, he stepped outside and walked toward a block of large brick buildings. In the centre was a narrow storefront with a pane of curtained glass on each side of a richly appointed wooden door. Turning a brass handle, Bert pushed open the door and with a slight bow, he ushered Sidney across the threshold.

Carpeted stairs and polished wooden handrails greeted Sidney's gaze. Confused, he turned to a smiling Bert who gestured for him to ascend. Murmured voices and laughter floated down the stairway, male voices mingled with the higher pitch of feminine speech and laughter. The aroma of sumptuous meals tightened Sidney's stomach with hunger pangs.

Atop the stairs, a long hallway illuminated by wall lights led them onward. To one side, a doorway adorned with a beaded curtain opened onto a small dining room and the décor made Sidney feel like a pauper appearing before a royal court. He looked at Bert again and the big man smiled while pressing a button.

Down the hallway, a door opened, and the most beautiful woman Sidney had ever seen began walking toward them. His jaw dropped, and his mouth went dry. The desire he felt left him light-headed. The woman glided - her movements were far beyond walking.

Midnight black hair fell in symmetrical rolls save for two dangling curls framing her delicate ear lobes. Two thin-strand jade chain earrings swung in perfect rhythm. The sweep of her neck melted into the flawless white skin of her bare shoulders.

A floor-length, emerald dress clung to every curve of her body. A sheer, long-sleeved open jacket of black lace caressed her arms. The bodice swept low and revealed the cleft between her breasts.

Her lips bore tastefully applied red rouge. She wore a hint of black kohl eyeliner and a near translucent dusting of face powder. The maxim a truly beautiful woman does not need large applications of makeup, was never so true.

The perfect symmetry of her nose precisely separated green eyes flecked with gold sparkles; her eyes an undercurrent from which a man might never surface. A man might wish to drown in those depths.

As the woman approached, she halted and made a small curtsey. Flashing a dazzling smile, she amazed Sidney by offering her cheeks for Bert to kiss.

"My darling Bertie, how wonderful to see you. You were so clever to send a message. Your dinners are almost ready."

She spoke with an exquisite tonal lilt and Sidney felt certain the sound was music, not words. The accent reflected her birth in French-speaking Quebec and her English pronunciation pointed to a refined education.

Releasing Bert, she offered a hand to Sidney. Blushing deeply and too flummoxed to speak, he bowed to kiss her hand. To his delight, she rewarded him with pleased laughter. Bert smiled to see Sidney's unexpected display of manners.

"Madame Desiree, I am honoured to present my young companion and friend. This is Master Sidney Turner, lately of England. Today is his first day on Canadian soil. Where else would I bring him except to the finest establishment in all the land? It is my wish he remembers today for the remainder of his long life."

A knowing look passed between Desiree and Bert. Taking his arm, Desiree guided Sidney through the doorway. Candles were set on an elegant dining table flanked by two high-back chairs. Sweeping a delicate arm toward the table, Desiree invited them to sit and then left the room.

The table sat in a bay window overlooking the street. Curtains allowed an outside view while shielding the interior. When seated, Sidney curiously examined the room. He had never seen such splendour. His hazy notion of a restaurant did not square with this room and one table.

"Bert, I've never seen anything like this and I just have to ask, where are we? I thought we were going to a restaurant." Bert's expression revealed nothing, and he sat silent as the Sphinx.

"After three weeks of ship food, the cooking smells are driving me crazy. Are they cooking our dinner now? How would this place know what we want to eat? I don't see other people and even the pub back home has a chalkboard menu." Sidney looked over his shoulder before asking the next question.

"That woman knows you. How did you meet someone so beautiful? No offence, but why would she even know you? It looks like there are things about you I know nothing about. Come on, tell me what is going on here. Or as much as you can. I think there is more going on than maybe I should know about." Bert smiled and leaning forward, spoke quietly.

"You are quite right lad. There are things you don't know about me, and let's keep it that way. You're a fresh-faced boy with little experience in the big, bad world. After tomorrow, I won't be around to keep an eye on you. You'll have to rely on your wits, but luckily, you've got enough to manage most situations.

"When something comes along out of the ordinary, there's a true saying I've learned. Experience is what you get when you don't have it and find out you need it. If that doesn't make sense, it will one day and hopefully, learning it won't be too painful. I met Desiree a few years ago over business with the boat and she is a trusted partner." A questioning look crossed Sidney's face and Bert chuckled.

"Don't ask so I don't have to tell you not to ask questions." He slid an envelope across the table to Sidney.

"That's your pay and before you count, it's more than you were expecting. It's meant to help get you where you're going."

"Thank you, Bert, but why?"

"The *Angus Celt* doesn't usually attract men with dreams or goals. Having you show up thinking you had to work for your pay, was an unexpected pleasure." Unaccustomed to accolades, Sidney squirmed at Bert's words of praise.

"Most of the swabs are running from the cops and work just enough to buy booze for their next piss up. Most aren't worth the shit paper we have to buy them. I always have to kick one of the useless apes out of the sling for work." Grinning at Sidney, Bert reached over to tousle his hair.

"It was a pleasant change when you showed up. The little extra is to say thanks for a job well done, especially for a lad who had never sailed before."

Unable to resist, Sidney peeked in the envelope. With shock, he saw double the expected wage. Not only that, Bert had paid for the three days Sidney was laid low with seasickness. About to protest, Sidney held his tongue when Bert wagged a silencing finger.

"One day lad, you'll understand. You ain't been out enough in the world yet. Your turn will come to be on this side, and you'll remember our talk. Now listen, I'm going to be serious, but keep it to yourself. I've got to keep my reputation as a mean bastard."

As though remembering a detail, he paused and rang a small bell. A waiter appeared, and Bert ordered Jameson whiskey and Sidney a ginger ale.

"You ain't really said why you left home. That's your business, but I've been around a while and have probably heard it all. The little bit you did say was about your mom, brothers and sisters but nothing about your father.

"I guess you had trouble with him and that's why you're in Canada. Apart from me, you don't know anyone here. When you get on the train tomorrow, that bit of extra cash is my way of helping you get started."

"You need to know I'm grateful Bert. One day, I would like to pay you back." Bert waved it off and smiled.

"When a man has a bit of spare cash, it can help him from getting into a scrape or out of one. Keep your money in your boot. And keep your yap shut about having it. If anyone asks you friendly like about money, they ain't thinking about what's best for you. No one cares more about you, than you. Sometimes you need to be a bastard, but it should only be when someone forces you.

"Life works smoother if you remember it's easier to catch flies with a spoon of honey than with a bucket of vinegar. Play nice with folks, but if you must fight for your life, you fight to kill. Got that straight?"

Sidney fidgeted, knowing Bert so clearly read the situation. This grim man understood how vulnerable Sidney might be surviving on his own. While inexperienced, Sidney knew not to expect such generosity every day.

In time, he would understand Bert's respect and admiration came from Sidney's solid effort under difficult circumstances. He did not yet realize the enormity of the challenge ahead of him. Bert appreciated his pluck.

"I've taken the liberty of ordering dinner. I trust you'll enjoy the meal. And I hope you'll like, even if you're not legally old enough, wines be served. You've guessed this is not a restaurant in the regular sense. However, I doubt you will ever have a finer meal anywhere."

"Well, what did you order and when do we eat?"

"Be patient, dining here takes several hours. I may be the boiler room boss of an old rust bucket, but your friend Bert knows a thing or two about life's better things."

The finely dressed waiter reappeared with two long-stemmed glasses of champagne. Murmuring "Bon soire, monsieurs", he placed a glass before each of them. Sidney's first impulse was draining the glass in one gulp and sensing this, Bert proposed a toast.

"Raise your glass and salute your journey and continuing adventures. I hope you find all you want. Here is to fame and fortune for Sidney Turner." With a clink of the glasses, Bert guffawed, drank it in one swoop and Sidney followed suit.

"Now lad, that isn't how you usually drink champagne. But you only toast a man's first day in a new land once. Just remember such magnificent nectar is usually sipped, preferably with caviar."

The waiter returned with bowls of French onion soup. With a flourish, he draped a sparkling white linen napkin on Sidney's lap so quickly the youngster had no time to feel self-conscious.

Placing the bowls on the table, the waiter presented a bottle of wine. Gaining Bert's approval, he drew the cork and placed the bottle on a sideboard.

Sidney viewed the soup with hesitation, unsure about the creamy substance atop his bowl. Looking to Bert for direction, he saw him clear a small opening to allow steam to escape.

"Don't fret lad. This is French onion soup with melted cheese. I don't suppose you ate this back in England?"

"No, and I never heard of it before either." After tasting the soup, Bert nodded his approval to the waiter.

"I'm willing to bet this meal, and all else tonight, are new to you. We have all evening to enjoy ourselves. Life is too short not to indulge when the chance comes along." Sidney would have never guessed, in a lifetime of guessing, this man so grim at sea, could be such a polished gentleman.

Sidney followed Bert's lead the remainder of the meal. When they finished their soup, the waiter returned to pour wine. He asked in French if all was well and Bert answered with his rudimentary French. The waiter nodded and smiling at Sidney, excused himself.

"Bert, I loved the soup. I've heard about French cooking but never had it before. Maybe I should have moved to France."

"No boy, you made the best choice coming here. Anything else?"

"Well, I noticed you, Desiree and the waiter have all wished me a very good evening. I wonder what you're talking about. Want to tell me, or will you say the less said, the better?"

With a pleased chuckle, Bert gazed at his young friend in the way one does just before presenting a surprise gift. Looking over Sidney's shoulder, he nodded. Before Sidney turned, rustling sounds spoke of someone entering the room.

Sidney's senses were incinerated by the woman standing beside Desiree. Apart from her rich burgundy gown, the woman was a mirror image of Desiree. Standing beside Bert, Desiree smiled proudly.

"Monsieur Sidney, this is my daughter Mystique. She is your hostess. You have only to ask, and she will attend to you." Red-faced, Sidney rose half way from his chair as he stammered good evening to this stunning young woman.

Sidney could not fathom a reason for this goddess to serve as hostess to him. Bert chuckled softly, and grateful for the diversion, Sidney shot Bert an enquiring look.

"Careful lad, turn any redder and you'll burst into flame. Relax and enjoy this young lady's company. When I come to Montreal, Desiree and I catch up on all that is worth catching up on. Her establishment is the only cure for what ails a weary sailor." Comprehension began to dawn on Sidney and he felt very nervous.

"We are in good company and the ladies only request, is that we enjoy ourselves." Bert knew Sidney had not entirely twigged to the reason for their visit but by morning, he would be a different man.

"Mystique, my friend seems uncertain. Perhaps you can help by speaking first." The young beauty gazed at Sidney and opened her lips to speak. Although her words were simple, rapture took hold and he followed only the music of her words.

Her voice held the same timbre as Desiree although with a hint of smoky contralto. Sidney sat spellbound; he could have sat there the rest of his days even if she just read train schedules to him.

"Monsieur Sidney, please do not be nervous. It will make me think you are uncomfortable and will send me away." Summoning his courage, Sidney croaked out several words.

"Please forgive me Mystique." While he furiously blushed, she rewarded him with a smile. Taking heart, he plowed ahead.

"Mystique, I hope you can sit with me, with us, I mean."

"Of course. That is why I am here. I wish to make you comfortable, so you enjoy your visit with us. Please Monsieur Sidney, anything you wish, you need only tell me."

Seeing his colour deepen, Mystique failed to hide a smile. Her smoky eyes were a deep well of sensuality. Helpless as a child, Sidney could only nod, his throat too dry for words. Taking pity on him, Desiree broke the spell.

"My fine gentlemen, please relax and we can talk while you dine. After dessert, Mystique will entertain you by singing."

Desiree rang a small bell and the waiter appeared with a serving cart. Removing the polished silver lids with a flourish, he put a plate before each man. Confused yet again, Sidney had no idea what the dishes might be. Bert leaned forward and quietly offered some guidance.

"This is veal cordon bleu, thinly sliced veal and ham with cheeses, spices, eggs, butter and a mushroom sauce. Here at Desiree's, they are famous for this dish." Sidney nodded and pointed to the other entrees. Potatoes Julienne, carrots Lyonnaise, springtime peas and polenta corn. Take your time, lad. I know you are hungry, but gulping it down, is considered poor form. We have plenty of time. Let this be your introduction to fine dining - one of life's great pleasures."

Watching which utensils Bert used, Sidney began eating. He had never tasted such food before. The meals at home had been simple, sturdy fare. A professional chef, trained in Paris, had prepared tonight's meal. It was served in stages which allowed time to eat leisurely. Sidney enjoyed the wine and drank several glasses quickly.

"Easy lad. I'm guessing you don't drink much French wine at home. Drinking two glasses that fast might have you half plastered. After dinner, we'll have dessert and then a liqueur, so you may want to slow down." Slightly chastened and feeling uncultured, Sidney put a full glass back on the table. Taking pity on the youngster, Bert softened his tone.

"This is not the night for you to get drunk for the first time. Mystique would be unhappy and Desiree mad at me for letting that happen, so take it easy, lad."

Thinking of Mystique encouraged Sidney to ask a question. The answer might be obvious, but he felt unsure and hoped Bert would not laugh. With the women momentarily out of the room, he asked.

"Bert, what is this place? Having this dinner is unlike anything I ever imagined. Desiree and Mystique are gorgeous beyond the telling. How does Desiree know you and why are they serving dinner and sitting with us? I don't understand. Oh, and by the way, I'm guessing my mother probably wouldn't approve of my being here either."

"Lad, you're near manhood. You're big enough to punch out your old man, leave home and sail across the ocean. Good for you, and I'm proud to call you a friend. Most men don't have the balls to do any of those things. Matter of fact, I'm probably one of them." Quelling Sidney's objection by raising a hand, he continued.

"It's true. I've thought of it, but never had the guts to leave England. I'm twice your age and been around the world but haven't done anything as ballsy.

"But you don't know about some things a man should. So tonight, I've taken the liberty of adding to your education. Consider yourself the guest of Desiree and myself."

"Your guest as what? I don't get it."

"I don't have time to tell you more beyond keeping your eyes open, and your mouth and wallet shut. Remember, when you're in a strange place, stand with your back to a wall."

"Yeah, you've told me that already. Anything else?" Shifting in his chair, Bert spoke in a more solemn voice.

"Yes, and it's something that has been getting men into trouble for thousands of years. I'm sure what the answer is but I'll ask anyway. You ever been with a woman?"

Unsure of the nature of Bert's question, Sidney wondered how to answer. Turning red again, he lowered his eyes and stammered.

"Bert, if I'm right in guessing what you're asking, I've not even kissed a girl, never mind the other thing. I only figured out how babies are made by watching farm animals." Bert laughed and snorted wine. Bashfully smiling, Sidney plucked up his nerve and continued.

"The only way you got anywhere with a girl at home was marrying her and I was too young for that. Never mind I would rather kiss a cow than any of them. So, does your question have anything to do with our being with Desiree and Mystique?"

For all his shipboard ferocity, Bert had a compassionate side to him. That Sidney had not received his education on the docks as had Bert, might be a blessing and a curse.

Sidney grew up in a home where he did not sleep with one eye open to survive until morning. He had not fought for food, clothing or a place to sleep. On the other hand, Sidney was naïve about the wicked ways that waylaid young men.

Bert learned early on about sex from prostitutes who worked the Portsmouth docks. Those experiences led him to believe women were good only for one thing. Not until meeting Desiree on his opium delivery, did he change his opinion.

A handsome young man like Sidney, would attract women of the shady trade. What might befall him? A young man far from home might yearn for companionship and prostitutes were the wrong company for a youth and his money.

At sea, Bert saw Sidney owned the heart of an oak. He intended to leave the ship in Montreal and take the train west to stake his claim.

When the ship docked in Montreal, Bert sent Desiree a note asking her to arrange a special evening for Sidney. He knew Sidney would gain some needed insights.

"Lad, I asked you that question for a reason. Now listen up and remember what I'm telling you. You're going to meet women on your travels. Some are good and some, not so much. The ones who are not so good, will tempt you with their bodies but offer little beyond that. They want to find a decent man like you, so you can provide for them."

"The little you're talking about, is it in the bedroom?"

"Exactly. When that type marries you, you find out she is too lazy to be much of a wife or mother. Other women's hearts and souls are so frozen by religion or prudish mothers, they can't make a man happy." Sidney had only a foggy notion what that meant.

"You have zero experience with women. Before you take that innocent mug of yours away, you need to hear a few things." Failing to hide his unease with the conversation, Sidney blushed yet again and spoke in a whisper.

"The church taught fornication is the path to eternal damnation. I'm guilty of cursing and disrespecting my father and I will have to pay for that. Maybe when I make my home out west, the Lord will forgive me once He sees my willingness to work hard and live a life worthy of salvation. So, don't take this the wrong way ..." Seeing the smile on Bert's face, Sidney stopped.

"Lad, just trust me on this score. In the morning, you will see the world in an entirely different light. Let's finish our dinner and then we will have a brandy and a cigar. Well, I'll have a cigar. You've never smoked before and it might make you sick."

The remaining courses were served with Gaelic flair. When the waiter uncovered a deep skillet, Sidney saw skinned peaches, brown sugar, several sweet confections and he smelled alcohol.

The waiter struck a match, and touching it to the liquid, stepped back when it flickered to life. After a minute, the flames died, and the waiter uncovered a container of vanilla ice cream. He scooped ice cream into bowls, added the flambé and served them. Cautiously sniffing, Sidney sampled the confection and then ate the dessert with greedy relish.

"Bert, this is the most amazing meal. How will everyday food taste after this? Thank you for bringing me here."

"You are welcome lad, glad you're enjoying yourself."

"Bert, I'll trust you know best about the rest of the evening. I don't have a clue what to do though and, well, you know."

"Not to worry lad, nature will take care of itself. Forget all the church crap you heard. There's nothing wrong with enjoying the finer things in life, especially when it involves a beautiful woman who likes you."

On cue, Desiree appeared, and Bert rose from his chair. Bowing low, he bid Sidney a good night.

Chapter Nine

In the soft candlelight, Sidney struggled to slow his pounding heart. Full of nervous curiosity, he wondered if the snickered comments he'd heard about sex were true. He hoped not to disappoint Mystique, or even worse, find the church was right about souls burning in hell.

Deep in thought, he failed to note the scent of rich Parisian perfume. Standing beside him was a heart-stopping, modern-day, Aphrodite. Mystique watched Sidney through half-lidded eyes while a hint of a smile played at the corners of her mouth. The perfume enthralled him, and he surrendered to whatever form of control she might choose to exercise over him.

"Monsieur Sidney, may I join you?" Again, that smoky voice cast a spell.

"Yes, of course mademoiselle Mystique, please," he stammered.

She found his awkwardness and manners appealing. It helped that he stood six feet tall and had deep blue eyes. Her body stirred in a manner she never felt around older men.

Like Desiree, Mystique was a courtesan in the old world meaning of centuries past. Such women exercised free choice about whom they entertained with their song, wit, beauty and bodies.

Desiree entered the business in her late teens and although she took precautions, discovered one day she was pregnant. Knowing whom the father was, she spoke to him about her predicament.

Fabulously wealthy, the man aspired to high political office and the potential for scandal could end those hopes. He relieved any financial concerns Desiree might have with a large cash payment. With that anxiety removed, she withdrew from view and moved to France for the pregnancy.

To make Desiree's absence plausible, she circulated the rumour a physician had diagnosed her with tuberculosis. The prescribed treatment required isolation at a sanatorium in the south of France.

On a spring morning, she brought a baby into the world. Seeing her daughter's angelic face, Desiree ignored all advice and kept the child, which she named Mystique.

After returning to Montreal, her rich patron provided, at Desiree's suggestion, money to purchase the brothel where she worked. With control of the operation, she changed the business from brothel to gentleman's club.

Accordingly, she sought out young girls from a background like herself and educated them. The girls were taught to sing or play a musical instrument, and more important, never to discuss their patrons. To further differentiate her establishment, Desiree added a five-star dining room, likely the only dining salon in the country closed to the public.

She interviewed the men wishing to enjoy the upscale environment her establishment offered. The high entertainment fees purchased the company of the lovely women. The patrons all knew the girls never spoke of their gentlemen acquaintances. Following that business plan, Desiree slowly became wealthy.

One evening, Desiree met Bert in the dining room. After discussing the nature of his business, she pointedly refused to allow transactions on her premises. However, for a fee, she arranged introductions to patrons who wished to establish trading relationships of one kind or another.

Desiree's patrons would have been astonished knowing she kept records. This precaution helped protect her from legal problems should patrons disagree. It worked in large part because many of the clientele were politicians and high-ranking police officials.

Mystique was born into this environment but lived away from her mother's business. She received a first-class education from tutors before Desiree exposed her to the business. Taught to play classical piano, she played public concertos to critical acclaim.

At sixteen, Mystique entered the business and Desiree arranged the introduction of her richest patron. The man understood the evening was Mystique's entry into the world of adult pleasures. Following that, Desiree limited the number and frequency of her liaisons. This evening's rendezvous, however, would be different. Knowing she was to be a reward for Sidney, Mystique did not consider the evening an assignment.

"Monsieur Sidney, I am your companion this evening. I must be certain you are comfortable and relaxed." Swallowing self-consciously, Sidney tried to breathe slowly and prayed for his body to embarrass him no further.

"Mademoiselle Mystique, call me Sidney. I am not old enough to be called mister, sir or monsieur. It makes me nervous, if you understand what I'm trying to say." She rewarded with a smile.

"Of course, if that is your wish, Sidney. But you must call me Mystique." With a burst of courage, he took one of Mystique's impeccably manicured hands and she softly squeezed in reply.

While she had long behaved as an adult, Mystique responded to Sidney in a way she did not with older patrons. She could see he had never been with a girl and was pleased to be his first love.

"Come to the parlour. Let me play the piano and sing for you."

She guided him down the hall and opened the door to her room. A richly decorated parlour and an electric chandelier provided mood lighting. In the corner stood a baby grand piano with silver candelabra perched upon it.

An accordion divider sectioned the room and barred his view of a claw foot bathtub and large bed. Dusty rose wallpaper traced with trailing green tendrils covered the walls and red velvet curtains adorning the windows, added to the intimate atmosphere.

Sitting at the piano, Mystique lifted the keyboard cover and motioned for him to join her. The bewitching scent of her perfume ambushed Sidney's senses. With adoring eyes, Sidney found his place without stumbling, and silently gulping, faced the young beauty.

His eyes painted her beauty on his brain for all time. Her eyes shone, and he blushed deeply, knowing she knew his thoughts. When she touched his wrist, he twitched as though shocked.

"You are so sweet, Sidney Turner. I hope you always remember tonight, no matter where you go."

He barely moved for fear of waking, for surely, he was dreaming. Mystique leaned close and fleetingly caressed his lips with her rich, full mouth.

Sitting back, she saw him blush once more. Hungry desire shone in his eyes. He might be inexperienced at lovemaking, but she knew his body would not fail them. She enjoyed building the anticipation vital to creating the mood.

Sidney marvelled while watching Mystique caress the piano keys. He did not recognize the tune and as she sang in French, he could not follow the words.

None of it mattered. Never had he seen such elegance and manners. Despite his youth, Sidney wondered if the evening might ever be equalled. In his imagination, he saw himself a wealthy lord living in a castle with Mystique. Having not ever seen a naked woman, his fever had them locked in a passionate embrace. While he mused, Mystique ceased playing and watched him with a knowing smile.

Placing her fingertips under his chin, she kissed him again. She allowed her lips to play and bathed his face with her breath. Parting her lips, she delicately traced the tip of her tongue along his lips.

"Sidney, I want tonight to be very special." His heart thumped when she took his hand.

"You have had a long journey so let me treat you like a king. I will consider your every wish a command." Sidney's face turned crimson and Mystique smiled at how aroused he had become.

"Do not be bashful. Behind the screen is a tub of hot water to bathe and silk pyjamas to wear." She already knew he would not wear the pyjamas.

"I will wait here for you." Knowing how the plot would unfold, she smiled once more.

Nodding to this goddess, he rose and stepped behind the screen. Nervously slipping off his clothes, he folded them neatly and listened. Hearing nothing, he wondered if she had left the room.

Tentatively dipping a toe in the water, he found it much warmer than at home, and far cleaner. Every Saturday evening at home, the family bathed in a galvanized tub. The established bath order meant his mother went first, then his two younger sisters, then his father, the two older brothers and Sidney. He found consolation, knowing Albert went last.

Still nervous, Sidney appreciated bathing in a tub not constructed from rough galvanized metal. Sliding into the water, he stretched out and luxuriated. Critically examining himself, he hoped Mystique liked his body. Imagining her naked made him erect again, and once more, he felt light-headed.

Sidney's father never discussed sex with his sons. Those conversations took place in juvenile gossip sessions with friends. The boys learned in school that touching themselves was sinful and harmful and Sidney heeded these admonishments.

When he awoke at night with his pyjamas soaked, following dreams about the neighbour's daughter, he felt ashamed. In the morning, he tried to wash away all evidence of forbidden thoughts.

Despite fearing heavenly retribution for the dreams, he had to admit the physical release was pleasurable. Could the act with a woman be anything like this? He also heard whispers about other sexual activities that simply could not be true. What sort of person engaged in such practices?

Certainly, a young man raised by the tenets of a God-fearing church would never stoop to such behaviour. He did his best to live up those ideals and congratulated himself for maintaining a moral superiority about sex. But this evening, he had miserably failed to banish sinful thoughts. The village vicar and his mother would disapprove.

Scented perfume stole into his reverie and a slim arm slid over his shoulder. He tried covering himself with a washcloth to preserve a morsel of dignity, but a delicious giggle rebuked him.

"Sidney, don't hide your body. You are beautiful. I want to bathe you and how can I do that if you cover yourself? Move your hands please."

Sidney's face turned flaming red. From the corner of his eye, he saw Mystique's face close beside his. On impulse, he kissed a corner of her mouth. She stopped the caresses, slowly faced him and softly pressed her lips to his mouth. The tip of her tongue traced a sensuous line. She slipped her tongue between his lips to unlock his teeth.

He had never kissed a girl, although he heard how the French did it. None of the village girls held his fancy nor had he thought of kissing one this way. With Mystique kissing him, he thought her mouth tasted like fresh spearmint. Not knowing what to do, he copied the languid movements of her mouth.

A soft sigh escaped from somewhere deep inside her. Sidney felt his body would burst. Now nearly frantic, he needed to release this primal desire, but Mystique knew exactly when to slow down.

Breaking off their kiss, she swabbed his brow to slow his breathing. His erection refused to soften beyond half readiness but that would do for the moment. Rising to her feet, she moved to the front where Sidney's feverish eyes devoured her.

Mystique wore a full-length, white gossamer negligee and the luxurious mane of midnight black tresses, fell in waves upon her shoulders. Fixing predatory eyes on Sidney, she stepped into the tub.

Taking a silver pitcher from a stand, she knelt and filled it with water. To Sidney's continuing amazement, she stood and slowly tilted the pitcher, allowing the water to course paths along her curves and the negligee instantly clung to her perfect body. Once more, Sidney felt weak as the blood drained from his brain.

Coyly, while softly biting her lip, she shook her head and allowed the obsidian tresses to sway across her breasts. Tilting her head, she ran her hands through the long hair and shook her head to settle the black mane in casual disarray. She wanted Sidney to recognize her own genuine desire.

Sidney laboured with dry, rasping breath. At this moment, he wanted her more than life itself. Knowing that, Mystique knew the time had arrived for them to explore one another.

Lowering herself into the tub, she kissed his throat. When Sidney gripped her shoulders, she gently, but firmly, pulled his hands away so he could caress her shoulders and back. While he did that, she continued to kiss his throat.

Her upper body rested on his torso and he felt the heat of her breasts. She began planting soft kisses on his chest and teased his nipples with her tongue. In unbridled passion, Sidney sucked her fingertips.

His warm mouth inflamed her, and she nearly reached orgasm. Her mouth continued across his ribcage and she felt his erection. Taking him in her hand, she bowed her head.

Sidney had heard about this and thought the idea repulsive, but the sensation was amazing. Mystique had barely begun when Sidney released with an anguished moan. The violence of the moment astonished him.

Through half-open eyes, he watched Mystique rinse her mouth. After daintily spitting in a basin, she took a peppermint and let it dissolve in her mouth.

Sidney felt confused by the act she had just performed. Taught that lust was sinful and the road to ruination, he accepted this missive without question. Now, not only had it happened, he had enjoyed Mystique's actions. With a pang of guilt, he realized he had committed another sin by partaking of flesh outside the sanctity of marriage.

His thoughts betrayed him, and he saw Mystique searching his face. She stood and peeled the wet negligee away from herself. Curling her naked limbs against him, she laid her head on his shoulder.

"Sweet Sidney, listen to me. Please do not think we have done something wrong. I can guess what you were told about sins of the flesh. The nuns taught me the same fables.

"Once I got older, I decided these stories couldn't be true. If God made us in his image, and he gave us these feelings, how can it be wrong? Love between two people must not be considered a sin.

"You are a beautiful man and I truly wish to make love with you. When I stand before God, my question will be the same. You are perfect, and you made love and peace. How then can the act of making love be wrong?"

Sidney pondered Mystique's words. This young beauty amazed him. In his experience, girls never expressed themselves so eloquently. She had read his thoughts and eased his mind.

With the weight of her body upon him, his body recovered, and desire grew again. Mystique helped him to his feet, so he could take her in his arms. She kissed his lips, and soft lips parted again, and her tongue teased him. Sidney enthusiastically returned her kiss.

She led him to the bed. Continuing to kiss passionately, Sidney moved between her thighs but was unsure about entering her. However, Mystique wanted to teach him how to pleasure a woman.

Mystique gently guided him while softly moaning, and breathlessly, she explained how he should touch her. With her coaching, he brought Mystique to orgasm. In amazement, Sidney watched as her mouth contorted, and her eyes stared at the ceiling before she pulled him up. Her sex was quivering, and he thrust himself deep inside her. With a gasp, she wrapped her arms and legs around him and bit his chest in ecstasy.

Pounding his hips against hers, Sidney was far too aroused to last long and once again, his body shuddered as he released. Mystique cried his name aloud as she reached another orgasm. She kissed his throat and whispered he was a wonderful lover.

Raising his head to look at Mystique, Sidney was dumbstruck to hear her words. Thoroughly infatuated, he would have never thought such a perfect creation might have feelings for a simple country boy.

Exhausted, they collapsed in one another's arms. Sidney felt overwhelmed by his feelings for Mystique. He was fully prepared to lay beside her for the remainder of his days. Having known such pleasure with her, never again would he believe it was a sin to make love.

A new confidence beat inside him. When the ship docked that morning, he was an awkward youth. Now he was a man, lying in the arms of this dazzling girl.

He gently stroked her face and she rewarded him with a warm smile. Raising himself on an elbow, he kissed her, and she wrapped slender arms about his neck. She parted her legs to allow his hips to fit between hers. The rhythmic movement of her hips encouraged him to move in time with her.

Mystique moaned while enthusiastically returning Sidney's passionate kisses. She rolled him over, straddled his hips and impaled herself. This position was immensely exciting for Sidney. He felt her contract around him and his body built toward another release. She cried his name and he erupted moments later.

Collapsing on his chest, she gasped for air while he held her close. Their perspiration mingled as their bodies cooled. Mystique buried her face in the nape of Sidney's neck and he was astonished to realize she was crying. With a depth of tenderness that was a revelation, he held her face in his hands.

"Mystique, why are you crying? Please tell me what I did to make you cry." She smiled sadly before replying.

"Oh Sidney, you've done nothing wrong, I'm just a foolish girl. My life for the last year has been training to practise love." Sidney nodded in partial understanding as she collected her thoughts.

"Sidney, my life is good, but I've never acted like other girls. They play skipping rope, hopscotch and have friends. My life has been learning to be a courtesan. Perhaps when Mama is older, I will inherit this place but for now, this is what she wants me to learn. I've been taught not to have feelings for anyone and now look at me!

"Tonight, is all we will have. Tomorrow you will go west and forget about me. So now, you know why I was crying. Mama would be furious if she knew I was talking like this. I'm a girl who just met the most wonderful boy and in the morning, he will go away forever." Sidney knew virtually nothing of women, but he saw this beautiful girl was vulnerable and needed him to hold her close.

"Mystique, this morning I was just fresh off the boat and had never been with a girl. I guess that was pretty obvious though." Offering him a wan smile, she kissed his cheek to encourage him to continue speaking.

"I never dreamed anyone could be as beautiful as you, never mind ever kissing her, and well, all that we did tonight ..." Blushing with misplaced chivalry, he looked deep into her eyes.

"I'll write you letters and we can stay in touch that way. Maybe I won't like Manitoba and will come back here. Especially if you want me to."

The bed was soft and comfortable. Although he entertained further thoughts of romance, his body betrayed him. The combination of clean sheets, luxuriant pillows and her massaging his neck, sent Sidney to sleep.

Light shone dimly around the curtains shielding the room from the world outside. Sidney's head lay on goose down pillows where he slept. Mystique lay beside him, smiling at the face of her lover. She had been awake for hours thinking of how she wished to change her life.

Sleepily murmuring, he tried brushing away the tickle on his ear lobe, but it continued. Opening an eye, he discovered Mystique playfully nibbling. Even before being fully awake, his body wanted to resume the festivities and Mystique obliged.

"Sidney, let's talk. No, please don't stop. I can talk and do this at the same time."

Sidney offered an unintelligible reply while gently sucking on her neck. He mumbled they were doing exactly what he had been dreaming of doing before he awoke. Their activity ended pleasurably, and Mystique excitedly sat up.

"Sidney, I'm coming with you. Mama will say no if I ask, so let's get going."

"You're coming with me? I don't even know where I'm going except to this Manitoba place." Mystique's lips compressed, and her brow set in a determined line.

"I won't argue with you or mama. I won't wait months for your letters and no girl out there is stealing you from me."

Far too besotted to believe another girl could capture his fancy, he listened in astonishment as Mystique continued.

"You'll like it out west and will want to stay, and staying with you, is what I want. So, hurry and bath and we'll leave. I'm already packed, so let's get going."

Mystique's eyes shone excitedly as he struggled to get hold of his mind. Once again, he thought back twenty-four hours to when he was still working on the *Angus Celt*.

Yesterday he had just arrived knowing very little about this country or women. A day later, the most beautiful girl in the world wanted to run away with him. The enormity of it all staggered him, but he now wholeheartedly believed he would kill to keep this girl.

"Mystique, you can't be serious. I don't really know where I'm going except to some place called Winnipeg. I don't know anyone there, don't have a job and or anywhere to live. Thanks to Bert, I have enough money for a bit, but it won't last long. What about your mom and everything here? Oh, please don't cry."

"Sidney, if you don't want me, just say it. Thinking of you with another girl just kills me, so let me come. I'll make you happy."

"Mystique, I do want you, but you have a good life here and I can't offer anything like this." Fearful of talking her out of the plan, he quickly added, "At least right now I can't..."

"Sidney, you are alone and need someone with you. Maybe my life has been easier, but I didn't work for it, so let me finish. You do understand how we make our money here?" When he cautiously nodded, she continued.

"Mama has done well and has been very smart. I just started in our business and before yesterday, I accepted that. But since meeting you, my feelings have changed." Sidney blushed and became aroused again.

"No Sidney, we have to leave. If you can forget about the short time I worked, I will make you happy. I have money to help us start in this Manitoba place. Please take me with you. If you don't, I will die."

Youthful hormones and exuberance has launched many a person on an adventure and it proved no different for these two. Swept along by her enthusiasm, he knew his life now included her.

"All right. Yesterday I didn't know you but now life without you is simply not possible. Let's leave right now." With a dazzling smile, Mystique flung herself upon him and giggled.

"I'll bath quickly and then you have one too and let's get dressed. We'll take the back stairs and the station is only two blocks away." After bathing and dressing, but before they left, he enthusiastically kissed her.

"Mystique, thank you. I promise to make you happy. Now let's go before common sense makes you change your mind." Cautiously opening the door, Mystique saw the empty hallway and they silently crept down the outside stairs to an alley.

Manitoba

Chapter One

Sidney and Mystique crossed the vast railway station hall and halted at the ticket counter. Mystique showed her planning ability by stopping Sidney before he enquired about tickets.

"Put on this ring and we'll tell the ticket man we just got married."

Slipping a heavy gold band on his finger, she flashed the ring she already wore. An older patron had proposed but she and her mother had declined. The disappointed man had hoped she would change her mind and would not take back the rings, a detail she did not share with Sidney. Gathering his nerve, Sidney asked for two tickets.

"Will that before first class, berth or coach?" asked the ticket clerk with an air of condescending disapproval.

Sidney did not know such terms, but Mystique saved him with a bright smile that concealed her wrath the clerk had not addressed Sidney with more respect.

"We were married just yesterday and we're on a budget. Can you offer us any advice?"

After an explanation of costs, they bought tickets for a shared sleeping berth. Mystique happily smiled, ensuring the clerk would remember her. The clerk asked their names but before Mystique could offer an assumed name, Sidney blurted out.

"Mr. and Mrs. Sidney Turner."

The clerk dutifully added them to the passenger list and passed two tickets under the wicket. Mystique beamed at Sidney and they boarded the waiting train.

"Well, more new experiences for me, Mystique. I've never been called a married man nor been on a train. New for you too?"

"No to married and yes to a train but only day trips. Oh Sidney, this is so exciting, please say you're excited, too."

"I am beyond excited. I've no idea what to expect. My life has changed so much this last four weeks. I lived in England a month ago and look at me now. Whatever Bert had in mind yesterday, I doubt he thought I would be taking you out west." Lowering his voice, he whispered.

"Not to mention what we did all night and this morning." Blushing again, he kissed Mystique.

They took a seat on an upholstered bench. Mystique leaned against him and he put an arm around her shoulders. Kissing the top of her head, he gazed at the rail yard. The large steam locomotives huffing on nearby sidings fascinated him and he wondered about the destinations of the trains.

A conductor broke his line of thought by calling out, "All aboard!" As the distant engine tugged the cars forward, an excited thrill ran down Sidney's spine.

Clear of the city, a broad panorama unfolded, and the wide fields fired Sidney's imagination. He envisioned owning a vast farm, building a fine house and raising a family. Shaking his head again, he chuckled and said to himself, *'You just got here and already think yourself a lord. Oh, wasn't last night the most amazing thing ever?'* He saw Mystique watching him and he squirmed guiltily.

"Sidney, tell me what you're thinking. Is this how love feels?" He shrugged and hoped to hide his surprise to hear Mystique speak of love.

"If this is how love feels, it's wonderful. I want to sing and don't care who hears me. Are you happy, Sidney?" Burying his face in her tresses, he inhaled her intoxicating perfume.

"Mystique, I can't believe how fantastic my life is now. I came here thinking about farming in this Manitoba place. And now my life is this mad adventure."

"You mean our life?" Mystique chided him.

"You're right, our life. Thanks to you, I'm a man today. I can't imagine ever feeling more strongly about anyone than you."

How quickly he had come to trust Mystique with his innermost thoughts. He feared awakening to find himself back in England with only the memory of this dream. Reading his thoughts, Mystique told him her English gentleman was special.

The rail line followed a broad river and Sidney marvelled at the vast forests; the English forests were never so large. From the little Sidney knew about Canada, the forests stretched hundreds of miles. Perhaps he could make his fortune by logging?

Then his thoughts returned to farming under the vast prairie skies. Excitement bubbled up inside and he thought *'Don't see any cattle here so you're going west. Like mom said, follow your heart.'*

Sidney had adult aspirations, but he was not of legal age. Doubts gnawed his exuberance and unease about his plans needled him. With impeccable timing, Mystique stirred and murmured sleepily. Kissing the top of her head, he silently mouthed he loved her. With Mystique at his side, the world would have to stand aside.

He resumed watching the countryside and the rhythmic rocking of the rail car lulled him to sleep. Passengers smiled at the sight of the couple, now so innocent, after tut-tutting at their display of affection only minutes earlier.

The train stopped in Ottawa at lunch and Sidney saw the buildings were far grander than he expected. *'Wow, these people are in a hurry to put the country on the map.'* Leaving the city behind, the train soon plunged into the legendary wilderness he had read about in books.

Mile after mile were wilderness landscapes that had existed for untold millennia. A lake came into view and he saw a moose, yet another first for Sidney. Other passengers barely noticed, and he wondered if one day, he might be so blasé.

Several hours later, the conductor announced the dining car was serving dinner. Astonished most of the day had passed, Sidney's heart skipped knowing he and Mystique would soon return to bed.

An hour later, Mystique slid backwards into the blankets and pulled Sidney after her. Finally spent, Sidney slid into deep slumber with Mystique in his arms.

Over the following days, they saw impenetrable forests and abundant wildlife. When the train reached Lake Superior to hug the water's edge, Sidney marvelled to see a horizon free of land. Towns hacked from the rocky shoreline occasionally came into view before the wilds closed in again. Sidney wondered if the land had even known humans before the railway's completion a quarter century earlier.

"Sidney, you're off somewhere else. Are you building a house and being a rich farmer?"

"Yes, I am. I can't get over how big everything is here. I can't wait to get to Manitoba. How big a house do you want?"

"It has to be two stories, so I can watch the sun rise." Sidney laughed; not once had she willingly left the warm bed.

"Laugh now, but when we have our own place, I'll be up first," she said.

Talk of building a house had long-term implications. Sidney's traditional English upbringing included Victorian morals and the stern edict one did not have sexual intercourse before marriage. To his mind, there was only one remedy to this conundrum.

With little privacy, Sidney tugged Mystique to the platform joining the railcars. Over the rush of wind, he bent on one knee and shouted above the din.

"Mystique, this might not be the most romantic place to ask but it sure is the right time. Marry me! Please be my wife." Wrapping her arms around his neck, Mystique's tears, eyeliner and lip rouge smeared Sidney's cheeks.

"Yes, yes, yes! What girl would ever say no to such a wonderful man? I will be your wife and have your children." Despite the roaring wind and shaking platform, they sealed the moment with a tender kiss.

"What are you two doing out here?" a white-haired porter shouted. "It's against regulations." Red-faced, Sidney bowed and stammered an apology.

"I'm sorry, sir. We'll go back inside. I just asked her to marry me and she said yes!" The porter's countenance softened, and he smiled at an old memory.

"Congratulations on finding such a beautiful young lady. Now, please, off with you."

Back inside, Mystique excitedly chattered, planning their life together and Sidney grew thoughtful. Neither he nor Mystique had spoken of her mother and leaving home, but surely, it must be on her mind.

They each had left home abruptly, and Sidney did not like how they left Montreal. Mystique never said goodbye to Desiree and Sidney had not bid farewell to Bert.

Without Bert, Sidney would not know Mystique or have a cash reserve. Feeling guilty, he had no doubt about Bert's wrath. All he might offer was he and Mystique were in love, and that would sound juvenile to Desiree and Bert.

"Mystique, I need to talk about how we left Montreal. Please hear me out until I'm done talking, okay?" Mystique squeezed his hand, signaling she would listen without interruption.

"I feel bad leaving Bert without saying good-bye. The only money I had was for a ticket and I would have been sleeping on a day coach bench. In Winnipeg, I might have gone hungry before finding a job.

"Your mom will be worried, and Bert pissed off with us, mostly at me. When we get settled, we need to write them a long letter. This isn't how I want my life with you to start, feeling like we've snuck off and done something wrong."

"Sidney, if they are mad, let it be with me because it is my idea. Mama will be angry, but she knows about love. When I tell her that we are married, it will be fine. You'll see."

Later that day, the dense stands of trees thinned and soon after, they saw the open prairie. Towns appeared and the tall wooden silos at the trackside mystified Sidney. After questioning a porter, he learned the structures were grain storage elevators. Built by grain companies, area farmers brought in their grain to sell. Once the elevators filled, rail cars loaded the grain and moved it to markets.

The information fired Sidney's spirit and he imagined bringing in a rich bounty grown on his own land. Now high summer and past the planting season, he hoped to find work bringing in the fall harvest. Perhaps he might work for a farmer over the winter before claiming a homestead.

As the land flattened, wide horizons stretched in every direction. Farms dotted the land and rows of shelterbelt trees edged fields. Men worked with large steam tractors and teams of horses stood hitched to flat wagons.

Arrow-straight gravel roads bordered the fields and Sidney realized these separated farms. His heart soared. This was farming on a much larger scale than he had imagined.

Mystique's face was full of disappointment. Having never been away from home, she presumed the west would be the same. Seeing a land of dusty roads and open vistas, it was a desert to her. Looking at Sidney, he clearly believed this was the Promised Land.

The vision of happily ever after in their grand house had been so appealing. Mystique had no work experience except her mother's business. The people of Mystique's world were not the day-to-day working class, and she was the proverbial princess.

Sidney was so different from her usual liaisons. He was polite, handsome and strong. Certain of love at first sight, Mystique did not doubt her feelings were genuine. However, this place was unlike anything she expected. She trusted he would do what was right and if they did not belong here, he would find a better place. Squeezing his hand, she summoned a bright smile.

"Never mind me. This is just so different. It must be strange for you, too, from what you've said about England. Is this what you were hoping for?"

Searching her eyes, Sidney saw fear but also signs of determination. Her luxurious home in Montreal made this rough country appear primitive. Perhaps she just needed time to adjust.

"To be honest, I didn't know what to expect. The poster in Southampton didn't look like this. I mean, how do you tell what it looks like before seeing it? England is nothing like this and the farms are small." Comparing the two realities, he became enthusiastic again.

"This is grand on a scale beyond the telling. Thirty years ago, there was no railroad and these people were still in Europe. There are millions of acres to farm if a man is willing to see it through. I wonder when we'll reach Winnipeg."

As though answering his question, a conductor announced their arrival in ten minutes. They sat closer to the window, peering ahead for a first glimpse of the city. Streets appeared with houses closer together as the train pulled into a large station. Hefting their bags, Sidney followed Mystique down to the platform.

Seeing a station far grander than expected, Winnipeg was clearly an important city. A large wall map of Canada caught his eye and he walked over to examine it. Winnipeg lay mid-point across Canada and that seemed the best of omens. Looking closer, he saw a town west of Winnipeg named Shilo. Saying the name aloud, he liked how it sounded and pointed to it on the map.

"Want to get tickets for this Shilo place? Just the name sounds like an adventure waiting to happen. The main train line is near it. Sight unseen, it sounds about right."

Mystique saw several towns had names of French origin. It comforted her to know other French-speaking people lived in the vicinity. She signaled her agreement with a kiss and Sidney bought two tickets. In answer to the ticket agent's query, he did not hesitate to give the names of Mr. and Mrs. Sidney Turner of Shilo, Manitoba.

Chapter Two

Upon reaching Shilo, the station appeared to be the town's most solid building. Dirt streets lined with small stores, a blacksmith shop and livery stable accounted for most activity.

Across from the station stood a hotel, and owing to the time, they decided to stay there for the night. A bored desk clerk showed Sidney where to sign the registry book and handed him the key for a second-floor room.

"The bathroom is at the end of the hall and only six other rooms share it." Sidney shrugged and carried their bags upstairs to the room for their first prairie evening.

"Well, it's nothing fancy but it will do. In the morning, I will make my claim at the land office and look for work. It's harvest time and farmers need men."

"Don't worry, Sidney, I have lots of money."

"That's all well and good, but let's hope I find a job quickly."

"You will my love. Now, come here and comfort me."

Opening an eye, Sidney saw morning's glow around the curtain edges. Mystique lay asleep and Sidney could not resist nuzzling her breasts. She stirred, and smiling sleepily, opened her arms to him. Soon after, his hunger pangs and impatience to begin the day, drove him from the warm bed.

"You go for breakfast while I bathe. I can't wait to see the spot where you make your claim." While Mystique chattered on, Sidney laughed.

"Go order breakfast and save me some, then we'll go to the land office. Oh Sidney, I can't wait to get started!" Noticing his blossoming desire as he stared at her, she pushed him out the door before their urges hijacked common sense.

Over a breakfast of ham and eggs, Sidney scanned a local paper. He wanted details about finding and filing a homestead claim. In the paper were advertisements for land, but not free land. The asking price for farmland was far beyond his reach. *'Well then, I'll check at the land office instead.'*

Putting the paper aside, he concentrated on breakfast while planning to marry Mystique. Neither had a birth certificate but they could always state their age as twenty-one. Thinking of Mystique and marriage, caused him to wonder why she had not come down for breakfast.

In their room, Mystique applied some make-up and styled her hair. She felt a bit off colour but paid it little attention. Then breakfast smells wafting from the dining room, triggered a wave of nausea.

She shrugged it off, but the nausea returned more forcefully a minute later. Taking deep breaths failed to calm her stomach and reaching for a washbasin, she retched and sat down. What had triggered this? She had not been sick in ages and it was summer. Perhaps last night's dinner had been bad, but Sidney hadn't been ill. Then like an approaching storm, a cloud began clamouring for attention.

Looking at the wall calendar, Mystique counted backwards and realized her period was very late. Fear quickly washed away the joy budding in her heart. The initial thrill she might carry Sidney's child, vanished. "Please God, no ..."

Basic arithmetic ruled out the possibility of this being Sidney's child. They had been intimate only for the last week. Her last period was two months ago, and that spelled trouble.

Mystique never drank while entertaining but her last client had insisted. At his behest, she drank too much red wine while playing the piano. Groggy from the wine, she submitted to the man's advances without exercising her normal care. Hungover in the morning, she awoke alone with little memory, but her body offered evidence of sexual activity.

Disgusted by the man, and disappointed with herself, she considered leaving the business. Knowing her mother would demand an explanation, she kept the incident to herself. Most of her reluctance stemmed from fearing Desiree might tell Bert.

The news would outrage Bert. He would confront the man and possibly beat him, maybe to death. A police investigation would certainly follow.

Then Sidney Turner walked into her life. Smitten instantly, she did not want to risk having another girl ensnaring him and demanded to entertain him. A wish to be with Sidney was her desire and their ardour brought them west.

Any thoughts she carried Sidney's child had become a nightmare. How could they marry now? She could never try hoodwinking him into thinking the child was his.

Although not an active parishioner, Mystique knew tenets of the Catholic Church ruled out terminating the pregnancy. However, having the child of a man she now hated, nauseated her. If she was pregnant, her mother would insist she put the baby up for adoption.

Desiree had candidly shared the details of how she bore Mystique. Against the wishes of her protector and closest friends, Desiree kept her baby. She decided on the name Mystique because of the mystery surrounding Desiree's whereabouts.

Mystique did not want to be a mother. Having a child born out of a financial transaction would be a nightmare she did not want to face. Her only option was returning to Montreal and she refused to deceive Sidney. Perhaps several years later, he might still wish to marry her. But as her fear grew that his love would be replaced by hate, tears trickled down her cheeks.

'Why now, God? Why punish me for loving this wonderful boy? I want to be married and live a good life. Do you want me to have a child? Is this what you want? Is it not a sin to take him away and leave me alone?' Wrapping her arms around herself, she slowly rocked and cried.

"Mystique, why are you crying?" Curious why she had not joined him, Sidney had returned. Taking her in his arms, she collapsed against him while tears stained his shirt. When Mystique's breathing steadied, she dried her eyes and faced him.

"Sidney, I'm being silly. I miss Mama and I'm homesick. These stupid tears started on their own, so don't worry about me. Come on, let's go and find this land office."

Giving him a smile far braver than she felt, they went downstairs. He opened the restaurant door, but Mystique stopped. She did not trust her stomach.

"I'm not hungry. Let's go and stake our claim."

Mystique knew she needed an excuse to return to Montreal. While they made love that morning, she had pledged her eternal love. How could she tell him an hour later of her wish to leave? Perhaps providence had a solution to her dilemma.

At the land office, Sidney saw no other applicants. That seemed odd, but striding to the counter, Sidney spoke the words he had been rehearsing for weeks.

"Good morning. I'm here to apply for land to homestead." His heart jumped while voicing the request but moments later, he knew only disappointment.

"By your accent son, you just got over here. Sorry to rain on your parade but there hasn't been homestead land here for a long time. Americans snapped up the last of it and the only land available, will cost you plenty."

With those words, the clerk burst Sidney's naïve bubble. But the clerk did have a scheme for lining his own pockets.

"Son, I can check for you, but it will take time." The clerk then desultorily sifted a pile of papers on his desk. Older people recognized the sly request for a bribe, but Sidney knew nothing of that game and at any rate, he did not have the money.

Sidney turned to Mystique. Her heart filled with pity seeing him so deflated, but she smiled and pulled him toward the door.

"Thank you for your time, sir. Sidney, we'll go back to Brandon. In the last week, all we saw is land."

She wore a brave face because right now, he needed her. The time to speak of leaving had not yet arrived. They had barely stepped into the dusty street when Mystique felt nausea sweep over her. Quickly excusing herself, she went back inside the land office to use the washroom.

A prairie vista beckoned to Sidney. The gentle breeze wafted a smidgen of dust while opening a door to the past. Through a dusty mist, shadowy silhouettes became visible. He heard faint shouts and words of a strange tongue while drums beat hypnotically. Tremors in the earth rattled his boots. The vision became clearer and he saw Indians on horseback among the shadowy silhouettes.

The magnificent horsemen shot arrows at other silhouettes that were buffalo. Transfixed by the spectacle, he dared not move for fear of breaking the spell.

The massive herd sped away with yipping Indians in hot pursuit. Dust hung in the air and the voice from his first vision returned to speak again. *"You will have a son of our blood. A maiden will find you."*

Without even knowing it, Sidney nodded. In the swirling dust, the face of a Sioux warrior became distinct and the power of his quiet authority mesmerized Sidney.

He knew the face from some faint memory. The man's eyes beseeched him to accept a knowledge requiring no words. Something felt so familiar, Sidney grew frustrated he could not name it. Then in a flash, he knew the blue eyes came from the past – and they were his eyes.

The warrior smiled, knowing Sidney had discovered their connection, and promised to reveal more of the future. His promise came with a caveat: Sidney had to stay in Manitoba.

The vision began fading. The brown shadow galloped from sight along with the thrumming of thousands of pounding hooves. The buffalo spirits had returned to their haven.

Only a few seconds had passed, but it felt like hours. Trying to calm himself, he smoothed his shirt in wonder. Was he losing his mind? Had the fresh air of the ocean, and now the prairies, affected his brain? Perhaps he was not getting enough sleep. Like the shipboard vision, he knew not to share the moment.

"Well Sid old boy. Best get your wits back before Mystique comes."

"Sidney, who are you talking to?" Mystique had rejoined him. Caught completely off guard, he blurted out the first thoughts that came to mind.

"I'm feeling on top of the world and the words have to come out. For some reason, this land is talking to me. You know, it's like I've been here before. I know it sounds crazy and don't think I'm off my rocker – at least too far off, anyway."

"No, you don't. I've felt that way sometimes and I'm glad you feel at home here. Let's get you to the Brandon office." Mystique hoped Sidney had not noted the singular reference. When they reached Brandon, she needed a reason why she could not stay with him. She had to confide in her mother. This was not a decision to make on her own.

At the Brandon train station, Sidney saw a poster advertising homestead land, but it was north of Saskatoon, Saskatchewan. About all Sidney knew about the place was how to pronounce the outlandish sounding name.

By the wall map, it looked to be nearly five hundred miles. That presented a problem because only an hour earlier he had promised to stay in Manitoba. He decided to check at the Brandon land office, but a huge hand suddenly clamped down on his shoulder and spun him around.

Chapter Three

"Bert, wake up! Mystique and Sidney are gone!"

Scrambling out of bed, Bert threw on his shirt and pants. Quickly looking around Mystique's room, he did not see Sidney's sea bag. A partially empty closet meant Mystique had also packed. Desiree knelt and opened the bottom drawer of a large wardrobe to hunt for a small metal lock box. The box normally lay under bulky winter garments but not this morning.

"It's gone - a thousand dollars I told her to save. What is she thinking? Where are they? Did she leave a note?"

Seeing her icy fury, Bert knew some of the anger was with him. He cursed Sidney and then found a note under the candelabra on the piano. Desiree snatched it from his hand and rapidly read it. With clenched fists, she looked ready to scream but not a sound escaped. Standing motionless, she passed the note over to Bert.

'Dearest Mama, I know you will be angry, but please, do not be. I always thought being here would be my life, but meeting Sidney changed that. I left with him to go west. I will write so you know everything is all right. Love forever, Mystique.'

Despite his anger, Bert felt a grudging respect for Mystique's pluck and for Sidney being smart enough to take her with him. There could be no doubt they were off to Manitoba and he meant to find them. He hoped Sidney would not travel under an assumed name. If he had, there would be no record at the train station.

Nevertheless, he needed to do something. His conscience also nagged him because his business arrangement with Desiree might be in jeopardy. From experience, Bert knew a woman angry with her man, meant anything could happen. His business venture had been very profitable, and Bert did not want that train going off the rails.

The original idea had been for Sidney to spend the night with Mystique before his journey west. As he had introduced Sidney to Mystique, he felt responsible for this drama. That the two would run off together, had never crossed his mind. He had little choice other than going after them.

"I have to tell Thompson to sail without me. Then I'll head to the train office and ask some questions." He paused for a moment, considering his next words.

"Sidney is dumb enough to give his real name if he is asked. At least I hope so. If he did, I'll go after them. He is going to regret being born when I find his sorry ass. I'll bring Mystique back even if I have to throw her in a sack and tie it shut." Bert rushed out the door and ran to the docks.

Now somewhat calmer, Desiree knew Mystique would refuse to return if only Bert went. She had seen Bert's ferocious temper, and it would be monstrously unfair if he beat Sidney for an escapade Mystique hatched. Forty-five minutes later, Bert breathlessly returned to see her valise at the front door.

At the station, Bert studied a wall map of Canada and softly whistled to see the distance. Once more, he felt a sneaking admiration that Sidney left England with only a pittance and the clothes he wore.

'Well, the young bugger has Mystique. If I was seventeen again, she'd be the girl I'd choose ...' He wanted to thrash Sidney, but days spent tracking him down, would cool the anger.

"I'll ask these agents if they saw them." He reached for his wallet; memories always improved with cash, but Desiree stepped in front of him.

"Give me your wallet and I'll ask. Your face is still thunder, and you'll scare people. Let me try charm and explain why I'm asking. I'll only use money if I must but let me try first." Bert knew if Desiree failed to get answers, so would he. When she turned on her charm, an agent would be putty.

The white-collared ticket agent looked up from his paperwork to see a beautiful woman standing before him. He felt the immediate attraction that Desiree had learned long ago to use to her advantage.

"Excuse me, I wonder if I might have your assistance with a delicate matter. Were you on duty earlier this morning, perhaps at opening?" Rarely did people ask personal questions and he wondered where her question might lead. Noting his hesitation, she hastened to explain the reason for asking.

"I don't mean to cause problems, but what I wish to know is urgent. Do you remember if a young woman and young man were here earlier this morning?"

While the clerk vaguely remembered a young man, he clearly recalled the beauty claiming to be the young man's bride. The woman now standing before him must be an older sister. The young couple now appeared to be travelling against family wishes and being a family man, the clerk wished to help. First though, he needed to protect his position.

"Madam, these are normally not the questions people ask me. My function is to sell tickets and help people route plan. I do not mean to offend, but please tell the reason for your questions."

Desiree's cheeks flushed. Fearing the agent would not help, she slid some bills across the counter. Reading her thoughts, he quickly clarified his position.

"I only ask to satisfy my concern about divulging information regarding passengers and their travel destinations. The nature of your reply will determine how much, if anything, I can say."

"The young woman is my daughter and she left home without my knowledge or approval. I fear she eloped with the young man and they may be on the way to Manitoba and I desperately want her home. Can you help me sir?"

"Madam, I will help you. If one of my daughters did such a thing, my reaction would be identical." He opened a passenger register for the morning express that had departed hours earlier and ran a finger down to the page.

"A Mr. and Mrs. Sidney Turner purchased two tickets to Winnipeg. I overheard the man say that in Winnipeg, they would buy tickets for the town of Brandon. Madam, you may wish to know they each wore a gold wedding band."

Hearing that news, confirmed Desiree's suspicions Mystique had planned the escapade. Doubting Sidney had concocted the outlandish marriage tale, she nevertheless felt relieved knowing where to begin the search.

The agent smiled knowing he helped comfort this beautiful woman. She still held the bills and he raised both hands in a gesture of denial. "Madam, I am happy to have helped you."

"Thank you so very much, sir. May I buy tickets for the next train now?" The agent checked over his shoulder before replying conspiratorially.

"Madam, I could lose my job for this bit of information. Our next express does not leave for several days. However, a train with that other railway leaves for Toronto in two hours, and in the morning, it goes west." Desiree squeezed his hand smiled.

"Madam, please do not repeat what I said, it would mean my job. If you employ the same manner of asking for information as with me, tracking them will not be difficult. Especially since your daughter is as memorable a beauty as her mother." She turned and saw Bert raise an eyebrow.

"Bert, I just knew it! This escapade is Mystique's idea. Promise that when we find them, you will not punish Sidney." His eyes narrowed but Desiree raised a finger to silence him.

"Mister, you listen while I tell you my news. The ticket agent said he sold two tickets to a newlywed couple. They each wore a gold wedding band and I know where the rings came from. Mystique refused a wedding proposal from a very wealthy patron.

"The man never thought his proposal might be refused. Mystique must have kept the rings. I doubt Sidney had such rings or that he expected to get married on his first day in Canada." Bert snorted derisively at the scenario.

"Get married? Until yesterday, he didn't know he could use his pecker for anything except taking a leak."

"Don't be crude. I demand you promise that as a man of honour, you will not hurt him. I will accept no answer other than yes."

By nature, Bert did not accept restraints. But he knew that once Desiree decided something, she would not change her mind. He also knew that despite her cool demeanour, she had a mile-wide sentimental streak.

Bert knew if he broke his promise, it would end their relationship. Staring down at her, he capitulated with a mock growl.

"You have my word, but I can't let him get away with such a boneheaded move free and clear."

"Bert, you already gave me your word."

"Hear me out please. I won't beat him, but he needs to have the fear of God put in him. I'll put him up against a wall and I'm positive he won't hit me. If he does fight, I'll pin him on the floor and threaten to kill him if he makes another move. But I promise not to give him the ass-kicking he so richly deserves."

"For all your wicked temper, Bert Westhaven, you do have a kind side. Yes, I'll agree to you giving Sidney such a lesson."

"Thank you. Most men would shoot him, you know."

"Yes, yes. It's no surprise my daughter so easily led him astray. As you have proven repeatedly, my love, men are no match for a woman's wiles." Bert smiled, conceded the point and listened to the rest of her proposal.

"I didn't get much of a chance to know Sidney. By now, they are miles away. We can take a Toronto train in an hour and in the morning, take the express to Winnipeg. The agent heard Sidney mention a place called Brandon. Let's have breakfast. Now that we have a plan, I'm hungry." Arching an eyebrow, she smiled.

"Soon you'll be in Toronto for the first time and tonight, you will always remember."

Several days later, the train stopped in Brandon. Bert and Desiree saw a town spread along the dirt roads radiating from the station. Only a few people stood on the platform as the train had been virtually empty.

Bert swung down from the coach before the conductor placed a small footstool to assist passengers. Putting their bags on the ground, he helped Desiree down. After a quick look around, he strode to the station door and opened it for her.

The open door rewarded Bert with the quarry he sought. Almost too much to believe, Sidney and Mystique were ten feet away, studying a large wall map. In a heartbeat, Bert closed the distance and spun Sidney around.

"You ungrateful prick! I ought to break your fuckin' neck!" Grabbing Sidney by the lapels, he lifted him clear of the floor and rammed him against the wall.

"The only reason I don't kill you right now is I promised Desiree I wouldn't. But don't even think of raising a hand against me or I will!"

Sidney's face turned white knowing his life would end if he struggled with this enraged bull. His bowels threatened to turn liquid and that would be worse than death. Desiree and Mystique vainly tried to insert themselves between the two men, but Bert's enormous strength stymied them.

"You betrayed my trust and friendship, you ungrateful bastard." Bert seethed while ignoring Mystique's panicked shrieks.

"I take you on in good faith, look out for you, and you run off like a thief in the night. When I let go, get down on your knees and beg forgiveness or I'll drag you outside and lay a whipping on you."

Bert relaxed his grip and Sidney's knees buckled. While Bert waved a huge fist under Sidney's nose, he half stammered, half sobbed an apology. "Madame Desiree, please forgive me for ..."

"No Sidney!" Mystique screamed, and she furiously whirled to face Desiree and Bert.

"Stop treating him like this! He did nothing wrong. Blame me if you think anyone is to blame. This was all my idea. I love Sidney and he has asked me to marry him, and I said yes."

Regaining his feet, and although terrified, Sidney stood before Bert prepared to fight for Mystique. It nearly happened but Desiree stepped forward and spoke in a voice clipped with anger and fear.

"Sidney, I accept your apology. Very little of my anger is for you. I suspected this is Mystique's doing. Come outside with me, away from this audience in the station." Marching to the door, she pointedly waited for Bert to open it.

Bert stomped through the doorway, and towering beside Desiree, stood silently. Waving aside Mystique's hand, Sidney smoothed his shirt and walked outside.

Angry and frightened, Mystique hated Bert with every fibre of her being. Knowing of Bert's ferocity, she still trembled at how he manhandled her young lover. Mystique's guilt included fear she might carry the child of another man. Now was not the time to inflame passions such news would surely provoke. Taking several deep breaths to steady her nerves, she joined the others.

Seeing a small park further along the street, Desiree walked to it. She pointed for Bert to sit on one bench and directed Mystique and Sidney to the other.

"All of you will listen while I talk. Have I made that crystal clear?" Without pausing to offer an opening for the others, she continued.

"Good, I see you all understand. First, thank God, we found you. Mystique, I will not ask what possessed you to run off. I'm still too angry to hear you out.

"Bert, thank you for keeping your promise to not beat Sidney. You will not threaten him again. Sidney, I am sorry about all this. My daughter is headstrong and independent. I fear she is far too much like her mother for there to be much hope of redemption.

"We are far from home, and that is where we are going on the next train. Sidney, you decide where you should go. From what Bert tells me, your family has no idea of where you are. I know what your mother must be going through. Returning to England is my recommendation, although your future is for you to decide. Before Bert and Mystique speak, do you want to say anything?"

"Madame Desiree, I am sorry for all this. My mum would be very cross with me." Red faced, Sidney turned to Bert in hopes of receiving the big man's forgiveness.

"Bert, you have been a great friend and I am unworthy of it. All I can say is I'm sorry and ashamed for not being man enough to say farewell." Bert's terse nod served as his reply.

"Mystique, I love you. If you still want me, please be my wife." His earnestness helped soothe some of the raw emotions.

Desiree's eyes filled with tears to hear his words. Never would she allow Mystique to leave Montreal and she planned to buy her loyalty. It would cause heartbreak for the two young lovers, but she hardened her heart to that likelihood.

Mystique's face dissolved into tears. Her brave young man loved her despite earning the wrath of his only friend and her mother. He was so decent and good. How could she tell him the truth? She had promised to marry him before realizing she might be pregnant. How could he possibly love her if he knew the truth?

Bert's anger cooled and as Sidney shared his feelings, the big man smiled as his inner voice spoke. *'Well mate, if you have to listen to the small brain, at least you fell for the most beautiful girl I've ever seen. Good luck taking her away from her mama...'*

Desiree gave Sidney a look of pity and took a deep breath.

"Mystique, come with me. Bert, please stay here with Sidney, we will be back soon." Extending an arm to Mystique, they walked along the rough board sidewalk.

Chapter Four

"Listen to me young lady. I cannot imagine what possessed you to pull such a stunt. If you were so unhappy at home, you gave no sign. The only reason we found you is the ticket agent in Montreal remembered you. I know you have not had a normal life. Oh, the times I asked God to forgive me. Who raises her child to be a concubine?"

"Mama, forgive yourself. I have no regrets about my life, at least not until now. I might not have had a normal childhood, whatever that is supposed to be. The few times I have been around other girls, I've been glad about all I know. How many other girls speak two languages, play piano and read literature?" Smiling sadly, Desiree linked her arm through Mystique's and resumed walking.

"Thank you, my precious child. Perhaps one day when you're a mother, my words will have more meaning."

Relieved that Desiree did not see her cheeks redden, Mystique did not trust herself to reply as her mother continued.

"Anyway, you cannot stay in this wild place. You are used to civilization. What life could you expect to find here? Bert tells me Sidney wants to homestead and farm. Does he know anything about farming? Does he have any idea what winter is like in this country? Where would you live? A log cabin, or worse, in one of those sod huts?" Desiree needed to paint a bleak picture of life as a farm wife; it was time to fight fire with fire.

"Honestly Mystique, is that the life you want? I know you think you are in love. Will love keep you from freezing to death in the winter? Will love plow the fields to grow food, so you don't starve? You're a city girl. You can bathe twice a day if you want.

"Where would you take a bath in a sod shack? How often could you bathe? Once a week or God help you, once a month? Have you thought about what it means to be a mother out here? You'd be chopping wood to cook meals while raising children."

Mentioning children returned the colour to Mystique's face and Desiree saw it.

"Why is your face red?" Grabbing Mystique's wrists, Desiree's eyes bored deep for an answer to an alarming suspicion.

"You're pregnant," Desiree said more as statement than question and Mystique collapsed in her arms. Desiree held her while a multitude of thoughts whirled. *'How can she be pregnant? She's only been with Sidney a little while.'*

"Mystique, calm yourself. You only left home a week ago, and there's no way you can be pregnant in that short time."

"Mama, it isn't Sidney's! I haven't had a period in over two months. If I am pregnant, it is because of that pig Raymond Cloutier."

"How Mystique? You know how to keep from getting pregnant. Why didn't you make sure?"

"He got me drunk first and I didn't make him use a rubber." Desiree angrily rounded on her and hissed venomously.

"Why didn't you tell me this before? Why?"

"I know what you would have done to him. He is connected at city hall and knows guys on the other side of the tracks. I decided to forget the whole thing. Now you know why I didn't want to see other men."

"You should have told me right away. I know people at city hall and on the other side of the tracks, too. He will be told to enjoy his pleasures elsewhere."

Desiree had considerable behind the scenes influence at city hall. Those connections ensured the authorities left her alone. So long as the business operated with discretion and her girls did not use drugs, the legal eyes looked away.

Desiree could also count on help in dealing with patrons who created problems. Soon one evening, two burly constables would pull Cloutier into an alley. Then a detective would tell the man not to visit the premises again.

Desiree knew how Bert would deal with the situation and that would draw unwelcome attention. Cloutier was a politician and well-known businessman. Were he to suffer a violent beating, people would clamour for a criminal investigation. Unless Cloutier disregarded the advice, Desiree knew to keep this news from Bert.

"Is Cloutier the reason you haven't entertained these last weeks? And is it why you ran away from home? Sidney was a good excuse for leaving?" Mystique said nothing, but her expression confirmed the truth of Desiree's assertions.

"All right, you don't need to say anything. You are coming home with me. I presume Sidney doesn't know about any of this?"

"No, he doesn't. This morning was the first time I got sick. Mama, how can I tell Sidney? I said yes when he asked me to marry him. If we get married right away, no one would know it."

"Mystique, now you are talking absolute foolishness. You cannot keep such a secret the rest of your life. Nor will I allow you to tell such a lie to him. He does not deserve your deceit. Life is difficult enough without living a lie." Mystique blinked away more tears while silently agreeing with her mother's logic.

"Tell Sidney, and please believe me, you are not going to marry him. Bert and I are making plans. I've been working for years and I want to slow down. You are young, smart and beautiful and it is time you began taking over.

"Years ago, I set aside a trust fund for you. I meant it so that one day, you would not have to entertain. Now that you seem to be following in my footsteps and are pregnant, you can pass the business down to another generation." She smiled sadly at the prospect.

"Mama, I can't tell Sidney the truth. I am his first love and he is so sweet. He would still want to marry me even with my news."

"Darling child, don't be so naïve. He would never accept it as his own. The baby would change his heart and he might start drinking because of it. Do you want to take that chance? That your young man might become a mean old man who thinks his wife is a whore?"

"Do you really think Sidney would get like that, mama?" Desiree shook her head recalling old memories.

"He would remember you were with other men and that his first love was pregnant, from another man, when he married you. That is what will happen and it's the wrong start to a married life." Mystique quietly absorbed the weight of her mother's logic and life experiences.

"Mystique, I have heard the same stories over and over, and it never ends well. Men come to our business to take comfort in the arms of women who give what their wives deny them. They all have the same stories. Their wives are unattractive, or do not like the marriage bed. Maybe the marriage was for business reasons.

"Whatever it is, these people are not happy. At least in Montreal, there is a diversion from their troubles. Where would Sidney find that out here? Please listen to me, Mystique. I know a thing or two."

"Mama, you are making so much sense I can't stand it. I know you're right, but I don't want to believe you. How soon are you going back to Montreal?"

"On the next train, with you. If you are pregnant, we must be at home to plan our next steps. And Bert has a ship to catch. So, what will you tell Sidney?"

"I don't know mama, I told him this morning we should get married right away. Now two hours later, I must tell him we can't get married and I'm going back to Montreal without him. What a fucking nut case I look like."

"Mystique, please do not use such language. Now listen to me while I give a speech, and please remember some of it. Affairs of the heart are difficult because emotion is involved. It makes smart people jump on a train to go somewhere with a person they met only the night before.

"When I was your age, I thought I knew what love was, but I was wrong. Bert and I have taken years to get to where we are now. You've known Sidney a week." They walked in silence, each busy with her own thoughts.

"Mystique, tell Sidney you do not want to get married. If you tell him you are pregnant, do not let him think the baby is his. Be quick because we are taking the next train back to civilization. I will wait with Bert while you two talk." While the women were away having their talk, Bert shared some of his thoughts with Sidney.

"Lad, I was not putting on a show or bullshitting you. I would have kicked your ass if Desiree hadn't made me promise not to do it. Now I have some things to say, so be quiet until I'm done. Even then, I don't want to hear what you think.

"Mystique is going back to Montreal with her mother and me. You are staying here. Desiree wants Mystique to take over in a few years but this half-cocked nonsense you pulled moved up those plans. Mystique will be very well set up financially, as in a millionaire.

"I don't think she'll throw that away just to live with you in a sod hut on the bald ass prairie. That's not what you want to hear but somebody has to talk sense to you. Just so you don't think I'm completely a heartless bastard, let me tell you about my plans for you. Still willing to listen?"

Sidney sat with bowed head while his heart broke. Knowing Bert was right did not make acceptance easier. The only good in this moment was not making a decision. Order was being imposed on him.

"That old sailing tub of mine has done well and I also have a side business you don't know about. It pays me way more than the boat and I saved all that money. What I was going to do with it, I hadn't figured out yet. Meeting you got me to thinking, what with all your grand plans." Sidney looked up to see the creases on Bert's forehead relaxing.

"You want to farm but I hear the free homesteading land is gone. So, you can either go further west or north and take your chances on finding a spot."

Earlier that morning, the vision told Sidney to stay. Perhaps now, he should forget the vision and look elsewhere for land. There were however, more surprises in store.

"Get a job working for a farmer and learn from him. Maybe in two or three years, you can go out on your own. From what I've heard, the land rush here has been going on for twenty-five years." Sidney groaned but missed the smile on Bert's face.

"I asked some questions on the train. Seems the land here is about the best for farming. So here are my thoughts for your future … and mine." Sidney looked up in surprise while hope flickered in his chest.

"I don't want to be sailing the rest of my life. Apart from the navy, I've never had a place to take off my boots and call home. Somewhere to hang my hat without asking someone if I could. You haven't either and now I'm coming to the part that concerns you.

"I plan on being done with the sea in three more years. The most water I want to see after that is in a bathtub with a beautiful woman scrubbing my back. I don't like cities and in case you haven't noticed, I'm not the most sociable person." Sidney could not help smiling and Bert did so as well.

"Go ahead and smile, lad. The thought of me trying to be a gentleman makes me laugh until I about piss myself. This place is about half way between the Pacific and Atlantic. So, if I get a crazy notion of going to sea, I've four or five days to sober up first. I reckon the best use of some of my money is to buy a spread and start farming."

"You want to farm, Bert? I would have never guessed that."

"Nor me, and I know less about farming than you. But unlike you, I've got somebody to teach me. That would be you, at least it will be you in three years. I propose that you stay here, work for a farmer and learn. Save your money and don't drink and whore it all away.

"I'll come out twice a year to see what's up, what you've learned and what you screwed up. If you do good, I'll buy a place and we'll go in as equals." Flabbergasted with what he heard, Sidney tried to protest but Bert hushed him.

"It will be my money, and you know I'm serious about my money. You can guess what will happen if you can't carry your end.

"This stunt you two pulled nearly made me think the whole idea is bloody stupid. I've cooled off and Desiree doesn't blame you, for some reason.

"What do you say, lad? Want to be my partner in a few years? If you're careful, you'll outlive me, and it will be yours someday."

Sidney sat in stunned silence. Once penniless and homeless, he had a chance to become a landowner. The next thought brought him crashing to earth. How would he live without

Mystique? Too young to differentiate between sex and love, he believed he loved her.

"Think it through lad. We can talk more later." Slapping Sidney on the knee, Bert took his leave. Sidney's nervousness returned as Mystique drew near. What had Desiree said to bring on all these tears?

"Sidney, please don't talk so I can say all I need to say. I'm going back to Montreal with mama. I can't give you all the reasons but, please believe me, it would not be fair to you if we got married right now."

"You're not staying here with me?"

"Please…if I stayed now, it would make things hard for mama. In a year, I can come back and marry you, if you still want me."

"I don't want to wait a year, Mystique. I want you now."

"I know you do. Mama says we don't know what love is, but she is wrong. With you, I found the meaning of love. But I must do this thing at home. It's family, Sidney. I have to go."

Mystique spoke the truth about returning to Montreal for family reasons. If she came back west, first she would write and tell him the real reason for leaving him. Today was not the day for that confession.

"Don't let some girl steal you. Please do not let that happen." Lowering her voice, she murmured.

"How is it no woman ever took you to her bed before now?" Hopes that he might smile at her humour vanished with his tears. Heartache almost overpowered her, and she had to end the conversation.

Sidney felt kicked in the stomach. He could not imagine living an hour without her, never mind a year. At his age, a year might as well be a sentence of eternal exile.

What was prompting her to leave? Whatever the reason, he would make it right, and beg if he had to beg. If there were another man, Sidney would kill him. He would accept nothing less than possessing her. Mystique broke into his feverish train of thought and implored him to listen.

"Sidney, there is no one else. Mama needs me at home for another year and that is why I must go back." Sitting still as a statue, Sidney cared nothing for her explanations. Nothing mattered now.

"Mystique, this morning you said we should get married right away and now you're leaving. Maybe you'll come back in a year?"

"Yes. Sidney, don't make this any harder on me that it is." Raising his hands in the air as though throttling an imaginary throat, Sidney groaned.

"I don't want you to leave and I feel betrayed. Please don't leave me." Mystique's heart broke anew to hear his anguished plea.

"Please, Sidney. You planned to come here alone anyway, and I would just get in your way. Get started and I'll come back when things in Montreal settle down."

"What if you don't come back in a year? Do I wait another year, or two, or three? How many?"

"Maybe you will understand one day. I have to do this, or we will regret it forever." The train pulled into the station and Mystique stood to leave. She bent down to Sidney, pressed her lips to his throat and whispered her eternal love. Extending his hand, Bert offered Sidney some final advice.

"Lad, this will all turn out the way it should. Do not jump on the next train to try bringing her back. That will create more problems than it would solve." Sidney just stared absently while Bert spoke.

"I keep my word, do well and one day you'll have your farm. Who knows? Mystique might even come back to marry you." In a fatherly tone, Bert summed up.

"I know what it's like to love a girl you can't convince to stay with you. It took me years to win Desiree over, but it was worth the wait, and you'll have to wait, too. Write me at the shipping office. If you don't, that's your loss. But I don't think you want to risk losing Mystique and a farm."

Bert climbed into the car, taking away everyone Sidney knew in this new country. Belching clouds of black smoke, the train pulled out and a forlorn Sidney shuffled off.

'Now what do I do?'

Chapter Five

The pebble bouncing off Sidney's brow jolted him from painful reminiscence. Three years had passed since that heartbreaking day at the train station.

"Geez old timer, remind me not to ask you anything tougher than whether the sun is shining!" John said. "Let's get back to work. I want to be done by supper. It's Saturday and you know what that means."

"Well Johnny, with someone normal I know what it means. For someone like you, sheep had best run and hide."

"Yeah, yeah, at least I'll get laid. I'll say the right things, buy a few beers and it's off to the races." Sidney snorted and shook his head at John's bravado.

"Sure John, so many women and so little time. At least there will be one less ugly woman on the dance floor tonight, so thank you mate."

"I might not find the prettiest girls, but it's better than nothing. You'll just be pulling your wire again, you cheap sod."

John laughed but looked closely at his friend. Sidney could be so withdrawn at times. They were young men who should be prone to outbursts of juvenile behaviour. While Sidney was good fun on most occasions, he sometimes retreated to a place no one else could reach.

John knew his young friend and recognized that today, Sidney wished to be alone. There might be little point asking him to come into town for some fun, but a pal's duty included trying to get a buddy laid.

"Sid, its Saturday night. Let's go town and see if we can't get into trouble. Come on, what do you say? I bet you haven't been off the farm for six weeks. It's time, man." Sidney laughed and rolled over on his stomach.

"So you can get punched out for making rude comments about some cowboy's girlfriend? Or maybe you mean getting arrested for passing out and falling into the punch bowl at the dance?"

"Well that doesn't happen every time you know."

"Or how about you scrounging beer money from your friends like you always do. And you'll get drunk and be so horny you'll hump anything that walks. My friend, you've got more tolerance for pain than ten other men."

"Come on Sid, they're not all ugly."

"No, you're right but screwing a pretty one once doesn't make you Casanova. Especially when it's some cowboy's girl and then he punches you out."

"I hardly remember that one. Thanks for sticking up for me though."

"Johnny, I'm only a few dollars short of having enough money to get a farm. With this drought, land prices are down. Even though it sounds like great fun to go into town, get drunk, get in a fight, get arrested and puke my guts out in jail. But tonight, my friend, I'll just have to pass."

John did not know Sidney had already made an offer to purchase a section of farmland. Sidney had not divulged Bert had sent out money for the purchase. They did not want locals thinking there could be cash backing up the offer.

Since he arrived three years earlier, Sidney kept his own counsel and listened when talk turned to land sales. In early July, the serious drought prompted Sidney to cable Bert.

A choice farm became available when the farmer fell behind with payments. Sidney made a cash offer and paid a deposit one day before the bank foreclosed. Some locals grumbled about the banks' cold-hearted business approach but where others saw misfortune, Sidney saw opportunity.

He fretted over telling the MacDonald family he would soon leave their employ. Within days of arriving in Shilo, Sidney was hired, and he had worked on the farm since then. Now, he and John were like brothers. He suspected the elder MacDonald knew about the land purchase.

Just as Sidney and John were about to resume their chores, Mr. MacDonald rode across the fields to them. John looked guilty for taking a long lunch break, but he need not have bothered.

"Easy lads, I didn't come out here to give you grief for laying about." The boys smiled, knowing the older man rarely raised his voice or grew angry. However, his arrival at mid-day was unusual and they were curious to know the reason.

"Sit down, these stooks can wait a bit longer. You boys haven't been following the news, but I have, and it concerns me. I didn't want mother listening, so I came out for us three to have a man to man talk." Surprised by the solemn tone, the boys sat down and listened.

"Remember about a month ago, some Austrian prince or whatever got shot dead in one of those backward eastern European countries? I didn't pay it much mind then because those idiots are all crazy anyway. The story dried up nearly right away and I paid it no more mind. We have more to be concerned about than their foolishness.

"Well, I just back from town. It seems things are a lot more serious than I thought. The Austrians want to start a war with Serbia where this shooting happened. So again, I'm thinking who really cares about what those crazy bastards are doing.

"Well, it turns out the Russians want to protect this Serbia place for some reason. Why, who knows? But the Russians don't want Austria to attack and are telling the Austrians to stay out of it." John and Sidney shrugged, and their interest faded. Seeing their responses, the older man grew agitated.

"Seems Austria will do what they want, and they told the Russians to bugger off. Well, the Russians won't bugger off and this is where things get serious. If Austria goes to war with this pipsqueak country, Russia might go to war on Serbia's side. And if Russia goes to war with Austria, all hell breaks out."

"Why does that mean all hell breaks out in Europe, dad? It doesn't have a bloody thing to do with us."

"I wish it was that simple, Sid, but it's not. See, I didn't know Russia and France have a treaty that says if one of them is attacked or goes to war with another country, the other is automatically at war."

"There's going to be a war over some dead prince?"

"That treaty got signed years ago, as a warning to the Germans. According to the newspaper, it means Russia and France would be at war with Austria."

"Well, it would be over pretty quick, wouldn't it?"

"Maybe, maybe not, but here is where it gets bad. The Austrians and Germans signed the same kind of treaty as the Frenchies and Russkies. So here you have a shooting in some pipsqueak place, that looks like it could bring war to all of Europe. I don't know where England stands, but I can't see the old country wanting Germany beating France again."

John still did not grasp the gravity of the situation, but Sidney had grown up closer to the murk of European politics. He began to understand the reason for Mr. MacDonald's concern.

"Now most people over there think a war won't last long. They say the treasuries couldn't support it and the shooting would be over in four months. I don't know if all that is right or not. These things have a way of turning out in ways no one thought about.

"If a war starts, it won't matter much to us unless England gets dragged in, and that's what scares me. Not much scares me – I've lived through plenty – but because of you boys." Completely puzzled, John shook his head.

"Us two? I'm staying right here with Sid." Mr. MacDonald stared at his naïve son who had never been further from home than town.

"Son, if England goes to war, so does Canada. And that means a call for all brave young patriots, like you two, to join the colours and fight for the Empire. The old fools who start these wars never go out and get killed. Nor do their sons. It's always the poor working stiffs the rich people otherwise never speak to, who suddenly become their best friends. I can hear it now.

"Young man, your country needs you! Step right up and put on this uniform. Then once the killing is over, they will forget all about those who are left. In case you haven't guessed it yet, I don't want either of my boys rushing off to die. Even if one of them is leaving home soon." Confused by the remark, John looked at Sidney.

"Sid, you're leaving home? Where are you going? You can't leave – you're my brother, for Christ's sake!" Sidney smiled as he answered John.

"Typical for you, Johnny. Dad comes out to talk about a huge war starting and for us not to join. All you think about is me leaving home." Sidney good-naturedly shoved John who angrily threw Sidney on the ground.

"You are leaving us then, you pecker head? How can you?" Mr. MacDonald pulled John away from Sidney and made him sit down.

"John, you knew this would happen. One day, I'll be gone, and the farm will be yours. Sidney knows enough now to have his own place. We've talked about this before. If my guess is right Sid, you won't be more than a mile away?"

"Quite right, Dad. Bert is coming with the money to settle matters. Next month I go over to get ready for next year."

"Next month? You're leaving us that quickly? You prick."

"Come on John, give me a break." Wanting to change the topic, Sidney switched back to the possibility of a war.

"Dad, do you really think this could blow up bad? I remember hearing back in the old country it had to come one day. Lots of people think Germany needs bringing down a peg or two. There are plenty of men who would be happy to fight a quick war and straighten up the Germans, as I've heard it put."

"Well boys, I'm not smart enough to see the future but my heart says this war will be very different than many people think. Except for America, all the world's most modern countries are squaring off.

"Millions of men will join an army to fight millions of men in the armies of other countries. I haven't even added in the British Empire either. That just adds to the numbers of men who will die.

"Now boys, listen to me. Our plans do not include you two going off to get killed. If the Germans invade Canada, then we'll pick up a rifle. I hope that's the only reason for either of you to kill another man."

"It doesn't sound like a bright future," John opined. "I never worry about anything except the farm and Saturday night in town. Dad, you raised us to respect the flag and Crown and I feel a real tug for England. Are you telling me not to fight for the Union Jack? Do you want me to stand back if Germany invades England? After all, it's where you and Sid were born."

Exasperated by John's logic, in part founded by his opinions, Mr. MacDonald organized his thoughts. What he would say next, might keep the boys from going to war.

"Listen lads, this will be a bit of a speech, but please let me finish. I don't pretend to know all the reasons why this war might start. But no reason is worth my boys dying in a war people won't remember in ten years. So, no, I hope you don't rush off to join.

"If you do, it will make life tough for your mother and me. Your sisters are too young, and your little brother is only ten. That's a two-edged sword. He's too young for man's work and he's too young for the army." Pausing for breath, he saw his words reaching Sidney but not John and he redoubled his efforts.

"My heart tells me this will be much worse than the politicians say it will. Plenty of mothers will be crying before it ends. Please talk to me before either of you do anything.

"Now, that's enough about this crazy world. The stooks won't get to the barn on their own, so get back to work. Just to show you I have a heart, finish these two rows and call it a day. I expect that beer and women are waiting in town." Feigning a cheery wave and wink, Mr. MacDonald rode away.

Sidney pondered the news. He could not imagine a huge war breaking out in Europe. The Germans were not stupid enough to fight the French, Russians and British Empire. Or were they? Time would soon give him, and the world, the answer.

Speaking of time, Bert was scheduled to arrive tomorrow, which ruled out going into town with John. Sidney did not want to meet Bert with a hangover and Bert would take a dim view of that. In all likelihood, John would have a wild time in town because tomorrow was the start of the August long weekend.

John resumed driving the wagon. Sidney stacked the stooks and kept pace with the horses. The easy flow allowed his thoughts to wander back to Mystique. She had not come back to marry him, and he had not received a letter from her in more than a year.

In stark contrast, Bert returned like clockwork to question Sidney about farming. Bert and Mr. MacDonald spoke freely and on Bert's last visit, Mr. MacDonald tipped him a neighbour might be in financial trouble.

Now capable of running a farm, Sidney was also an accomplished horseman. People knew him to be a serious young man and his life appeared well-ordered and free of distractions.

Despite appearances, Mystique was never far from Sidney's thoughts. Sidney had hoped Mystique would come west on Bert's first visit. Deeply disappointed that she didn't come with Bert, he put on a brave face but after three glasses of wine at dinner, he asked.

"Why didn't Mystique come with you? I know it hasn't been a year, but I want to see her again. Will she come?"

Bert pitied his young friend. Shortly after their return to Montreal, Desiree shared Mystique's reason for leaving Sidney.

"Bert, I am going to tell you something that is not to leave this room. Never, never, never and I mean it." Groaning, Bert wearily placed a hand on his forehead and looked askance at Desiree.

"Mister, don't give me that look. Mystique is pregnant, and she is going to the same French town where I had her. And no, Sidney is not the father."

"Well, the story certainly gets more interesting then, doesn't it?" Ignoring Bert's snide remark, Desiree continued.

"Please don't ask who the father is, and I have no proof beyond Mystique's word. Nor do I wish for the man to be involved. Tell those who ask, that she is at a private school in Switzerland. That should satisfy the busybodies."

Bert whistled. It meant keeping a secret about the woman who meant the world to Sidney. He consoled himself by thinking, *'If he doesn't know, it can't hurt him.'*

To answer Sidney's question, Bert said Mystique had left for school in Switzerland. Embellishing, he added the business courses took two years. He hoped that would satisfy Sidney and keep him from asking more questions.

Since Bert's fibs, Sidney had received just two letters from Switzerland. Mystique wrote of learning finance, history and geography. She claimed to miss him and asked him to wait and not fall for a wild western girl.

The ruse kept Sidney from thinking of visiting Montreal. Mystique wrote the first letter in France and walked the short distance across the Swiss border to mail it. After her return to Montreal, she wrote the second letter and mailed it to France. The elderly matron who delivered the baby, mailed it from Switzerland.

Desiree chided Mystique for leading Sidney on when there was no chance of their meeting again. Mystique clung to the hope she could tell Sidney the truth face to face. Despite deceiving him, she still believed in their love.

Her baby was born severely physically and mentally handicapped. That misfortune derailed all chances of a family adopting the child. On her return to Montreal, Mystique bought a nearby townhouse. A live-in nanny cared for the child when Mystique was attending to the business.

Despite the child's complications, and bitter memories of the father, Mystique loved her baby. She also came to understand another truth about the birth. A doctor advised her the chances of having another handicapped baby were high and Mystique bitterly mocked herself.

'You find a wonderful boy and now you can never be his wife. Do you expect him to accept you with another man's child? Sidney, the baby will always have to live with us. Oh, and Sidney, we can't have our own children. Still want to get married?'

Even without Desiree's reminders, Mystique knew the baby was her first obligation. She quickly developed a sense of responsibility that surprised and gratified Desiree.

Guilt also nagged Desiree because she had condemned her daughter and grandchild to a life dependent upon a bordello. She prayed God would forgive her for involving her family in such a life.

Mystique also laid awake pondering the course of her life. Now twenty, she had a child who could never leave home even though such children usually had short lives. It was cold comfort knowing the child would not outlive her mother.

Then her thoughts turned to Sidney. How he must hate her. She had broken all her loving promises, along with his heart. Memory returned her to the nights and days when they were together.

Mystique had not been with another man since Sidney. Alone at night, she sometimes closed her eyes to relive lying in Sidney's strong arms. Caressing herself, she tried to satisfy the longing while tears wet her cheeks. How she missed her young lover! He had probably forgotten her, and a wild western woman shared his bed.

Chapter Six

Another stook crashed onto the wagon and John looked back in surprise. "Easy, Sid! Throw any more on the wagon like that, you'll bust it in half."

Sidney mumbled an apology and reminded himself to settle down. John said nothing but looked at his young friend with concern. What was eating him? About to get the farm he saved years to buy, Sidney looked as though he had lost his last friend in the world. Sighing, John thought everyone born in England was truly just a bit odd.

The weekend had been a wild one for John, and this morning, he was paying the price. Becoming intoxicated on Saturday night, he tried picking up a cowboy's girl and got into a fight. The police promptly arrived and arrested him.

In a bout of over exuberance, he swung at the police officer and received a sound beating plus an extra day in jail. His furious father dragged him home and administered another thrashing in the barn.

When John arrived for work that morning, Sidney shook his head disapprovingly. Taking pity, he allowed John to drive the wagon rather than heave stooks. They normally switched off on this duty every week and today should have been Sidney's turn to drive. John had such a hangover, he was obviously incapable of physical exertion, so Sidney took his chores for the day.

The day carried on much like any other and the number of stooks in the fields slowly diminished. When a distant noon bell rang, the boys stopped for lunch in the same spot they always did. Beginning to recover, John could finally keep down water and food.

While they ate, Mr. MacDonald raced across the fields to them. The boys looked at one another, hoping no one at home was hurt. Clattering to a stop, Mr. MacDonald vaulted from the horse and held up a newspaper. That too was completely out of character, it was Tuesday and he only bought the paper on Saturday.

"Those crazy European bastards," he shouted hoarsely. "Look what happened on the weekend. The asshole Germans declared war on France and Russia and as if that wasn't bad enough, they invaded Belgium too!"

Sidney's heart plummeted, knowing England championed Belgium's neutrality. Germany's invasion meant only one thing and he dreaded hearing more of the news.

"All five major European powers, Germany included, signed a treaty, decades ago, guaranteeing Belgium's neutrality forever. Now that stupid bloody Kaiser Wilhelm has turned his armies loose to trample all over Belgium. England gave the Germans until tonight to leave Belgium or they're going to war!" He sank to his knees and tears rolled down his cheeks.

"Already thousands of young boys just like you two have probably been killed. The French, Russians and Germans have yet to really get into it. All over some ridiculous Austrian prince. How can people be so stupid?" In his anguish, he appeared years older and the boys were unsure what to say.

"Well, Dad, haven't they all said a war can't last more than a couple of months? That won't give Canada or the rest of the Empire time to get into it, will it?" Sidney asked. The older man sobbed and walking toward them, he fiercely gripped their shoulders and beseeched them in a raspy voice.

"Boys, promise me not to rush off to Camp Sewell and join up when the call comes for volunteers. This won't be the grand adventure people think it will. Both of you promise right now."

Sidney did not intend to be part of a war experts claimed would be over by Christmas and Mr. MacDonald's intense emotion puzzled him. The look of eager anticipation on John's face, though, ran counter to Sidney's wonderment.

"Dad, you can't hold me to a promise like that. It's fine for you and Sid to say don't go. You're both from there and have seen something of the world. All I've ever seen are these fields and the arse end of our horses."

"Son, the ass end view of a horse won't get you killed. A shooting war certainly can."

"Dad, this will be the adventure of a lifetime and I'm not so sure I want to miss it. Besides, aren't the strong supposed to defend the weak? That's what you taught me. A country is not the same as looking out for your little sister but isn't the principle the same? How can a small country like Belgium stick up for itself against Germany? If people are to live free, don't others have to help them do that?"

His father's face was a mask of agony. It was obvious no entreaty would dissuade John from joining the army if Great Britain went to war.

"Son, I may be wrong about this war lasting a long time. I pray to God I am wrong, and I don't often wish that. But my heart tells me it won't be a short, cheery war." Rubbing his chin, Mr. MacDonald seemed to be recalling a history lesson.

"Son, millions of men are picking up rifles and marching to meet millions of other men with rifles. When they meet, hundreds of thousands will be killed. Even if is a short war, far too many will be killed. If it lasts a year or longer, it will be millions. I don't want you to be one of the dead that in a generation, few would know you were alive."

John reached out to hug this man who suddenly appeared old and frail. Watching the scene, Sidney saw a future without John. Fear stabbed him and grabbing John, he shouted at him.

"Listen, asshole. For once in your life, be smart enough to listen to dad. He knows more than us two young pups put together ever will."

On the next day, the world learned Germany had ignored Britain's ultimatum to leave Belgium. The result was a state of war now existed between Germany and the British Empire. Canada was now involved in a world war.

Several weeks later, two men strode up the lane leading to the MacDonald house. Sidney recognized the big man carrying a valise in one oversized hand. Bert had come to settle final details on the farm purchase.

Squinting at the other man, Sidney realized with sinking heart who walked beside Bert. With a wide grin, John threw a salute and called out.

"Look Sid! You are now standing before one of His Majesties soldiers, so show a little respect."

The last emotion Sidney felt was joy that John had defied his father and joined the army. No one doubted John would join. He had virtually camped at the telegraph office for the last ten days.

John was fascinated by the news from Europe, which detailed the army movements of the countries known as the Allies - Russia, Belgium, France and Britain.

The communiques painted pictures of dashing French cavalry charges while the British army arrived in France to a hero's welcome. Plucky Belgium delayed the German advance, and all seemed well in hand for a speedy victory. Perhaps predictions the war would end before snow fell, were correct.

The reports failed to recognize the true scope of events unfolding on the plains of Belgium and fields of northern France. The truth was still several weeks away. For now, it all seemed a great adventure. Young Canadians flocked to recruiting centres by the thousands and there were more volunteers than spaces.

"You daft bugger, it's a serious offence to steal a uniform and parade about like that." Sidney joked but his heart was not in it and he worried about the parent's reaction. Before John could respond, there were footsteps on the porch.

"Oh, my poor boy, what have you done?" John's mother wailed. "Tell me this is a bad joke. Please don't tell me you joined the army!'

"Well, yes, I have, mom. I'm now a member of the Canadian contingent and ..."

"No you're not! We are going to that camp and telling them this has all been a big mistake. You can give back that uniform and boots and we will just forget all this nonsense." John's face turned bright red at his mother's outburst and he was about to argue when his father spoke up.

"Easy, my dear. I don't like this either, but it's time we accept our dear boy is no longer a boy. He is his own man now and can make his own decisions. So, how long did you sign up to serve?"

John's blank look confirmed he had no idea of the length of his commitment. He quickly tried to cover his confusion by repeating the prevailing wisdom.

"Oh dad, that's not important. Things are going well and the Heinies are already on the run. They told us at Camp Sewell this is probably a big waste of everybody's time because it will be over soon. So, there's no need to worry."

His parents looked on in exasperation, knowing further talk was pointless. Their son had joined the army out of a deep-seated sense of duty and love of country. Like multitudes of families on both sides of the Rhine, they had instilled those beliefs in their children. How could they fault them for following their teachings?

The catastrophe occurring on the fields of Europe would rock the very foundations of humanity. Millions of families were about to learn to their immense sorrow where this blind outburst of patriotism would lead their sons.

Chapter Seven

Three weeks had passed since John's announcement and he had already left to train at Camp Valcartier in Quebec. Rumours were a dime a dozen, papers reported the troops would soon sail for England. Reading that, Sidney shook his head in wonderment. *'So much for military secrecy.'*

Bert originally meant to stay out west but the outbreak of war changed his plans. When the crew of the *Angus Celt* learned of the war declaration, half of them jumped ship to join and there were not enough men to crew the ship. That forced Bert's immediate return to Montreal.

He and his partners planned to retire the *Angus Celt,* but war meant the old boat was needed to carry cargo. With the change of plan, Bert barely had time to complete the farm purchase before departing. The night before he was to leave, he and Sidney went for dinner.

"Well, lad, let's raise a glass to our future and to good fortune. We've come a long way since you were a seasick pup aboard ship. How do you feel about the life you've made?"

Sidney considered the question and looked out at the street. He had been thinking a great deal during the last three weeks. There had been a family send off for John when he left for basic training. It was an emotional farewell as several dozen men boarded the train. The war separated families and, in many instances, it would be forever.

He compared that to Mystique leaving three years earlier. She had not written for over a year. He bitterly supposed she had married a wealthy client and was living happily in a Montreal mansion.

"Bert, I'm happy with the hand set for me to play. You know some of my story, so I'll be quick. About all I knew the day my father threw me out was the road going to Southampton. This sounds sappy, but one of the best things was boarding the *Angus Celt*.

"I met you and our fortunes have been joined since then. Working my ass off had something to do with it but I sense something more at work. I don't understand but maybe I've been in the sun too often without a hat." The two laughed and Bert looked at Sidney before asking a question.

"Does that something have to do with these dreams you have? You've talked a few times in your sleep about a walking thunder and brother buffalo. Good Christ, lad, what the hell are you dreaming about?"

Sidney squirmed. He had been unsure about having such dreams, but Bert's comments confirmed he did. The dreams about thunder or walking in thunder, only lingered for moments but clearly, the dreams and visions were connected. The visions had not visited recently but Sidney felt certain of their return.

"I didn't know about the dreams, Bert. You'd think a young guy would dream about getting laid."

"Damn right. Mystique is never coming back and it's time you accept that. It was a bit much to expect you two to have life work out just by waving a magic wand. Get on with it, lad. Find a nice girl and get married."

"Maybe one day but not right now. I've too much to do." Raising an eyebrow, Bert searched Sidney's face.

"Lad, Mystique is too much of a city girl to be happy living out here and peeing in an outhouse. The farmhouse is nice, but it would cost a fortune making it fit for her. We don't have electricity and won't for years. Can you see her chopping wood?"

"I know Bert, but I liked that dream. Ah, what the hell. As usual, you are right, but now I'm curious. Desiree is a princess too and not the sort to use an outhouse. How will you cross that bridge?" Bert chuckled at Sidney's shrewd line of questioning.

"Ah lad, your brain is one of the things I like about you. Yes, Desiree is a princess, which is another topic. Desiree knows I want to be here farming, but she has a problem with prairie winters. So here is what we've decided, with your agreement, of course."

"Of course."

"She'll come out in the spring, stay until we finish the harvest, then go back to Montreal. I want to spend winters in Arizona, but she doesn't want to be away from family nearly all year. I'm not sure how that will play out."

Sidney cocked an eyebrow at the mention of family and waved a hand indicating he wanted to hear more about this family.

"Well, look at me turning into a blabbermouth in my old age. I'm obviously talking about the business and Mystique taking over. We'll work it out like we always do."

Bert had come as close to the truth as possible without revealing Mystique's secret. He hoped Sidney would figure out the unspoken part.

"Mystique is tied to the business and it's a full-time job. She has plenty on her plate, and with the war, business is booming. Sid, there hasn't been anyone else. She has too much else to worry about.

"One day, she will be fabulously wealthy and can cut the strings and be free. I can't see the future but doubt she will come back out here. You don't know what you might get if she did... Find a girl here and live your own life."

Sidney mulled over Bert's words, wondering about the references to family and what he might get if she returned. Bert sometimes spoke in riddles that became clear after careful reflection. Leaning back in his chair, he studied Bert's weathered face for a moment, then smiled.

"Bert, you have been as good a friend as any man can be blessed to have. You've never given me bad advice or steered me wrong. I won't speak of Mystique again, you have my word. And I'll think about finding a nice girl. So? What is next?"

Two months later, Sidney settled into the house on his new farm. For once, he had his own place. Based on their gentleman's agreement, he and Bert each owned an equal share of the farm, even if Bert did not live there much. His side business made that impossible which Sidney still knew nothing about it.

Bert pined to live far from the sea in the country and he wanted to be working outdoors at something of his own. His will stipulated all assets passed to Sidney but in typical Bert fashion, Sidney knew nothing of that either.

In the meantime, a letter from John arrived. He described his training to date and noted that disorganization appeared rampant. The men were all chomping at the bit to ship overseas and get into action against the Germans.

News from France over the past two months had been good and bad. The first exuberant dispatches had given way to news of setbacks for the Allies. For a time, it appeared the Germans might capture Paris. That was most definitely not the war strategy that had been planned.

There was a huge battle in France involving millions of men at a place called the Marne. It ended with a general German retreat, but the jubilation was short lived. In a series of running battles, neither side delivered a knockout blow. Both sides reached the sea and a year-end deadlock appeared inevitable. All the fighting had failed to produce a clear-cut result for either side.

Although not a general, Sidney could see by the map that neither side could get around the other. He presumed the generals would eventually figure out how to proceed.

John's letter claimed that when the Canadian contingent arrived, Germany would realize there was no hope and surrender. Sidney laughed but hoped this preposterous boast could be true.

Press reports issued by the combatants reported their losses were light while those of the enemy were enormous. Problem was, each side said the same thing. If both sides were suffering heavy losses, the true casualty figures must be hideous.

Maps indicated the Germans were having more success than the Allies. Most of Belgium had been overrun and large areas of northern France were occupied by Germany.

Sidney remembered the heavy autumn rain in England and the wet snow that followed. How would men cope in cold, muddy conditions in the countryside of northern France and Belgium? *'No thanks. Let's just get this crazy war over. The sooner John is home, the better.'*

The year ended with Sidney settled into his role as gentleman farmer. He chuckled while striking various poses before the shaving mirror.

"Jeeves, do pour me another brandy and bring in the newspaper. What is that, Jeeves? The coach has arrived to take me to the charity ball someone organized in my honour? Ah yes, Sid old boy. Life will indeed be grand one of these days. All you have to do first is get rich!"

Sidney had no idea how much time he needed to earn such fortunes. He tried not to think he might benefit from the deaths of his fellow citizens, but if the war lasted until the next harvest, he and Bert would earn a large profit.

The adage war is good for business certainly appeared to be true. Canada had sent tens of thousands of troops to fight and more were training. Those men needed to eat and prices for grains and beef had risen handsomely. Mr. MacDonald predicted a war of three years and that Canada would feed the vast Allied armies.

This was the good news, but the war created a problem for Sidney and thousands of other farmers. Many of the young men who joined the army were farmers and hired hands. Their absence created a serious labour shortage. In many instances, those left to work on the farms were old men and women. They worked slowly due to age and inexperience.

Sidney did not suffer those problems; his difficulty stemmed from the size of his farm. Without purchasing the steam machines now available, the farm was too large for one man to work.

In early March, he wrote to Bert in Arizona and asked him to come home and help work the farm. Bert laughed reading the plea for help, but he began packing.

"My young friend needs me to come and help on the farm. Let's start in the morning because it will take a week. Come along and see how much work farming is." Coming over to him, Desiree laid her head against his chest.

"I would love to come but I feel awkward about seeing Sidney again. Do you know if he still dislikes me? I can't blame him if he does." Chuckling at her discomfort, Bert planted a gentle kiss atop her head.

"I doubt Sid was ever angry with you. His heart is too big, and he likely still thinks he owes you an apology. I don`t think

Mystique will ever be out of his heart and I doubt another girl has been in his bed. Maybe with all the men away in Europe, Sid will see the hunting is good."

"Oh, you horrible man. Let's pack so I can see your farm." She started upstairs but turned back with the look Bert knew meant a serious question was next.

"Are you still involved in your little export business?"

When the war began dragging on, Bert was able to wrap up his underworld involvement for several reasons. Foremost, the direction of trade in opiates had reversed. The market, legal and otherwise, had become Europe. With plenty of business in England and France, the crime boss Bert served, no longer needed the trans-Atlantic trade.

Bert also knew many of the men he served with in the navy, were at sea prepared to defend England with their lives. Opiate prices had risen since the war began and his conscience nagged that he might profit from the suffering of his former shipmates.

The war politicians had claimed would end in four months, continued to drag on. Rumours circulated that more than one million men had been killed and millions more were training for larger battles.

"Darling, my smuggling days are over. I will now earn my fortune as an honest man. Maybe one day I'll tell Sid how I paid cash for the farm, but sometimes, he's too naïve for the truth."

"You mean he's too honest to think of getting something other than by hard work," Desiree replied with a mocking smile.

"Be careful about calling the kettle black, my little pot," Bert retorted with a playful tweak of Desiree's perfect backside.

Just then, the horseplay was interrupted by a knock on the door and the arrival of a telegram from Thompson on the *Angus Celt.*

"Broken propeller shaft in Montreal. Repairs more than boat. Send four men to work the farm?" Bert wrote a hasty reply: *"Keep them drunk a week, then send."*

"Good fortune always seems to find me when things look out of control. The *Celt* has sailed its last trip, just when Sid and I are up against it trying to work our farm. Thompson is sending out four older hands to help us. Don't you love it when a plan comes together?"

The next afternoon they rode a train north along the California coast. Although still winter on the Canadian prairies, here it was warm sunshine and breezes.

"My dear, if a man had any brains, he would not be heading north. Life here means never shovelling snow or chopping firewood just to survive. Maybe one day when Sid and I know more about farming, you and I can spend the winter here."

"You would get fat and lazy, Bert Westhaven. Then I would have to find a handsome young lover to keep me happy when you fall asleep after dinner."

"So long as he cut the grass while he's there, I'll let him live," Bert growled. Desiree poked him in the ribs and became thoughtful.

"Four men are coming to help on the farm? Could one or two work at the MacDonald's farm? With John in the army, his father must be in a bind."

"What a great idea. Sid and I don't need four men so sending two to the MacDonalds will work." Six days later, they arrived in Shilo. The two men shook hands and Sidney bowed low over Desiree's hand.

"Hello Sidney," she smiled. "Thank you for your kind welcome. I was concerned you still hated me."

"Madame Desiree, I never hated you. Now let's get home before dark." Bert smiled to see how deftly Sidney had handled the potentially awkward moment. He had matured and was wise beyond his years.

"Sid, did you get my telegram about the four men?"

"Yes, and it's a huge load off my mind. We'll have enough hands to get the fields ready for spring seeding. What a jolly good stroke of luck!" He remembered to add, "Even if it means the *Angus Celt* goes for scrap."

"Being melted into scrap is a fitting end to the old tub. It helped me become a gentleman farmer so no need for any tears. Desiree thought up the idea about the men coming here."

She explained her thoughts and Sidney wondered how much more luck might come his way. Would Mystique come out and marry him? *'Get a grip, man. If she wanted you, she would have done it by now, so quit bullshitting yourself.'*

"All right, that is settled. Any other news, lad?" Sidney pointed to his breast pocket to answer the question.

"Got a letter from John last week. It sounds like the grand adventures aren't quite so grand. His regiment spent most of the winter on Salisbury plain. Nothing but marching and learning to dig trenches. He couldn't believe all the rain and gales." Bert shuddered remembering England's ferocious winter storms.

"I remember our crossing on the *Celt*. I thought you were going to die, lad."

"Yeah, I remember. Anyway, John said the storms blew down their tents but now they have wooden huts. Half the men had colds or pneumonia and the other half were bored silly. He just got over his pneumonia. They are in Belgium now and if England was bad, Belgium sounds ten times worse." Bert smiled grimly and replied.

"The navy ain't any bed of roses, but at least you aren't up to your arse in mud, or being rained, snowed or shit on, all day. At night, you slept in a hammock, which is the lap of luxury compared to sleeping in a muddy trench."

"Yeah, John said they are somewhere near Ypres. A few days of front line, a few days in reserve and a few days of so-called rest. Sounds like the so-called rest is carrying ammo, wire and any other bullshit duty they throw at them. He said for being in the front line, things are quiet. Says when it dries up and gets warmer, the fighting will pick up."

The reality of trench life defied all rational explanation. Men stood for days in cold pouring rain, often up to their knees in mud and water. They ate tin cans of cold, greasy bully beef while lice infested their armpits and underwear. Rounding things off, the enemy sniped continuously, at times less than fifty yards away, and a strong man could hurl a grenade that distance.

"I'll bet John would pay for them to forget about him and come home. I'm glad he stays in touch with everyone here."

Chapter Eight

"Bias! Quit fucking around with that knife and fill those sandbags. You know that thing isn't standard issue."

"All right, all right, Sarge. Take it easy. I plan on being ready if the Huns come." The slender, dark haired private laid a razor-sharp skinning knife on the fire step and grabbed a spade.

"C'mon MacDonald, hold that bag open while I fill it. Hope Sarge fucks off. My blade isn't sharp enough yet. You know...just in case the Huns come over."

"Man, if the Huns find that, you're gonna be sorry."

"Only way the cocksuckers will get it, is off my dead body."

"Don't say that, man. It's bad, bad luck."

Louis Bias and John MacDonald were platoon mates in the 8th Battalion, 90th Winnipeg Rifles. Their battalion held trenches near the Belgian village of St. Julien. The Germans had attacked French troops with chlorine gas and the Canadians expected similar treatment.

Louis Bias was a mixed blood soldier from Portage la Prairie, Manitoba. During training at Salisbury Plain in England, he and John MacDonald became friends. Typical of young men, they bantered back and forth to pass boring camp hours. In the trenches, they continually kibitzed to ignore the dreadful realities of war.

"Still thinking of scalping a Hun? Can't say I blame you. Your chances of killing one with that knife are better than with these useless fucking rifles. Man, do I want a Brit rifle. At least then I'd have a chance."

Louis grunted his reply while ladling dirt into the sandbag John held open. Looking over John's shoulder, Louis saw the sergeant move down the trench and he flipped the spade away.

"You white guys call me a prairie nigger. Shit, my old man is white. My mom says Grampa didn't take scalps, but I don't believe that. What with him being a Sioux warrior and all. Ah what the hell, I'm gonna get me a Fritz scalp when they come. Hope they do." John shook his head knowing thousands had died in fierce fighting over the last two days.

"Well, buddy, I'm sure you'll get your chance." Louis grinned and rubbed his hands together in anticipation.

"When the Huns see their buddies scalped, it will scare the shit out of them."

Night fell, and a sinister silence descended over no man's land. While he stood watch, John mused, *'The calm before the fucking storm.'* The eastern horizon began to lighten, the stand-to order passed along the trench and then scattered rifle fire came from the German lines.

For the hundredth time, John checked to ensure a bullet was in his rifle's chamber. Fingering the safety, he clicked it on and off to calm his nerves while Louis continued sharpening his knife.

Their sergeant came along to make certain all the men were awake. Officers had already explained that peeing on their handkerchiefs, helped neutralize the chlorine vapours.

"Make sure you soak your hanky. Boys, I aint' crazy about that either, but if it saves my ass, it works for me."

A harsh flash lit up the horizon and a thunderous roar of artillery shattered the dawn. Hundreds of shells exploded, blasting trees, trench walls and men into pieces. John cowered and prayed his bowels would not let loose. Opening his eyes at a sharp tug on his arm, he saw Louis grinning maniacally.

"Come on Mac, get up here. Here's our chance to kill these cocksuckers. Man, let's get some scalps!" Through the uproar, their sergeant hollered for the platoon to get ready for a German attack.

"Fuck me boys, here comes the gas. Piss on your hankies."

Having to tie a urine-soaked handkerchief over his nose and mouth, brought John's blood to a boil and now he wanted to kill.

As the gas cloud rolled forward, German bullets swept men from the firing step. The enemy advanced behind the gas and shooting erupted along the line as the Germans closed in. A huge German jumped into the trench and shot at John. The bullet grazed his ear and Louis shot the attacker in the head.

"Fuck! I fucked up. Now I can't scalp him!" Ignoring his bleeding ear, John stood beside Louis, and gasping for breath, they shot at shadowy figures.

"Goddamn this piece of shit rifle," John screamed. Throwing it aside, he grabbed one from a dead mate. Then a shell exploded and killed the platoon's machine gun crew. Louis grabbed John and they pulled shattered bodies off the gun.

Swinging it into position, Louis called out targets and John fired until he ran out of ammunition. Their heroics had however, attracted German attention. A machine gun crew scampering across no man's land, began setting up directly in front of them. Louis screamed at John over the din and yanked him forward.

"Come on, man. We gotta charge the bastards or we're dead." With a wild whoop, he leapt from the broken trench with John in close pursuit. Before the crew finished setting up, the two screaming Canadians fell on them.

"Kamerad!" two Germans yelped while raising their hands.

"Fuck you, kamerad!" Louis yelled and drove his bayonet into a man. John bayoneted another, but two Germans bolted, and John shot them. Bullets snapped past and they ducked down behind the dead Germans.

"We gotta get back to our trench," John shouted.

"Wait a minute man," Louis yelled and pulled back a dead German's head. To John's astonishment, Louis brought out his skinning knife and with a scream of victory, took the man's scalp.

"You crazy son of a bitch! You made me wait for that? Come on, let's get the fuck outta here."

They began crawling back while bullets kicked up dirt all around them. Sliding into a shallow shell crater provided little cover. Louis held the bloody scalp overhead, waving it mockingly at the German lines and a rifle bullet snapped it from his hand.

"You fuckers! Now I gotta get another one. Wait here Mac." He scrabbled at the lip of the shell crater but then heard John scream.

"Fuck, I'm hit!" A bullet had shattered John's hip. The wound bled fearfully, and Louis doubted John would survive. Knowing he had to do something, Louis bound it with a field dressing.

"We're dead if we stay here. Can you move?" Through gritted teeth, John stifled another howl and nodded.

"Start back. I'm gonna kill those cocksuckers shooting at us. I'll be back." Louis scrambled from the shell hole and charged into the dust and smoke.

Crawling from the hole, John pulled himself past dozens of bodies. He finally fell into a trench, but the men took little notice of another wounded man. Knowing survival was up to him, John staggered upright and rolled over the back parapet in hopes of finding an aid station.

After creeping a hundred yards, he reached a support trench where strong hands pulled him in. Two men rolled John onto a stretcher and quickly examined him.

"He don't look too good mate. Doubt he'll make it." The other man nodded in agreement.

"We'll be lucky getting to the aid station with him still breathing. But come on, give him some morphine. Make the poor bugger's last minutes a bit less painful."

They gave John the morphine, hunched over and carried the stretcher to the rear. The powerful sedative eased John's pain and he closed his eyes.

Chapter Nine

When the new men arrived, Sidney put them to work preparing the machinery and harnesses for spring seeding. In mid-April, the weather broke, and warmth returned to cheer men's hearts. With the soil moist from spring snow, the outlook for a good crop was favourable. After dinner one evening in late April, Sidney, Bert, Mr. MacDonald and the hired men met in a field to chat.

"What do you make of the war news, Bert?" one of the hands asked. Due to his navy service, everyone presumed Bert was a military expert and the logical source for opinion.

Over the last days, the papers reported heavy fighting in the Ypres salient of Belgium. The Germans had used poison gas on Allied troops and there were conflicting rumours about the effectiveness of this new weapon.

The headlines screamed of Germany's descent into barbarism by using such a weapon. Canadian troops were in the thick of the fighting and had received loud praise for their heroism in holding the line.

Astute readers discerned through the censored words that casualties must have been heavy. They read that entire units had been withdrawn for rest and reinforcement, a euphemism for high rates of death and injury.

"Well, it sounds like the fighting is hot and heavy," Bert replied. "I was never in the army, but I know about artillery. An eighteen-pounder gun makes a hell of a mess of a building, never mind what shrapnel can do to men. I'm not religious but I pray at night for the souls of our men." Mr. MacDonald listened quietly and joined in the conversation.

"Well, my John is in Belgium. I hope to God he is nowhere near the fighting, but my heart tells me he is. Please God, don't let him think he needs to be a hero. I would feel no shame if he ran when the shooting started." Mutters of agreement sounded from the men; all were grateful to be in a peaceful farm field.

"I can't imagine how any man can hold his ground when poison gas is used. Boys, please say a prayer tonight for my John. Pray for all the boys on both sides and that it soon ends."

Sidney listened without comment and kept his eyes lowered toward the ground. When the war began, he wanted to join after seeing the posters urging men to rally and defend civilization. The first burst of enthusiasm eased when the government announced more recruits were not required. People no longer automatically asked young men not in uniform when they were joining up. Sidney tried to convince himself he served by growing crops and raising horses and cattle.

The war created a huge demand for horses in both the cavalry and transport use. Authorities at nearby Camp Sewell had already visited the farm and noted the quality of the animals.

The war originally forecast to be over by Christmas, had entered a second year. That Germany had gone on the offensive in Belgium, surprised many on the Allied side. Places that two weeks earlier were in Allied hands now belonged to German troops. The recent German assaults were paying dividends and some politicians questioned if the war effort might be in jeopardy.

Sidney could not believe the British Empire faced defeat. The weight of numbers would simply not allow for that possibility, but how it all would play out was beyond him. His head ached thinking about it.

One evening in early May found Sidney surveying his fields again. The next morning, he planned to harness a team of Percheron horses and begin seeding. The evening air still held some warmth and the scent of new leaves budding on trees floated in the breeze.

It was a perfect, quiet calm and the world seemed at peace. *'Well, it's peace here in my little corner, which suits me just fine,'* Sidney mused as he walked back to the house. Drawing closer, he saw a man sitting in one of the veranda chairs and with surprise, recognized Mr. MacDonald. What was he doing here?

Sidney called out as he stepped on the porch, but the face of his neighbour spoke of trouble. Mr. MacDonald looked as though he had aged twenty years in the last day. Ashen-faced and eyes rimmed red, he held an envelope in one hand.

Their eyes met and without a word, his trembling hand passed the envelope to Sidney. Fear tightened around Sidney's heart while he withdrew a folded letter.

The letter had come from the adjutant office of John's battalion. It expressed condolences for the death of Private John MacDonald on April 24 during fierce fighting near the village of St. Julien outside of Ypres. Sidney would become familiar with the wording of such letters; this was the first of many he would read.

The letter said John carried out his duties faithfully and cheerfully no matter the circumstances. Well-liked by his fellow soldiers, he always bolstered the spirits of those around him. Buried with full military honours, further details would follow should such become available.

But the letter hid the grisly truth of how John and hundreds of other Canadians died that day. Most of the dead lay on ground captured by the Germans. A common grave or ditch became the resting place of a fortunate few. Many more were blown to pieces by high explosive shells or disappeared into the mud of a Flanders field.

Warfare changed forever on those days in April 1915 when the Germans unleashed poison gas. Hundreds of men died while frantically gasping for breath the chlorine gas denied them.

The MacDonalds were fortunate. John died where the Canadian lines held, and his body went to the rear for burial. Although painful to learn his fate, it was far better than receiving a notice John was missing in action. In some instances, people clung to forlorn hope for years that missing men might return.

Tears ran down Sidney's face, and throwing his arms around Mr. MacDonald's neck, the two men wept together. Regaining his breath, Sidney rocked back to look his adoptive father in the eyes.

"Dad, we have to carry on and be brave. That's how he would want it, but you know that as well as me. We knew this could happen, but the idea was too scary to think about."

"I know, son. I just hope it was quick and that he didn't suffer." With a tremulous sigh, he tried steadying his shaking hands before speaking again.

"As you might guess, mother is taking it hard. One of her sisters is staying with her and the girls for a few days." Sensing that listening was the best option, Sidney nodded to encourage Mr. MacDonald to talk out his grief.

"Women mourn different than men. They go all out with their weeping and wailing. We men aren't so good at all that. We might shed a tear, but usually quietly, and women don't understand that. Because I can't cry so easily, she thinks I don't feel the pain as much. So, tonight lad, I want to be around men. We can talk or find something to do that may keep my mind on a bit of something else." Wiping away tears, he became angry.

"What the hell are our poor boys dying for over there anyway? Nothing in this world is worth millions of young boys, on either side. Surely to God, men have not taken leave of all common sense. Why can't the killing just stop and let men talk this thing out?"

Sidney had no answers. He found the death of a cherished friend a new and unpleasant experience. He could clearly see John's smiling face while cheerily calling for another beer.

Sidney rarely drank, and Mr. MacDonald took a dim view of strong alcohol. However, Bert liked a healthy shot of Jameson's Irish whiskey and kept a bottle in the cupboard. Sidney knew Bert would not object to them sharing his whiskey even if he was not home.

"Dad, wait here, I'll be right back. I want to honour John."

Striding into the kitchen and opening a cabinet, he found the whiskey. Taking two glasses from a shelf, he returned to the porch and handed a glass to his companion. Pouring two fingers into each glass, they stood to face east.

"Wherever you are, my son, the good Lord isn't telling me right now. So I can try and make sense of all this, in my heart is where you shall remain."

"My brother, I know you'll always walk at my side," Sidney added. Clinking their glasses, they tossed back the whiskey.

"Pour me another one, son. I want to have something to hold in my hand while we sit."

Sidney poured two more drinks and sat down beside his adopted father. Reaching out, he held Mr. MacDonald's hand. For several minutes, they sat quietly and drew comfort from the other's presence.

The shadows grew long as the sun dipped below the horizon. From the lane, came the thunder of a galloping horse. Bert marched across the porch and swept up Mr. MacDonald in a bear hug. The older man sobbed anew and wiped his face with a handkerchief that had seen too many tears that evening.

"Thanks Bert, hope you won't mind Sid and me sharing a drink or two of your whiskey."

"No sir, I'm glad you found it on this sad night. I've seen enough death to know there is nothing anyone can say to ease your sorrow. But I want you to know I'm heartbroken over the death of such a fine young man."

"Thank you, Bert. That means a lot to me."

"You are most welcome, Percy. I read the paper, and for once, they aren't trying to bullshit us. Looks like you were right, and this war won't be the short adventure politicians were selling us." Bert walked into the house and returned a moment later with a glass.

"Pour me a shot lad, and don't be stingy. Good Irish whiskey is for times like this and it will loosen our tongues to speak what is in our hearts. Keeping the sorrow inside only puts it off until the day it has to come out. And when that day comes, it ain't pretty seeing a man break down, so let it loose right now."

With the glass filled, Bert faced east and beckoned the other two to join him. He normally used Mr. MacDonald's nick name of Mac. This sad evening called for more formality and using the given name felt right.

"Percy, let me propose a toast to John, our departed warrior. We said this ditty in the navy when we fired the main guns. You never knew when things might blow up and the old mates taught me this one." Bert chanted the old Irish soliloquy into the warm evening air.

"May the road rise to meet you.
May the wind always be at your back.
May the sun shine warm upon your face,
And rains fall soft upon your fields.
And until we meet again,
May God hold you in the hollow of His hand."

Bert smiled, "I'd like to add two more lines that are often left unsaid at times like this. But I'm certain young John would laugh hearing these words.

"And may ye be in heaven a half hour
Afore the devil knows ye're dead!"

All three men broke into soft laughter with calls of "Hear, hear" and "Well and truly said, Bert."

"Thank you for that, Bert. I've not heard it in many years and had forgotten it altogether. Yes, John would be fortunate to be in heaven a half hour before the Devil knew he was dead. I'll not deny some of his shenanigans pissed me off mightily. But now they seem rather tame compared to this war that is sucking up the lives of so many good young boys."

They sat quietly for several minutes, each busy with favourite memories of John. Mr. MacDonald broke the silence first.

"You fellows know that I'm a bit of a religious man. Not enough for my dear wife, but enough so I am comfortable with the notion of church. I would be obliged, Bert, if you wrote out that toast you recited.

"The words will be a comfort on those days when I need a bit more strength. I'll give a copy to my wife but think it best to leave out the last two lines. Mother wouldn't like the notion that her little boy might be of interest to the fellow down below."

While they quietly reminisced in the gathering darkness, neighbours stopped by to offer their hands in friendship to Mr. MacDonald. Word travelled fast in the small farming community and the men met while their wives congregated at the MacDonald home.

Several men brought along bottles and one a banjo. After several drinks, the man played a familiar tune, and all joined in song. Stories circulated about young John. Percy had not heard some of the tales and shook his head to learn of some of his son's escapades.

Glasses were lifted in sorrow and heartfelt friendship. While most drank a little more than usual, no one became drunk as tongues loosened and tales were told. And so, the most dreadful evening the MacDonald family had ever known, slowly wound away and all present carried off a share of the grief.

Chapter Ten

Time never stands still and as the weeks passed, the demands of farm life drew their attention to other pressing matters. One sunny morning, Sidney hooked a team to the seed drill and hitched two other teams for Bert and a hired man.

Sidney led, and the others walked adjacent to the ground he seeded. They made good progress and Sidney was pleased. At this rate, they would finish in several days. With luck, they'd be swathing a good crop by mid-August.

While he worked, Sidney thought of how much he missed John. Last year he and John seeded the spring crop at the MacDonald farm. This year, Sidney was working his own land while John lay in a grave in far off Belgium. *'I should have spent more time learning from John instead of us larking about so much,'* Sidney ruefully reflected.

"No wonder adults say youth is wasted on the young," he counselled his team of horses. "Don't you fellows take life for granted," he advised. Looking over his shoulder, he hoped Bert had not heard. *'He thinks you're half-barmy now without you talking to the horses, Sid old boy.'*

"What the hell are you talking about up there, you silly bugger? The sun isn't that hot yet to bake your brains! Are the horse farts getting to you, boy? "

Sidney snickered and thanked his lucky stars to be friends with this man who terrorized most people with just a frown. If only Mystique had been so loyal. Very reluctantly, he had accepted Bert's admonition she would never return.

'Why the hell do you still love her? She was around two weeks but what an amazing two weeks.' He needed to accept that while the remainder of his life might not be as fiery, it could have satisfaction and contentment. Could it not?

They had almost completed seeding a quarter section when an automobile stopped. In 1915, cars were uncommon, especially in rural Manitoba, and it drew everyone's attention. The driver, a young soldier, opened a rear door for an older man whose red-tabbed tunic announced an officer.

Stopping the horses, Sidney walked to the car. Glancing over his shoulder, Sidney saw Bert coming to join him. Equal partners, they discussed all matters of the farm. People automatically presumed Bert the owner due to his imposing presence and age. To everyone's surprise, he always introduced Sidney as his business partner. Nodding toward Sidney, the officer stepped forward to meet Bert.

"Good day, sir. I am Major Steele with the Lord Strathcona Horse at Camp Sewell. Pardon me, gentlemen, over at Camp Hughes, as it is now named."

The major failed to hide his displeasure over the name change. Most military personnel and all locals disagreed with the renaming. The minister of defense was Sam Hughes. Local politicians trying to gain influence with the minister, had pushed for the change in hopes of being awarded contracts for war materials.

"I came to speak with you about purchasing some of your horses. As well, perhaps your man might consider joining our regiment." Bert smiled and waving a hand, interrupted the major.

"I'm glad you stopped to talk with us, but I must defer to the young master here. He is my partner on the farm and is the horse expert."

Surprised by such a display of respect for the younger man, the major atoned. He offered a slight bow to Bert and extended his hand to Sidney.

"Forgive me, young man. I assumed your companion was the owner of the farm."

"Well sir, he is part owner and I am the other. His name is Bert Westhaven and my name is Sidney Turner." With a firm handshake, Sidney politely asked how he might be of assistance.

"Mr. Turner, our battalion needs horses for the war effort. I am scouting the countryside and your farm is on my list." Bert laughed aloud that their farm could be of interest to the army but the major smiled and resumed speaking.

"First, are you willing to sell some of your herd, and if so, at what price? I am authorized to negotiate a price that is fair to you and the government. The second matter for discussion is whether Mr. Turner might join the regiment as farrier?"

"That is a flattering request, major. By my accent, you know I'm from England, where I learned about being a farrier. I would think a cavalry regiment has its own farriers."

"That is true, Mr. Turner. However, the war has made demands on our regiment and most of our trained men are already overseas. The war ministry, in it's, ahem, wisdom, saw fit to send nearly the entire regiment overseas. Because of the fighting in Belgium, the army suffered heavier casualties than expected.

"So, in addition to procuring horses, I'm also asking men to serve their country in this time of need." The major's face grew flushed at the prepared speech and he wore a somewhat sardonic scowl. Bert chuckled and drawing near, joined the conversation.

"Major Steele, I served in His Majesty's Royal Navy a fair number of years, mainly aboard battleships. You might guess I've seen my share of officers and learned to decipher when one is spouting bullshit and when it's genuine." The major's face reddened but he spoke up in his own defence.

"Mr. Westhaven, please do not assume my words were of such a governmental nature. It is true the army needs new recruits to return our units to full strength."

"Yes, I gather that, major. Reading between the lines in the newspapers tells me we barely held back Jerry last month. I don't know how many of our men were killed but if they stopped the German army, it must have been thousands. This war has gone badly for our side so far. Until we get some smarter minds working for us, I can't see how we can win."

The young soldier sniggered at Bert's words. Had the major been a career soldier, he would have reprimanded him. Fortunately, for the corporal, Major Steele had served in a militia unit before receiving the call to active service.

The major was a successful Winnipeg businessman with a large network of associates that extended to Ottawa. That network made him privy to information a major usually did not possess. He knew about the shocking number of casualties suffered by the Canadians in the fighting around Ypres.

There was more bad news which were the main reasons for the major's obvious contempt for Minister Hughes. The minister carelessly approved equipment purchases for the army. There were instances of poorly made uniforms and boots that disintegrated in normal use. The minister had sung high praises for the Ross rifle and authorized their issue to the troops.

In the field, the weapon frequently jammed and proved unreliable. Word quickly spread, and Canadians learned to depend on the British Lee Enfield rifle. The men scavenged British rifles and despite the minister's anger, they continued to favour the British weapon.

"Mr. Westhaven, your navy service gives you an edge into the military mind." Pausing, the major looked back to his driver.

"Corporal, perhaps you can take a stroll down to the crossroads yonder. Be back in about twenty minutes, would you?" The young man nodded, saluted, and left.

"Now, gentlemen, I can speak more freely. We did indeed suffer heavy casualties around Ypres. My understanding is our Canadian corps suffered six thousand casualties, including over two thousand men killed." Bert and Sidney were astonished so many men were lost in a single battle and sadly shook their heads.

"That is a stunning number considering our first contingent numbered less than forty thousand. These modern weapons are causing huge losses for all armies. I am not blind to our casualties and do not think of it as just bookkeeping."

Bert growled it would be grand if more officers thought that and the major nodded.

"These are the lives of our young men being spent in defense of our civilization. And it's not just our side losing men. Entire German divisions were annihilated around Ypres last fall. Prisoners spoke of their university students linking arms and marching into battle while singing patriotic songs.

"British regulars shot them down by the tens of thousands. The Germans call it the Death of the Children. Some of their troops question the wisdom of this war, just like some of ours do." Sidney and Bert looked at one another and Bert gave a low whistle.

"I appreciate your honesty, major. Those are terrible numbers and I pity the poor mums and dads. What in hell are our civilized countries fighting about? I hope peace comes before all the young men are killed." Glancing at his watch, the major shook hands with Bert and Sidney.

"Gentlemen, thank you for your time. Please come to a decision soon regarding the sale of some of your horses. Mr. Turner, you would be a fine addition to our regiment. Whether you would go overseas is not my decision to make. It would be fine with me if you stayed here to teach. You may contact me through the battalion orderly room." With a jaunty half-salute, he climbed into the staff car.

Sidney stared after the car before turning to look at Bert for an indication of his thoughts. But Bert was a master at portraying nothing. Any decision Sidney might make was up to him, but once he decided, Bert always chimed in.

"Selling some horses is easy to decide," Sidney said. "Prices are up and with the money, we can buy mares to make more horses. If this war lasts longer, we can sell them to the army or farmers to replace their old horses. Good idea?"

"Yeah, it is, and I'll leave it with you." Bert returned to his non-committal gaze to learn if Sidney had more to discuss.

"I know you won't say a word about what the major suggested unless I say something first. I remember yours and dad MacDonald's advice about joining the army. It sounded wise then, and still does, but here comes the 'but' part.

"I'm grateful for everything here. God knows what I would be doing back in England. Probably would have joined up just to get away. None of what we have here would have happened if I hadn't met you." Holding up a hand to stop Bert, Sidney carried on.

"I can't deny that I wanted to join the colours right away. If I had, maybe I'd be with John in some muddy Belgian field. I don't believe the army had time to give him a Christian funeral. At first, it didn't make much sense to go when the experts said it would be over quick. Guess the experts aren't experts after all.

"If I go to fight, will it help England? Probably not and my chances of coming home aren't very good. You served your country, Bert, and if you had stayed in the navy, you would be at war. This is the biggest war in history and if we're going to win, it seems everyone should help. I know we're doing our bit by helping feed the troops." He smiled shyly at his next thoughts and resumed.

"Maybe one day I'll get married and have some kiddies. One day if they ask what I did in the war, all I can say is, grow wheat for the army. Maybe that doesn't sound like a reason to risk your life, but it means something to me, Bert."

Bert regarded his young friend with a mix of pride, pity and concern. Sidney clearly wanted to join the army. Even with no military experience, Sidney knew a war was not an adventure. He had seen the black-bordered columns in newspapers announcing the latest deaths and injuries of Manitoba boys. He had no fanciful notions of a hero's death wrapped in a Union Jack flag.

John's death brought home the grim reality that war was a brutish enterprise with the sole purpose being to kill your fellow man. If men knew this, why did they still offer themselves up to die?

Sidney remembered reading an article disabusing the notion that a man who died for his country, would be remembered by a grateful nation. When tens of thousands perished battering against an enemy trench, how was it possible to remember all of them as heroes?

At what point did the boy next door become just another name in a long list of the boys next door? How long would it take before readers grew numbed by all those names?

"Lad, I can't deny that were I fifteen years younger, my thoughts would be the exact same. I've laid awake and thanked whoever is up there, that my time of service has come and gone. I'll admit to being relieved my ass isn't in a muddy ditch while some Heinie is trying to kill me.

"I don't believe this is a war to save civilization. That's just something somebody in government thought of to get young fellows like you to join. To me, this war is about saving somebody's royal family and empire. It sure as hell isn't worth having hundreds of thousands of brave British and colonial boys die. Nowhere near reason enough for my best friend to get killed."

"Bert, you sound positive I'm going to get killed if I go."

"For Christ's sake, boy! Didn't John's death tell you anything? Sure, he did his duty and fought bravely to save his pals and Belgium. But he's dead, and the people paying the price are his family. What should have been a good long life, sure got screwed over.

"He's lying in the ground while worms feast on his flesh. All the life his family gave him, ended in a muddy hole. It's so far away I doubt anyone from here will ever visit his grave. Hell, the Germans could attack again and break through. Where he's buried might not even be there after the war."

Sidney saw Bert's emotions were on full boil. He rarely displayed sentimentality and his affection for Sidney.

"Lad, I get it, I really do. A man wonders if he'll run when he is face to face with it. I was never face to face with it, but I fired plenty of rounds. We knew if the devil wanted you, he'd find a way to spark a powder bag.

"Any one of us would have thrown himself on a charge to try keeping it from exploding. Never mind all that bullshit about dying for the King, England and God. It's for shipmates, Sid, no other reason. The tars you sweat with, slept with, and cursed for their farts and bad breath. That is why you'd give your life."

Sidney had never faced such dangers but accepted Bert's words as truth. He knew beyond all doubt he would fight to the death to protect his friend. Bert's words struck a chord, but Sidney had not finished voicing his reasons.

"If that's the reason men stand together, it's reason enough to fight for your country. I've not met a man here who is dishonest or disagreeable. Let me change that, the only people I've met like that are English, sad to say. I've been helped by complete strangers and taken in and treated as family."

Bert thoughtfully scratched the stubble sprouting on his chin as he listened to Sidney.

"If this country is made up of such people, isn't it worth fighting for? After all, Germany declared war on France, Belgium and Russia. It's Germany torpedoing ocean liners and freighters, burning villages and using poison gas. If that's the nature of the Germans, don't we have to fight if they force us into it?"

"Lad, I can't disagree with anything you've said. I've been to a few German cities. Maybe their language hurts the ears, and yes, the Kaiser is a first-class asshole. They got a bit too big for their britches the last thirty years or so. Maybe this war was inevitable with such headstrong people." Bert held up a hand asking for a moment to finish his speech.

"By and large, they seem to want the same things we do - a home, food and looking after their families. England, France, Germany, Austria and Russia seem to be fighting a war mostly about annihilation. That doesn't make sense and this war looks to have taken on a life of its own. If men in Germany feel like you, this will be a long war."

"So, what to do, Bert? Should I go or stay and do my bit here?"

"Lad, no man should tell another what to do and I won't with you. But I can share what I think you might do. Years from now when you're on your deathbed, it's best to die without regrets. You've got one now, and that's enough."

Sidney blushed realizing Bert knew he still carried a torch for Mystique. His other regret would be not joining the army to serve his country.

"Bert, you guys are new to farming so it's not fair for me to leave now. If the war is still on next year, I'll go see the major. What do think of that idea?"

"Well lad, you staying helps get the harvest in and puts some money in the bank. That's always nice, you know. Christ Almighty, I sound like a farmer! Well, what do you say, sir? Shall we finish seeding?"

By working twelve and fourteen-hour days, they finished seeding in one week. Through the summer, rain fell when needed, hail skirted their fields and the crops flourished.

On horseback, Sidney surveyed the fields and no matter how often he looked, he still could not believe the sight. *'Not in a million years would you have this in England.'* Despite his gratitude, the wish to serve as more than a farmer continued to nag.

"Bert, I remember the major saying I could decide about going overseas. That doesn't square with my notion of the army giving men a choice about how they serve their time." Bert chuckled as he remembered the strict discipline of his navy days.

"I know the Canadian army takes after the British. The navy never asked how much butter I might like on my toast. All I ever heard was, stand at attention and speak only when spoken to. When you sign on the dotted line, your ass is theirs.

"Maybe in a specialized trade, you might have some wiggle room. I'd sure want a signed letter from the major. Hell, I'd want a letter signed by a general. Majors are a dime a dozen, generals are a bit scarcer."

Sidney considered Bert's advice and, as usual, it was sound. Talk often vanished on the breeze. Signed letters were not as easily forgotten. In a structured hierarchy like the army, Sidney wondered about receiving such latitude.

"Bert, won't an officer get pissed off if I ask for a signed letter? It would sound like I don't trust him." With a conspiratorial smile, Bert answered.

"Lad, you don't get to be an officer without knowing which way the wind blows. Officers below the rank of a fleet admiral or field marshal don't make decisions, they follow orders. I doubt the major made that offer without first talking to the colonel.

"The colonel won't decide something like that without talking to a general. Somebody screwed up royally if they don't have enough farriers. You might get an answer when we sell the horses. A high-ranking officer has to sign off on spending government money, so then we'll ask."

Sidney's trade was in demand but doubted he would enter the army as anything other than a private. If majors were a dime a dozen, privates were a penny per bushel. He had no desire to begin his army service on an officer's shit list. Although the army was a different beast from civilian society, soldiers were still human. He wondered how to frame his request and not offend the major but figured it all would work out. Bert would think of something.

Chapter Eleven

As summer progressed, farm work occupied most of Sidney's time, but his first love remained Percheron horses. Despite their great size and strength, they enjoyed Sidney washing them and brushing their manes and tails. They became privy to his secrets and regret that Mystique had not returned.

Sidney would have melted knowing Bert occasionally overheard these conversations. One evening, Bert heard Sidney in the barn talking to his equine companions.

"What do you think of that idea, Albert?"

Sidney sentimentally named his favourite horse Albert, after his younger brother. Back in England, he and Albert shared boyish thoughts. While no longer a boy, Sidney missed those talks.

"Do you think the major will put in a good word for me? Let me stay until Bert can run the farm? I would go right now if they promised not to send me overseas. It's not that I'm afraid, well not completely, just kind of afraid. It wouldn't do if a Heinie killed me. If that happened, Albert, we'd never see each other again and I could never marry Mystique. I'm going to have to give this some more thought."

When Sidney finished the grooming, he stood before Albert and solemnly addressed the horse.

"You haven't said a word, so now it's your turn to chime in." Chuckling self-consciously, Sidney whistled softly as he rubbed down the horse's great flank. Swallowing his laughter, Bert called out before entering the barn.

"Lad, don't forget we have more horses than just Albert. The others will get jealous at you playing favourites."

"I know Bert, but Albert is the best listener. At least he nods when I'm talking. The others just stand there and take a crap every now and again."

"Well, they're letting you know what they think of your stories. Albert is just kissing your ass to get extra feed," Bert chuckled.

"Lad, I've been thinking about you joining the army. They will take you in a flash, but I doubt you'll get any promises. That's just not how the big machine operates. If they do send you over, I can probably make a go of it here. But I'd be happier having you here, so I've come up with a solution."

Sidney sat down to hear Bert's idea. Bert considered matters from every angle and had answers for all questions.

"I rode past Camp Hughes last week and saw the soldier boys marching out to the train station. Couldn't help wondering how many of the cheerful fellows will be dead by year's end."

"Aren't you full of happy thoughts? Hope you didn't talk to them. Someone might have been so cheered up, he hung himself." Bert laughed and gave Sidney a finger gesture before continuing.

"No lad, I kept my words of encouragement to myself. They need to learn for themselves. Anyway, I saw a delivery wagon go in the main gate and a grand idea came to me. Go see the major to ask about being hired on as a civilian farrier. That way, you're part of the war effort. What do you think? Hell, just to sweeten the deal, tell them you'll work for free. Those cheap bastards in Ottawa would love that kind of bargain."

Sidney laughed aloud at the brilliant suggestion. Of course, it would work, although he balked a bit at the idea of working for nothing.

"Bert, as usual, you have come up with the best of both worlds. If it wasn't Sunday morning, I'd go see the major right now."

"Well, lad, you could go now. I bet the major is on church parade, so you could find him there. I'm afraid I can't go for safety reasons – the church might fall down if I stepped inside."

"You are so full of shit. You've never been in a church. Why not come with me? That is, Sir Westhaven, if you can spare the time away from your realm."

"I'm full of shit? It isn't me the army wants. Your gift of shooting the shit must interest them. Anyway, let the major enjoy his peace and quiet and see him tomorrow."

The following morning, Sidney saddled Albert and enjoyed the scented breeze on his ride to Camp Hughes. He felt grateful to be alive. Thousands of miles away, other young Canadians would not live to see another sunrise.

Bowing his head, he offered a prayer of salvation and gratitude for their service. Reaching out, he patted Albert's massive flank affectionately and received a soft whinny.

At the camp guardhouse, he reined in at a young sentry's challenge. Sidney thought the man barely old enough to be out of middle school. Despite the uniform and rifle, Sidney doubted the Germans would give up at the sight of him. Remembering Bert's advice to tell rather than ask, he replied.

"Good morning, private. My name is Sidney Turner and I'm here to see Major Steele. If you will point the way, I can conduct my business with the major."

The soldier guessed he and the visitor were the same age, but the stranger spoke with a quiet air of authority. Giving Sidney a quick look, confirmed he was unarmed. That was good enough for the sentry. Others could deal with the visitor if he created problems.

With a soft word and snap of the reins, Albert plodded past staring soldiers. The horses in camp were cavalry mounts, not massive dray animals. Sidney stopped at a white tent marked Adjutant's Office. At the open flap stood a corporal and Major Steele. The corporal looked at Sidney with curiosity and the major smiled.

"Mr. Turner, welcome to Camp Hughes. It's good to see you." The corporal was surprised the major would so respectfully address a man junior to them.

"Corporal, if you have no further questions, please carry on." With a sharp salute, the corporal turned on his heel and disappeared among the long rows of tents. Turning to Sidney, the major asked, "What brings you here on this fine morning, young man?"

One of the major's primary duties was overseeing the care and feeding of the regiment's horses. Ready to pull out his hair over the ineptitude of some soldiers, he prayed Sidney would join the regiment.

"Major Steele, you asked about us selling some horses and our offer is in this envelope. I trust you'll advise us of the army's decision?" The major took the envelope and asked if Sidney had more to discuss.

"Sir, you also asked me to join the army. Since my friend's death in April, the thought has never been far away. Patriotism aside, I have other things to consider before deciding."

"Well, tell me and perhaps I can address those concerns."

"We bought our farm less than a year ago. Bert and the hired men have no farming experience, which is the biggest problem. Most of what I know is from working on Mr. Percy MacDonald's farm the last three years." The major glanced at the piles of paper on his desk that required his attention.

"I'm not sure how this is pertinent to your serving in the army, Mr. Turner. Excuse my impatience, but will you be sharing your decision with me soon?" Sidney blushed and came to the point.

"Major Steele, I have a craft the army needs, but my farm needs me, too. Rather than hoping for special consideration not to be sent overseas, might I hire on as a civilian? I could work here during the day. Evenings and weekends, I could work at home. Kind of the best of both worlds."

Major Steele smiled. He had overstepped his authority by offering to keep Sidney in Canada and hoped Sidney would not follow up on the offer, or better yet, simply join up.

"Mr. Turner, your idea could work to everyone's benefit. Let me present your offer to the colonel and I will advise you of his decision. Have you considered the amount of your compensation?"

"I hoped the army would make that offer, sir. I don't know what farriers are paid in Canada."

"Let me suggest your rate of pay should be the same as a private's daily rate. The men would not like it if we paid you more and life will be much easier if you fit in with them."

"That is a splendid idea, sir. Thank you."

"We will issue you a uniform, you'll take your meals in the mess and essentially, you'll be a soldier in the field."

"Major Steele, I hope to be coming to work here soon." Leaving the tent, he rode home to share the news with Bert. Less than a week later, an army courier delivered a letter confirming an employment offer at the daily pay rate of a private.

Sidney quickly settled into a new routine, dividing his time between farm and camp duties. The days were long, but he felt a sense of purpose teaching by day and supervising at home. The only difficulty arose from a few older soldiers who resented the young man's familiarity with the major. Their resentment vanished however when Sidney proved his competency.

A month later on a Friday morning, the major sent Sidney and a purchasing officer to Winnipeg to inspect the work of a saddle and harness manufacturer. The officer wore his uniform and Sidney went in civilian clothing. After concluding their business mid-afternoon, the officer said good-bye to Sidney. His family lived in Winnipeg and he planned to visit for the weekend. Left to his own devices, Sidney decided to take a train for home.

He recalled being in the station with Mystique, a time that now seemed to be from another life. *'Remember, no regrets. Bert would blast you for still mooning over Mystique.'*

Unlike his first visit, the station teemed with soldiers waiting to board trains and families bidding them farewell. Posters portrayed gallant soldiers with rifles and urged men to be stout-hearted and remember the fallen. Sidney wondered what John might think of the appeal.

While making his way to the ticket counter, a slender woman barred his path. Mumbling excuse me, Sidney went to step past her, but she stepped in front of him. Biting back his exasperation, he tried again but still she blocked him.

"Excuse me miss, I'm trying to catch a train." Then he looked down and caught his breath.

At first glance, she bore an uncanny resemblance to Mystique, but she was not his lost love. This woman did however have the exquisite mouth, delicate nose and soft white skin that enthralled him four years earlier.

Her hair was the deepest ebony that she wore in the modern flapper style. She dressed modestly, although the cut of her clothing hinted at a slender figure. Not since Mystique, had Sidney been so captivated.

Fixing Sidney with deep blue eyes, the woman handed him a white feather. Sidney took it and the woman venomously hissed at him.

"You should be in uniform, you coward." Eyes ablaze, she turned on her heel and melted into the crowd. Sidney heard bystander comments while his face turned crimson.

The white feather phenomena began in London and spread to other countries of the British Empire. Young women handed white feathers to men not in uniform as an accusation of cowardice. Sidney was enraged at the insult. The woman had already had left the station and anger propelled Sidney out the door to confront his accuser.

"Excuse me, miss," he called but she continued walking away. "Excuse me, miss!" he called again.

Knowing he had come after her, she walked faster. Sidney refused to allow her the luxury of ignoring him and he broke into a quick trot. Jumping in front of her, he forced her to stop. Beautiful or not, he refused to be humiliated without speaking out.

"Did it cross your mind I'm out of uniform because I'm on leave? How dare you presume to know enough to humiliate me? Who in the blazes do you think you are to pass judgement on a total stranger?"

Never had Sidney raised his voice at a woman but now he was yelling at one on a public street. Had she been a man, he would have pummelled her on the spot.

Shocked by the loud exchange, several passers-by considered speaking up, but the fury of this young bull deterred them. Sidney towered over the girl with his fists clenched, but realizing how foolish this appeared, he stepped back. The woman had not flinched, and anger raged in her eyes.

"You coward! No wonder you aren't in uniform. If you were, you wouldn't yell at girls half your size. You bloody big ape, you haven't the balls to talk like that to another man! Yelling your fool head off, proves you're nothing but a bully. I have one more thing to say, and it's fuck off and die!"

Tears ran down her cheeks and despite his anger, Sidney saw they came from sorrow as well as anger. Gathering herself to her full but diminutive height, she sneered and stalked away.

Her outburst astonished and baffled Sidney. Using foul language defeated any point she wished to make and all within in earshot, knew it. It had been an ugly public exchange and bystanders lamented the decline of proper public behaviour. Sidney returned to the station for dinner before catching the train.

After dining, he boarded and stretched out his weary limbs on an empty bench. Looking around the car revealed his only company was a drunk passed out on a bench. The coach lights dimmed, and the train passed through darkness cloaking the countryside. Pulling his coat close to sleep, he heard a coach door open as someone entered. Despite the dim light, he saw his accuser from the station.

His anger simmered as he quietly studied her. The girl had earlier looked Sidney directly in the eye with absolute contempt. Now, in the car, curiosity won out over his wounded pride. Sidney rose from his seat in the almost-empty rail car and glided to the front rows where the girl sat. Without fanfare, he slipped onto a facing bench.

Tired and half asleep, the girl took little notice of him. Sidney silently stared, waiting for her to recognize him while hoping she would not start yelling again. She gave him a cursory glance and then, with a start, recognized him. Her eyes narrowed to slits.

"What are you doing here? Did you follow me? I've a switchblade in my purse, so don't try anything. Why don't you sit somewhere else?" That she had not cursed at him, encouraged Sidney.

"I'm doing the same thing you are. I'm taking the train to where I need to be tonight, just like you are. Presumably, you're going home. I'm going back to Camp Hughes." He waited for that information to sink in to gauge her reaction. A look of confusion passed over her face and she relented.

"So, you're in the army after all? You could have told me, you know," she said defiantly. "If you said you were just out of uniform, instead of yelling at me, it would have saved both of us embarrassment."

Sidney enjoyed her discomfort and regretted he had no audience to witness this scene. While the moment felt satisfying, conscience could not allow him to indulge in false pretense.

"Well miss, I was brought up not to interrupt people when they're speaking. Since you were going a mile a minute, I didn't have the chance to say anything." She blushed, and knowing he had scored a point, Sidney resumed.

"But all the same, you're right. I'm not officially in the army, but I do wear the uniform without a rank."

"I don't understand. You wear a uniform but aren't in the army? Isn't that against a law of some sort? Does anyone else besides me know about this?"

"It's no secret, miss. Wearing a uniform is the army's idea. You can tell I'm from England. I came to Canada four years ago and I farm near Brandon. I thought about joining up earlier this year when it looked like the war wouldn't be over soon." In a suspicious tone, the young woman broke in.

"That doesn't tell me why you wear a uniform you aren't entitled to wear. What gives?"

"I'm coming to that. I work with horses and the farm is close to Camp Hughes. We have some Percheron horses on the farm. The army asked if we would sell them some horses. The major knew about me being a farrier and he asked me to join up."

"Why didn't you? Are you afraid?" Seeing her questions bring a red flush to his face, she apologized.

"I'm sorry. I'm not trying to make you mad or insult you. I just don't get what you're talking about." Trying to keep an edge from his tone, Sidney resumed his explanation.

"My partner and I got the farm just before the war and I'm the only one who knows about farming. It didn't seem right to leave, and I couldn't decide what to do. We got the idea of working for the army as a civilian to teach the troops."

"So how long will you do that? Will you ever go overseas?"

"Maybe. Nearly all the farriers went over when the war started but things haven't gone the way the brass thought it would. So, the army needs me, and here I am."

"But why won't you join up?"

"Well miss, if I join, they might send me over before I can teach enough men. That would leave the army where they are now if I became one of the brave fallen."

Tears sparkled in her eyes at Sidney's reference to the fallen, but she blinked them away. He saw the fleeting display of grief but thought it best not to enquire.

Sidney sensed her animosity beginning to lessen. He guessed she was in her late teens or perhaps twenty. She was petite and delicately featured with obsidian hair and dazzling blue eyes. At least sharing blue eyes, was something they had in common.

Her features suggested mixed blood, but he was unsure what it might be. Each bloodline added to her beauty and now that they were on more civil terms, he was mesmerized. Not since Mystique had a girl captured his attention so strongly.

'Careful, Sid old boy, don't forget what happened the last time you felt this way.' Sidney looked out the window, but the full moon meant there was no place to hide his feelings.

She watched him through veiled eyelashes. That she had warmed toward him, came as a surprise, since she had hated him at first sight. Now somewhat calmer, she liked what she saw.

Tall, muscled and handsome, with a slow country charm, she thought. The blue eyes seemed familiar, although she did not know how that could be. She thought his accent delightful. That he spoke intelligently, did nothing to detract.

Her mother had sent her into Winnipeg to shop, not to meet a man. Since the spring, she had carried a feather in her purse. She nearly presented it several times but refrained until today. Something about the appearance of other men stirred feelings of pity rather than scorn. This young man's bearing, however, demanded she give him the white feather.

Now that she knew something about him, she regretted her action. Her instincts said his words were true. At any rate, she acted on an impulse and it proved to be an unsatisfactory experience. Trying to shame the man had not eased her grief and she pledged never to do it again. Deep in thought, she failed to realize he was speaking.

"Miss, I don't know how far you're going but it would be a shame if you got off this train and I didn't know your first name."

He extended his hand and after a moment's hesitation, she took it. They flinched as a spark passed between them. Sidney twitched, and he saw the hint of a smile playing at the corners of her mouth. Gathering his wits, he tried speaking normally but it came out nervously.

"I'm Sidney Turner and it's my pleasure to meet you."

"Thank you for your kind words, Mr. Turner. My name is Emma Bias from Portage la Prairie. Your timing is very good, because we're only about ten minutes from my station."

"Well, despite how we met, I'm glad to meet you, Miss Bias. Should we meet again, please call me Sidney. I'll go by Mr. Turner when I get old."

"All right, Sidney. And should we meet again, you must call me Emma. My girlfriends call me Gemma because my mother called me her little gem when I was little." She smiled and the change in her expression incinerated his senses.

"Emma, I hope to have the chance to know you well enough to be part of the inner circle that calls you Gemma."

"Well, that won't be easy, Sidney. I don't let just anyone into this inner circle, as you put it. It isn't easy, but it is possible," she replied with a saucy toss of her head. Quickly looking around, she lowered her voice and spoke in a conspiratorial tone.

"My middle name is Rose, and I love it most of all because that's what I really am. Maybe you'll find out for yourself one day." Enthralled, but a little wiser, he hoped not to be too easy to snare this time.

"Emma, in case I never see you again, please tell me why you gave me that feather."

She replied with tears and her head slumped forward. The change stunned Sidney and he could not imagine the reason. He shyly touched her knee in hopes of comforting her. Sidney offered a linen handkerchief and she dabbed her eyes. Recovering her breath, Emma spoke again.

"Oh, for Christ's sake, what the fuck is the matter with me?" Her cursing shocked Sidney again.

"Sidney, forgive me. You were just in the wrong place today. I've been carrying that feather for months waiting to give it to a man I thought deserved it. You got it even though now I know you don't deserve it. Want to know why I did something so mean?"

"Yes, because it humiliated me and really pissed me off. So yes, tell me the why and the what for." Offering her a friendly smile, he hoped it would encourage her to share the secret.

"I don't claim my reason is an excuse. My brother died in Belgium at St. Julien around April 24, and that is about all we know. Some of our men saw him and a buddy charging a German machine gun. One of his pals wrote to say he would have been killed doing that. For now, he's listed as missing but we're sure he's dead."

"I'm sorry to hear that, Emma. A man who was so close to me I considered him a brother, died at St. Julien that day. He was his family's eldest son and before he went, I promised to help with their farm. Between them and us, I guess a few people depend on me. His name was John MacDonald and he served with our Winnipeg regiment."

"So did my brother, Louis. What a tragic coincidence. He joined up at Camp Hughes. Your friend and Louis probably met. My folks didn't want him going but he said the same things as all these other young fools. It would be a great adventure and he didn't want it to be over before he got there. I suppose your friend talked the same damn fool way?"

"Yeah, that's what John said. He said if I joined after him, he would have licked the German army by himself and all I needed to do is count the prisoners. We know he is buried on our side and not missing somewhere like your poor brother."

"I was heartbroken and so pissed off when Louis died I thought my insides would blow up. My handsome, smart brother all the girls fainted over, was dead. The anger was more than I could stand, and I needed something to make me feel better." Dabbing her eyes, Emma offered a brave smile.

"One day, I read about the white feathers and decided to do the same thing here. I wanted my brother home safe and I was angry that other people's brothers were alive. When I saw you, it was like why the hell are you walking around happy when my heart is broken? I'm sorry. It wasn't right that I tried screwing up someone else's life."

He sat attempting to figure out this girl with the stunning looks, a fiery temper and a vocabulary that made Bert sound like a Sunday morning preacher. Sidney thought horses easier to understand than women.

A conductor opened the coach door to announce the next stop was Portage la Prairie. Emma stood and offered her arm for Sidney to escort her. The evening air held a hint of frost and she shivered while drawing her coat tightly around herself.

The car stopped, and the conductor placed a footstep on the platform. Sidney stepped down and extended his hand to her. Emma descended two steps but stopped on the last one.

"Sidney Turner, it was nice talking to you. You know my name and where I live. So whether you ever see me again, is up to you."

Leaning forward, she pressed her lips against his before drawing back, her face bathed in the glow of the platform lights. Seeing the surprise and desire in his eyes, she let slip a girlish giggle, bounced off the step and walked into the darkness.

Chapter Twelve

"Lad! Watch what you're doing with that swather! You're way off course, so just park it and I'll finish this field."

Stung from his reverie by Bert's sharp words, Sidney saw how far he had strayed. A band of Durham wheat still waved in the breeze. Face aflame, he brought the four-horse team to a stop. Bert parked his team and strode over. He did not know whether to be angry or concerned with Sidney's careless work this morning.

"All right, should I fire you for the rest of the day or just pull your head out of your arse? What happened in Winnipeg that you're so off kilter? If I didn't know better, I'd think you stashed a jug of whiskey in your lunch box." Looking back at the crooked crop line, Sidney sighed and faced Bert.

"No, I don't have whiskey in my lunch pail. It's much worse than that. I met a girl in Winnipeg and I think I'm in love."

"Oh, I see. So, you do have your head up your arse. Well, lean forward and I'll pull on your shoulders to get you back to normal. Here I thought you had lost your mind." Sidney laughed in exasperation. Bert could be so hard-nosed about affairs of the heart.

"Bert, let's take a short break and I'll tell you about my day. All last night, I lay in bed thinking about this girl." With a loud guffaw, Bert rejoined.

"You were pulling your wire all night, you mean. No wonder you're useless today." Uncomfortable with the accusation, Sidney blushed.

"Okay, lad, let's rest the horses and have some water. Now, what about this girl? You went to Winnipeg for saddles and tack, not a girl. But you didn't do too badly considering what the army wanted you to do." Sidney's excited grin warned Bert to be ready for a long explanation.

"Here's the short form, then the rest at supper. We finished the buying trip and the lieutenant went to visit his family. I was in the train station when this gorgeous girl walks up to me. Without saying a word, she hands me a white feather and takes off. Took me a second to twig and when I did, holy shit, I was mad. I didn't care if she was a looker." Groaning silently, Bert thought, *'Here we go again.'*

"She was already outside, and I ran after her to spout off. She calls me a fucking coward right to my face. Says I'm too chicken to talk like that to another man."

Only in the roughest bordellos had Bert heard women use such foul language. This girl sounded as though she could out-curse him – truly a feat.

"I never would have guessed a girl would pop off like that. I didn't know what to say and thought she might slap my face, but she just walked off."

"So, that's why you think she could be the girl you're going to marry?"

"Smart ass. After supper, I catch the train and there's only one other guy in the car and he's passed out. Well bust my balls, she comes into the car and sits down up front. I want to know what's with her calling me names, so what the hell? I sit down in front of her and because it's kind of dark, at first, she doesn't see it's me. Then she does and says there's a switchblade in her purse if I try anything."

"Lad, it must be true love."

"Yeah, you're funny. So, we talk, and I tell her about farming and working for the army. She calms down a bit and tells me why she did the white feather trick. Turns out her older brother got killed at St. Julien the same day as John. She read about the white feather and it seems a good way to get over her anger and I'm the guy that gets it. Now that I know why she's so barmy, I can't stay mad at her now, can I?"

"No, and she knows you're putty and can do what she wants. Look out lad, that's how it starts."

"Uh huh, let me finish. Her name is Emma she lives in Portage la Prairie. At her stop, I help her down, like a gentleman. She smiles, then she kisses me. Right on the mouth, too!"

"When a first meeting goes that smooth, it's a match made in heaven. But in the meantime, Mr. Turner, let's finish up here." The remainder of the day passed with Sidney's thoughts centred on a young girl with sparkling eyes.

In late September, Sidney visited Major Steele at Camp Hughes and found the major packing his personal and military kit.

"Good day, Mr. Turner" the major boomed jovially. "I trust the harvest is done and you can resume your camp duties?"

"Yes, sir. The harvest is done, but it looks like you and the fellows are leaving. Can you say where you are going?"

"Yes, my guess is you locals knew we were off to England before we did. The British are expanding their army and they have accepted our offer to provide more troops."

Sidney mused that as the need grew for the Canadian army to increase in size, it might lead to conscription. He wondered how farmers would cope if more men were called away.

"I expect there will be a big push next year and our boys will likely be in it. The Germans have millions of trained men with very good equipment. We will need a much larger effort than we have made so far to push them back to Germany.

"Well then, major, does that mean my services here are no longer required? Can you tell me anything about that?"

"Not to be pessimistic but I wouldn't count on our arrangement continuing far into the future." Extending a hand, the major concluded.

"I've enjoyed working with you, Sidney. I hope you join the regiment because you would be an excellent soldier. For that matter, you would be a good officer!"

Sidney rode home while comedic scenes of himself as General Turner, played in his mind.

"Yes, Albert, I rather like the sound of General Turner. My first order will be promoting you to major. Between the two of us, we will win the war and I can marry Emma. Won't she be pleased?"

That idea brought him around to thinking if he wanted to marry Emma, he should visit her. He hoped she had not forgotten him already. After all, Mystique had apparently forgotten about him.

"Yes, Albert, I think it is high time to call on Miss Bias."

The next morning, he swung aboard the train in Brandon and watched the sunrise spread across the prairie. Bert had already scolded Sidney for his delay in calling on Emma.

"Lad, there's more to life than this farm. Life is too short, and Mystique isn't coming back. Go see Emma."

Sunshine set a low ridge of hills ablaze with golden fields and emerald trees. While Sidney watched, the panorama transformed, allowing present day to slip into the past. He saw a herd of buffalo flow over the hills, raising clouds of dust, and in the dust, Sidney saw the Indian warrior who had a message to share.

"Our Spirit chose you to be with our people. Take this woman and child and help bring peace between our peoples."

'A woman and child? Which peoples am I supposed to help? I don't understand.'

As earlier visions eventually made sense, perhaps this one might. He would ponder it another time. Today he had other plans.

Sidney impatiently tapped his foot as the mile markers slipped past. All he knew was Emma left the train in Portage la Prairie. Did she live miles out of town? He would feel a complete fool if he could not find her.

Portage la Prairie finally came into view and the train huffed to a stop. Unsure where to begin, he brightened upon seeing the telegraph office. Doubting the clerk would offer directions to a stranger, he decided on a bit of subterfuge.

"Excuse me, sir, I wonder if you might help me? I'm off to Winnipeg to join up. Before I do that, I want to pay my respects to the family of a chum of mine who was killed at Ypres. Can you help me sir?"

"If he is a chum of yours, how is it you don't know where he lives?" The obvious question caught Sidney flat-footed but fortunately, his quick wit came to the rescue.

"Well, like I said, he was a chum, but we hadn't known one another very long. I farm near Brandon and we were weekend drinking buddies when he trained at Camp Hughes." The clerk sniffed disapprovingly but relented and asked for the name.

"Louis Bias, and his family apparently lives here in town." The clerk shot Sidney a look of disapproval hearing the family name.

"Some of them live in town. The others are across the tracks on the reserve. I could have guessed Louis Bias after hearing about the boozing. You don't look the sort he hung around with, but if you had whiskey, he would" the clerk ended contemptuously.

"Well, sir, as I said, we were more weekend chums than lifelong friends. Can you give me directions, please?"

"They don't live too far away so you'll be there quick. This time of year, the whole works of them might be around."

Armed with directions, Sidney walked from the station. Why had the station agent remarked so caustically at the mention of Louis Bias? And what about the reserve? Only Indians lived on reserves.

Several minutes of walking brought Sidney to a modest two-storey home. He saw a well-kept yard with flower beds lining the walkway and rose planters beside the front door. Crossing the veranda, he took a deep breath and knocked. For several moments, he heard nothing. Then came heavy footsteps and a man opened the door.

"Good day sir. May I help you?"

A handsome, bespectacled middle-aged man wearing a high collar white shirt and narrow black tie stood before Sidney. His black hair was greying at the temples. Doffing his hat, Sidney introduced himself with a firm handshake. His calm exterior hid the butterflies frantically trying to escape his insides.

"A pleasure to meet you, Mr. Turner. I am Alexander Bias. Perhaps you can share your reason for visiting our home?"

Alexander treated everyone with respect. A trader with the Hudson's Bay Company, he knew everyone within a hundred miles, but not Sidney.

"Papa, do I hear Sidney Turner?" The voice which belittled him weeks earlier, now sounded as if it belonged to an angel.

"Sidney! How nice to see you." Alexander raised an eyebrow with a look of amused patience.

"Papa, this is the young man I told you and mama about after my last trip to Winnipeg." Alexander faced Sidney as wonder gave way to embarrassment.

"Mr. Turner, Emma spoke of her behaviour. On behalf of my wife and me, please accept our apologies. I assure you we did not raise our children to be disrespectful. Nor to use the foul language Emma does when she is angry."

"Mr. Bias, Emma told me why she did and said what she did. I accepted her apology although there wasn't time to say so before we parted company. So yes, Emma, apology accepted and no lasting harm."

Twisting his cap in his hands, Sidney blushed when she rewarded him with a bright smile. Alexander opened the door wider and invited Sidney into the parlour.

"Please sit down, Sidney. Would you care for a cup of tea? I am home for lunch early today and have a little time yet before I go back. Emma, please put on the kettle and bring your mother to meet Mr. Turner." Flashing Sidney another smile, Emma left to do her father's bidding.

"By your accent, you haven't been in Canada more than a few years. I'm guessing you hail from southern England?"

"Yes sir, my village is about halfway between London and Oxford on an old Roman road. But I've been here four years and I'm a Canadian now, sir."

"I hear you own a farm and help your adopted family. You have done well, young man, and I salute you. Congratulations."

"Thank you, sir. I've worked hard, and I had a lot of help. When I got to Brandon, a man hired me to work on his farm. I learned how to farm with him and his son, John, but the war changed our plans. Sir, I'd like to offer my sympathy to you on the loss of your son."

"Thank you, Sidney, for your concern. Yes, the war certainly changed the plans of many people," Alexander offered wistfully.

"My son Louis rushed off to join almost the moment we were at war with Germany. It upset his mother, but I said Louis had the right to decide matters for himself. Since his death, I've berated myself many times for saying what I did."

"My mate John, joined in Brandon. His father begged him and me not to join. I listened, but John didn`t. He died the same day and near the same place as Louis. A major at Camp Hughes told me thousands of our men died there, but they stopped the Germans from breaking through. The war might have been lost except for those men."

The light click of heels heralded the arrival of Emma and her mother. Much to Sidney's astonishment, the mother was a full-blooded Indian.

"Sidney, this is my mother, Florence Helen Bias."

The older woman's cheekbones confirmed her lineage. Her long, black hair was tied in a braid that cascaded down her back. Middle-aged, Florence remained attractive with indigo eyes that matched the warrior eyes from Sidney's visions. Sidney sensed Florence came from the warrior's lineage. Perhaps she might explain the visions that had perplexed him.

Taking Sidney's hands, she greeted him in her native tongue. Sidney understood not a word, but the lilt and cadence of her speech fascinated him. A ripple of the softest laughter escaped from Florence's lips and she switched to English.

"Welcome, Sidney Turner. An old sprit brings you to be part of our circle. I gave you my name in our native language. To my people, I am Laughing Maiden." Emma hugged Florence and beamed at Sidney.

"This is the young man I was so mean to, mama. I apologized, and being a gentleman, Sidney accepted it. Even though papa is still unhappy with me."

"As he should be, Gemma. You will have a chance to be forgiving like Mr. Turner. Then you must be gracious and accept that others will trespass against your spirit. You must learn it is important for all to walk in peace." While Sidney digested those words, Alexander moved the conversation to a less lofty plateau.

"Emma, you and Sidney should talk without us listening. Why don't you go for a walk while your mother and I have lunch? Sidney, it's a pleasure meeting you. Emma, be gentle with this young man," he admonished with a twinkling eye.

Taking a shawl from the coat tree, Emma opened the door and waited while Sidney bid adieu to her parents. When he joined her, they went out to the street.

"I was interested by how mama behaved with you. She acted as if she knew you and was expecting you. Did you notice that?" Sidney had noticed but did not know how to answer.

The visions confused him, and he questioned their validity. '*If the woman I'm to take is Emma, I can live with that. Are the two peoples her mom and mine? Does he mean Indians and whites?*' He wondered if Florence thought him to be the piece of a puzzle she needed to find.

"I thought maybe she is that kind to everyone," he replied lamely. Emma's eyes searched his face, wondering if he was being forthright.

"She isn't usually like that with strangers. Let me tell you a story but it might take a few minutes." Happy simply to be in Emma's company, Sidney would have listened to a day-long story.

"Mama was born in the late 1860s, in a spring when the buffalo didn't come because the whites killed so many of them. White people took their lands and forced them onto reservations."

"In England, people would have gone to war to keep their lands."

"Easy to say, but we were outnumbered. How could they win with a bow and arrow against rifles?"

"I hadn't thought of it like that. Guess we would have lost too if the French had rifles and we only had swords."

"Exactly. We lost everything. Now most white people think Indians are just drunks, thieves or cheap whores. It's true that some Indians are like that, but not Mama's family. Louis sometimes drank too much and got in fights.

"When people called him a no-good Indian, he punched them out. Papa's blood makes me look white, but mama's blood made Louis look Indian. It pisses me off white people called him and mama names, but I'm very proud of my people. Some whites think we should be pushed right off the land."

Sidney had never spoken to anyone of native ancestry. The few Indians he saw around Brandon seemed to be troublemakers. Other than that, however, he never gave Indians a second thought. Now, he had met a girl who was half-Indian and half white. He wondered if she felt torn between the two races.

"Forgive my saying so, Emma, but I never would have guessed you are half-Indian."

"I know. Looking white helps me get along in the white world. But when I'm on the reserve, they call me an inside-out apple, white on the outside and red on the inside. It's supposed to be an insult. I get it from both sides and some days I just want to move where no one knows me. People are just such a bloody nuisance sometimes. Do you ever feel that way?"

Sidney considered the talk that would have passed around the village gossip circle after he and his father had exchanged blows.

"Yeah, sometimes I do. Before I came to Canada, in our village, people didn't have much money. It seemed all they could afford to do was talk about each other. But I bet it was nothing compared to what your family gets."

"From the little mama and papa have said about it, Papa's friends said terrible things about him marrying what they called a squaw. Mama's side said she was too ashamed of her people to marry an Indian man. Some people in town don't think they're really married and won't even speak to them."

"Sounds like the Montagues and Capulets all over again, but out here instead of in Italy." Surprised by the reference, Emma regarded him with heightened appreciation.

"Sidney, you've read Shakespeare? That's a surprise."

"Well even though I'm a boy from a small town, I am English. I have heard of a few things in life, you know."

"Oh, that isn't how I meant it. Except for papa, I don't know anyone who knows anything about Shakespeare. Hearing someone talk about Romeo and Juliet is a real surprise." With a laugh, Sidney back-pedalled several feet.

"Well, don't think I'm some sort of bookworm because I'm not. My best mate Bert and his lady Desiree are why I've read outside normal limits. Desiree reads a lot because society expects a lady to be cultured." He decided not to elaborate why this particular lady needed culture. Perhaps another time.

"On cold nights at home, I pass the time by reading. I always thought Shakespeare was for stuffy, rich people. I have to say, I quite like the bit I've read."

"Good for you, Sidney. Lots of people don't even know how to read or write." Grateful his mother insisted he learn his letters, Sidney had another question to ask Emma.

"Where on earth did you learn to swear like you do? You can out-swear Bert and he was a gunner in the British navy." Turning bright red, she giggled.

"I got bored around the house in my early teens. Mama said I was a giant pain in the rear end. Is that the language you mean?"

"That's pretty tame compared to what you said in Winnipeg."

"I know but let me finish. Some days, Mama asked Papa to take me back to the post, so she could have some peace and quiet. Sometimes he took me on his trade route for a few days, too."

"Sounds like fun. Was it?"

"Yeah it was, but around the forts, you see and hear a lot of rough things. You know, from the drovers, cowboys and Indians. There was always whiskey and arguments about who was screwing somebody's wife or girlfriend."

"Really? It sounds like the wild west."

"That's because it is the Wild West, silly. When we got home, I talked the same way. Mama had a fit! I got such a spanking and she tried washing my mouth with soap."

"Yuck. My mom did that to me once. Not much fun."

"Mama was so pissed off. Now that I'm a bit older, I don't talk like that except when I get mad. Guess you know that."

"Yeah, I do. I hope not to be your target ever again."

Emma linked her arm with Sidney's as they strolled through the area considered downtown Portage la Prairie. Sidney knew he was near the point of no return with this vivacious young woman.

'You've only met two girls and you fell for each of them. You really don't have any idea what you're doing.' Emma peeked up at him from under a jet-black curl of hair.

"There is far more to you, Sidney Turner, than I first guessed. You try to pass yourself off as a simple country boy. The truth is, at twenty-one, you own a farm, you help neighbours, you teach soldiers about horses, and you read Shakespeare. How much more there is to learn about you?"

Chapter Thirteen

"I pronounce you, man and wife. Son, you may kiss the bride." Opening his hands in greeting, the minister made the official announcement to the congregation.

"Beloved family and friends, allow me to introduce Mr. and Mrs. Sidney Turner."

A gentle peal of laughter rippled through the church at the young couple who were totally enthralled with one another.

Sidney wore a pale grey suit and azure tie. A red rose had been pinned on the lapel by Bert, the best man. Emma wore the white wedding gown her mother wore at her wedding nearly thirty years earlier. A fine white lace veil flowed over her jet-black locks to lay weightless on her shoulders.

Sidney raised the veil and saw her blue eyes filled with love. Her soft lips were crimson rouge and a thin gold neck chain held a tiny crucifix that lay in the cleft of her bosom. Sidney greeted her upturned mouth with the gentlest kiss while murmuring his undying love to the fairest of all roses.

"My handsome husband, I want you to show me the joys of love tonight" Emma whispered shamelessly.

She had offered herself to him before their marriage, and despite his desire, he tore himself away. This evening she wanted to discover the reasons for whispered laughter among her girlfriends. Seeing colour rise to Sidney's face, she felt a wave of desire that left her light-headed.

Turning to the congregation, Emma and Sidney took their wedding march down the aisle. Sidney was ready to challenge the world. He now had a family that confirmed his place on earth. *'Making babies is going to be fun and I can't wait to start. Down boy, can't be standing up here with a hard on.'*

The lavish wedding dinner and dance Bert and Desiree arranged, flew by in a flurry of toasts. Seeing Desiree returned

Sidney's thoughts to Mystique and he admonished himself for mentally straying off course on his wedding day. Florence beckoned Sidney to follow her for a quiet word.

"Sidney, I want to share a story my father passed down to me. It will not take long, and Emma and Alexander know I want to tell you this. I didn't understand the whole story until we met. The instant we met, I knew you were the answer to my questions.

"Now that you married my sweet girl, it's time you know. And Sidney, please call me mom, I miss that. My father was Walking Thunder of the Santee Sioux. He was a warrior, but his real gift was seeing and understanding visions."

"Walking Thunder is quite the name. I hope you tell me why."

"Young Sioux men have to seek a vision to know their manhood name. Father went up a mountain for his and there was a thunder and lightning storm. The people were sure he would die up there."

The old woman's eyes unwound like a slow-motion newsreel as she shared the vision. Hearing about the lightning strikes, Sidney flinched and squeezed her hand.

"Sorry mom, I hope that didn't hurt, but that would have scared me to death."

"After they saw my father walking down the mountain through the storm, they called him Walking Thunder."

"What a great name. Only an Indian could have that name. People would laugh at me if that were my name. He must have been very proud of it."

"He was, and he met my mother a few years later. I was born sometime in the spring of 1868." Not knowing the date of your birth puzzled Sidney.

"How do you know when to have a birthday party?" Florence smiled and shook her head.

"Sidney, that is such a white man question. We have a birthday party, as you call it, on the first nice spring day. I still keep some of the old ways."

"Can you show me some of them?" The question confirmed her new son-in-law was a special white man.

"In the spring of 1876, we went south to find father's people. We were in a big camp when the army soldiers found us. There was a great battle called the Little Big Horn where Custer had his last stand.

"All the soldiers died and some Indians, too. My father was one. His body fell nearly on top of Custer and they think he shot him. After the battle, we came back here but I hardly remember my father." Florence touched a fist to her heart and then Sidney's.

"My mother married a white man and my name changed to Florence Helen. One day I had a vision of my father and he said to remember where I came from and to tell my children." She paused to search Sidney's face and read his thoughts.

"You have visions you do not understand, tell me what you see." Sidney wondered how to tell a native woman, things he did not understand.

"I don't know what these dreams or visions are telling me. I saw the first one at sea coming over here. It looked like I was hunting buffalo and it was trying to tell me a story. To be honest, it scared me, and I wondered if I was crazy.

"People in England don't see such things or if they do, I've never heard of it. Sometimes I see dust clouds and buffalo running in them and I see an Indian man. He looks at me like he has a message." Florence hugged Sidney after hearing his story.

"You've seen my father. My dear boy, he does have a message for you. In my dreams, he tells me he has spoken to you. Be wise and learn from him. You are a special white man who can hear this way and it is rare. Tell me more."

"If this gift is rare, I hope he slows it down a bit for me."

"Some of my people will say it is strange a white boy crossed the ocean to join our circle, but I do not question the Great Spirit. We all walk under the same sun, on the same grass and breathe the same air."

"So, Emma is the granddaughter of a great warrior. That certainly explains a great deal." Sidney chuckled and then grew serious.

"Will you help me understand?" Florence's reply caused Sidney to wonder about the future.

"Whites will tell you not to listen to the beliefs of savages. I have been to white churches and heard priests and ministers preaching about their God. The bible accepts no word except the white word. There are good words in that book, but it never speaks of the spirit joining all things.

"I believe Walking Thunder sees the future and he says you might go into terrible danger. I think you know what that means and please listen to him. Louis did not listen, and he went to the war where white men killed him. Just like white men killed my father and many of our people.

"The whites have been very hard on our family. Become someone who leads others. Show them the right path with your good heart. I've kept you long enough, go back to your bride." Kissing his cheek, Florence Helen released him.

Back in the hall, Bert wrapped Sidney in a bear hug. The Irish whiskey had unlocked a torrent of sentimentality.

"I'm beyond happiness and the word unbelievable comes to mind, too. You go from being homeless in Southampton to owning a farm and marrying a beautiful girl. I'm honoured you're my best friend and I insist on being godfather to at least one of your children," Bert spouted in joyous abandon.

Several hours later, Sidney lay panting in Emma's arms as their frantic breathing slowed. Kissing his cheek, she ran one hand through his damp hair while the other traipsed along his spine before coming to rest on a buttock. To her surprise, intercourse had not been the painful experience she expected.

Church teachings claimed the only purpose of sex was bringing children into the world. Her mother said sex between a wife and husband improved with practice. After her first experience, she could not wait to try again. Brushing a lock of hair from her face, she leaned on an elbow and gazed intently at him.

"I hope you are pleased with me, my sweet husband." A wolfish smile left no doubt.

"I heard so many different things about what to expect. I felt nervous, but I wanted you. Now I want to ask you something and please don't think I'm nosey or jealous." Male instinct warned Sidney to listen carefully before replying.

"When you were being fitted for your suit, Bert dropped by my parents' house. I poured him a couple of drinks to loosen him up a little."

"Damn him. What did he say?"

"Never mind being annoyed. There is a room inside you I knew you would never open, so I asked Bert about when you first came to Canada. He told me pretty much the same things you've told me, but I knew there was more. I poured him more whiskey and he swore me to secrecy upon pain of death. Well, I promised him but inside, I poo-pooed the part about death." The look in Sidney's eyes said she knew that which he swore never to reveal.

"Do we have to talk about this on our wedding night?"

"Yes, because it has something to do with our wedding night. Bert told me about Mystique and please, don't be mad."

"I'm not mad. It just isn't something I want to talk about, especially on our wedding night."

"I knew you had a story you would never share with me. When we made love just now, I knew she taught you what you did."

Clearly embarrassed, Sidney laid a forearm across his eyes until Emma finished speaking.

"Are you done, Emma? I certainly hope so." She playfully slapped a butt cheek and laughed.

"You know what you hear at church. That sex for the fun of it is against God's commands and all that baloney."

"Yes, I heard that in my school boy days. Now are you done?"

"Just about. After we did it just now, I knew what Bert said about you two was true."

"Oh Lord, are you ever going to stop?"

"No wonder she was so good, being a courtesan and all. Bert showed me her picture. No wonder you were head over heels. What a beautiful woman and I don't blame you for loving her. In all honesty, I could see myself with her" Emma blushed.

"Now that's getting weird, Emma. Are you done yet? I'm ready again if you care to look."

"You waited years for her to come back. I am so grateful she didn't come back. Okay, now I'm done. So, let's screw again, my horny honey."

Morning sun turned the red velvet curtains crimson and bathed the room in a bordello glow. Sidney opened an eye upon feeling the pain of a limb gone to sleep. An arm lay trapped under his sleeping bride.

A hint of a smile played on the faint trace of rouge on her lips. As she breathed, her breasts rose and fell beneath the covers. The blankets hugged the contour of her shoulders, descending to the slim waist before rising in a graceful arc over her symmetrical hips and dissolving along the length of her shapely calves.

'Thank you for wanting to be my wife. You've filled the hole in my heart and I will be the world's best husband.' With his free hand, he stroked a curl of black hair that fell on the nape of her neck.

For all her efforts to be an untameable prairie filly, Emma possessed a sweet innocence Sidney's touch had stirred into wakefulness. Blessed with a delicate, well-proportioned face, her willowy figure hinted at smouldering sensuality. All had burst into a mad dance of uninhibited flame during the all-night passion of their wedding night.

He smiled at the contrast between the fawn peacefully sleeping beside him and the vixen who demanded, in shocking language, what she wanted. Moments later, Emma's eyes opened and without a word, wrapped her limbs around him to welcome his body.

An hour later, she joined him for breakfast in the dining room of the grand hotel. A sunny spring day brought a soft breeze through lacy curtains decorating the long windows. Hunger had tormented Sidney while he waited for Emma to make an appearance.

Heads turned as the glowing young woman, threaded a path between tables and dazzled Sidney with a beaming smile. Rising from his seat, he pecked her cheek and whispered, "I love you so much, my darling."

He eased out her chair, as proper gentlemen should, and she sat. A waiter took their orders and Sidney could not hide his disdain when she asked for coffee. Sidney held fast to some old country customs and at breakfast, tea was his preferred beverage. Try as he might, he had not entirely shaken the

English snobbery for all things American. Emma nudged his arm and teased him for his attitude.

"You aren't in England any more, old chap," she needled in a poor imitation of his accent.

"Yes, I know that, my darling, and for nearly everything else I'm eternally grateful. However, I wish this blasted custom of drinking coffee would go the way of the dodo bird," he answered in exaggerated English prose.

"You do know my fine gentleman, I am making it one of my life's ambitions to knock off some of your stuffy Englishness." Lowering her voice, she leaned forward to whisper. "The other is screwing your brains out, so don't say you weren't warned."

"Kindly stop trying to embarrass me in public, my dear. I've lived in the wild west long enough to make love to you right now, on this table, if you don't stop."

"Go ahead, big boy, I dare you. In fact, I'll make the first move."

"Don't you dare, Emma Rose Turner," Sidney hissed. "I'll never get it up for you again if you make a scene."

"Oooh, you big strong man. Just when I find out how much fun screwing is, you don't want to play," she mocked.

"Let's just eat breakfast. Then we will go home where I'll deal with your condition," Sidney muttered. Emma thoughtfully gazed out the window to organize her thoughts.

"When we said our vows yesterday, I was happy and sad."

"That was your chance to say no to marrying me. It's too late now, my darling."

"Sidney Turner, there are times when you are funny and times when you aren't. Don't make jokes about my marrying you," she scolded.

"I was sad Louis wasn't there, but his spirit was standing right beside me. Mama said she saw him, handsome as ever, while we said our vows. And I thought about your family in England not knowing about our special day. You never talk about them, but I know your mama would have loved to have been there. Did you at least write and tell them about our getting married?" Through the toast in his mouth, Sidney mumbled an unintelligible reply.

"Do you expect me to believe that was a yes? You've got that stupid look on your face again so don't hand me a line like that. You are so full of shit, Turner. Just admit you didn't write them."

"I was very busy, in case you forgot. I had to seed, look after cows and keep the farm running smoothly. Not to mention working at the camp, too."

"If you were that busy, how is it you were in Portage la Prairie so often? Don't tell me it was on army business. Don't make me have to tell you twice in one morning, you are full of shit."

"I thought a good wife was supposed to honour and obey her husband, not verbally abuse him on the morning after their wedding night," he finished with a leer.

"Well, we'll just have to go upstairs so you can punish me," she taunted.

An hour later, they released one another, finished packing and returned to the train station. Emma leaned against Sidney's shoulder and held his hand.

"I wish it didn't take four hours to get home. That's a long time to wait for you to screw me again." With a heavy sigh, Sidney leaned back and shook his head.

"Emma, where did you learn to talk that way? I know it wasn't at home. Please be more ladylike, would you?"

"For you, my handsome husband, I'll try. But if I behave, how will you recognize me?"

While Emma and Sidney were away, Desiree helped Bert move from the house he shared with Sidney. He had firmly rebuffed Sidney's entreaties to continue living with them.

"Lad, Buckingham castle would be too small for me to live under the same roof as newlyweds. You are a little slow catching on at times, so trust me on this one. Emma will appreciate it more than you think."

The hired-man house on the MacDonald farm had stood empty since John joined the army. Bert planned to stay there until he and the hired hands built a house for him. While they packed, Bert and Desiree had a discussion.

"The lad has grown up right before my eyes. He did everything on faith and came to Canada because he liked a poster. Can you believe that? I'll say one thing for him, he wasn't smart enough to know he should be afraid," Bert chuckled. Desiree smiled wistfully. She still carried guilt for her behind the scenes manipulation of Sidney.

"Sometimes I think it was wrong to keep them apart. Maybe they could have handled it. Bert, don't take me the wrong way. I'm happy Sidney found Emma and has more to his life than the farm." Draping an arm across her shoulder, Bert shook his head.

"You did what you thought was right. Sidney might have agreed to a baby, but I'd bet ten thousand dollars that after a few years, he would have felt gypped. You made the right call, and if Sidney ever finds out, he'll thank you."

Returning for another load of furniture, they found Sidney and Emma at the house. Bert opened the French champagne he had bought months earlier. After toasting the newlyweds, Desiree and Emma busied themselves sorting wedding gifts. The men sat with two glasses of Irish whiskey.

"I bought the Winnipeg paper," Sidney said. "Man, the war news is tough to follow. Half the time I can't figure out if we're winning or losing." Leaning back in a chair, Bert sipped some whiskey before offering his analysis.

"I doubt anyone will come out ahead. Who will rebuild France and Belgium if the young men are dead? How many years will it take to repay the war debts?" Sidney nodded and denounced the politicians of the warring nations.

"They've been fighting for two years. France is hanging on at Verdun but even the papers say it's a close thing. Sounds like tens of thousands of Frenchmen and Germans were killed. It reminds me of two drunks punching each out. Neither remembers what started it but they keep swinging."

"You're right, lad, and it looks like a big navy battle happened in the North Sea. The Germans and England both say they won, but if you count the ships sunk, the Huns came out on top. Some of the men I served with are dead now, I'm sure."

"Bert, you might have been one of them. Our boys are in a big fight again at Ypres and the Brits are supposed to make a big push soon. I can't understand why everyone knows about it weeks before. Doesn't surprise mean anything anymore?"

"Well lad, the biggest surprise is that the war is still going on. I'm all for beating Germany but it will be a shitty victory if most of our young boys get killed and the country is bankrupt. Don't ever think that because you aren't in uniform, you aren't helping. Someone has to feed our boys."

"Yeah, I know, Bert, and you know what I'll say next. But ten years from now, I don't want my boy asking me, what did you do in the war daddy, and my answer is, swathing grain."

"Listen up, lad. At least you'll still be here in ten years. John MacDonald will still be dead. I'm proud of you, boy. Don't ever think you're a coward. Finish your drink and we'll say good night so you two can do what newlyweds are supposed to be doing."

Chapter Fourteen

The summer slowly wore away. Emma and Sidney settled into their routine as man and wife. After completing a bountiful harvest, they visited Florence and Alexander for Thanksgiving dinner. The rich aromas of a lavish turkey dinner greeted them at the door.

"Do you smell that?" asked Emma. "No way our turkey would smell that good if I cooked it."

"That's because I would have distracted you and while we were busy, supper would have burned to a crisp."

"Sidney!" Alexander boomed. Taking Sidney's arm, they went to the living room. "I'd like you to meet Mr. Arthur Meighen, our Conservative Member of Parliament. Arthur, this is our son-in-law, Sidney Turner, from Shilo."

The dark-haired Mr. Meighen was of medium height. His suit and polished shoes spoke of a man accustomed to success. Sidney wondered at the reason for the man's presence.

"A pleasure to meet you, young man. Alexander tells me you have a farm and serve at Camp Hughes too."

Sidney provided a quick overview of his activities and expressed appreciation that Canada had provided him with such opportunity.

Since Mr. Meighen did not plan to stay for dinner, he quickly came to the point. He always prospected for young men to join the political party and perhaps stand for election. Hard-working young men like Sidney made ideal candidates.

"Manitoba became a province nearly fifty years ago. For me though, one disappointment is the lack of progress at bringing the white man and Indian closer together. We wanted to integrate Indians into our society but for the most part, we are failing. Maybe it will take several generations and the passing of those, both white and red, who still remember the old ways."

Sidney listened but did not understand why Mr. Meighen would speak to him of such things. Seeing Sidney's puzzled look, Mr. Meighen explained.

"We need bright young men in politics. I mentioned the failure to bring Indians closer to our society because you married into a family of mixed blood. When Alexander married Florence, most whites thought he had lost his mind.

"Sidney, you married a beautiful young woman because of who she is. I think you could help bridge this gulf between the white and red man. Please consider joining our political party, and after the war, consider standing as a candidate for Member of Parliament."

The notion took Sidney completely off guard. Government was far removed, both physically and from his day-to-day life. He had enough to think about without involving himself in the affairs of government.

"Well, sir, what you are talking about is as far from my thoughts as the moon. My plans are to raise a family and pass the farm to my children. Government is a long way away for me." Mr. Meighen nodded in understanding but pressed his point.

"Years of dealing with people with conflicting ideas wears down a man. Fresh blood keeps people thinking and that is the reason I hope you will think about it." He rose to bid farewell and shook hands with Sidney.

"It has been a pleasure to meet you, son. The older generation worries about the younger generation running the country, but you have renewed my hope. After all, your generation did not get us into this war, even if it's the young men who are dying."

Sidney went into the kitchen and though Florence stood with her back to him, he knew she was smiling.

"I've thought about how you can help our people. We talked to Mr. Meighen the last time he was in town and that is why he wanted to meet you."

"So, mom. You talk about me behind my back?" Florence nodded and kissed his cheek.

"Of course, precious boy. I want you to do this because it will take special white men to change things. I hope one day you can be a powerful man in government. So please stay out of the army. You have more to offer than your life."

Back at the farm, Sidney spoke with Bert about the conversation with Mr. Meighen. If he were elected to government office, that meant absences of several months in Ottawa. It was only fair to discuss the notion with his best friend.

"Lad, is there no end to surprises with you? Member of Parliament, the Honourable Sidney Turner. It has a noble ring, does it not? Should your subjects refer to you as sir?"

"Piss off, smart ass. I'm being serious and you're being a wanker. Being in government is the last thing I ever thought of doing. Most of those assholes aren't worth two dollars, never mind how much they're paid. Emma's mom thinks I could help the Indians."

"Lad, you've come a long way. People can tell straight off that you're honest and dependable. Seems those aren't qualities a politician needs though. Anyway, everyone knows everyone else out here so it's not like you're a stranger. If people think they need you, they will elect you. I can run the farm, and when I have questions, Percy will have answers. So, go be our representative down east. Make us proud or you'll get my boot up your arse!"

The first snow fell in November and the pace of life slowed. Sidney and Emma felt blessed but were disappointed that Emma was not yet pregnant. Neighbours said to be patient, it would happen in good time. After six months of trying nearly every day, they grew impatient.

"You'd think with all our trying, you'd have been pregnant a dozen times. I don't get it, we do it nearly every day. Good thing we're young and horny." Sidney smiled as Emma leaned against him for a hug.

"I think we need to hump at least twice a day," she teased. She loved behaving like an imp, knowing her foul language bothered him. It was also true that when she used words he frowned upon, he surrendered to an urge to ravage her.

"It's already early afternoon and you didn't even rub up against me while I washed the dishes. No wonder I can't get pregnant if my husband won't have his way with me,'" she whimpered with mock petulance.

In response, Sidney turned her to face him and hoisted her onto the kitchen counter. He gently pulled her hair back and kissed her deeply. Youthful energy took over and they shoved clear a space on the counter top. Later, gasping for breath, they clung to one another as he slowly dissolved inside her body.

"Well, my husband, do you think that will finally get me pregnant? I'd love to tell our daughter about the time her madman father screwed her mother on the kitchen counter." Sidney shook his head in mock disgust.

"We need to do it again tonight, my hot little number. Don't forget you are to produce a boy first. You're a wild one. Next thing, we'll be doing it in the barn like the farm animals."

"Well why not? After all, you are my stud."

True to their word, they made love again that night and many others that followed, hoping Emma would conceive, but each month brought disappointment.

"My darling, it's time for a check-up. It's wonderful fun trying but by now, we should have the pitter-patter of little feet."

"Well, my sweet man, maybe you're shooting blanks. If the doctor says you're the problem, I need to take a lover. I hope you won`t mind."

"Just for that remark, you're coming upstairs right now!" With a mighty heave, Sidney threw Emma over his shoulder and marched upstairs to her peals of laughter.

Several days later, a specialist in Winnipeg conducted thorough examinations and questioned them closely. He promised to inform them of his diagnosis when the test results were ready.

A letter arrived three weeks later. The test found Emma to be infertile and she would never conceive. Bitter tears stained her cheeks and Sidney held her until she fell into an exhausted sleep. An angry Sidney, whispered questions into the night air.

"I don`t get it, spirit. Aren't I supposed to be the bridge between our two peoples? What about all your talk of my unborn son? Guess you don't know any more about how the world works than me. Any time you have an answer, will be fine. Other than that, just bloody well leave us alone."

For millions of other families, the news was far worse. The bloody Battle of Verdun finally sputtered out in the rains and snows of November and December. After ten months of dreadful slaughter, the French army had pushed the Germans back to near their starting point.

The Germans original plan meant to bleed the French army to death in a merciless artillery assault. Their initial successes lured them into a false sense of success. They committed large numbers of troops to the fight, just as French resistance stiffened. On the hills around Verdun, Germany also bled.

Verdun wasn't the only tragedy. At the Battle of The Somme, the British Empire suffered nearly a half million troops killed, wounded and missing. After five months of vicious fighting, the "big push" had stalled a few miles from the starting point.

Thousands of dead khaki figures lay scattered about the landscape or hung on barbed wire. Their bodies mingled with the multitudes of German soldiers who died counter attacking. The butcher's bill eventually totalled over a million casualties. Only dreadful winter weather stopped the large-scale slaughter that men seemed powerless to end.

Huge numbers of wounded men returned home to speak of the horrors of close quarter mechanized warfare. In many small towns, the grim truth was that most of the young men who rushed to join the war in 1914, were now dead, wounded or missing.

Canada suffered heavily during the Somme offensive and new soldiers were needed to replace the dead. As 1916 gave way to 1917, talk of conscription began making the rounds of government and was reported in newspapers.

Divisions over the issue appeared along urban/rural lines and in Quebec. The predominantly French-speaking populace was largely under-represented in army ranks. Quebecers viewed the war as a foreign misadventure and many families vowed to hide their sons rather than allow them to serve. Farmers also opposed conscription knowing the policy would create further manpower shortages.

The spring of 1917 became a defining moment in Canadian history. In northern France, the Canadian Corps attacked and captured Vimy Ridge. Held by the Germans since 1914, the ridge had remained in their control despite ferocious French and British attacks. The German high command believed the ridge impregnable and they continued to fortify it.

The Canadians planned and stockpiled the myriad of equipment and supplies required for the monumental undertaking. Unlike previous attacks that merely launched troops toward the German lines, the Canadians prepared meticulously.

On April 9, in semi-blizzard conditions, Canadian troops stormed the ridge and held it despite desperate German resistance. The success earned them their reputation as shock troops and henceforth, Canadians often spearheaded British attacks.

The Germans adopted the saying, 'Prepare for the worst' when Canadians appeared opposite them. While the Canadians richly deserved their reputation, only adequate reinforcements ensured they remained a potent force. To be the sharp point of a spear that mauled the enemy, commanded a high price.

By the spring of 1917, it became obvious conscription was coming. With mounting trepidation, Sidney read newspaper editorials calling on the government to enact the legislation. He realized the time to decide about joining the army had arrived.

To be a conscript did not sit well with him. He wanted to decide for himself. In early May, he sat down with Emma.

"Rosie, we need to talk."

"This will be serious," Emma replied. "You only call me Rosie when it's tough talk time." She fixed him with a steady eye and dreaded what she would hear.

"You know all the talk about conscription. For sure, there will be an election over it, but no matter, there's too much support for it not to pass."

"Sidney, don't tell me you're going to join, or even worse, you already have."

"No, my darling, I haven't already joined. I would never do anything like that without first talking to you. When it does come, they will send a notice telling me to report wherever they want, and I don't want that. I want to choose my regiment."

"Sidney, please. You know how hard it was for me, mama and papa when Louis died. I'm just starting to feel normal and I don't want my heart broken again. Even if I can't get pregnant, let's keep trying." She smiled wanly.

"I know that, my darling. I remember when John died, even if at the time, it seemed he died for a noble cause. The war has gone on nearly three years and we don't look any closer to winning than in 1914. I don't know what it will take for Germany to surrender. Let's pray it won't take another three years."

"So, you're going to join the army. Why, Sidney? You might die and that will just leave me broken again and a widow besides," she stammered while beginning to sob. Coming around the table, Sidney wrapped her in a hug and waited for the sobs to subside before speaking again.

"Bert doesn't want me going either. He says it's up to me so let me say what I'm thinking. Want to hear?"

"The only fucking thing I want to hear is that you're staying home with me, where you belong."

"Rosie, please. If I don't go, they'll come and get me. Am I supposed to hide like a criminal? I've never done anything dishonourable and I won't start now."

"There's a first time for everything." Sidney kissed her forehead.

"Able-bodied men will have to go. If not, I might wind up in prison. Either way, my darling, your husband will be taken away from you." She began crying again but they were tears of defeat.

"I don't want to be here alone. I'm really, really scared. No, I'm terrified of losing you to this shitty war." Sidney sighed again but determined to make his point, he continued.

"The Brits made conscription law last year and we will too. Mark my words darling, they will force men to register. Then who knows where a fellow will wind up?" Emma whispered through her tears.

"At home, with his wife? What about you running for parliament and all? You can't do that or anything else if you're dead."

"In a perfect world, being home with my wife is where I would be. Too often life isn't bloody fair. Anyway, here is my idea, so please listen?" Straightening in her chair, she summoned a brave face to hear him out.

"If conscription comes, and before they send out notices, I'll join up. That way, I have a bit more say in which regiment I join rather than going who knows where."

"Well, even if I hate you being in the stupid army, that makes sense. Can you be in some part that doesn't fight? Then I'd know my husband will come home to me."

"Aha, my girl, you understand what I'm getting at. I didn't think of something like the medical corps seeing I don't know much about medicine. My thinking is being a farrier and with all this trench fighting, there aren't any cavalry charges. Think it will work?"

As Sidney predicted, later that spring the government announced conscription. As a farmer, Sidney could ask for an exemption but with Bert and hired men on the farm, he doubted he would qualify.

Days before conscription became law, Sidney saddled Albert and rode to Camp Hughes. Morning sunshine painted the sky a blue only the prairies can colour. A choir of singing birds were a stark counterpoint to the errand Sidney planned.

Reaching a crest in the road, he saw Walking Thunder's face over a line of trees. His expression was dramatically at odds with previous visions. Like a slap across the face, Sidney felt Walking Thunder's anger for his rejection of the way of peace.

'Return home. One day you will be a father.' A final warning advised that ignoring this edict would end his life and make life more difficult for those who followed. Sidney beseeched the spirit.

"I understand, but if I am from two peoples and both need my help, how can I help one and not the other?"

Walking Thunder vanished, leaving Sidney to sort out the quandary. In the end, Sidney's sense of duty and honour won over an apparition he did not fully understand.

He arrived at camp and presented himself at the recruiting tent. There he swore an oath to serve faithfully and in moments, he was no longer civilian Sidney Turner. He was now Private Sidney Turner of the Lord Strathcona Horse, and eligible for overseas service.

Chapter Fifteen

"All aboard!"

Conductors shouted over the din raised by hundreds of voices and a huffing steam locomotive. Khaki clad soldiers hoisted heavy packs. Most wore a brave face for teary-eyed women and shook hands with men. Three years of war had cured most people from any illusions of glory.

Emma buried her face in the rough wool of Sidney's tunic and struggled to hold back tears. She had no words left and heartbreak was evident on her ashen features. Her parents were grave as they recalled a farewell, three years earlier.

On that long-ago day, all cheerily waved small Union Jack flags while a band played 'God Save The King' and 'The Maple Leaf Forever.' Three years and thousands of deaths later, people realized many of those boarding the train would never return.

Bert took Sidney's hand in a crushing grip, he did not trust himself to speak. Forgetting when he last shed a tear, he fought them back. The two needed no words and Sidney drew Bert near to kiss his cheek. Desiree found a small opening to give Sidney a farewell kiss. Alexandre's tears disappeared into his grey moustache. He hugged Sidney and kissed his cheek. Sidney saw hope in Florence's eyes and over the din, she shouted in his ear.

"My child, remember our spirit's words. Do not throw your life away being a hero. That is not your path. In battle, saving your friends is the path. You will come back if you remember our spirit ancestor."

Sidney turned to take Emma in his arms. She hugged him fiercely while her hands were busy at the back of his neck. Weeks earlier, she purchased a St. Christopher charm and thin gold chain bearing the inscription 'Forever and ever, Emma'.

"It's St. Christopher and it keeps people safe on a journey. I know this isn't really a trip, but it can't hurt. Wear it every day and never take it off. My love will keep you safe until you come home to me."

She tried smiling but failed like all the others. Burying her face against him, a deluge of tears soaked his collar. There were no words, only tears and quick kisses punctuated by whistle blasts.

A piercing shrill announced it was time to depart. Sidney swung onto the coach steps and jauntily waving his service cap, disappeared inside the car. The train whistle shrieked once more and there came a clanking of wheels as the connection slack drew tight. Slowly, the cars rolled away to fluttering farewells of waving handkerchiefs. Most of the throng stared down the tracks as the cars faded into the vast Manitoba prairie.

Emma stood silently, instinct said she would never see him again. She searched her mother's eyes looking for hope of a reunion. Softly stroking Emma's hair, Florence hummed an ancient Sioux mantra for departing warriors. The chant beseeched the Great Spirit to bestow good fortune on the young man headed into battle.

"Gemma, I've sent prayers asking our ancestors to watch over Sidney. He is a special white man, and few are worthy of the protection of our ways. I cannot see the whole future, but I will know more in days to come. Be brave my angel, and trust he will come home."

Her encouraging words did not reflect the truth Florence felt but she did not want her precious child to suffer. Emma was not convinced but grasping for any hope, she accepted the spoken salve.

"My love, do you think we'll see him again?" Desiree asked Bert. "I know you pray he comes back, but what does your heart say?"

Bert continued staring down the tracks although the train was lost to view. Out of earshot from the Bias family, he shared his thoughts.

"I know him better than most. He's smart and will think things through before taking a chance. What concerns me is his temper when people get pushed around. Then he flies off the handle and comes out with all guns blazing. That will get him into trouble." He did not add *'Especially where he's going...'*

Desiree had a confession to make but did not tell Bert until Sidney departed. After bidding farewell to the Bias's, they climbed into their carriage to begin the journey home.

"I have to tell you about something I've done. I'm not sure if it was completely wrong but I need to tell you." With a sideways glance, Bert knew she would not rest until sharing her thoughts.

"It's bothered me for years I kept the kids apart. If I could turn the clock back, I would do things differently. I know Sidney is happy with Emma, but I still wonder. I would rest easier if Sidney knew the truth."

"Okay, let us hear it. As usual, I know you think you did the right thing. No matter how outrageous it is."

"Well I'm glad you know I'm always right. Every now and again, I do make a mistake, but I hope this isn't one." Turning on the driver's seat, Bert examined her with a critical eye. Desiree sounded serious and he hoped it did not mean trouble.

"When we got to the station, remember I excused myself for a minute?"

"A minute? It was nearly ten and I was about to come looking for you."

"I'm glad you didn't because that would have wrecked my plan. I sent Mystique a telegram with the train number and told her..."

"No, please don't say you told her to meet Sidney in Montreal. Don't tell me that. We know what will happen. Not a good thing to do. How do you think Emma would feel if she knew?"

"I thought about it, honest I did. It isn't right Sidney doesn't know the truth about someone he loved as much as Mystique. I leave it up to Mystique about meeting the train. Sidney won't be there long anyway if she does go."

"Desiree, Desiree, Desiree...please let this turn out the way you hope it will. I don't want to get a letter in a few weeks asking me for advice about whether he should tell Emma something."

A thousand miles to the east, a messenger boy leaned his bicycle against the railing of an unassuming apartment block. Checking the address, he ran up several steps and raised a heavy brass doorknocker. A maid in a black domestic uniform took the message and closed the door.

"Madam, a telegram for you." A telegram was unexpected, and the Brandon station struck a note of fear. Her mother was in Brandon with Bert.

'Please no, don't let anything be wrong with mama.' Standing beside a parlour window to catch a remnant of fading light, Mystique tore open the telegram.

"I owe you this and you must tell him. Sidney arrives in three days on troop train 342. Tell him the truth. Love always, Mama."

Mystique stood stock-still and looked out at the street below. Memory returned her to an evening six years earlier. Now twenty-three years old, she felt middle-aged, so much had happened in that time.

Her daughter was almost five, but cruel fortune saddled the child with physical and mental deformities. She could never live an independent life. Medical opinions believed the child would not survive to adulthood. Mystique loved her baby, but the heartbreaking situation had closed her heart. She vowed to remain chaste and not expose another child to such risk.

Mystique had focused on running the business Desiree ceded to her control. Since the war began three years earlier, business had flourished. High-ranking officers and politicians patronized the establishment and Mystique astutely invested the windfall. The war would not last forever and she had learned not to try predicting the future.

Although she had no shortage of suitors, Mystique respectfully but firmly rebuffed them. She heard whispered gossip she took only women as lovers or she awaited the return of a long-lost lover. The rumours proved convenient and Mystique did not dispel them.

However, while lying in bed late at night, loneliness visited. Her thoughts replayed the days of joyous freedom and intense passion with Sidney. She recalled the happy conversations, the sights they saw and the blazing love that lasted until dawn. Then her perfect body stirred, and she softly caressed herself.

Covering her mouth with one hand to quiet soft moans, the other brought pleasure. At times, she shed bitter tears at squandering the opportunity to win Sidney's lasting affection. After the blood cooled, she rebalanced her loneliness against finances and caring for a child against an unknown future with Sidney.

"You will soon be here again," she whispered. "I want to see you, so you know why I did not stay with you."

Lifting the burden would be a relief. How Sidney accepted her news, was his to decide. From Desiree's letters, Mystique knew Sidney had married the year before and that Emma was infertile. The irony of the situation was not lost on her.

'I lost the man I loved because a pig fathered my child. Sidney finally stops waiting for me and marries a woman who can never give him children.' Mystique believed God had punished her for practicing the profession she had been born into.

'You punish me for my sins, but why punish Sidney too? It's not his fault he loves a woman you think is evil.'

As the train rolled east through the night, men drifted off to sleep. Sidney gazed at the moonlit countryside slipping past, his thoughts a kaleidoscope. Short of actual combat, the men hoped they were sufficiently trained for the realities of a war they would soon fight.

The odds of survival were on a man's side but who survived was a game of chance. A bullet meant for one man might miss by an inch and end another life instead. Nothing could be certain, and Sidney hoped if death struck, it would be quick and offer him a chance for a proper burial.

Louis Bias remained missing and presumed dead. The chances of finding his body were practically zero. Sidney did not want the heartache over his death compounded by being one of the thousands of missing in action. He remembered the adjutant's pledge to keep him in the rear on farrier duties. *'That is until the adjutant gets blown away and the new one won't agree to me staying behind...'*

'Montreal, what a memory' he mused as the wheels brought him closer with every turn. His only night there, had been in the arms of Mystique and death alone would erase that memory.

'Well at least all we're doing there is changing cars for Halifax.' Still, it would be amazing to hold Mystique once more. He wondered yet again about her reason for leaving and if she still loved him.

Conscience tugged, knowing his marriage vows were to honour and love Emma until death do them part. He eased his inner turmoil knowing he truly loved Emma. She had been right about one facet of Sidney's life. Emma knew there would forever be a room in Sidney's heart where he housed his love for Mystique.

Affairs of the heart are often difficult to expunge, and Sidney accepted his attraction for Mystique remained. *'Thank Christ you'll never see her again. Some things will always be but that doesn't mean you have to do anything about it.'*

When he arrived in England, he wanted to visit his family. Not once had he written to let them know he was alive and well. For all his mother knew, he had fallen off the earth and vanished. He would love to see his mom, younger sisters and Albert again. There were mixed emotions about his father and brothers; some hard feelings persisted. *'Well Sid, you'll see what's what when and if you get there.'*

He fell asleep to the rhythmic rocking of the train speeding through the night. The only relief from the monotony were occasional stops for more troops to board. Sidney did not recognize anyone; the newcomers were from across the country.

The tight quarters and stuffy air did nothing to alleviate the boredom everyone tolerated. Hearing they were only twenty minutes from Montreal quelled Sidney's fear he might go mad. The day had been long with little to see except dense timber stands crowding the tracks.

After three days of bland train food, Sidney hoped for a break of several hours to find a good restaurant. The train stopped at the station and a commotion at the car entrance drew his attention. A military policeman entered and signalled for quiet.

"Listen up. Rain east of Montreal washed out part of the main line a couple hours ago." Raising his arm, he tried silencing the wild cheers.

"Sorry for the bad news but it looks like we'll be stuck here about two days while the track is repaired. I haven't heard yet about billets but I'm sure army efficiency will sort things out." Rude peals of derogatory laughter echoed through the car in reply.

"Form up on the platform outside for further orders."

They formed into ranks to learn what the army had in store. The onboard train officer had neither planned nor anticipated an unexpected exigency. It was his unfortunate luck to have spent his day playing cards and drinking whiskey. Now he was in a drunken stupor.

A wildfire rumour dismissing the men with orders to return in forty-eight hours, spread like wildfire. Like a prairie wind scattering leaves, the troops vanished before a garrison officer arrived to order them to remain on the platform.

Sidney was among those who disappeared. Having money, he wanted to stay in a hotel and be comfortable. Walking through the downtown, he savoured his short spell of freedom from orders and army routine.

His heart raced, what had been idle fantasy aboard the train, was now reality where so many thoughts dwelt. While wondering where to stay, he trusted it would be simple to find quiet lodgings.

While he walked, a slim figure discretely followed. A brimmed hat and a veil shielded the face. When Sidney paused to cross a street, the person also stopped to see where the soldier might walk. The shadowy follower was surprised when the soldier turned a familiar corner. Despite the pleading of his common sense, Sidney could not resist walking by the establishment.

'It's not like you're going to walk upstairs and ask to see Mystique. Just satisfy your dumb ass curiosity. Then go find a room and get a good sleep. Who knows when you'll sleep in a decent bed again?'

Stopping directly across the street, memory returned him to the most enchanting evening of his life.

Chapter Sixteen

"Hello Sidney." The voice he could never forget instantly rooted him to the sidewalk. Hearing the voice from hundreds of dreams brought his blood to a boil and days of endless longing vanished like a wisp of smoke in a strong breeze. Despite his leaden feet, Sidney found the strength to turn around as she raised the veil.

In an instant, their bodies crushed together, and Sidney kissed her as though he would never relax, and Mystique returned his blazing kiss. A need to breathe finally forced them to break but they held one another tightly. Finally recovering a speck of composure, Sidney gasped.

"What kind of miracle is this? I never expected to see you again. How is this possible?" Placing a finger to his lips, Mystique silenced him. She did not want the evening consumed by talk. In the morning, they might talk but tonight, she wanted to hold him close.

"No Sidney, tonight we will not talk. Please come home with me. In the morning, we can talk. I want tonight to be about making the love we have missed all these years." Completely aroused, Sidney longed to lie in her arms, but his conscience refused to allow such duplicity.

"Mystique, please no, that can't happen. I have to tell you something..." Cutting him off again, she pulled him across the street to a small café. Sitting in a dark booth, she reached across the table for his hands.

"I know what you would tell me Sidney. Please forgive me, but it doesn't matter. I broke my promise to you and now another woman shares your bed. Tonight, I want you in my bed. Tomorrow you will get on that train and go away to war. Losing you is more than I ever wanted to know about in life. There has been no other man since you."

"How can that be? I've never forgotten being with you. You're more beautiful than ever. Surely men here have gone blind."

"Sidney, I must explain why I did not come back. It's not easy but finally I can, and must." While Mystique laid down her burden, Sidney said nothing. When she shed several glistening tears, Sidney swept them away with a fingertip.

"After that horrible night with Cloutier, I wanted to quit the business. And then Bert had to bring you into my life. I loved you at first sight and I really did want to marry you. But when I found out about being pregnant, Mama said you would never forgive me."

"You had nothing to forgive Mystique. I could have said it then, and I can say it now."

"Yes, you can say it now. I'm not sure you could have accepted me being pregnant by someone else and still want to marry me."

"You don't know that, being pregnant wasn't your fault or idea." Mystique shook her lovely head at his ongoing naiveté.

"Sidney, people would say you married a pregnant whore. Between that, and mama bribing me to take over, I didn't seem to have much choice. The truth is, I felt dirty and didn't deserve a wonderful man like you. I was too ashamed to tell the truth and afraid you would hate me if you knew." She paused and weighed her choice of words before continuing.

"Sidney, my daughter was born crippled, mentally slow and cannot be left alone. I took it as God's punishment to change my ways. The thought of having another child like my daughter, drove me into celibacy. That is the reason, and because I still love you, I never took up with anyone."

"Mystique, I've never stopped loving you either. Emma knows and when she saw your picture, she understood how I fell so much in love." Mystique's eyes shone with tears and she leaned forward to kiss him.

"Sidney, I've missed you so much and I'm sorry for all the heartache. I can't make that go away. Tonight, let me show you my feelings are still alive."

"Part of me wants to say yes, but please Mystique, I can't. I promised to be faithful. Betraying that would break her heart...and mine. Please understand, put yourself in Emma's place. Tell me how you would feel if she asked me to forget about you." Mystique bowed her head and sighed in resignation.

'Him and his damned honour.' There was no getting past the logic of what he spoke. Mystique would be outraged if the situation were as Sidney portrayed.

"Hearing you speak like this breaks my heart and makes me love you more. Yes, I would be furious if another woman tried to take you into her bed, even just for one night."

"Thank you. The men on the train would think I'm crazy and trample me to be with you."

"I only want you Sidney and if I can't, there will be no one else. I threw my chance away because I was afraid." In the silence of the booth, their eyes made love and sharing sad smiles, they had no need to speak.

"I have to find a hotel room before it gets any later." Mystique regarded him wistfully.

"It's late on Friday night and the hotels will be full. Come home with me and stay in the spare room." The unspoken invitation made him uncomfortable.

"Staying at your place won't make this easier." The smoky depths in her eyes still bewitched him but she set her mouth in a firm line.

"Yes, I'm sure. Come home with me, I'll pour you a drink and make you supper. Let me enjoy your company tonight and if you change your mind..." As his face flushed, she smiled at her small triumph and pulled him outside.

In a few minutes, they arrived at a row of townhomes. Mystique climbed several steps and unlocked the heavy oak door. Inside, he saw a tastefully appointed interior of understated elegance where she lived comfortably.

Hanging his army great coat in a closet, she led him to the parlour. Lighting two long stemmed candles, her eyes sparkled in the soft glow while searching his face. Sidney saw her love and he drank in the moment of standing before this impossibly beautiful woman. With a smile, Mystique poured fine whiskey into a crystal glass.

"I understand you like Jameson's. I will be right back so make yourself at home." She sensed his embarrassment to be dressed in the rough woolen of his service uniform.

"Would you care to change Sidney? There is a pair of coveralls in the closet one of the painters left. It's not fancy but it's clean and might fit you."

"Thanks, guess if I knew ahead of time, I would have bought some normal clothes. I'm a bit embarrassed. I've had this on four days and might be a tad fragrant."

"Don't worry about that. Have a bath while I make supper and then we can talk."

Hearing the running water, she resisted an urge to sneak in on him. Sidney carefully disrobed in the bathroom, but his body remembered a night, years earlier.

"Down boy. I know what you want. I'd love to but little brain, you can't take over. Maybe this wasn't such a good idea after all... well, no shit Sherlock."

Squeezing his eyes shut, he slid into the tub. In the hallway outside, he heard Mystique's light footsteps pass the door and half hoped she would enter, half hoped she would not. Mystique smiled mischievously knowing he struggled to control his desire.

'Oh Sidney, please change your mind.'

'Please don't come in here, I won't be able to say no.' Sidney knew if she came in, his resolve would disappear like an avalanche clearing a mountainside.

The silence relaxed him while the warm water eased his tight muscles. Long days of travel caused his eyes to close but when he began snoring, a soft knock on the door startled him.

"Sidney, are you all right? Please don't drown in there. Dinner is nearly ready." Reaching for a thick towel, he dried off and wriggled into the painter coveralls.

'If you get a hard on, you'll rip this thing wide open.'

Tantalizing aromas led him down the hallway to the kitchen and he doubted a more desirable chef ever graced a kitchen. A chair creaking under his weight dashed hopes of surprising Mystique.

Mystique shot him a smile over her shoulder and his nostrils flared. Pleased with herself, she settled on a homey approach that might encourage him. Quickly setting the table, she brought their dinners and sat down.

"Thank you, Mystique, this looks delicious." In the charged atmosphere, he again regretted their parting. *'No man, no.'*

"Sidney, tell me about Manitoba. Tell me what happened after I left. How you learned to farm; I knew you would be fine."

Over a glass of wine, Sidney spoke of his life but made little mention of Emma beyond describing how they met. Mystique's eyebrows knit together and her anger over Emma's outburst was palpable. Recognizing that her reaction may be hypocritical, she said nothing.

Sidney glowed while speaking of Percy and John MacDonald and stressed he learned about farming from them. He also expressed his gratitude that because Bert fronted the purchase, they had their own farm. Mystique had long known of Bert's lucrative sideline business but kept that from Sidney. She wondered if his naivete would object knowing that illegal transactions provided the cash for the farm.

Mystique spoke about her trials and despite her child's difficulties, she felt fulfilled caring for her. The business thrived under Mystique's stewardship and she had repaid her mother's faith and generosity many times over.

"I know it's too late to wonder what might have been. I have a good life Sidney and my business does well. Despite my little girl's problems, she is the light in my heart. There hasn't been a day that I haven't wished you were her father. If it had been you, I would have married you and stayed in Manitoba. Mama might not have liked it but, no matter what, I would have been your wife."

"Mystique, I'm pissed off you didn't tell me. I might have been able to handle it and we could have had kids of our own. Ah what the hell, Desiree did the right thing. Now that I've been through a few prairie winters, I couldn't imagine you living in a farm house with me."

"Sidney, let's not talk about this anymore. Go sit in the living room and pour us a glass of wine while I clean up."

Sidney was impressed Mystique lived in a building with indoor plumbing. She always had hot water at the tap. In contrast, he drew water from a hand pump in the kitchen and boiled it on the wood stove. *'Wonder how long she would have put up with that?'*

He relaxed on the overstuffed chesterfield in the softly lit living room and drew further comparisons. Electric lighting meant no kerosene lanterns or candles.

Sidney took a long sip of wine and closed his eyes. The long travel days in cramped quarters, the fine dinner, a bit too much wine and the quiet surroundings, sent him to sleep.

Pale morning light seeped through the curtains and brought him to semi consciousness. Opening his eyes, he found himself under warm blankets in a comfortable bed. Scratching his chest, he discovered, to his surprise, bare skin. To even greater surprise, Mystique lay asleep beside him. A wayward blanket and her sheer negligee, created a physical reaction for him.

'Oh no.'

Rapidly flipping through his memory, he did not recall intimate relations. His fidgeting awoke Mystique and she offered a sleepy smile. She caressed his shoulder but did not move closer to him.

"Good morning Sidney, I hope you slept well." His discomfort was obvious, and he raised an eyebrow by way of question.

"You were sound asleep on the chesterfield, so I brought you into the governess's room. I took your coveralls off but that is all. When you go to sleep Sidney, you are really asleep."

"Thank you, I kind of remember, but it seemed a dream. What time is it?"

"Just after nine."

"What? Holy Jesus. I have to get to the station. I'll be up shit creek if the train goes without me." Mystique calmed his fears. She had already taken care of that uncertainty.

"I phoned the station and it doesn't leave until two this afternoon. That is when the track is supposed to reopen." Heaving a sigh of relief, Sidney's stomach growled. Mystique rose and putting on a dressing gown, padded into the kitchen to make breakfast.

After putting Sidney to bed, Mystique had washed and pressed his uniform. Such domesticity firmed her resolve to confront

Sidney in the morning. With one remaining opportunity to state her case, she was determined to use it.

Sidney found his clothing neatly folded and her kindness touched him. *'Ah Mystique, you're not making this any easier.'* Images of Emma's sweetness played before his eyes and cooled the growing desire. Knowing death was a real possibility in the coming months, he wanted a clear conscience.

The awkward silence while they ate pressed Sidney to leave before desire overtook good intentions. Mystique cleared the table and then sat down with a determined expression.

"Please listen to me Sidney. I love you and you still love me. You don't have to leave. Nobody knows you're here. Quebecers are hiding their sons from the army. Stay with me and be safe." Raising her hand to forestall his objections, she plunged on.

"Don't leave, not now and not ever. I know it's selfish of me. You have Emma and the farm. But if you stay, I know people who could make things easy for you. And I have money, lots of money."

Sidney felt the pull of longing but knew it could never be. Too much held him in Manitoba. He could not deny feeling cheated that Emma could never have a child, but they shared that heartache. Had fortune made him a father, he would have applied for an exemption from the army.

Emma loved him with her whole heart and their life together fulfilled him. There was no chance of him turning his back on Emma, Bert and the farm. His love for Mystique simply had to remain unfulfilled. Knowing most men would never experience the love of two such women, he felt honoured.

"Mystique, you know I can't hide here until the war ends and then for years after. Desiree and Bert would be here on the next train if the army came looking for me. Everyone would know I deserted and then what? The police would be here and what would that cost you?" His words sounded braver than he felt, and her ashen face spoke of heartbreak.

"Mystique, I'll always love you, but I can't stay here. I made promises and one is serving in the army. When the war ends, I want to come home and live as a free man. If I deserted, who knows how long I'll be a wanted man. Please accept that, it breaks my heart saying it, but I can't do this. You have to let me go my darling." Her eyes glistened hearing the unassailable truth and she whispered her reply.

"I had my chance and didn't take it. When you put it like that, I can't put you in danger. I'm losing you again but let's not be sad this morning. At least I have your beautiful memory."

France

Chapter One

"Attention!"

The sound of hundreds of boots striking the station platform followed the shouted command. A general stood on the steps of a rail car and sourly surveyed the troops before him.

Numerous faces proved they had partaken of big city temptations. Many of Sidney's comrades were downtown drinking, whoring and fighting. Jail cells were the accommodation for some who celebrated their brief taste of freedom too energetically.

"You men are a disgrace to the uniform you wear. From this moment on, you will conduct yourselves as soldiers instead of an undisciplined rabble."

The general disappeared inside a first-class coach and shouted boarding commands quickly emptied the platform. Within minutes, the train pulled out and began the last leg of the journey to Halifax.

Two days later, Sidney stood dockside before a gangway waiting to board the ship taking him and thousands of other men to England. On the bow high above, he read RMS *Olympic*. *'You're going back to the old country in fine style Sid.'*

The *Olympic* was a sister ship to the ill-fated *Titanic,* which had collided with an iceberg and sank five years before. *'Here's to hoping my luck lasts for at least another week.'* He recalled his first ocean voyage six years earlier before aboard the *Angus Celt.*

'Now you're going the other way. Might not be a millionaire yet but I'm way better off now. Not sure if I'm smarter though...might not come back.'

The troops filed aboard and found their assigned bunks. Since the men were not paying passengers and did not tip, the crew chose not to exert themselves beyond normal duties. Sidney stood at the stern railing watching the coast recede in the gathering dusk.

'Wonder if I'll ever see Canada again?' he mused while distractedly stroking his St. Christopher medallion.

Images of Emma, Mystique, Bert and his extended family in Manitoba flashed through his mind. Bert disagreed with Sidney joining the army when he had other options. However, he respected Sidney's decision, knowing he too would have volunteered were he younger.

Emma was frightened thinking of him fighting in a war that had already claimed tens of thousands of young Canadians. Every month she prayed to be pregnant knowing that would compel Sidney to apply for an exemption. Emma could not escape feeling that due to her infertility, she had failed him. While Sidney never resented Emma, he did feel betrayed by life's arbitrariness.

'Figures, I can't have a child with my wife but the other woman I love could. Christ, why does life have to be so bloody complicated?' He balanced that angst knowing he had kept his marriage vows and could return home honourably after the war.

The steel deck thrumming beneath his boots reminded him black gangs below were shovelling tons of coal. He remembered the nightmarish heat and how sweat, mixed with coal dust, stung his eyes. Still, he felt no compulsion to go below and offer his services. *'Let's hope not to get seasick like the first time.'*

Before leaving Halifax, Sidney read about a major battle near Ypres that involved the Canadian Corps. Flanders had become synonymous with bloody fighting and Sidney hoped it ended before he joined the regiment. The troops knew torrential rains had turned the battlefield into a quagmire where men drowned in shell holes and field guns sank in the mud.

The battle began in July but four months later, it had degenerated into a muddy slugging match between two cold and weary armies. Despite firing millions of shells at the Germans, and tank support for the infantry, forward progress was measured in yards.

Press reports rarely detailed the tens of thousands of dead, wounded and missing who paid the price for these measly gains.

Rumours began circulating the Canadians would move north to play a role in the madness. Their objective would be the town of Passchendaele, a name soon to be equated with the word senselessness. *'Christ let it be over before I get there.'*

The voyage remained uneventful and even the weather cooperated. Six days on, a smudge of land on the horizon indicated the trip was nearly finished. Sidney watched the land take form and he recognized the entrance to Southampton harbour.

From here, he left England six years earlier. However, he no longer thought of himself as English but rather, a Canadian. Returning to the land of his birth, felt much like returning to a foreign country, albeit a very familiar one.

'You're a Canuck now Sid, this place belongs to the past.' Through determined and disciplined hard work, he achieved more than he ever dreamt possible. None of his achievements would have been possible had he stayed in England; Canada provided the opportunity to make his dreams a reality.

"We'll soon be in Shorncliff pal," muttered a soldier standing next to Sidney. "From what I hear about Ypres, they better teach us how to walk on water if we're supposed to break Fritz's lines."

The man chuckled harshly and flicked a cigarette butt into the dark water below. Sidney grimly smiled and caustically responded.

"Yeah, sure sounds like you're right mate. Guess the shell craters are so full of water the place looks like a lake. Mud up to your arse and if you fall in a shell hole, you drown. Wonder which stunned brass hat general thought it a good place to fight in?"

Common soldiers in the ranks were not privy to the secret reports of the general staff in London. In the spring of 1917, a French offensive along the Chemin de Dames, failed with huge losses. Even before the offensive ended, many regiments mutinied and paralyzed the French war effort.

Three years and millions of deaths had not purchased victory and on both sides, many soldiers had grown disillusioned. The French troops promised to oppose any German advances but refused to take part in more senseless attacks. By a miracle, the

German high command failed to discover the demoralized state of French armies. At top-secret meetings, the British agreed to attack in the Ypres salient.

The first attacks showed great promise, but torrential rain turned the battlefield into a bottomless swamp. Artillery pieces sank into the mud after firing only a few rounds. With Herculean efforts, crews levered the guns back into position. After firing several rounds, the men had no choice but to repeat the exercise.

Soldiers huddled in trenches full of muddy, diseased water and thousands suffered from painful trench foot. Adding to the horror, thousands of corpses carpeted the mud.

Attack followed attack against German positions for little or no gain. The attackers' bravery earned their opponents respect and astonishment. Following British attacks, the Australian/New Zealand army corps tortuously inched forward toward the pulverized village of Passchendaele.

Defying all predictions, rains increased, the assault stalled in the mud and overflowing streams before the shattered town. Desperate to salvage even a symbolic triumph, the British high command ordered the Canadian Corps from France to the blood-soaked Flanders morass.

The Canadians attacked in late October, which coincided with the arrival of Sidney's reinforcement draft. Everyone heard rumours of the dreadful fighting and some were true. Most knew they might soon be there and they prayed for the battle to wind down before winter arrived.

Autumn rains falling along the English coast, heralded winter's approach. As the *Olympic* sailed into Southampton, clouds broke while a watery sun struggled to shine. After passing the Isle of Wight, the liner docked. Sidney's return to the old country included a surprising yearning to see his family.

Before that happened, he would train at Shorncliff in neighbouring Kent. Most men of the reinforcement draft were new to army life and the training would further prepare them for the brutal realities of trench warfare.

Sidney had prior training at Camp Hughes in Manitoba and for the most part, this was a refresher course. *'Let's hope this refresher takes the rest of the war.'* After completing their training, most of the men would enjoy a short leave. After that, they would cross the English Channel and come face to face with the war.

Company by company, the men marched to waiting trains that delivered them to camp several hours later. Heavy rain began the moment the men left the train, and all were soaked when they marched through the gates.

Grouse as they might, the situation was far better than from three years earlier when chaos reigned primarily because of poor Canadian and British planning. Troops were bivouacked in tents for weeks during one of the worst autumn rains in recorded history. Thousands became sick and many feared they might perish before facing the Germans.

Learning such painful lessons led to improvements as the war dragged on. Proper shelters, mess halls and indoor classrooms for specialist trades training were built. On the firing ranges, men learned about the intricacies of this new form of warfare.

Sidney was billeted in a hut with other men of the regiment's replacement draft. Sitting on a bunk, he sorted his kit and hung the wet coat and trousers to dry. In the dank atmosphere, he doubted anyone might be dry again.

The funk created by all these men, wet uniforms and muddy boots nearly made him gag. Driving rain hammering the hut's western façade provided a small mercy by allowing them to open east-facing windows.

"Close the door asshole!" greeted a wet and dishevelled soldier as he entered the hut. Sidney sat at the far end and saw the man questioning several troopers. They pointed in his direction and the soldier navigated along the crowded aisle.

"Private Sidney Turner?"

"Yeah, what do you want with me mate?"

"I'm to fetch you to the adjutant's office right away. Don't know how you managed to get his attention so quick seeing as how you just got here. Better that's your problem than mine but come along smartly."

Slogging through the driving rain on a gravel path, they reached a hut with a white board sign announcing various battalion offices. Opening a door, the guide beckoned Sidney to enter and the man smiled.

"Good luck mate, whatever you've done to wind up here already."

Peering down the hallway, Sidney saw several doors and walked along until he found the adjutant's office. Knocking on the glass-paned door, he entered and saw several clerks typing or answering telephones. The room had an air of efficiency that spoke of important proceedings. A corporal glanced at Sidney and nodded for him to speak.

"Private Turner reporting as ordered sir." The clerk smiled patiently. *'When will these recruits learn?'*

"Private, I don't know how long you've been in this army but surely by now, you know not to address a corporal as sir. Corporal works every time."

"Yes corporal, I know that, but I've not been ordered to the adjutant's office before. Can you tell me why I'm here?" A familiar voice pre-empted the corporal's reply.

"Corporal Higgett! Send in Private Turner and then close the door if you would please."

The voice belonged to Major Steele, now the leader of the farrier-training program. With a smile, the major extended his hand.

"An officer does not normally shake hands with an enlisted man, but this is different Private Turner."

"Well sir, it's certainly a surprise to see you again. It's been some time since I last saw you at Camp Hughes."

"It has been a long time, too long. You know how time flies when you are having fun? Not that the last two years were fun, much of it has been dreadful. However, let's not scare you off before you cross the Channel. Stand at ease, there are a few matters I want to discuss with you."

Sidney worried about being brought up on charges for disappearing in Montreal although that made little sense. If that were the case, his welcome would have been a provost marshall, not an escort to the adjutant's office.

'Let the major do the talking. Play dumb and you should be able to walk out of here without going to jail.'

"First, let me congratulate you on being promoted to corporal. When I saw your name on the new draft list, I spoke with the colonel and he agreed to promote you."

"Yes sir. And thank you, sir."

"You did a fine job in Canada and your joining the army meant something to us. We haven't operated most of the war as cavalry because of this infernal trench fighting. Winter has ended large operations and we, and the enemy, will take time to rest and recuperate. I'm sure you know about the Flanders battle. Officially it's known as Third Ypres though most call it Passchendaele."

"Thank you for your kind words, sir. Yes, I heard about the battle. It sounds like it was tough going."

Widespread opinion held the fighting was a senseless slaughter. Some believed the Allies must be trying to lose the war by conducting such a battle.

"You spoke carefully corporal. Well done. So long as you are respectful, you may speak your mind with me."

"Thank you, sir."

"The Flanders battle made little sense to me and most of my fellow officers. Rumour has it General Currie and Field Marshall Haig had a serious disagreement about committing the Canadian Corps to this mess. Between us, the Brits, the Aussies and New Zealanders, we did push the Germans back several miles from Ypres. I suppose that is one positive result for our efforts."

"Well, sir, gaining a few miles for all those casualties does not seem much of an accomplishment. Most men I spoke with believe it should have stopped when it turned into a mud bowl."

"I can't disagree with you corporal. I spent several weeks there with the Princess Patricia's Canadian Light Infantry during the battle. There is no way our regiment could operate there as a mounted unit, so I went on a look and learn basis."

"You're lucky to be here, sir."

"Yes, I had some close calls although I didn't get away untouched. Got a mild case of trench foot even if, as an officer, I could dry my feet every night. Little wonder so many of our men have it. I've just enough time to get caught up here because I'm going back to France around Cambrai.

"Anyway, it's best not to say too much more. Some of my fellow officers don't think it proper to speak so freely to an enlisted man. Please keep my comments to yourself?"

"Certainly sir, I appreciate you sharing your views. It gives me an idea what to expect hearing from someone who was there. Sir, is my promotion why you ordered me to your office?"

"No, it isn't. Most of the regiment is in France now, just south of Ypres. Now that America is in the war, large offensives are undoubtedly in the planning stages for next year. If it gets back to being a war of movement, the cavalry will return to traditional uses." Sidney guessed where the conversation was heading.

"We need to get back to form and that's why I summoned you. You will be a farrier again and perhaps do some instructing. But you must finish your own training before Christmas. When you complete the course, you will be given a one-week pass. Then you go over and join the regiment. All understood corporal?"

"Yes sir. Thank you for your confidence and the Christmas pass. I hoped to have time to visit my family here."

Sidney had trained in Canada but spent little time firing a rifle. He now hoped to achieve the fifteen rounds per minute standard set by the professional soldiers of Britain's pre-war army. Their expertise with the Lee Enfield rifle had become legendary at the battles of Mons and First Ypres in 1914.

Sidney's prowess with the weapon surprised both himself and his instructors. Upon attaining the fifteen rounds a minute goal with a high degree of accuracy, the rifle instructors urged him to train as a sniper. *'Lay out in no man's land, in the mud, hoping I don't get shot? Screw that.'*

He sailed through the four-week course with positive reports posted to his service file. After receiving the week-long pass, he prepared to face his family after a six-year absence.

Carefully packing his kit bag with a change of uniform, he brought cash too. In London, he bought some civilian clothes and Christmas gifts for his mother and two younger sisters. He wondered if his brothers were at home and whether his father would allow him in the house.

Chapter Two

The next morning, a husky soldier intently eyed his surroundings from the carriage platform. His collar and shoulder badges identified him as a Canadian but rarely were 'colonials' seen in this small English town. Swinging down from the carriage, the soldier began walking to the nearby town of Chinnor.

Sidney saw little had changed and reminded himself the pace of change here was glacial. Except for the occasional automobile passing through, people from two centuries earlier would immediately recognize the place.

It was a stark contrast to Canada. Two hundred years earlier his farm was home to Indians and buffalo. Only a generation earlier, his farm had not existed. By comparison, stone fences bordering the English fields were hundreds of years old.

He reached the road leading to his boyhood home and rounding a bend, saw the shop and living quarters above. Wishing to hold the moment, he stood quietly for a moment beside a hedge. Six years away had softened his attitude toward his father and he wanted to see everyone again.

The house looked smaller and he marvelled that eight people once lived in such cramped quarters. Life on the open prairie made him forget the scarce living space in the old country.

Firmly knocking on the thick wooden door, he waited for it to open. For several moments, he heard nothing but then came tentative footsteps. How odd. The girls always rushed to answer the door. It finally opened part-way and a grey-haired woman peered around and stared at him.

"Yes, what do you want?" his mother asked in a shaky voice.

'What the hell is going on here?' Why was his mother frightened and hiding behind the door?

"Ma! It's me, Sidney. I've come home to see you," he boomed. Her expression changed from suspicion to bewilderment and then tears. Crossing the threshold, he swept up his mother like a child and held her close. As emotion overcame Emily, she began sobbing.

Her cries carried inside, and two young girls charged to the doorway. Seeing this uniformed man holding their mother was completely unexpected. He looked familiar but due to recent events, it appeared a cruel joke was playing out.

Sidney was just a distant memory to Victoria and Constance. He left so long ago, it seemed he never existed. Sidney was only seventeen years old when he left and just beginning to grow into full manhood.

Six years later, he was a muscled young giant of six feet, two inches. The girls stood with mouths agape realizing their mother's tears were joyful rather than sad. They were still uncertain about the man, but his features marked him as family.

Smiling broadly, Sidney beckoned the girls to come to him. The smile masked his surprise to see the girls so thin and pale. Their grey frocks were threadbare, patched many times and far too small. Emily obviously still ruled though. The girls were clean, and their auburn hair was neatly brushed.

Earlier in the year, Germany commenced open warfare on all shipping in waters around the British Isles. For a period, so many ships were lost that England stood on the brink of defeat. After introducing the convoy system, sufficient supplies now reached England, although shortages continued.

A blessing lay hidden within the submarine terror when the United States declared war on Germany. America repeatedly warned Germany to halt the policy when U.S. ships and lives were lost in the surprise torpedo attacks. In April 1917, America finally entered the war and it was only a matter of time before the Allies achieved victory.

However, it still shocked Sidney to see the girls and his mother in such a condition. Beyond the scarcity of young men, Sidney had not seen shortages in the land of plenty known as Canada.

"Come on, Vic and Con. It's been a long time, but don't you remember your brother, Sid? Come on, let me give you a big hug."

The girls looked at one another and encouraged by their mother, shyly crossed the hall. Sidney hugged both girls and caught the scent of soap in their long hair. It had been a very long time and he had missed them.

For their part, the girls had all but forgotten Sidney. They were young when he left home and over time, they rarely heard his name. They grew accustomed to a family dynamic of two parents and only three older brothers, not four. Upon first sight of Sidney, they thought their brother Thomas had returned.

"Sidney, I can't believe you're home. I've been so worried about you. All this time and not a word about or from you. How could you stay away so long and not even write us?"

"Mom, that was wrong and I'm sorry to worry you. I'll explain in a bit. Where is everyone else?" The question opened a world of heartache millions of homes had experienced during three years of war.

A man's voice answered part of the question. Sidney's brother Reg looked up at Sidney from his wheelchair with a smile of sorrow and resentment. The moment felt awkward until Sidney shook his brother's hand.

"Hello Sid, good to see you. Guess you can see things have changed a bit for me. Maybe I should say things have changed completely for us in the last while."

Reg wheeled around, and they followed him into the kitchen. Putting on the kettle for tea, Reg motioned the others to sit at the table. Emily had begun crying again and Sidney knew at least one of the family was dead. After asking Constance to let the others know about Sidney's return, Reg began to talk.

"Things went well for us after you left, Sid. We opened another shop and then the war started. Right away, there were shortages of beef, mutton, sugar and such things. It was tough to make a go of things when we couldn't get meat to sell and make a go." The contrast between Canada and England was stark and Reg continued the story.

"There were calls to join up and many lads did. You know, do your bit for king and country. Thomas joined right away and people coming in the shop always asked when I would go. A man can only hear so much of that so finally I joined the navy. Can you believe that? Me, afraid of water and here I am in the bloody navy?

"I wound up on the Lion below decks in the midship turret powder room. We didn't see much action because Jerry wouldn't come out and fight. That changed at Jutland when a German shell hit our turret. The flash went down the barbette tunnel and killed most of the men there.

"I was lucky, if you can call losing your legs lucky. The explosion knocked a shell over and crushed my legs at the knees. The ship's surgeon cut them off before I bled to death and that was the end of my war." He finished his story bitterly, but Emily stirred and spoke up.

"You be grateful you made it home alive Reg. It's far more than your brother Thomas got for his efforts." Reg's face reddened, and he nodded in agreement before softly speaking again.

"You're right, mom. Sid, Thomas got killed last year on the Somme, at least we think he was. I only just got home and a few weeks later, we got a telegram saying he was missing." Sidney offered a sliver of hope.

"Reg, maybe he was wounded, and the Huns have him." The others shook their heads sadly and Reg deflated that hope.

"We all hoped that too, Sid, but too many notices have gone out to have much hope. A month later, one of his mates wrote us a letter from a hospital here in England saying Tom and his platoon were wiped out in Mametz Wood. A Hun machine gun got them, but his pal couldn't get their bodies. For now, the army has listed them as missing in action. Bastards couldn't tell us the fucking truth."

Glancing at Emily, Sidney's shock increased seeing his mother's reaction to such profanity. Where once Emily would have used a switch on Reg for such language, she now merely nodded. Times had indeed changed when she tolerated profanity in her home.

"Sorry to talk that way, guess you could say I've got a bit of anger in me these days. That isn't all either, Sid."

Halting footsteps on the stairs ended further comment. Sidney stood when another man entered the room. At first glance, he did not recognize his younger brother, Albert. Through his terrible disfigurement, Albert was smiling at Sidney. Switching a walking cane to his left hand, Albert extended the right.

"Hello Sid, always knew you'd come home sooner or later," he said in a laboured voice.

Sidney carefully shook hands before embracing his frail younger brother. To see Albert in such condition was doubly shocking. Albert had shown signs of becoming a strong young man just like Sidney. Albert's army service permanently changed his life and broke the heart of his family.

After Thomas's death and Reg's traumatic injuries, Albert could not overcome his anger with the Germans. Despite the frantic pleas of his parents, he joined the army to avenge his brothers.

In the spring of 1917, the British army attacked around Arras, France. Several days after the first assault, Albert and his battalion went over the top to exploit gains achieved through the initial attacks.

Braving withering German fire, surviving members captured a length of enemy trench. While they consolidated the position, German infantry counter-attacked. As Albert's platoon set up their machine gun, several shells exploded. Albert survived only because the men standing in front of him took most of the blast.

Knocked unconscious, he lay under mangled bodies when the Germans attacked. When their attack was repulsed, the Germans shelled the British with mustard gas. When this gas contacted flesh, it caused painful skin blistering and burns.

Fortunately, for Albert, the dead bodies shielded him from a lethal dose of gas, but it clung to his exposed flesh. When the Germans retreated, British reinforcements began clearing the trench. It was too dangerous to leave the trench and the men simply hurled corpses over the back edge.

"Fuck me, mate. Look at this poor bugger's face. Lucky he's a goner, he would be a freak if he lived." The two men picked Albert from the tangled mess and went to heave him out.

"What the hell? The poor bastard is alive. Jesus Christ, now what do we do with this mug?" They waited several hours until night fell, and stretcher-bearers took Albert to an aid station. Albert would survive but bear scars and physical difficulties for the rest of his life.

The room fell quiet. One brother was dead, one an amputee, one horribly scarred and frail. Only Sidney remained whole. He knew they would think him mad to risk life and limb after seeing the cost his family had paid. Perhaps he had made a huge mistake by not applying for an exemption. While he sat deep in thought, another person entered the room. Silently watching Sidney was his father.

Thomas's appearance shocked Sidney. He looked to have aged twenty years. His black hair had gone silver and thin. Years of toil and loss had taken their toll.

Crossing the kitchen, Sidney reached out to hug his father. Thomas flinched and relaxed only when Sidney did not strike him. Sidney held Thomas several moments before planting a kiss atop his father's head.

"Hullo, Dad, good to see you. Truly, I mean it with all my heart. Sorry for leaving the way I did and not writing so you knew I was alive. I hope all of you will forgive me."

Unable to contain his emotion, Sidney began crying. The sight of his aged parents, crippled brothers and hungry sisters overwhelmed him. His emotion stirred the others and they gathered for a family hug.

Tears were a perfect icebreaker and the day passed in harmony. After abundant prodding, Sidney spoke of his life, marriage and good fortune in Canada.

"Glad to hear it and I'm proud of you, son," Thomas offered. "The odds were not in your favour when you left even if you had more money than I knew about." Emily smiled at the reference to her giving money to Sidney.

"Never mind that, Thomas. A mother's love is nothing to trifle with. You must know that by now."

"Yes mother, I finally know that. I'm glad one of our family struck it rich."

"Well dad, I wouldn't exactly call it rich. If not for meeting Bert, things would be quite different. Still though, I can't deny things have gone well. You can't imagine the size of Canada and how much land is there for people to live on and farm.

"Over here, the overnight train from London to Edinburgh is a long journey. The train from Montreal to Winnipeg takes four days and that is only half-way across the country. All I saw for days was trees. Just when it seemed I might never see open land again, along comes Lake Superior, which looks like an ocean."

"What about wild Indians and wolves? It must be dangerous over there. Do you have a rifle? Can you get food?" Albert asked. Sidney tried to hide a smile but failed.

"No wild Indians or wolves, at least not around the farm. And I haven't gone hungry either. Anyway, let me tell you about my wife, Emma." Filled with excitement, the girls begged for details.

"Is she pretty? How did you meet her? Does she have a big family? Do they have servants?"

Taking a wedding photo from his wallet, he showed it to everyone. The girls curiously examined the photo and squealed in delight seeing Emma's sweet features. Emily looked up in quiet satisfaction with a question in her eye and Sidney felt certain he could guess it.

"Well, you can see how pretty Emma is. Her family is smaller than ours and they don't have servants. Ma, I see you're wondering. She is half-white and half-Indian."

Everyone looked surprised, his father and brothers with a touch of disapproval, but they held their opinions. Sidney anticipated such a reaction; it was also common in Canada. His brothers appeared more curious than judgemental and neither could believe Emma's native ancestry.

"Her father, Alexander, is white and a trader for the Hudson Bay Company, which you know about here in England. Her mother's white name is Florence Helen and she is Assiniboia Sioux. That tribe is part of the Sioux you've maybe heard about." Reg then asked Sidney a history question.

"They were the ones doing most of the fighting out in the wild west, right, Sid?"

"Well, they certainly put up the biggest fight. Her mother's father was a Sioux warrior who was killed at the Little Big Horn, Custer's Last Stand. Emma's mom was about eight and she remembers things about her dad. I can't remember how to pronounce his name but in English it means Walking Thunder." Incredulous, Thomas guffawed and asked.

"What kind of name is that?" Sidney's face stiffened at the question.

"Dad, Indians take their names differently than us and when you know the reason, it makes sense." Feeling somewhat intimidated, Thomas shrank back. Sidney spoke of Emma's family history, Indian beliefs and stories about their past.

"They even know how to read and write, and they live in a real house in town." Emily blushed and took his hand in apology.

"I'm sorry for what I was thinking. Emma is lovely, and I hope she makes you happy." After kissing her cheek, Sidney shared his only disappointment with married life.

"She is a wonderful girl Mom and I'm very happy, but she can't have children. The doctor says it's a problem that can't be fixed. Emma cried for days and said I could divorce her, but that's not happening. It's not her fault she can't have a baby. When I get home, we'll adopt a baby."

Constance looked at the picture again and asked a question reflecting her tender years.

"She's very, very pretty just the same. Does she have a brother who could marry me and take me over to Canada?" Normally such a question might be amusing but the times were not normal.

"No little sweetheart, she doesn't have a brother you can marry. Her brother Louis died in Belgium two years ago when the Huns used poison gas."

"Hope that answers these socialist bastards screaming for the war to end, and never mind if the Germans started it" Reg opined.

"They ignore that the bastards invaded France and Belgium, slaughtered old people and children, shot nurses, sank ocean liners, bombed London, used poison gas, shelled our coastal towns and sink unarmed merchant ships. Do they want the Kaiser sitting in Buckingham Palace?" Murmured approval circled around the table that ceased when Emily held up a hand.

"Reggie, my heart will always ache over how our family has suffered. One of my sons is dead and two are crippled. Today a long-lost son returns home in a uniform. I cannot believe rational men could not stop this slaughter with a few words." Reg went to speak but Emily silenced him with a glare.

"Hear me out. It's all well and good saying we must defeat Germany but at what cost? When all the young men are dead? When nations go bankrupt? When nothing is left for the future? We must learn how to get along without killing millions of people. If this war will really end all wars, then yes, we must win. Otherwise, let it stop now."

Silence followed for several moments following the short speech. Emily rarely spoke of politics but many women in the warring nations were now speaking out against the war and the immorality of sacrificing an entire generation.

Censors tried sanitizing the war but hundreds of thousands of wounded men returning home, told the true story. Millions lay dead, their bodies ground into the mud without a trace.

"You speak the truth my dear. Too bad women like you are not running the governments" Thomas offered while turning to Sidney.

"I'm glad you've come home son. I'm proud you're in uniform but worried you won't come back safely. Promise you won't be a hero?"

"No heroics for me, I promise." Remembering the charm Emma gave him, he fished it out from under his collar and Victoria held it close to read aloud.

"Forever and ever, Emma. Your wife gave you that, so you'll remember her?"

"Yes, she gave it to me when I left, and I never take it off. Every day I think of her so far away. But back to what you said Dad, I've not exactly been trained as a front-line soldier," he partially fibbed.

"I worked for the army teaching men how to be farriers and when I joined, they left me doing it."

Smiling at the white lie, Albert nodded. Sidney had trained for trench warfare and his brothers knew it, but the gentle falsehood comforted Emily.

"Well, I shan't worry so much then, dear, if you are not in the front lines. We've had enough heartbreak in this house."

Chapter Three

Three months later, the Germans launched their largest offensive since the outbreak of war in 1914. With Russia withdrawing from the war, it allowed Germany to transfer a million men to the Western Front. Their first blow fell on the British in northern France and a break through to the English Channel appeared imminent. It was Germany's last bid to win the war and both sides knew it.

The commander of British Empire troops, Field Marshall Sir Douglas Haig, ordered his soldiers to fight where they stood. The troops obeyed and died by the thousands, but their sacrifice ensured thousands of German soldiers also died in the desperate fighting.

Sidney's reinforcement draft of men for the Lord Strathcona Horse reached France and was bound for the British lines near Amiens. The men were packed into cattle cars pulled by a huffing steam engine.

They had no idea where they were, and the only constant was an unceasing rumble of artillery. Each minute the train plodded east brought the sound of guns closer. No longer was it a murmur over a distant horizon. Sidney heard the roar of heavy guns and saw muzzle flashes outside the rail car walls.

Everyone knew of the desperate fighting as Empire troops struggled to slow the German advances. Most men rated their odds of survival as low, but with few exceptions, they were grimly determined to meet their enemy in battle.

Shortly after midnight, the train mercifully creaked to a stop. Hours of being crammed like sardines in a tin left Sidney's legs painfully cramped. He wearily clambered to the muddy ground and hefted a heavy pack. While the calendar proclaimed it was spring, cold rain and sleet pelting the men contradicted that fact.

Their woolen great coats soaked up rain and made for an unwelcome burden. The choice was throw away the coat or stay warm, but struggle under the weight. More experienced men knew the coats doubled as a blanket when they finally got to sleep.

Wherever that might be, it would not be in warm, dry barracks. With a bit of luck, a barn filled with straw might be their shelter while mice foraged in their packs. If luck were in short supply, bed might be a hole scraped in the wall of a muddy trench with rats for company.

Luck was on their side that dreary evening. After a short march, the platoon entered a stout barn. Shucking off their heavy packs and greatcoats, the men settled in for a well-deserved sleep. Veteran soldiers heated tins of stew. Experience taught their next chance for warm food might be days away. Sidney viewed the rations with distaste and his reaction earned him laughter.

"Turn your nose up now if you want, boy. In a couple days, you'll be hunting in your pack for another tin of Mac!" Knowing the man spoke the truth, Sidney sat down to heat a tin of the greasy bully beef. Rain and sleet accompanied the continuous artillery fire. After eating, most of the men wrapped themselves in greatcoats, and burrowing into the straw, they fell asleep.

Sidney restlessly tossed and turned while scratching the lice in his crotch and armpits. After an hour of fruitlessly striving for relief, he rose to stand in the doorway and look at the night. The small village was far enough behind the lines not to be endangered by German artillery. He felt the turmoil of a world gone mad, of ordinary men killing one another simply because they wore different coloured clothing.

A mile to the east, a battery of heavy guns fired on distant German positions. Faint flashes on the far horizon proved the Germans were answering. Fingering Emma's medallion he wondered, *'How many poor bastards are dying out there in all that tonight? Sid, old boy, you'll soon be hoping to dodge all that shit so let's hope your luck holds.'* Returning to the straw, he kissed the charm and pulling close his damp greatcoat, fell asleep.

Rough calls roused the troops to fall in before dawn and prepare for inspection. An officer checked each man's orders and directed him where to report.

Sidney would rejoin the regiment somewhere to the east near Moreuil Wood. Rumour was the Canadian Cavalry brigade had charged heavily armed German troops at the wood. Casualties of men and horses were high, but their valour had stopped the German advance. If even half the rumours were true, Sidney would have a great deal of work repairing the cruelties of war.

The men began marching toward the front lines. Several hours later, Sidney reached the regiment and immediately went to work. The long hours his specialized work demanded, meant time flew by but he did not begrudge the pace. He cared deeply for the horses and did his best to help the regiment recover from their recent battle.

Tending the innocent horses became Sidney's oasis of tranquility during this human madness playing out in the fields of northern France. He trimmed and shoed hooves, massaged leg muscles and groomed when time permitted.

Try as he might, Sidney could not contain his morbid curiosity to see actual front-line trenches. He had trained in Canada, England and France and now he wanted to see it. His regiment was close enough to the front lines for long-range German guns to inflict harm, but he had not yet come under direct fire.

This part of France had witnessed vicious fighting during the Somme battles of 1916. The troops cleaned out old trenches, placed new duckboards and strung barbed wire. More bloodletting would take place on this tortured landscape.

Early one evening, an officer walked through the stabling area looking for volunteers to carry supplies forward. Before the old hands could stop him, Sidney raised his hand and volunteered.

"You dumb shit, you've been around long enough to know you never volunteer," came a whisper of disgust. Another low voice chimed in to berate Sidney for his foolishness.

"Got a death wish, dumb ass? Better learn quick, asshole. That is, if you live through it. You'll be taking wire up and then go on a wiring party, you bloody big ox. Then you'll see how smart you are...asshole. For the love of Christ, Turner, I thought you were a bunch smarter than that." In protest at the verbal hectoring, Sidney spoke up.

"I've been in the army over a year and all I've done is look after horses. Lots of men have done their bit and I've never even seen a German." Muffled laughter was his reply.

"Hey Marty, asshole says he's never seen a Jerry. Can you believe this shit? Listen, bud, I've been here nearly three years and the only Huns I've seen were dead, which suits me fine. Way better those bastards than me. Keep your head down, shut your yap or get a bullet in the head." Sidney's dull stare proved the message was getting through, but the harangue continued.

"Never mind getting it in the head, get in the bag. If you screw up, some poor bastard who's doing things right might get it instead. If that happens, one of his buddies might be so pissed off, you'll get a bayonet up the ass as payback. So, Mr. 'I've never even seen a German', don't screw things up tonight."

With that advice, Sidney followed the officer. Small piles of supplies awaited, and each man would carry at least one article. A sergeant saw Sidney's size and, as predicted, he was given a roll of barbed wire. He made the mistake of easily hoisting the wire and the sergeant gave him a box of machine gun ammunition.

'Jesus Sid, no wonder those guys think you're stupid! Didn't take you long to prove them right. Stow the heroics and pray you live to morning.'

The men inched forward and descended into a zig-zag trench where another sergeant halted them. Putting a finger to his lips for quiet, he inspected each man. Anything that might clink, they left behind and removing their steel helmets, the men donned green woolen toques. A tin of burnt cork passed along the line for each man to blacken his face.

There followed another signal for silence because the communication trench ended at the actual front line. The only sounds were muffled breathing and the tread of boots on wooden duckboards as they struggled forward. Star shells randomly fired into the night sky and everyone froze in their tracks. Out here, the training paid off. Apart from the occasional bark of a howitzer to the rear, there was little noise.

In the rear areas, Sidney occasionally caught the scent of death, but it surrounded him here in these front-line trenches. The very atmosphere seemed to be an oily, invisible vapor that stuck to a man's face and refused to be washed away.

The stench of decaying bodies defied description. The dead littered no man's land and few men risked leaving a trench to bury them. Thousands of men were dying in the titanic struggle raging across northern France. Sidney would come to ascribe the stench as a giant scavenging animal that feasted on corpses before belching putrid and astonishingly pungent stomach gases.

The reek of death was not just that of men. Thousands of horses, farm animals and rats by the millions, were also victims of this frenzied human madness. To the disgust and horror of all soldiers, rats gorged on dead men, burrowing under uniforms and gnawing until only bones remained.

The stench nearly brought up his dinner. Stopping in his tracks to gulp air, he forced his stomach to settle. Ignoring the muttered curses at his back, Sidney willed his body not to betray fear and loathing.

Just when he felt the worst had passed, a man in front vomited and Sidney automatically followed suit. Several other men threw up which elicited an outburst of fierce anger from the sergeant. Bullying his way along the trench, he berated the sheepish men in a ferocious whisper.

"You candy ass fuckers! Get used to that stink, that's all there is in this shit-hole country. Couple of days ago, a horse spooked, ran up here and got killed by shrapnel. Between the sun, rats and goddamn flies, it stinks like hell. There's dead Huns, too, and the sausage-eating bastards stink after a couple days." One of the men retched again and vomited on the sergeant's boots.

"The only way you could be more goddamn pathetic is if you were all girls! You assholes are the best Canada can send? Don't those useless recruiters know we're fighting real men?" Sidney had heard enough and though still feeling queasy, he threaded his way forward.

"Enough of your foul mouth, sergeant. I don't give a shit about your three hooks. Mouth off again and I'll kick the shit of you.

I'm here to fight the Germans but if I warm up first by kicking your ass, that's fine with me. And if I do, these guys won't back you up."

The sergeant considered bluffing his way out but thought better of it when the other men crowded round. They were not about to side against a young giant who looked big enough to thrash everyone at once. Turning away, the sergeant muttered for them to follow him.

Soon they could go no farther. One hundred yards away were the Germans. Almost immediately, a bullet thwacked a sandbag an inch from Sidney's head. A hand pulled him down onto the trench boards.

"Careful mate, you're so tall, you make a great target for a Jerry sniper," came the urgent warning. "This trench ain`t deep enough for tall buggers like you. Don't ever stand up straight again unless you need a permanent cure for a headache." It happened so quickly Sidney had no time to be scared and his saviour hollered towards the German lines.

"Missed him, you sauerkraut bastard. You've pissed off my young friend and he's coming over to kick your stinking Prussian ass!" From the German trenches came mocking laughter and a stream of unintelligible taunts. A young captain hissed up the stairs of a dugout after hearing the threats.

"Silence! Have you men lost your minds? I will shoot the next man who endangers our lives," seethed the captain. "For Christ's sake, this war is dangerous enough without asking for more."

The officer checked the trench for casualties or damages to the position. Satisfied, he beckoned several sergeants to follow him into the dugout. Before doing so, he passed word to maintain absolute silence.

A few minutes later, the sergeants reappeared with their orders. The sergeant Sidney threatened earlier, called the working party together and with great satisfaction, shared his orders.

"The captain wanted you all out straight away but with all the commotion, we'll hold off for half an hour. You fine fellows sit quietly until you're called. Oh, and by the way Turner, the captain noticed how big you are. Just the kind of man to carry wire and screw pickets into no man's land."

With a satisfied sneer, the sergeant disappeared down the firing line. Sidney sank down with his back against the trench wall and tried to avoid being riled by the cards dealt to him. His hand strayed to rub the medallion around his throat.

'Well, Sid old boy, someone has to carry the wire and guess its natural the captain figures you're just the man for the job. Especially when that cock-sucking sergeant volunteers you...'

Distant rumbling behind their lines followed the flashes of shells exploding in the distance. Conventional wisdom among the troops was "some fat ass general wants to keep Jerry awake. Meanwhile he's asleep in some fancy chateau way back." Moments later the sergeant returned and called the squad together.

"Listen up, we've got a good trench line and the bastards haven't broken through. They're just over there, mostly in those trees but they dug in to get their asses out of sight. It's goddamn dangerous so keep your heads down. You're gonna find some bodies. Most are Huns but a few of our boys are there, too.

"Now listen up. You find a breathing Hun scumbag, knife him and make bloody sure he's dead. And don't get all fucking girly. One of you has to die, and better him than you. And for Chrissakes, don't make a load of noise or the bullets will fly.

"I'll go first. Keep your bloody eyes open, don't get split up, keep close to the man in front and shut the hell up. If shooting starts, stay where you are until it stops." The sergeant saw the men nod and he hoped everyone made it back alive.

"You've all heard this before but you're gonna hear it again. If a flare goes up, drop right away or freeze. So long as you don't move, Jerry can't tell if you're a tree stump or a wiring post. If you panic and run, that's when you get a bullet in the back. You picket men might have to do it on your knees so be careful.

"Now this is the most important part. If you get lost out there, don't start calling for someone to come get you. Nobody will and all that does is give everyone a shit fit. The Germans will know a working party is out and they'll send up flares.

"Keep still and look for the North Star. If it's on your left, our trench is behind you. On the right, you've turned around so keep going straight. There's no moon and a clear sky, so no excuse for getting lost. Anybody dumb enough to get lost and wind up in a German trench, deserves what he'll get.

"When we get out far enough, I want each man to crawl the length of his body to my left. The man after him, does the same until the last man. That man taps the man to his right, all the way back to me so I know everyone's where they're supposed to be.

"Then I tap the man beside me to screw in his picket. When he's done, he taps the man to his left for him to do the same. When the last man is done, you guys tap all the way back to me. I hope nobody hits a dud shell and blows us up.

"Once the pickets are in, Corporal Turner will string the wire on the pickets until he gets to the end. Then he taps the man beside him back to me and that's the signal to get out of there. You follow each other, and I'll wait for everyone before I go back. Got that and everyone understands? No questions? Good. Let's get this done."

Everyone hoped the instructions would make more sense when they got out there. The sergeant looked back again and signalled for the men to follow him. A shallow listening post forward of the trench, allowed sentries to watch the enemy lines. It also served as a departure point to crawl into no man's land. The sergeant listened before cautiously sliding under the wire and as each man passed, a sentry whispered the password.

The only sound was sporadic artillery fire. Gunners usually did not fire into no man's land at night because each side had working parties out. That knowledge gave small comfort to men working in the dark while praying not to draw attention.

For all the bullying, the sergeant knew his business. About fifty feet out, he waited for the man behind him to draw level. Using hand signals, he directed the men to crawl to his left. He knew by the silence, that their presence remained unnoticed and he tapped the man beside him to continue.

The first man quietly screwed in a picket and tapped the man to his left. Each man followed suit and carried out his duties. The last man finished, and the sergeant signalled Sidney to string the wire.

What Sidney discovered in no man's land shocked him. Shells craters left the ground a pockmarked sore filled with metal fragments. Helmets and weapons lay everywhere. Knowing men would not discard either, it came as no surprise to see corpses. Most were Germans killed a day earlier, when they stormed the Canadian positions.

Empty tin cans, broken wooden ammunition boxes and shattered remains of farmhouses and barns littered the earth. Combined with dead bodies of men and animals, it created a reeking mess of decay and despair. Sidney thought if government leaders could experience this insanity, the war would have ended years earlier.

Sidney quickly discovered it was nearly impossible to pull a heavy roll of wire without snagging it on the myriad of obstacles. Several times he tangled an unseen object and made noise while freeing the roll.

He finally reached the sergeant, who made obvious his displeasure with a hand signal. Biting back an angry retort, Sidney could not resist offering an upturned finger in reply. The sergeant glared and waved Sidney along the line.

Carefully rising to his knees, he tied wire to a picket screw and slowly reeled out the wire. It was exhausting work and despite the cool night air, he began sweating. Reaching the next man, he stopped to regain his breath.

The man signalled his impatience for Sidney to hurry. Lying on his back, Sidney reached up and wound wire around the curled steel rod. He finished and offered an upturned finger to his impatient comrade. His impertinence angered the man, who decided not to wait. When Sidney moved away, the man tapped his mate to follow him back to the sergeant and from there, to their trench.

The need for silence meant Sidney took more time stringing wire than the others needed to screw in the pickets. Becoming impatient, no man waited upon receiving the premature return signal. Their actions went unnoticed by Sidney while he completed his task without drawing German attention.

'Christ, how bloody far do I have to go along this line? Bugger that, will I ever find the asshole sergeant and our trench?'

He reached the last man who, courtesy of Sidney's efforts, disappeared using the wire as a guide. Tying off a length of wire, Sidney snipped the wire and then grasped that he was alone in no man's land. Choking back white-hot anger, he debated whether to follow his orders and string more wire.

'Gutless bastards. Every one of those cocksuckers weaseled back. You're the only dumb bastard left out here. Maybe I should leave this goddamn wire and crawl back too. Hope I find the gap in the wire. Hope someone's waiting for me. Christ, hope I don't get shot. Wouldn't that be a bitch if the squad tells the sentry everyone's back. The sentry will think I'm a Heinie and shoot.'

Uncharitable thoughts flooded in while anger and fear crowded him. *'It won't be a pretty sight when I get back...if I get back.'* Taking several deep breaths to calm his nerves, he decided to follow orders.

'At least you can look in the mirror and know you weren't some coward who wouldn't follow orders.' His sense of duty directed him to string more wire, but events would conspire against a safe return.

Chapter Four

The Germans planned to attack at dawn. Working parties were out to cut the barbed wire guarding Canadian trenches. A faint scraping noise alerted Sidney he was not alone, and he froze. Furious whispering followed but after several moments, the scraping noise was repeated. Once again, whispering reached Sidney and then silence.

A German solider using an entrenching tool to scrape under the wire, had made the noises. Lying prone on the cold earth, Sidney dared not move and hoped the enemy soldier missed him in the dark. After gulping several times to slow his breathing, he came face to face with a huge rat.

The rodent's whiskers tickled his face and revulsion at this filthy scavenger nearly made him ill. The creatures often fed on soldiers who were too badly wounded to defend themselves. Sidney hoped his menacing glare would frighten off the rat.

A Canadian sentry also heard the scraping noise. Flares fired overhead, transformed night into day. Sentries on each side were ready to fire at anything that moved. The rat's beady red eyes were only inches from Sidney's face and it bared long yellow fangs. In that moment, a teenaged German soldier thirty feet away, panicked and ran for his lines.

Machine guns instantly opened fire and bullets spun the man around several times before he fell on the barbed wire. The firing continued, and Sidney flinched as bullets passed inches above his head.

Terrified by the gunfire, the rat vanished but Sidney was too petrified to be grateful. His bowels threatened to turn liquid as he lay with eyes shut tight. To buttress his resolve and avoid panicking, he clenched Emma's medallion and prayed.

As quickly as it began, the firing stopped. If it continued, the artillery would open fire and none of the troops wanted that.

Silence descended like a heavy woolen blanket and for a moment, Sidney thought the worst had passed.

Feeling as though he had not breathed for hours, he stiffened at hearing frantic panting. The sound nailed Sidney to the ground knowing it must be a German soldier.

'Jesus Christ! Now what the fuck am I gonna do?' The sergeant's words rang in his ears. "One of you has to die and better him than you."

'Let's hope it doesn't come to that but best be ready just in case.' Slipping the razor-sharp farrier knife from a trouser pocket, he brought it close to his chest. *'Maybe Fritz will bugger off to his trench and let me do the same thing.'*

Fate had another plan for the lost and frightened sixteen-year-old German boy crawling toward Sidney's hiding place. Willing the German to turn back failed and seconds later, the boy slid down into the shallow scrape. Gasping in surprise, the boy reached out to determine the identity of the soldier.

When hands closed around Sidney's collar, he plunged the knife into the boy's neck. A torrent of warm blood gushed over Sidney's hands. Adrenalin-fueled, he pushed the German's face into the dirt to muffle any cries. Through the gurgling breath, came a pathetic mewling that sounded like "Mootee, mootee."

The boy convulsed several times as his life force evaporated in the cool night air. Sidney squeezed his eyes shut and feverishly imagined he was home on the farm. He wanted to be anywhere but lying on this filthy battlefield.

Minutes passed and then the enormity of his action weighed on him. He had killed a human being and literally had blood on his hands. An overdose of adrenaline soured his stomach and he vomited bitter bile. Spitting out the mess, he wiped his mouth on the dead boy's tunic sleeve. Revulsion swept him again and he remained dazed and disoriented.

Ever so slowly, a sense of order re-established itself in his mind. The lifeless German soldier confirmed the hideous reality of this place as Sidney processed the event that had just occurred.

Relief that he still lived shared centre stage with sorrow he had deprived a mother of her son. He recalled his own mother's heartache over the death of a son and in the quiet moment, his emotions had time to play.

'Kill or be killed doesn't seem reason enough to take another man's life' Sidney forlornly decided.

Lying in the shallow depression, he let loose tears over the horror of killing and for a minute, sorrow left him oblivious to the world. Guilt sickened him over his relief he did not lay dead on the poisoned ground.

For all his size and enormous strength, Sidney had broken his sentimental heart. Light from another star shell only served as an unwelcome reminder of where he was. The dead German lay inches away, jammed face down into the dirt.

"I'm sorry, mate. Christ, what the hell are we doing to each other out here?" Sidney knew millions of men had slaughtered one another in the years of constant carnage. He had wondered how it might feel to pull a trigger and kill a man.

In a moment of self-defence, he answered the question of whether he could take a man's life. And the sad truth of this personal discovery was unlike anything he might have imagined.

It was one thing to squint along a rifle barrel and shoot a man at two hundred yards. Killing a man by slitting his throat, literally face to face, was intensely brutal.

Sidney might not have struggled with this burden under different circumstances. An enemy artillery barrage had not threatened him while he watched comrades blown to bits. After surviving a vicious shelling, men were full of rage. When the enemy attacked, they fought wrathfully to exact revenge for their suffering. Once the attack was defeated, the fortunate survivors leaned on one another for moral support.

Alone in no man's land, the blow Sidney had struck was very personal. There were no mates slapping him on the back in congratulation. This burden was Sidney's to deal with, but he hoped to find the trench and commiserate with his fellows.

'And when I find that gutless sergeant...'

Another star shell lit up the night and the dried blood on his hands felt like a stain on his soul. Taking the dead man's canteen, he twisted off the cap and washed his hands. With no other option, he dried his hands on the German's tunic.

'Sorry to make more of a mess of you, mate. Guess that's the least of your worries now.' Tipping back the canteen, he offered a silent toast to his fallen foe. Sidney's sergeant forbade the men to carry a canteen into no man's land. The German soldier's sergeant apparently overlooked that detail, which cost the soldier his life.

Leaving the man face down in the dirt seemed disrespectful and Sidney easily turned the small body over. In the flickering star shell light, the face became visible and it was a pitiful sight. The dead man was not a man. He looked no more than seventeen years old.

'Christ mate, you aren't even old enough to shave.'

Anger shook him to see a youth who should be at school rather than in a uniform. Had Germany really become so desperate they were sending boys to fight? No wonder the youngster made so much noise. He was a just a frightened schoolboy.

'You didn't even live long enough to become a man. I'll bet you didn't even get laid. Well, I don't want you disappearing and I'm the only one who knows what happened to you.' Sidney rummaged through the boy's uniform looking for identity tags but found nothing.

'Yeah, those clowns took your tags off but not your canteen.' Then inside an inner tunic pocket, he found an army issue postcard with a name and address on it. Although he could not read it, someone back in his lines would be able to help.

'I'll write his family, so they won't wonder like we always have for Louis and Thomas.' Tucking the card inside a pocket, he realized he had lost all track of time. A mist slowly rose around him and in the star shell light, a luminescence grew.

'What the hell is that? I've seen enough strange shit for one night.' An answer to his question quickly came when the face of the Indian appeared. From his conversations with Florence Helen, he knew Walking Thunder had come and his eyes blazed with displeasure and reproach.

"This is not your path. You were not to go to war. You have followed the white ways. I come to guide you so choose wisely."

If Sidney heeded Walking Thunder's advice, he could go home. And right now, he was in a place where a man could lose his life in a heartbeat. Sidney decided to follow the advice. After all, he had killed an enemy and in these few hours, he had seen enough of war to last a lifetime.

A star shell bursting overhead broke his reverie and from the dubious safety of the hollow, he surveyed the surroundings. To his dismay, tendrils of fog slithering across the ground now obscured the place marks he noted earlier. A clammy quilt of fog descended and made him shiver.

Lying back, he saw stars. By sitting up, he might see a way back. When the light faded, he cautiously peered in all directions and the tips of shattered trees poking above the fog, looked familiar. Certain he had passed those skeletal remains hours earlier, he knew it was now or never.

Checking for barbed wire that might snare him, he raised his head. Pinwheels of fear rolled down his spine and he knew his only option was standing. The shoulder height fog would work however to both advantage and disadvantage. He could see above the fog and the tree landmark was directly in front of him. But in the murk, the ground was invisible, so he couldn't see objects that might trip him up and create noise.

Sentries on both sides strained to hear any sounds in no man's land. Fog was perfect cover for a trench raid to capture a prisoner to interrogate. With the fog thickening, Sidney decided to risk walking before all sense of direction was obliterated.

Although he gingerly tested the footing before placing his weight, he slipped on a patch of mud and fell into a string of barbed wire. The wire saved him from tumbling to the earth, but a steel picket jabbed him in the ribs.

Hearing the jangling wire and his muffled curse, jumpy sentries tossed grenades into the darkness. A grenade exploded twenty feet away that stunned, and partially deafened him. Sidney tore ragged holes in his uniform pulling free knowing he had to run or die. Another grenade exploded, and red-hot shrapnel bit his legs. Primal fear overtook reason and he shouted toward the Canadian lines.

"Don't shoot, I'm a fuckin' Strathcona!"

Several more grenades detonated behind him, but he was far enough away that the new wounds were only skin-deep. A sentry called to warn he was nearly at the trench when the ground vanished beneath Sidney's feet.

Tripping over ankle-high wire, he fell across the breadth of a trench and struck his head on a steel revetment. Stunning white light burst behind his eyes and he knew nothing more.

Chapter Five

Air scented with spring flowers and a hint of sea breeze teased the heavily sedated Canadian soldier. White bandages wound around his forehead. A sling lifted his right leg off the mattress. Doctors had expertly sutured numerous shrapnel wounds on his legs and buttocks. Fluids flowed into his veins from two drip bottles. A chart hanging from the bed frame allowed staff to record progress of the man's recovery.

The soldier was one of hundreds convalescing at Number 10 Canadian Medical Hospital in Brighton, England. His skull was fractured and for nearly three weeks, he had lain comatose. Doctors wondered if he would regain consciousness. X-rays showed blood clots and only time would tell if they dissolved.

Over the last several days, the swelling lessened which was an encouraging sign. The shrapnel wounds in his back and buttocks were easily treated. But when Sidney fell into the trench, he landed awkwardly on his right leg and broke the femur. The young man was extremely fortunate to survive the fusillade of grenades and the resulting broken leg and skull fractures.

From the depths of heavy sedation, Sidney's eyelids flickered several times. Accustomed to constant darkness, the light stung his eyes like hot needlepoints.

Like a sleeper swinging a foot from bed to a cold floor, he opened and closed an eye until the light felt kinder. With one eye having led, he opened the other. Now that he was willing to endure the stabbing needles, light vanquished the darkness.

Along with a return to consciousness came pain. Unsettling images of his actions returned. Had he really stabbed a German boy in the neck? Perhaps the morphine cocktail brought on hallucinations.

Stitches in his body spoke to the reality of exploding grenades on that foggy night and by gingerly touching the bandages on his head, reintroduced pain. Looking down, he understood why he could not stretch both legs. What in hell was with the cast?

'Well, dumb ass, they usually put on a cast when something is broken.' The throbbing pain was unwelcome, and he did not recall breaking his leg. After finding no other damage, he laid back. The vision of Walking Thunder flashed back to him. Had he used his last chance?

Perhaps his injuries warranted a medical discharge from the army. If so, he could go home to Emma and the farm with his sense of duty and honour intact. He had fought for King and country and suffered serious wounds. There was no denying he had followed orders and conducted himself as a soldier before the enemy. The more he considered Walking Thunder's words, the more he wanted to go home and live in peace.

"What a delight to see you finally awake, Corporal. We thought you might never wake up. How are you feeling?"

The melodious voice belonged to an attractive young woman standing before his hospital bed. Sidney tried speaking but his mouth was too dry. Smiling warmly, she poured a glass of water that he gratefully sipped.

"I'm Mildred but everyone calls me Millie. I volunteer here, to help look after you brave men. Do you need anything else, Corporal Turner?"

He regarded this wisp of a girl who looked not much older than eighteen. *'Just a bit older than that German boy.'* Millie was pretty but to his surprise, he thought she was too young for him.

'Here you are all wired, bandaged and tubed up but your dick is still thinking. Jesus, have I been gone that long?'

"No, I think I'm all right, Millie. Thank you. Can you tell me where I am, how long I've been here and what my injuries are? Oh, and call me Sidney, it makes me feel a bit more human."

"Sidney, you are in Brighton at Number 10 Canadian Military Hospital and today's date is May 18. I'm not supposed to talk about your medical condition because I'm not a nurse or doctor. I can fetch someone who can tell you more. I'll be right back, Sidney."

She disappeared, and Sidney heard wounded men occasionally groaning or crying out from the depths of sedated sleep. Millie soon reappeared with an older, rather severe looking nurse.

"Corporal Turner, I understand you have questions regarding your current medical condition. On April 23, you were taken to a casualty clearing station. They determined your injuries were too severe and evacuated you to a field hospital near Doullens. Your wounds were treated there before you were brought here aboard a hospital ship."

"I don't remember any of that." The nurse scanned his chart and continued her update.

"You have been in a coma because of multiple skull fractures. Bleeding inside your head put pressure on your brain and caused the coma. The swelling has gone down the last two days, which means the bleeding has stopped. That will ease the pressure on your brain. How are you feeling?"

"Somewhat groggy, ma'am, and a bit bed sore as well. I guess from all the bandages, tubes and this cast, I won't be up dancing any time soon?" he said ruefully.

"No, you won't corporal. But we'll have you on your feet in about six weeks. When you can stand again, you will exercise to recover your strength. You can also expect headaches for the next while. Your other wounds are clean, the shrapnel is removed, and the punctures are stitched. You will have scars for the rest of your days, though." The nurse paused before speaking again in a softer voice.

"You're very fortunate to survive such serious injuries, young man. I've seen men die of lesser wounds than yours." Reverting to her usual formality, she concluded.

"Now, if there are no other questions, I must return to my duties and patients." Without waiting to learn if he did have more questions, she walked away.

With a low whistle, Sidney realized he had been unconscious for nearly a month. *'Well at least you woke up again. That's way better than that German boy.'*

Although conscious just several minutes, he had already thought twice about killing the young German. Why should he worry about that any longer? He knew men who boasted of killing dozens of Germans with no more regard than swatting flies.

Once, he'd heard a Canadian soldier bayonetted a German and licked the blade clean. Some men seemed to regard killing as sport, others saw it as payback for the death of a comrade. Surely, he could not be the only man who felt remorse over killing.

Perhaps he had not been in the line long enough to see friends die and thirst for revenge. How could men behave in such a primitive manner? Perhaps men were not even as civilized as the animal kingdom. After all, animals had not invented a machine gun capable of killing hundreds of men.

Coming back from his ponderings, he saw Millie still at the foot of his bed. She smiled shyly; obviously, she wished to talk. Unsure what to say, and to cover his uncertainty, he asked for a glass of water.

She handed him the glass and he smelled soap and her clean clothes. What a refreshing change from the stink of soldiers in dirty uniforms. He sipped the water while considering how to ask her another question.

"Millie, what is done with a soldier's belongings when he is brought in? And at the risk of sounding indelicate, when are we bathed? I certainly wasn't this clean when I got here."

"Well, to answer your first question, your belongings are likely in the table beside you. You would have been bathed before the operation. They are very fussy about cleanliness."

"Do male orderlies bathe the wounded men? Surely the women nurses don't bathe the men...do they?" Millie's face grew red discussing the notion of naked men.

"The nurses bathe the men. They can't spare men just for that and besides, thousands of men have been in here. I imagine the nurses are very used to seeing naked men." Sidney smiled and could not resist a bit of teasing.

"Have you seen many naked men here, Millie?" Turning beet red, Millie stammered out a reply.

"Of course not. That would never happen since I'm not a nurse." The question clearly embarrassed her, and he changed the topic.

"I can't reach the drawer beside me. Would you mind handing me everything that is in there?"

Millie passed over a small canvas packet. Inside were a few coins, his wristwatch, and the post card tucked inside his pay book. Withdrawing the card, he looked at it with curiosity. The handwriting and the printed salutation were unfamiliar. It depicted a German soldier bidding farewell to his stoic appearing mother. Although he could not read the words, the meaning was clear.

Millie wondered how this Canadian had a German post card in his possession. An explanation was in order and Sidney decided to sugar-coat the truth.

"The night I got wounded, we were in no man's land on a wiring party. Some star shells went up and I took cover in a shell hole. Well, a German was already there but he was dead. He might have been sixteen, maybe seventeen at the very most."

"Sidney, the Germans are terrible for putting boys in the army."

"You're right, Millie. I'm sure his mother didn't want him in the army. One of my brothers went missing on the Somme. It's hard on my dear mom and I thought this German's mom should know he's dead and not just missing. I found this postcard and luckily, he had already addressed it. There's been so much hate and we'll need to get past that when peace comes." Millie thought it a wonderful gesture and gushed appreciatively.

"That's such a sweet thing to do Sidney. I'll help you anyway I can, but it might be difficult getting a letter to Germany. I'll ask the hospital chaplain, he should know how to mail a letter." She gazed at him wistfully and her naiveté unsettled him.

"Millie, there is one thing you might be able to help me with."

"Yes, anything at all, Sidney, and I'm happy to do it."

"There's a good girl. Since it would be difficult for me to do it, would you please take down a letter to my wife?" Her jaw dropped, and she flushed in embarrassment.

"Why of course, but right now I must tend to some other patients. Let me see how my time looks later this afternoon, all right?" Nodding tersely, Millie walked away.

'Well that went rather smoothly Sid old boy' he mocked. *'Guess you're going to find out how well you can write lying on your arse.'* Several minutes later, another volunteer walked past, and he beckoned to her.

"Hello, I'd like to write a letter home, but I don't have a pen or paper. Is it possible to be given some?"

The attendant appeared to be in her late sixties. No problem here, he thought. She asked for several minutes grace and then, true to her word, sat down while he dictated a short letter.

Emma would have received a telegram advising her he had been wounded. That would be worrying for her as it offered little information. He wanted to reassure her while glossing over the actual circumstances.

"Dearest Emma, by now you know I've been wounded. The wound is minor so not to worry, my darling. Just tripped in the dark and injured my right leg. I am in a splendid hospital near Brighton in jolly old England. Lovely view of the sea and the grounds here are like a garden. Nothing like England for fantastic gardens, you know!

The medical care is first rate and for a hospital, the food is quite good. Anyways love, I will be here about six weeks to get some strength back after all this lying about. You know me, always on the go. Will write again soon. All my love and thoughts, your Sid."

He knew the cheery, shallow note did not sound like him. Bert would tell Emma that if Sidney offered in-depth details, censors might not pass the letter. The attendant promised the letter would go out in the next mail.

An hour later, an older, soft-spoken man in grey vicar cloth introduced himself. Millie had spoken to the vicar about mailing a letter to Germany, and he wanted more information.

Sidney explained while omitting full details of how he found the postcard. That Louis remained listed as missing in action still affected the Bias family and Alexander still clung to a sliver of hope. Perhaps this note to a mother in Germany might bring a measure of solace.

The vicar nodded and praised Sidney for his charity. He would send the card and Sidney's note to a colleague in France who would mail it through neutral Switzerland to Germany.

The vicar's knowledge of German confirmed the soldier meant the card for his mother. He claimed to be doing well and was proud to defend the Fatherland. Sidney grew uncomfortable with not revealing the truth to a man of the cloth and he confessed to killing the young man. The vicar sighed.

"War is the devil at work, and please God, let it end soon."

After agreeing on the wording of Sidney's accompanying note, the vicar promised to translate it into German before he mailed it. The letter explained Sidney found the body and, adding a white lie, that he buried the boy. He hoped God would overlook the falsehood.

"Please, sir, just one more thing. That boy was saying something that sounded like mootee, mootee. Do you know what he was saying? Maybe he was cursing me?"

The vicar shook his head sadly and explained what a German boy said with his dying breath.

"Mother, mother."

Chapter Six

Thousands of miles away, Emma read a telegram. It advised her husband, Corporal Sidney Turner, suffered wounds on April 23 and had been evacuated to a hospital in England.

After sharing the telegram with Bert, they went to Camp Hughes. Several weeks later, Emma and Bert learned about Sidney's shrapnel wounds, fractured skull and broken right leg. His recovery would take until at least mid-July.

"For Christ's sake Bert! I told him not to be a hero. And look what the hell he does on his first goddamn day in the front lines! He goes out in no man's land alone at night, and nearly gets killed. I just can't trust that man. He promised to stay back looking after the horses, not go running around where he can get killed. Why is it you men think you have to prove you've got balls of steel?"

She burst into tears of anger and fear. Sidney's injuries resurrected the pain of her brother's death three years earlier. Seeing her distress, Bert wrapped Emma in a fatherly embrace. He and Desiree had already discussed an idea, and this was an opportune occasion to raise the topic.

"Emma, Desiree and I already decided this, so all you need to do is listen. Sid will be laid up for quite a spell and we're sending you over to England to see our hero."

"Oh Bert, you can't do that. Who will look after the farm? I have money and Mama and Papa will insist on helping me."

"Emma, in case you've never guessed, you're like my daughter. You're married to the best friend I've ever had. To me, he's part son and part brother. Don't worry about this trip, okay? I'm going to let you in on a little secret Sidney still doesn't know about." Emma laughed, knowing all about her naïve husband.

"What? My Sidney doesn't know all your secrets? Who would ever believe my simple country boy could be that way?"

"Hey, little sweetie, that country boy side is one of the things you like best about our boy."

"You're right, of course." Now bright-eyed and curious, Emma begged to hear the secret.

"While I had the boat, I also ran a side business. Don't ask what it was. Let's just say it's not something the law might like. It paid me very well and that's how I had the scratch for the farm. I've got more than enough money to last the rest of my life.

"Some might say I've lived a wicked life and maybe they're right. But I can look any man in the eye and say I never took anything that somehow, I didn't earn. Now, whether the law liked it, is another story."

Emma thought it over. Sidney had never mentioned Bert's past might be shady although it did not come as a great surprise. She knew better than to ask him for more details. Bert would just laugh and change the subject. However, she did not think it right for him to pay for her trip overseas.

"No sense arguing with me, girl. It's already paid for so now you have to go."

"But Bert..." He held up one hand and wagged a finger.

"Listen, honey, Sid got hurt about three weeks ago. He's flat on his ass in Brighton. I know the place. It's a resort town on the English Channel and at this time of year, the weather is grand. Just the place for a healthy young couple to spend a few weeks, um, getting reacquainted."

Emma blushed at 'reacquainting' with Sidney and it stirred a desire to lay with him again. Bert laughed seeing the change in her complexion.

"It's not a sin, girl, never mind what the church says." Blushing furiously, Emma laughed.

"I can't deny that's something I've missed since he's been gone. Mama told me it's one life's most special things when a man and woman truly love each other."

"Your mama is a wise woman. Now listen up, you're already booked on next week's train to Halifax. It takes about six days to cross the Atlantic. The boat docks in Southampton, which is only a hop, skip and a jump from Brighton."

"Oh, that sounds so exciting Bert. Then what?"

"Then what? What we were just talking about girl?" Slapping Bert's forearm, Emma growled ferociously and laughed.

"You'll be there in two to three weeks. The big lug should be getting around on crutches or even a cane. Maybe you can go up to London on a week's leave. I'll do my best to pull some strings, so he can spend some time with you. I've got friends in London who can arrange a hotel, so not to worry."

Emma hugged Bert. No wonder Sidney thought so highly of him. She knew something of Bert's legendary temper and terrifying ferocity in a fight. However, he possessed a kind and generous side she guessed few people ever saw. To be one of Bert's friends, was far grander than being his enemy.

Ten days later, Emma stood at the railing of a trans-Atlantic liner in Halifax harbour, where the scars from a devastating munitions explosion the previous December wrenched her heart.

It had been the biggest man-made explosion in history. Nearly two thousand people died, and thousands of homes were damaged or destroyed. Emma had never seen such destruction and the sight made her grateful home was far from the ravages of war.

Emma knew the Belgian town of Ypres had suffered continuous shelling since 1914. Ypres had not suffered a single catastrophic explosion like Halifax. Each day, the Germans slowly reduced it to rubble by artillery bombardments.

Turning to happier thoughts, she wondered what England would be like. Her curiosity was nearly overwhelming. Perhaps she could persuade Sidney to visit his parents, brothers and sisters.

Many Englishmen believed themselves superior to all other nationalities and races. Emma worried that Sidney's father and his brothers, might regard her as a half-breed savage. He had tried explaining they based their opinions on more than Emma being half-blooded.

"You're also Canadian. Many Englishmen think Canadians are nothing but poorly educated colonials." Sidney had never seriously considered the possibility Emma might one day meet his family. Reminding herself the primary reason for sailing to

England was to meet Sidney, she put aside pre-conceived notions.

One sunny afternoon, Sidney was lounging in a comfortable lawn chair on the hospital's front lawn. Over the last week, he began hobbling around with canes after weeks on crutches. Due to his robust health and enormous strength, his recovery was progressing well, but he knew that meant a quicker return to the front.

'Never mind rushing back to do your bit and all that drivel. I bet the war will still be going on a year from now. The Yanks are coming so let them do their part for now.'

Hundreds of thousands of Americans were now in Europe. Sidney heard a million were training to meet the Germans in battle.

It could not come too soon. Britain and France had been bled nearly white in four years of non-stop killing. How Germany continued pouring men into battle was beyond Sidney's reckoning. He knew they did not have the manpower the Allies now possessed. Eventually, the law of averages would defeat Germany.

For now, he was content to rest on this comfortable chair and enjoy the warm sunshine. Although it was hospital food, the meals were certainly an improvement over tinned McConachie stew. Except for an occasional sharp pain as the leg bones knit back together, his wounds did not bother him.

The doctors advised the leg was not yet strong enough to support his weight. After another four to six weeks of rest, they expected he could return to duty. Closing his eyes, he wriggled into the chair and sighed aloud.

"So, let the sun shine and everyone can just bloody well leave me alone."

"Well, that isn't much of a way to greet someone who came thousands of miles to see you." The voice sounded familiar but having dozed off quickly, he kept his eyes closed.

"Keep this up and in another minute, I'm going to find someone who will talk to me."

"Emma! Oh my God! Emma!"

Vaulting from the chair, he wobbled precariously while the canes fell to the grass. It could not be true, yet his beautiful young wife was in his arms and soaking his dressing gown with tears.

Hugging one another tightly, their delight bubbled over in a shower of ecstasy. Emma's tears smeared her face and streaked Sidney's cheek with black eye liner. He swayed on his feet and Emma leaned back to steady him.

"Hey, my darling, guess its best that I sit down again. It must look like I'm drunk." His face grew red as he panted.

"Not only that, but there's a danger I'll be pointing at you through my pyjama bottoms. Although I must admit, it's a relief knowing all my parts are working again..." Emma giggled at her own racy thoughts.

"Yes, my sweet man, let's do sit you down." She eased him back onto the lounging chair and looked back toward the hospital.

"Too bad we aren't alone," she whispered huskily. "It's been awhile since I've seen your private parts..."

"Well, we won't find much privacy here, unless we find a broom closet. Besides, the head nurse is quite the stickler for rules and regulations. She would take a very dim view of you even being this close to me. I think she believes patients belong to her."

"Any idea how much longer you will be stuck here? Oh Sidney, I so want to be with you and see England. Your head wound looks to be healing nicely. There's barely a scar and your hair is growing back. Want to tell me about that?"

"The doctor said my skull fractured in the fall. I guess that in another month, they will spring me from this prison. The big concern is making sure my leg is strong enough, so I can get around again."

"Sidney, the telegram scared the hell out of me. Thank Christ Bert was with me when the messenger brought it. They don't give many details. Just that Corporal Sidney Turner was wounded in action on such and such a date."

"Sorry to worry you, my darling. I know the army doesn't tell you much about what we're doing over here."

"I imagined you with both legs missing, or badly burned or blinded by poison gas." Sidney smiled seeing her concern.

"Nothing that dramatic, my dear. I just fell into a trench in the dark, hit my head and landed with a leg under me. Nothing exciting." She let him finish but her expression hinted at smouldering anger.

"Turner, you are full of shit. Think I don't know you? You always get that stupid look when you try bullshitting me. I don't understand why you still think you can get away with it." She paused to catch her breath and calm down before resuming the tirade.

"The telegram didn't offer much so I pestered Bert into taking me over to Camp Hughes. I don't know how he knows so many people, but he does. He already made inquiries before we went. A couple of bottles of whiskey probably changed hands. At the adjutant's office, we heard about the working party, whatever that is. We heard a bit about what went wrong and that you were almost killed. The adjutant said you might get discharged from active service and I've been praying for that."

Sidney studied his hands while considering her words. He too hoped for a medical discharge, but his strong constitution worked against that possibility. After his return to the regiment, he would ask to serve only farrier duties. Three hours in the front line had cured him of all curiosity about trench warfare.

"Well, my darling, at least you know I'm not a very good liar." He paused, collecting his thoughts. *'Please don't ask about the train trip from Winnipeg to Halifax.'*

"I won't be returning to the regiment for a while. When I know more, so will you. Now, let me guess. You coming over here was Bert's doing. Knowing him, he bought the tickets and gave you hotel and spending money?"

"Don't get all righteous about it. You listen to me, buster. It was your bright idea to join and on the very first day, you nearly get killed. I remember hearing you wouldn't be anywhere near the fighting. You remember Louis and John MacDonald? Your best friend wants you to come back safe."

"All right, all right. You've outmaneuvered me again. Yes, by now, you'd think I would know that. Now enough about me, do you have a room in Brighton?"

"Yes, my sweet man," she smiled with mock contriteness. "I have a nice room with a big, comfy bed. We might even sleep in it..."

"You have no idea how much I'd love to tear your clothes off. If I had known you were coming, I could have asked a few questions. As it stands now, if I'm not in my hospital bed by dinner, it's considered being absent without leave." Emma stood up in amazement Sidney could not spend the evening with her.

"Honest, my darling, that is how the army would view it. The only excuse is a medical emergency. And if it was a medical emergency, I should be here at the hospital."

"Well then, what do we do? I didn't come all this way to watch you sit in a lawn chair."

"Leave it with me, darling. I'm much better and the doctor hardly takes the time to check on me. They need beds for newly wounded and that gives me an idea. I'll talk to the doctor to see about staying with you to free up a bed.

"I'll ask him to check on me every day, or better yet, every second day. I won't be lying in a bed and wasting the nurses' time. Besides, I've got the most desirable nurse on the planet to bathe me." Leaning over, Emma kissed him gently and teased him with the tip of her tongue.

"Oh, you can be a smart boy Turner...sometimes."

"Well, then let your sometimes-smart boy ask a few questions. Doubt I'll get out today, but I can aim for tomorrow."

Chapter Seven

Sidney's guess proved correct that the hospital needed his bed. The doctor listened while Sidney presented his case.

"I understand your wife came from Canada but there is a precaution to remember, Corporal. Your leg is still healing, and forgive the, ahem, imagery but prolonged activity is not advisable. I would appreciate your cooperation in my not having to explain to my superiors why you've taken a turn for the worse."

"Yes sir, completely understood. I will conduct myself with care and caution. I am to present myself daily at 1100 hours for the first week and after that, at 1100 hours every other day the next. Thank you, sir, your kindness is much appreciated." With a snappy salute, Sidney hobbled from the examination room.

Earlier that morning, Emma asked the hotel concierge about securing more affordable accommodations. Like all good concierges, and for a modest stipend, he arranged the rental of a seaside cottage on the edge of town.

"The gentleman who owns it is an officer in the navy. He hasn't been home much the last few years."

Emma bought some groceries, tidied the place and then went downtown to shop at a women's store. Satisfied with her purchases, she fetched Sidney.

"It's a cute little place, exactly how I always imagined an English cottage. No electricity or running water but there is a coal stove for heat and a small tub, so we can bathe but unfortunately, only one at a time."

"Bathing me is quite the rigmarole with this bloody cast. Not a challenge we can't figure a way around, I expect. In case you haven't noticed, I'm rather looking forward to your being my nurse and meeting all my needs."

A bus stopped near the cottage and despite Sidney's pace, they soon arrived. After surveying the interior, he commended Emma on the choice. The kitchen had a table and two chairs, and a small sitting room held two overstuffed chairs and a small settee. A silkscreen divider separated a four-poster bed from the rest of the place.

Sidney knew the next four weeks would be a time to treasure the remainder of his life. How had he ever found such an angel to marry? *'Actually, it's more like how did you ever find two angels who wanted to marry you?'*

Dropping his canes into the empty brass shell casing that served as an umbrella stand, he faced Emma. She was a spectacular sight, backlit by sunlight pouring into the room. A white summer dress streamed with red roses and green circlets hugged her slender figure.

She offered her mouth and their passion built. He swayed unsteadily and leading him to the bed, she gently pushed him down. Sidney watched transfixed as Emma slowly unbuttoned her dress and pulled it over her head. Alluring French perfume wafted, and Sidney's stomach knotted with desire.

Emma wanted the lovemaking to be more than a moment of frantic coupling. "All right sweet man, let's make this special," she purred.

"For God's sake! Seeing you like that is so special I'm ready to finish all on my own."

"Don't spoil this Sidney. It will be special if we take our time. So, don't touch me, just be still." Nearly frantic, he reluctantly followed her command.

Playfully breathing her way along his chest, she gently nibbled the pulsing tendons in his neck. Tickling his ear lobes with her tongue, she whispered lewd descriptions of acts they were about to perform.

"Please, please, please do that now before it all happens in my underwear," he moaned.

She ignored his pleas while massaging his chest and thrilling to the power of his muscles. His arousal electrified her. Reaching under a pillow, she pulled out a cloth shopping bag.

The bag held a mask to enflame a soldier who had not seen his wife in nearly a year along with French silk underwear, racy garters and white stockings.

During their long separation, she often fantasized. Wearing the sexy underwear and mask, she gyrated slowly but Sidney could not hold back a shuddering release.

"Oh Sidney, you're weren't supposed to do that already. I didn't even get a chance to take off my garters yet. When you get hard again, we'll try that once more." She traced a fingertip along a thigh to caress her femininity. As Sidney watched, she closed her eyes and climaxed.

"If I had a dollar for every time I've done that since you left, well, I'd have a lot of money. When you're ready, you can look after my needs..."

By dinner hour, Sidney's injuries and recent inactivity had drained him of energy and he fell asleep. While he slept, Emma prepared a hearty stew for their evening meal.

After supper, Sidney sat on the settee to stretch his leg while they talked. The delightful meal and quiet surroundings relaxed him and in mid-sentence, he fell asleep again. Tugging him to bed, Emma lovingly tucked blankets around him.

He barely moved all night and at first light, Emma slid an arm around his neck. In an instant, his hands closed around her throat and squeezed. Terrified by his reaction, she slapped his face, but he continued. Mustering the last of her strength, she kneed him in the groin. Groaning in pain, he awoke to see Emma's bulging eyes and red face.

"Jesus Christ! Emma! Oh shit! Are you all right? Please God, I didn't hurt her." Gasping for breath, she pushed him away and scrambled out of bed. Leaning against the wall, her eyes mirrored those of prey cornered by a ferocious predator.

"Sidney! What the hell? Are you trying to kill me? You're scaring the shit out of me!"

Sidney struggled to his feet, but Emma raised her hands to warn him away. After coming so close to death, her heart was racing.

"Please, my darling, I'm sorry for hurting you. Please don't think I would ever hurt you."

"Just go sit at the table. I need to get my wits together. You scared the shit out of me and right now, I don't trust you."

Like a whipped cur, Sidney wobbled to the sitting room. Peeking around the divider, she saw him crying at the table. Resisting the urge to hug him, Emma hesitantly sat down and spoke after several seconds of silence.

"Sidney that is the closest to death I've ever been. I'm scared, and you need to tell me what's going on. All I did was hug you and you tried strangling me. If I hadn't kneed you in the nuts, you would have killed me.

"Were you having a nightmare? Is this something from the war? Tell me, because I need to know. I'm won't stay if this is how you'll be if I touch you while you're asleep." Emma saw his desperate expression while he thought, *'Jesus Christ asshole, you nearly killed her.'*

"I have to tell you about my night in the trenches. Maybe then, you'll understand what just happened. Shit, maybe I'll understand."

Emma only interrupted twice to ask for clarification of some detail. She wept hearing Sidney's panicked reaction to the German soldier, and how he killed the boy. Face in hands, Sidney loosed howling sobs, remembering the lad's pathetic mewling while he died.

Lost for words, Emma's heart broke while he spoke of killing a man. She could not square that scenario to Sidney's gentle nature. It was confusing and discomfiting. Was he someone she no longer knew? With no ready answer, she needed to rebuild her shaken trust in this man she loved so deeply.

"Get dressed while I make breakfast. Then let's go for a walk while I think about what you told me." They walked and for nearly an hour, he talked about his war, sparring no detail of what he witnessed during his short time in the trenches.

Emma saw her beloved Sidney had changed, but his heartfelt outpouring encouraged her. The gentle man she loved wholeheartedly would return home. With her love and support, he would resume being the man she married.

"Until I get past this darling, please be careful putting your arms around my neck."

The next four weeks passed in a blur of seaside walks, enjoying afternoon sunshine, long talks and holding one another. Knowing his return to active duty loomed, they savoured each day, but she also noted the times he seemed far away. Catching his eye during such episodes, she saw an ocean floor, flat and featureless.

Newspapers reported the Allies slowing, and finally halting, German advances. The huge numbers of American soldiers arriving in Europe had dramatically shifted the odds and the Germans knew the Allies would counter attack. Thoughts of the coming storm were on Sidney's mind.

Three weeks into their holiday, they boarded a train to visit Sidney's family. As foreseen, his father was condescending toward Emma. Although his brother Reg was barely better behaved, Albert appeared delighted to meet his sister-in-law.

Sidney's sisters, Constance and Victoria, were very inquisitive and asked Emma a myriad of questions about Indians and life on the prairies. Their child-like curiosity encouraged Emma to invite them along on a walk with her and Sidney.

The day passed quickly and soon it was time to bid farewell. Emily and the girls walked them to the train station. On the way, Emily voiced her embarrassment with Thomas over his treatment of Emma.

"Sidney, I don't understand your father. There are times I want to hit him over the head with a shovel. For all the years you were gone, I blamed him."

"Well, mom, in all fairness he wasn't the only one in the wrong. I had something to do with it too."

"No Sidney, don't think that way. You were still a boy. It was terribly unfair of your father to treat you and Albert as he did."

"Thank you, mom, that makes me feel better." Squeezing his arm, Emily offered him a brave smile.

"When your father makes up his mind, he will not listen. Emma, please accept my apologies. Too many people in this country think if you are not English, you aren't much of anything. England has done a great deal of good in the world, but we've also brought harm to people in many countries.

"I'm getting old. All my life seems about is cooking, cleaning and raising children. It would be wonderful to see Canada, to see this place where my Sidney has done so well." Taking Emily's hand, Emma smiled warmly.

"Promise you'll come and see us when this awful war is over. We could even take the train and see the Rocky Mountains. You girls must come too." On the return to Brighton, Emma rested her head on Sidney's shoulder.

"None of them will come, will they?" Sidney kissed her quickly and answered.

"No, they'll never leave England. Mom went to London once when she was a teenager. My father left town just once to go to Spithead in 1897 for Queen Victoria's diamond jubilee.

"My brothers only left home because of the war and you see how that turned out. Heaven knows if the girls will ever see more of England, never mind the big world outside. My darling, the people in this town don't see much of the world. Far as I know, I'm the only person who ever left England."

The following week, doctors approved Sidney's return to his regiment in three weeks. It was now early August and Sidney heard about an approaching big push against the Germans. All available men were heading to the front.

The Canadian and ANZAC army corps would spearhead the British effort. Everyone hoped the battle would finally break the German army and bring peace. Knowing he would soon be back there, Sidney planned for one last special memory with Emma.

On his final week of leave, he took Emma to London. Sidney had never seen London and although he considered himself a Canadian, his heart swelled with pride to see the grand sights.

The city, still considered the greatest in the world, enthralled Emma. The cathedrals, government buildings, and statues thrilled her. One morning she stood before the gates of Buckingham Palace to watch the changing of the guard. They rode the subway, or underground tube as Londoners referred to it, and she marvelled at the system's ingenuity. They went out for dinner, and on two occasions, the theatre. It was a far cry from their Manitoba farm.

"Sidney, I get it why people here think they are better than everyone else. Here we are in London on a Saturday, we've been out to dinner, seen a show and now we're riding the tube back to the hotel. Try doing that in Brandon on a Saturday night."

"I agree you can't do all this at home on Saturday night but Emma, don't think this is normal. Look around and tell me how many so-called average people you see. It takes big money to live this way and the working class don't have it.

"Not everyone in Canada does this either but at least they get out sometimes and live it up. If I still lived here, this would be way out of my reach. That's one of the reason I'm so grateful to be a Canadian." It was their last night in London; the morning marked the end of Sidney's leave.

In Brighton, doctors cleared his return to the regiment and they rode the train to Southampton. Emma's ocean liner would sail after sunset due to the submarine threat. She had not considered that danger and the precaution brought home more realities of war.

They held one another at dockside, oblivious to everything around them. After seeing the multitudes of injured soldiers in hospital and London, Emma feared letting go of Sidney. Her husband was returning where millions had died. Steeling her courage, she smiled and dabbed her eyes. To her surprise, Sidney's face was streaked with tears.

"Come on now," she wheezed, "I thought big boys don't cry."

"They don't, but right now, I don't feel much like a big boy. This fucking war, I hate it." He had not intended to blurt that aloud, but he had, and she saw he was frightened.

"Well, my dearest sweet man, at least you're finally smart enough to be scared. That means you'll keep safe and come home to me."

"I guess you saw enough wounded men to know this isn't some boyish adventure. But, I'll be on farrier duties, which is the safest place to be. So be my brave girl and tell everyone you saw me off to do my duty and all that bullshit," he cynically intoned.

"Sidney, I mean this. Don't get killed or I will be so mad. If you think I'll be mad, see what mom does to you! Wear your St.

Christopher medallion and never take it off. Come home to me so we can keep trying for that baby."

After kissing him once more, she strode up the gangway without a backwards glance. Sidney wasn't offended. He knew his wild prairie girl did not want him seeing her fresh tears.

Chapter Eight

On August 8, 1918, the Allies launched the great offensive to finally end the war. The Canadian Corps helped spearhead the attacks. From bitter experience, the Germans knew the fighting would be bloody. Their soldiers took to heart the warning, "The Canadians are coming, prepare for the worst."

The Allies advanced eight miles the first day and Ludendorff, the German quartermaster general, declared it, "the Black Day of the German Army." Believing victory was no longer possible, he urged the Kaiser to open peace negotiations.

Allied soldiers were not privy to that information, but the ground and large numbers of prisoners captured, signalled the war was changing. In many instances, German soldiers threw down their weapons when attacked. Sometimes entire battalions, officers included, surrendered to a single company of Canadians. Disappointment with the failure of their spring offensives, had created a precipitous drop in German morale.

Many Germans no longer believed in the call of duty or that their deaths might serve a higher purpose. Stories of widespread food shortages at home sapped many a man's will to fight and they simply wanted the war to end. The high ideals they marched to war with in August 1914 had died, along with two million German soldiers.

Their soldiers died in battles ranging from muddy Flanders, in the flats of Artois, along the murderous Somme, on the ridges of Champagne, at the Marne, through hideous Verdun and into the Vosges. Very little martial spirit remained which became more apparent daily. The killing, however, would continue for several more months before the guns fell silent.

Sidney rejoined the regiment two weeks after the August offensive began. After years of static trench fighting, the war had again become one of movement again. His regiment belonged to the Canadian Cavalry Brigade.

The troopers usually had little idea where they were, and Sidney simply followed them, attending to the horses. The war was not far away, and the roar of guns was deafening. On nearby fields, he knew men and horses were dying. As the Canadians chased the Germans, his heart broke to see the carnage left in their wake.

The close Allied pursuit did not allow the Germans time to establish strong points. Whirlwind artillery barrages, closely followed by infantry attacks, broke German lines and forced a withdrawal. Despite their crumbling front, some Germans fought to the death and inflicted thousands of casualties in the process.

A carpet of dead men told the tale. Advancing formations might not see a camouflaged German machine gun until it opened fire.

Men crawled beneath the bullets whizzing overhead and closed to within yards of their enemy. A brave soul or two tried judging when the gun was firing in another direction. Rising, they hurled grenades or charged, firing their rifles and bayoneting the gun crew. Yard by deadly yard, the Canadians and their allies pushed back the enemy.

Sidney's heart ached at seeing the dead in Canadian uniforms as he trailed along behind the front-line troops. As the men moved forward to attack, one occasionally looked at him like he was a coward. Their contempt bothered him, but he consoled himself knowing he too, had fought in the front line.

When some troops went into action for the first time, many did not live to see another day. Once Sidney's unit moved forward, he found their bodies, and too often buried a fellow Strathcona.

His heart hardened at the callous, impersonal death of so many young men. With loathsome regularity, he scooped up body parts or rolled corpses into a shallow scrape. Often, he could not determine which part belonged to the fragmented dead. Near misses of bursting shells infuriated him and he screamed curses at the unseen dealers of death.

"Don't you Hun pieces of shit ever stop? For God's sake, leave us alone to bury these poor souls. No wonder the whole world hates your fucking guts!" The war cared little for his feelings, the killing simply continued day and night.

He strove to show a measure of compassion to the dead of his own side. With the front moving once more, many fell to bullets rather than high explosive and shrapnel shells. Bullets usually did not savage the body in the same manner as artillery shells, so Sidney could lay to rest a poor lad with a modicum of human dignity.

For dead Germans scattered in a field or in a pulverized machine gun post, he mustered no sympathy. On particularly gruelling days, he kicked their bodies into a hole. Sometimes he dragged a dead German under a bush and left him for the rats and crows. Such was the price Sidney paid in losing some of his humanity to the vulgarity of war.

He never buried horses, leaving the carcass as a protest against all the death. *'If only we were as good at finding cures for diseases as killing each other.'*

While in hospital, he had read sanitized newspaper reports of battle. After four years of war, how could anyone still believe it was a grand adventure? *'Guess if the recruits knew ahead of time, no one would go.'*

August became September and optimism grew that the war might end in 1918. The fighting moved into areas of France and Belgium the Germans had occupied since 1914. In early October, the Canadian Cavalry brigade moved forward to support attacks east of Cambrai.

Sidney knew little about the grand scheme and movements of hundreds of thousands of troops. He had heard about Cambrai and had a general idea of where he and the regiment were located. One morning, his regiment assembled to be part of an attack to capture Le Cateau.

The British army fought a delaying action there in 1914 to slow the German advance into northern France. In a reversal of fortune, now the Germans were fighting a rearguard action to slow the British advance.

The British general staff knew the Germans meant to establish formidable defenses near Le Cateau. Breaking those defences would be difficult and the generals were determined to prevent it.

The Cavalry Brigade moved up to support the British attack and the Strathconas would take part. While tending a horse tied to a picket line, a sergeant reined in and shouted at Sidney.

"Turner, get your rifle and sabre. We're supporting the Brits at Le Cateau and we're going right bloody now! Get a move on."

"Right Sarge, I'll be ready in a minute." Not once since his return to France, had he been concerned with anything except farrier duties. Surprised by the order, Sidney dashed to his tent for his rifle, sabre and gas mask.

Lashing the gear in place, he swung into the saddle and raced to join his company. Once there, he discovered he did not have his identity discs or wallet. Those items were a nuisance when he worked, so he put them in a pouch. Apart from the Canada buttons on his tunic, he was anonymous.

"Shit, shit, shit! Sarge, I forgot my discs and wallet in all this bloody rush." The sergeant shot him a look of exasperation. A bugle sounded, and the regiment began moving.

"No time for that. Get it when we get back!"

The horses broke into a trot and Sidney saw other Canadian cavalry regiments also forming up. In the distance were sounds of battle and they were heading directly toward it.

Canadian field guns opened fire, making many horses skittish. When his horse nervously bobbed, Sidney patted his mount on the neck and muttered.

"I don't blame you, mate, for being scared. I'm wondering what in hell I'm doing here. Best not ever tell Emma about this."

To the north, British troopers waved and to the right, other Canadian cavalry squadrons advanced. Sidney became more apprehensive as they drew closer to the fighting. Directly in front, stiff German resistance held up the British infantry attack. The cavalry received orders to pass through the infantry and charge the Germans.

They came under machine gun and artillery fire while several German aircraft swooped down to strafe. As the troopers madly galloped, bullets and shells howled past.

"Jesus H. Christ! That was close. I'm gonna get killed out here!"

Their charge helped break German resistance and it took them clear of the fighting. Several villages appeared, and patrols went to each. The sergeant who detailed Sidney to join the attack, ordered him along. After fording a small river, they approached a village.

A broken signpost for the village of Neuvilly lay on the ground. Then suddenly, they came under fire from enemy soldiers crouched behind a low stone wall. A kilometre further back, German artillery fired over open sights. The troopers whirled around to race away from the hail of death. Shrapnel shells burst overhead, and a man and horse skidded to earth near Sidney.

"Goddamn it! Let's get the hell out of here." Stretching out along the neck of his horse, Sidney screamed for it to run faster.

A second later, another shrapnel shell burst sent Sidney and the horse crashing to the ground in a bloody heap. He lay staring up at the sky while his mount shuddered and died.

Badly wounded, the pain was merely an irritant as the lifeblood drained from his shattered body. His final lucid seconds were a slow fall down a deep well, dropping from the circle of light as darkness squeezed it to a vanishing pinpoint.

Sidney felt his body growing numb and realized he was dying. His bloodied hand fumbled to grip the charm Emma prayed would keep him safe. Through the blood bubbling in his mouth, he wheezed his final words.

"Emma, Emma, Emma, Emma..."

He coughed in a vain attempt to spit out the blood running down his throat. At the pinpoint of light, a white haze formed and slowly gave way to the image of Walking Thunder.

"You gave away your medicine. Now you will join me... and your son will take your place."

'My son?' As the light left him, a tiny smile played upon his lips.

Chapter Nine

Emma sat in Doctor Evans office, awaiting an examination. She had returned from England two months earlier and prayed daily for the war to end. Sidney's cheery letters arrived regularly, urging her not to worry.

"I'm doing well, the leg bothers a bit, but the other wounds healed up nicely. I'm well to the rear with our horses and that suits me fine." Knowing not to believe all he wrote, she nevertheless appreciated his efforts to mollify her.

This past week, she had felt ill on several mornings. Perhaps she had caught the Spanish influenza bug that was sweeping the globe. Although no locals reported being sick, she might be the first to come down with it. Bert and Desiree took her to see the doctor and afterward, they planned to splurge on lunch.

In the exam room, Doctor Evans smiled at Emma. Now in his late sixties, his grey hair had long ago vanished from atop his head. Wire rim glasses perched on his nose and red suspenders bookended a pudgy belly.

"Well young lady, it's safe to say you don't have that awful Spanish flu bug." With a delighted smile, he took Emma's hand.

"Against all odds, you are going to be a mother, Mrs. Emma Turner. No doubt about it, April or early May, I should think."

Emma sat rooted on the exam table, afraid to breathe in case it broke the spell. An electric thrill flashed through her and then she screamed. Bouncing off the table, she fiercely hugged Doctor Evans as tears streamed down her cheeks.

"Oh, Doctor Evans, are you sure? It's supposed to be impossible for me to get pregnant."

"Young lady, I've delivered most of the babies around here. I doubt any man knows more about babies and pregnant women. You are going to be a mother in the New Year." Squealing in delight, Emma hugged the old doctor again.

"Careful honey, don't kill me before the baby comes."

"Sorry, I guess you can tell how excited I am."

"Yes, but let me finish. Whatever caused that egg to shake loose, well, I know what causes that," he chuckled. "Go home and tell everyone your wonderful news. You'll be back often to see me, and I expect you to take care of yourself."

Desiree and Bert had already guessed the reason for Emma's happy shriek. Bursting from the doctor's office, she flung an arm around each of them. Bert uncharacteristically let slip several tears.

"Just to keep you two company...of course." Linking arms, they decided to return home. The fall day was spectacular and unseasonably warm.

'How can life be any better than this? That's easy, having your husband at home would make it perfect.' The news from overseas was encouraging with rumours the war might end before year-end.

"Oh, Bert and Desiree, I'm going to be a mommy. Do you think Sidney will be home before the baby comes? You have to help me think of a name, something special."

"Sidney, if it's a boy. He couldn't have a better man to follow than your husband. And I insist on Desiree and me being godparents."

"Of course, he has to be Sidney. Bert, you're always right. Sidney always tells me that and it's true." An hour later, they reached the farm and Desiree forbade Emma from entering the kitchen.

"You and Bert sit outside while I make some sandwiches and tea. Go on now, please do as you're asked."

Emma and Bert sat on the porch swing and he held her hand in a fatherly manner. No words were necessary. The bond between them would never be broken. It was a moment Bert wished could last forever but then he heard a motor car in the distance.

"Probably another dumb sod who's lost. Bet he pulls up and asks if he's headed the right way for Winnipeg."

When the car drew nearer, they saw it was painted khaki green. A young soldier drove while an officer sat on the rear seat.

Bert's stomach knotted in fear. Daring a sideways glance at Emma, he saw her smiling and he prayed the smile would still be there in a few minutes.

Stopping at the steps, a private opened the rear passenger door. To Bert's surprise, Major Steele stepped out with the aid of a cane. He nodded and walked toward them holding a leather valise.

Emma's smile froze, sensing something terrible was about to forever change her world. Major Steele leaned against the porch rail and shook hands with Bert before turning to Emma.

"Mrs. Turner, I thought it best to come in person. We received a telegram this morning from the war office, and I'm afraid it concerns you."

Emma rose from the swing to stand at attention as tears started down her cheeks. She did not want to hear this, but if she had to, she would stand tall.

"It is my sad duty to inform you that your husband, Corporal Sidney Turner, has been missing in action since October 9, 1918. We have few details so far. He was on a reconnaissance patrol near Le Cateau, France, and none of the patrol returned. That is why I have so little information and the reason for the delay in notifying you."

Emma sagged at the dreadful news and sobs wracked her body. Steadying her with one arm, Bert stroked her hair. Desiree had quietly come to the screen door and hatred for the army coursed through her veins. How could a day of such joy and promise, become one of heartbreak and despair?

"Please accept my sympathy on this news madam. I knew your husband well. He was a good soldier, a good man, and he may yet be found. The patrol went missing near the village of Neuvilly. It stayed in German hands for several days before our troops captured the area. It is possible the men were taken prisoner and if that is the case, the Red Cross will notify us."

Desiree glared with such hostility, the major blanched. Holding Emma close, and not wishing for the soldiers to witness her sorrow, she pulled Emma inside the house. Bert held the door and turned back, grimly shaking his head.

"Major, I know you mean well, but please don't offer us false hope. Hoping the men are prisoners, doesn't do anyone much good. I presume the men were killed and that's why you have so few details?"

"Sir, in all honesty, I cannot definitely state the men died in action. All I am permitted to say is they are missing. We learned this terrible piece of news just this morning." Major Steele paused and fixed Bert with a determined air.

"I lost my right leg at Cambrai last year. Mr. Westhaven, I have seen my fair share of battle. Speaking off the record, I doubt any of those men are alive. After the Brits captured the village, they found some fresh graves but there is no word on whose remains they might be there. This next bit of information is unconfirmed but apparently, local villagers buried the men.

"Sidney was supposed to stay back tending to horses. A private claimed a sergeant ordered him and Sidney to saddle up. Before the private could get ready, Sidney left with the regiment and the private stayed behind. That is the only reason we know Sidney went forward. He left his wallet and identity discs behind, that is how quickly he left." Bert stared heartbroken at the implication of the major's words.

"Sid might have been killed and even if they find him, there's no way to know it's him?"

"Yes sir, I'm afraid that is very likely what happened. Unless a member of a burial party, who knew him, finds his body, it's highly doubtful he will be identified. Maybe after the war ends and we have time for such formalities, then, perhaps."

The major obviously shared their grief. Standing tall as possible, he saluted Bert before returning to the car.

"Whatever I can do for Emma, yourself, and the family, you have only to ask."

Epilogue

Less than three weeks later, the guns fell silent on November 11, 1918. The Allies were victorious, although the price paid in human life was staggering. Millions of men died on the western front and Corporal Sidney Turner was among them. On May first of the following year, Major Steele visited with news.

Within days of the capture of Le Cateau, a small Commonwealth military cemetery at Neuvilly was created. The Germans had originally ordered villagers of Neuvilly to bury the slain. Most of the dead were British, although the only unidentified body was thought to be that of a Canadian cavalryman.

The man wore a Maple Leaf collar badge and a battered brass shoulder patch. Villagers had found his body with the remains of a horse and the saddle bore the etched letters, LSH.

A search of the soldier's body revealed no identification or rank. Subsequently, the British re-burial party remarked that, whoever he had been, the soldier was a big, strong man. The grave was afterward marked. . . A Canadian Soldier of The Great War.

At dawn on the eighth day of May, Emma Rose Turner gave birth to a healthy baby boy. With such a petite stature, it proved a gruelling process, and sorrow had left her weakened.

Florence and Desiree stayed the entire thirty-six hours of Emma's labour. Doctor Evans came to the house the night before. Desiree woke him several hours before dawn when it became clear the waiting had nearly ended.

Emma had never experienced such excruciating pain and she was exhausted when the baby finally emerged. Perspiration plastered hair to her face and she felt physically abused. Then a slap on a bare bottom created a lusty howl of indignation that rose in crescendo. With the last of her energy, Emma gazed at the child wrapped in a warm towel.

Florence, Desiree and even old Doc Evans, shed tears of joy mixed with melancholy. The child's father, lay in grave thousands of miles away but now lived on with the birth of his son.

Gently laying the baby on Emma's breast, Florence cleared the wet hair from her daughter's flushed forehead. Kissing Emma's cheek, she beckoned Desiree to join them.

"Life goes on, my precious child. You have reason to live with this little miracle. I pray that one day you too, will know how it feels to become a grandmother." Smiling wanly, Emma kissed her mother's hand and whispered.

"I love you mama, and Desiree, I love you too."

"Have you thought of a name for your son, my child?" Emma smiled sadly but with pride.

"Yes, but I want Papa and Bert to come in when I tell you." Before Desiree could summon them, they entered with sheepish smiles. They had obviously been listening at the door.

"Well, you can't expect us to wait around wondering what is going on without us," Alexander exclaimed excitedly. "It's not every day a man becomes a grandfather. Come on, Bert, let's look."

"Mama and Papa, pick him up and look in his eyes when I tell you the name of your grandson. Desiree, you and Bert hold one of his hands. You are his godparents." Emma waved over Doctor Evans to hold his hand before making her announcement.

"Let me introduce Sidney Louis Turner. The name came to me seconds after Doctor Evans said I was going to be a mommy." Her voice broke and tears rolled down her cheeks.

"I didn't know yet Sidney was dead and that he'd never know he would be a father. I'll always be grateful Bert and Desiree sent me to England. I didn't know it would be the last time to see my Sidney. Deep down, I'm sure he never expected to come home. This little miracle is a reward for all of us.

"I make this vow before all of you. My son will never go to war. I name him in honour of two men who gave their lives, so my son will never suffer such a fate."

Thousands of miles away, in northern France, clouds blocking the sunshine were breaking up. One sunbeam peeked through and warmed a patch of ground over the grave of an unknown soldier.

About the Author

The son of a career soldier, Gary developed a keen interest in military history at a young age. His family lived in various locations in Canada and also a three-year posting to Germany. Over the years he developed a passion for writing short stories and essays. Several of those essays have been published in a national magazine. His grandfather fought in The Great War and four decades ago, Gary began researching Canada's involvement in that conflict. Another obsession of his, which began fifty years ago, is riding motorcycles, naturally enough without his parent's knowledge. In 2011 he toured the old Western Front in Belgium and France on his BMW. That trip of a lifetime, led to the germination of his new novel, I'll Take My Chances.

We would love to hear your thoughts on I'll Take My Chances: Volume 1. Feel free to visit our website www.bluemaxchronicles.com and send us your feedback.

Made in the USA
Monee, IL
14 August 2021